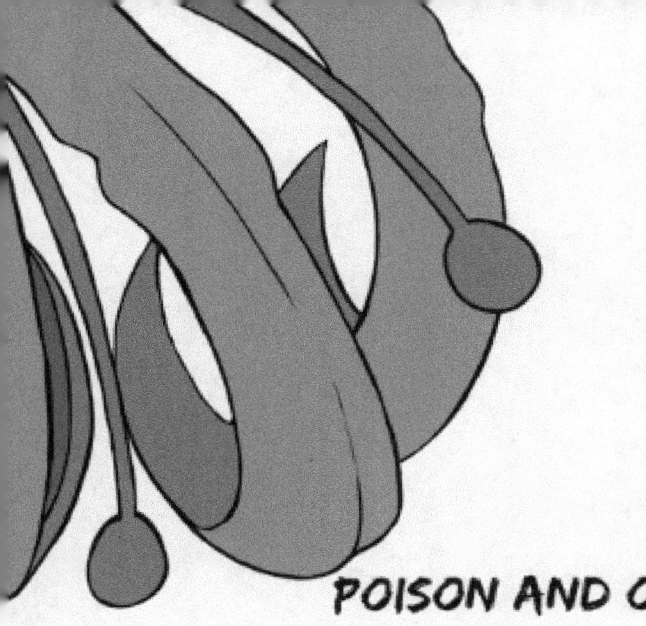

POISON AND OPIUM

ACT I

DANCE OF DEMONS

ALYSSA LAUSENG

Dance of Demons (Poison and Opium, Act I)

NOTE FROM THE AUTHOR

This book contains material that may make readers uncomfortable. This list is to give everyone a broad idea of what they can expect to find, but not necessarily comprehensive. Let's dive in:

Depictions of slavery
Depictions of child abuse
Blood
Murder
Death
Animal Death
Self-harm
Drinking
Smoking
Drug use

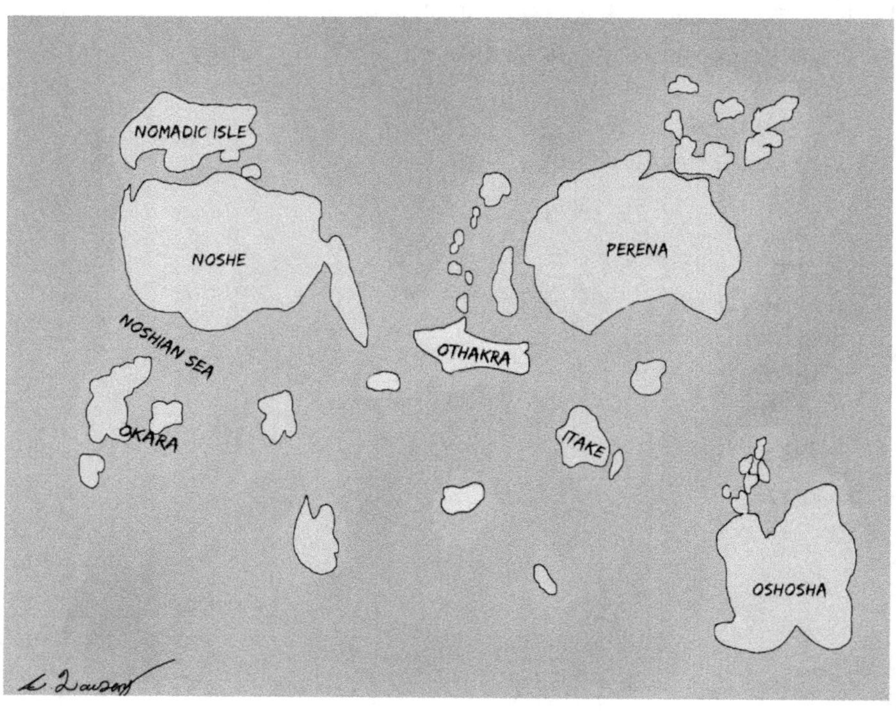

NOMADIC ISLE
NOSHE
NOSHIAN SEA
OKARA
OTHAKRA
PERENA
ITAKE
OSHOSHA

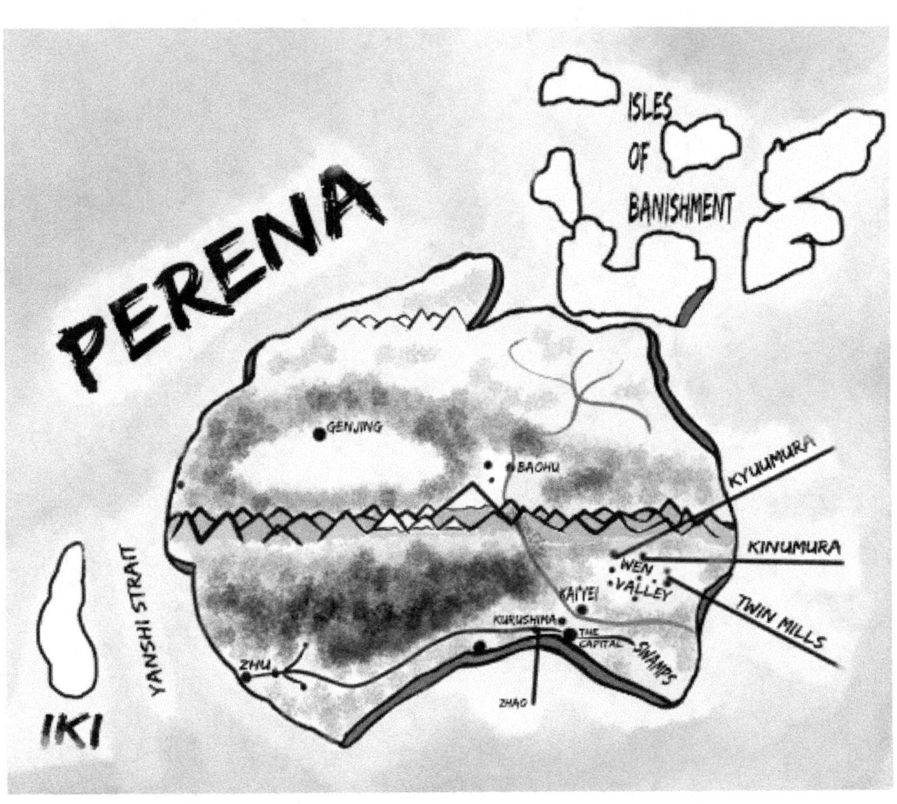

PERENA
ISLES OF BANISHMENT
GENJING
BACHU
KYUUMURA
KINUMURA
WEN VALLEY
KAIYEI
TWIN MILLS
KURUSHINA
THE CAPITAL
SWAMPS
ZHU
ZHAO
YANSHI STRAIT
IKI

CONTENTS

1. Surfacing — 1

2. Shattering the Fractal — 14

3. Rough Silk — 27

4. The Opened Gate — 36

5. Hive-Minded — 48

6. Solstice Night — 58

7. Priestess of Shadows — 68

8. Blossoming — 79

9. Fateful Gamble — 86

10. The Interwoven Threads — 95

11. Higanbana — 104

12. Whispers of Deceit — 114

13. Cutting Teeth — 125

14. Jinchu — 137

15. Interlude — 145

16. The Bridge at Kai'yei — 156

17. Warmth   171

18. Late Summer   181

19. Ominous   191

20. The Westbound Road   200

21. Kill the Messengers   215

22. Harvest   226

RAVENOUS HOUNDS BAYED IN the distance. Their haunting calls rose into the darkness like moaning ghosts of the island's perturbing past as lanterns flickered in relentless gusts of windswept rain. Stolen generations shamefully marked Okara's sesquicentennial history, its bricks molded from their blood and mortar, mixed with salty sweat from thousands of exploited lives. Few acknowledged the ugliness in that truth, and fewer could accept it. The dogs howled again in their miserable, chillingly offkey chorus, beckoning to wandering guidelights hovering above the ground. After a round of indistinct shouts, nearly muted by the weather, the lights dipped past the silhouette of a guard wall protecting the inner complex, down a slope, and toward the tobacco fields.

From the safety of indoors, it wasn't hard to determine that this escape attempt looked thwarted. The slaves whose labor powered the backbone of the Giahatian Empire frequently fled the enormous plantation imprisoning them; rarely did they make it to the freedom they longingly sought, but no threat of violence or death from those who boldly dared to call themselves "master" was sufficient to prevent some despairing souls from taking the chance.

A flurry of wind hit the warped window glass at the same time as a hissing spray of rain, causing a raven-haired boy to jump back and muffle a yelp under his hands. Terrified at the noise he'd made, his violet eyes nervously darted around the dimly lit room, worried that someone had heard him and would find him awake, watching as events unfolded below. As if they were the unspoken curse of an ancient, vengeful god, autumn storms typically waited until after the annual slave auctions, bringing high winds and torrential downpours. This year, the monsoons raged early in the Noshian Sea to the island's north. Although inclement weather created hopeless circumstances for those who dared to try escaping, Daisuke understood why that unidentified person chose tonight to run.

He felt the same bone-deep desperation as every inch of his skin prickled with the urge to flee.

He should've gone to bed hours ago, but sleep became a predictably useless endeavor when he tried closing his eyes. Instead, anxiety kept his mind incessantly buzzing, wired with the awareness of an auction creeping closer with each passing hour. He glanced out the window again, then padded toward a candle beside his parents' unoccupied cot. He'd been awake so long that it had burned down further than what would escape his father's notice—or, worse yet, wrath. Trembling with another bout of silent panic, Daisuke reached under his mother's side of the bedding and extracted an extra, slightly less used candle he stored there for such reasons. If Honda and Akane were busy attending to their assigned duties at later hours, he liked staying awake in the rare comfort of a quiet night. After all, the tiny room wasn't often devoid of yelling, arguments, or a palpable, gut-wrenching tension as he and the rest of his family tiptoed around his father in futile attempts to avoid Honda's explosive temper. Most silences created by his absence meant safety, reprieve, and a chance to exist in peace.

Daisuke shuddered and tried not to think about the physical side of that terrible disposition, gently blowing out the flame on the first candle before licking his fingers to dampen the wick. Despite the small calluses his fingertips had developed from performing the ritual, he winced as heat briefly prickled against his skin. After a few touches to his inner wrist to test the temperature, he determined he could put it away safely; he'd made the mistake of not doing so once and didn't intend on reliving the incident that had followed when his parents returned for the night. He picked off as many wax drippings as possible and then switched it for the spare.

Lightning illuminated the room as he stretched out beside his younger brother, who slept soundly on their shared bed. As much as Daisuke wanted to join him in his restful state, his eyes remained on the dark ceiling above them for a while, mind on high alert as he listened to the storm. The outside world's noises gradually faded, and the relief of dreamless sleep eventually took him under, finally shutting out his racing thoughts and frayed nerves.

As it went with every day, morning rose too soon and summoned a different storm than the one that had left gusty winds and leaden skies in its wake. It didn't take long for him to realize how anger had already found its way forward, threatening to leap onto his tongue and wreak havoc, opposing the way he usually tried to guard his emotions. He waited until he was confident he could only hear his mother's steady, sleep-laden breathing, then cautiously peeked through a cracked eyelid.

"Daisuke, wake up."

The unexpected whisper of his name startled him into opening both eyes. After calming himself, he turned toward his younger sibling's voice with a withering glare as he rolled onto his back from his stomach. "What the hell, Kulako? Are you *trying* to kill me?"

Kulako merely shrugged, his young face indifferent as ever toward Daisuke's tone, though a prolonged look at his expression revealed a deep worry he couldn't articulate. Not that he would've talked about it if he had the words to explain it—their parents made sure they both knew emotional displays of any kind weren't tolerated, and he'd already taken those lessons to heart. "We need to make the bed. Dad said he'd be back soon."

Trained hypervigilance compelled Daisuke to confirm Honda's absence; an instinctual habit, no matter how he trusted Kulako's assessment. He braced on his elbows, which propped him up enough to search the room. "What do you mean? Where did he go?"

"To get a—" Kulako hesitated, gaze darting between his older brother and the bare walls around them. He'd forgotten the word. Then again, getting information from one as young as five probably wasn't the wisest choice. An anxious pair of violet eyes strikingly similar to Daisuke's finally settled on him apologetically.

Daisuke chuckled and moved off the cot.

"Don't worry about it. I remember, now," he said, forcing himself to sound calm. He didn't want to scare his skittish brother with how much rage he felt boiling beneath the surface. It was hardly Kulako's fault—only their father was to blame for how this year's auction day would unfold.

If Grandmaster Norio chose someone to sell at the auction, they wore a collar that marked them for the exchange. Since Daisuke had turned eleven during the spring, he'd been deemed old enough to join hundreds of others who were also on the unfortunate side of the selection process; it wasn't a secret that his father intended to offer his sons to the Grandmaster when they each came of age, but he couldn't accept this plan for his life. While he longed to see the world outside of Okara, it sure as hell wouldn't be with a slave collar latched around his throat while he was dragged along by some witless, smug-faced noble. He'd never be able to live with himself if that happened. He *would* become more than someone else's property, no matter what it took to claw his way out of his current situation.

The room's sliding door rattled open seconds after they finished smoothing the thin, frayed blanket over their bed, frightening both boys. Daisuke pivoted and pulled Kulako behind him in one motion, creating a physical barrier between his brother and Honda Akahana, the kind of man who could take an overseer's whip and still choose to use it on other slaves. He wore his fiery red hair back in a tight ponytail to pull it away from his face and hate-filled brown eyes, regarding his sons with the same utter contempt he always did.

"Get ready," he commanded shortly, unhooking a leather collar from the belt of his plain brown yukata. "The auction begins in the afternoon once the Grandmaster's luncheon ends, and I expect you to look your best."

Daisuke felt Kulako tug on his sleeve, a non-verbal reminder not to react to their father's words. Unfortunately, his fear gave his older sibling's temper leverage. It shouldn't be acceptable for either of them to feel that way. None of this...*horseshit* should be tolerable. Now, he *wanted* to make trouble—this *would* become an argument for the sake of it. *Someone* would listen to his displeasure, starting with the source of every miserable experience he'd had.

"And what do *you* plan to do with Kulako if someone *actually* buys me? Did you bother to think about that?"

"We'll manage, boy. It's none of your concern."

Daisuke rolled his eyes despite knowing what it'd do. "Sure. I've seen what you call 'managing,' Dad, and—"

"Daisuke," his little brother begged, though the strained, quiet plea came seconds too late, as ire had already ignited across their father's face. Honda backhanded his older son without a second thought, sending the room into a tense, heavy silence with only Akane's breathing interrupting.

"I don't have time to argue with you. Put this collar on and get ready," he seethed with indisputable finality after giving the strike time to sting. He shoved the collar into the stunned boy's grasp. "You will *not* humiliate me in front of Grandmaster Norio today."

Daisuke's head stopped ringing and allowed him to regain his bearings as his father turned away; usually, it was a sign that the conversation wouldn't escalate further. Nevertheless, he didn't dare let a slight twinge of inward relief distract him, recalling the rare occasions he'd misread the man's body language in the past. It was how his father responded to perceived disrespect—among several other things—and, realistically, he knew he'd gotten off easy this time. Honda didn't want to bruise him too badly before the auction.

"To hell with Grandmaster Norio," he muttered as the sliding door slammed, wiping his forearm across where a red spot would inevitably form on his cheek.

Those who had become more indoctrinated said Grandmaster Norio was the sole reason they could live, and that they'd have nothing if not for him; they'd say everyone should be grateful for the generosity he spared by feeding and housing them—poorly, one might add—while asking for nothing more than a bit of hard work in return, but Daisuke disagreed. It didn't make sense. There couldn't be a redeemable thing about a man who honestly believed his birthright called for him to own other human beings, trading and selling them like cattle, while thriving off their back-breaking labor. Unfortunately, there seemed to be a surplus of people whose ideals aligned similarly with the Grandmaster's. They demonstrated their support through willing participation in the yearly auctions, owning Nomads in faraway lands, or parroting beliefs from generations before them.

Daisuke often wondered if he'd ever find a place in the world where Northern Nomads had their dignity, let alone their autonomy, but the outlook was rather bleak. Even being allowed the traditional Nomadic ear piercings they received during infancy and upon adulthood was a privilege that had to be granted by their masters.

Gods, Daisuke hated that word. Agitated, he fiddled with the lower black stud in his left ear, then sighed heavily, glancing at the leather collar in his right hand. It was an infuriating sight. Now fuming, he threw it across the room as hard as possible without warning, scaring his brother when it flew past his face. Kulako stared at him after it hit the opposite wall, until he eventually won their wordless argument about whether the outburst warranted an explanation; he also hated it when his younger sibling was right. Unlike their father, Daisuke tried to rein in the physical side of his temper and instead traded it for longwinded, irritated tirades against whoever slighted him.

He retrieved the collar and sat on their bed, then gestured for Kulako to join him while he tried to find a way to describe his thoughts in a manner a smaller child could understand. Daisuke held out the worn leather to examine it, trying not to imagine how many others had worn it ahead of his time, no doubt wrestling with the same terror he experienced at the sight of it. "Disgusting thing, isn't it?"

Kulako looked afraid to give a response. "I guess."

"No one else will ever tell you this, but you *are* allowed to have an opinion, Kulako." Daisuke sighed as he set the collar down in front of them. "Dad left, so it's safe to say something, and you always tell me what's on your mind."

"Only because you make me."

"Give it over, little pest."

Kulako rolled his eyes, then softly answered, "You look tired...and mad...and scared."

"That isn't the opinion I wanted." He cringed. If his younger sibling was perceptive enough to discern it, so was Honda; he hated the man more than his insufficient vocabulary had words to describe, but could hardly call him unobservant.

"...*Are* you?"

"Does it matter?" Daisuke rolled his eyes, then sighed and glanced over at their mother's slumbering form, balled up with her back to them as if subconsciously guarding herself against them. She hadn't always been so despondent, but displays of maternal affection and warmth were things he'd never come to expect from her, no matter what he did. Unfortunately, Kulako was worse off when trying to develop any bond with Akane; she barely spoke to him beyond making him help her with basic tasks. Looking after his brother had become his responsibility since their grandmother died when Kulako was around two years old, which added to why he refused to leave before he was ready. He wanted his younger sibling to come with him.

The only thing worse than one unwanted child is two. Daisuke thought as he gritted his teeth to oppress his bubbling irritation; not *everything* was his parents' fault. Their union wasn't a choice they'd made or because they preferred each other's company over that of anyone else's. To put it bluntly—and the way Daisuke heard the process described—Grandmaster Norio had arranged them as a "breeding pair" for Honda's red hair and Akane's violet eyes. The most expensive slaves had both traits, while cheaper ones looked more like him; although all shared the Northern Nomadic hallmark of fair, alabaster skin, those born with black hair and brown eyes got sent to the silk farm across the small strait running along Okara's eastern side. It made his stomach churn. He was sure he wasn't supposed to know any of this, but neither Honda nor Akane minced words during arguments, and he'd involuntarily listened to plenty of those.

As if his mother's ill-fated circumstances weren't enough, one of the other slavemasters had the idea to mix opium into an entertainer's tea to make them more compliant and cheerful for guests ever since an attempted stabbing during a previous year's auction. Although Daisuke still didn't think that woman had done anything wrong, he knew she'd faced swift execution afterward. Upon the slavemasters' agreement to take no further chances, entertainers got to keep less of their self-respect than before. Now, Akane broke into cold sweats when forced to go without her singular means of escape from such a bleak reality—he wished he could hate her more for it.

I guess I hate this place enough to make up the difference. Daisuke turned his attention out the window, head tilted as he tried to pinpoint exactly where he'd seen the lanterns the previous night, but their room was at an odd angle to get an unobstructed view of the main path into the fields. With a terrible sense of morbid curiosity taking hold, he turned to Kulako, unable to believe that searching for the person who attempted an escape last night would be less depressing than staying around their mother.

"Time for a walk, little pest. We'll wake Mom if we stay here—you know how that goes for us."

Kulako finally looked away from that damned collar and nodded, obviously welcoming a distraction from their tumultuous morning and everything he couldn't possibly absorb yet. The boys already wore their usual black trousers that cut off at the knee, and after they'd pulled on their only clean shirts, Daisuke took Akane's brush from the dresser to run it through Kulako's hair first, then his. He used a piece of twine to keep his back in a ponytail. Once ready, they quietly slipped out of the room and made their way through a long corridor before descending rickety stairs, which eventually met better construction as they neared rooms where the Grandmaster's family and guests typically stayed. Finally, they stepped onto the whitewashed courtyard stones, near a koi pond where they and other children were sometimes permitted to play in the cooling waters on the hottest summer days. Grand homes encompassed the yard and the grandmaster's house in a semi-circular formation; if Daisuke remembered right, one of Norio's brothers, an adult son, and his business partner occupied them. A wall of iron and stone kept everything inside, including sheds, stables, and four long buildings where tobacco, cotton, and rice were processed.

A gate marked the main entrance to the inner complex, usually operated on command by slaves, but today, it stayed open for guests to come and go at their leisure. Despite the outward show, it didn't provide the invitation to wander off as some might hope. A path into the plantation fields followed the slope from the gate, and a narrower one wrapped around the wall, leading directly to the nearby town and converging with another that came from the back of the complex, where mules hauled cartloads of product away.

Daisuke examined the rows of withered tobacco plants as he stood with Kulako at the hillcrest, then glanced at the solid gray skies above. Something like a sixth sense warned him not to go further. Perhaps it was the admonishing sneer from an overseer leaning against the wall several paces away, enjoying a jug of sake to himself while he waited to greet stragglers late to the festivities, but he'd received that look plenty of times and managed to ignore it. No, it had to do with whatever they were about to find. He second-guessed his choice to bring Kulako along for it, too, though there weren't many other places he could go. Especially not when all these extra people milling about compromised his favorite hiding spots. The wind tousled their hair as they picked their way down the silent path.

"Got you!" a voice erupted behind him as someone grabbed his arms and nearly sent his soul to the heavens.

Daisuke forced his tense shoulders to relax and huffed, hoping an air of annoyance would disguise the fright he'd received. "Shun, I've asked you not to do that *several* times—it scares Kulako."

Of course, getting the younger boy to play along rarely worked without explicit instruction. Demonstrating the stubborn streak he'd learned from his primary influence, Kulako shot his older brother a most unimpressed look, which Daisuke mirrored.

Shun smirked and slung an arm around his friend's shoulders, jostling his heart rate again. "Looks like he'll be fine. Now, then, what are we up to?"

"Didn't you hear the hounds last night?"

Shun's light brown eyes sparkled with interest. Being Daisuke's closest friend meant he was no stranger to misadventure. It was one of the few ways to entertain oneself without going mad, but it came with risks; their excursions rarely ended well for Daisuke if Honda caught wind of what they were doing, making discretion an absolute. The fallout of an incident from last summer, when their antics accidentally caused a loaded cart to roll away, still haunted him.

"What are you hoping to find?" the other dark-haired boy ventured after they'd walked for a bit.

"I'm not sure," Daisuke confessed, then turned to Kulako, who warily trailed the older two. "Come on, keep up."

"Can I go back?"

"Sure, and then when Dad catches you by yourself, *you* can tell him why." Daisuke glared. Kulako knew he wasn't serious, but when an instinctual fear rushed into his eyes all the same, it twisted his heart. "That was a bit harsh, wasn't it? Come on."

Kulako hesitated at first, but soon came to his side. With his brother now safely nearby, he turned toward his friend again, only to be met with a sharp jolt to the chest.

"Daisuke." Shun had elbowed him—hard—and brought their little group to an abrupt halt. Daisuke nearly snapped at his friend as he regained his senses, but his voice left him. Instead, he sharply pulled on Kulako to bring him closer and used the same hand to cover his sibling's eyes while he and Shun stared in shock at the sight before them.

At a crossing of footpaths between the tobacco stalks, tied to a hastily erected post, was the mangled figure of a man. Flesh dangled in strips from his bones, and the vicious, gnashing fangs of the hounds had torn away half of his face. Small clumps of red hair stuck to pools of dried blood on the damp ground, swaying in the wind like blades of grass. Kulako and Shun whimpered. Daisuke retched.

SHUN REFUSED TO SPEAK to—or look at—Daisuke and Kulako after they discovered the body. He went directly to his mother once he'd regained control over his limbs, meaning she'd likely forbid them from playing together again, but that was the least of Daisuke's concerns at present. Auction time came far too soon for his liking, though he'd been anxiously monitoring the preparations for days. After ensuring his brother would remain safely tucked away in an isolated hiding place, he approached a throng of other Northern Nomads with the collar in hand. His knees adopted a slight wobble with each step closer. Looking around, most people wore similar expressions of uncertainty or sorrow; like any other year, his rage and disgust absorbed these mental images into an archive of reasons why the world should burn.

I can't do this. Daisuke swallowed, his trembling and sweating fingers sticking to the leather as they clenched around it. He glanced to his left, hoping to find an opening in the human wall made by overseers—no escape. He still had to try. Just as he was about to move, someone grabbed the collar from his hand and callously latched it around his throat. An overwhelming wave of anxiety shot through his veins. Another person stepped forward to strip the shirt from his back and shackle his hands together at his front. Heart pounding and still in shock, he was forced to abandon his idea of running away as the overseers yanked people into neat lines and herded them toward the courtyard.

Children weren't part of the actual "excitement" of the fast-paced auction headed by the Grandmaster's paid staff. Instead, they were positioned at the edge of everything, made to stand in neat rows toward the front of the courtyard for convenient browsing, as if they were any other item at a market. Rigid with fear, the open gate behind him barely registered in Daisuke's mind—by now, a patrol of hounds ensured no one could pass through without permission, anyway. He tried ignoring it, but the urge to vomit weighed heavily on his tongue.

Maybe I can time it right and throw up on a nobleman. He sighed wistfully. While it meant he likely wouldn't be sold, doing something like that guaranteed a beating from Honda later, and it'd be much worse than the single hit he'd already received today.

Nothing happened for a while, as Grandmaster Norio had an entire introduction he liked to bore everyone with, which gave Daisuke too much time alone with his imagination. Someone might drag him away from home today, separating him from the life he knew and the few he loved; he hadn't even spoken to his mother yet. While he never believed he'd miss the plantations, the cruelty touted on full display never failed to feel unbearably heavy on his heart. This auction was the will of Hikari—a goddess of love, light, and creation, who supposedly didn't mind when certain factions of human life were treated shamefully. Either Grandmaster Norio was entirely too comfortable speaking for the goddess, or the values everyone said she stood for were a lie.

Daisuke became aware of a long shadow now towering over him, though he had no idea how long the man stood there. He slowly raised his eyes, not intending to look directly at whoever this was, but he needed to tilt his chin back to get a proper assessment. The Raven God of the Nomadic Isle had gifted Northern Nomads with the ability to withstand frigid temperatures, and granted them otherworldly dreams of insight, but they weren't a tall race compared to others in the world. Judging by what he knew of hair and clothing customs on Perena—which was minimal, but enough to identify the social classes with some accuracy—he determined the man was a merchant of sorts. His long jacket's lack of intricate embroidered designs and silk embellishments indicated he likely wasn't very wealthy; owning a slave would elevate his social standing, which would, in turn, help his financial status.

The merchant stared at him for a long moment. Annoyed, he eventually said, "Tempting price, but this one's too scrawny for outdoor work, and I'm not interested in a house slave."

"We'll keep going, sir. There's plenty more," his accompanying guide reassured, then began ushering him further along the line. Daisuke's eyes found a rock resting between his feet. Gods above, how he wished he could lob it at those men.

Soon after, another shadow appeared, attached to sturdy boots made from quality leather. Daisuke's spine stiffened when the nobleman's fingers abruptly and carelessly clamped around his jaw, still smelling like the fried duck served earlier that afternoon. He managed to swallow the reflexive revulsion that prickled under his skin at being touched. However, he couldn't force down the anger consuming every inch of his rationality when his head involuntarily jerked backward and then to the side as the man examined him.

"I don't usually allow my slaves to keep their piercings," he murmured as if Daisuke couldn't hear. "But this one *is* younger. Healthy nails and hair. Black hair, unfortunately, but that's better for my coin pouch than a red-haired one since I won't recover the expense on this investment for a bit yet. Besides, if I know Norio, he'll say this one's already priced fairly because of the violet eyes and age."

Daisuke trembled as he struggled not to buckle under the strength of his emotions as they uncontrollably slipped away from their tight seal. He didn't think he'd ever felt more humiliated, not even when Honda struck him in front of others.

The fingers around his chin abruptly invaded his mouth to check his teeth, triggering an explosion of wild rage. He bit the nobleman's fingers hard, then spit bloody saliva into his eye when that foul-tasting hand wriggled free, followed by the most soul-soothing, wounded yowl he'd ever heard. It wasn't nearly loud enough for Daisuke's liking, but he knew how much negative attention he'd already drawn to himself. With the dread of realization beginning to trickle in and his feelings still rampaging, it was time to brace for impact.

"What's going on over here?" Everything racing through the boy's mind froze at the sharp snap of Grandmaster Norio's voice.

"Possessed! This one's possessed!" the man cried, holding his bleeding fingers. "He *bit* me, for Hikari's sake!"

Grandmaster Norio quickly pieced things together. He fixed a dark, dangerous glare on Daisuke that he couldn't ignore, then grabbed him by the collar and forcefully pulled him into a bow at the waist. Blood rushed into his ears at the motion, which stirred the anger still boiling through his veins and blocked out whatever stupid apology the grandmaster uselessly spewed at the nobleman. Anger, hatred, desperation, humiliation, and—

"Are those tears?" the nobleman abruptly scoffed, still nursing his injury.

Tears? Daisuke stupidly glanced in the grandmaster's direction, not understanding whom he was addressing at first—*he* didn't cry. Honda would never have it.

"If you're sorry enough to cry, boy—" Hot leather squeezed at Daisuke's throat to tug him upright, then slacked before Grandmaster Norio hit the space between his shoulders to shove him forward. "—then I suppose you'll have no issues giving this man a proper apology of your own. Go on, now. Show our good friend you mean it."

Daisuke shook as he fought with his pride, and once more, the urge to vomit churned in his gut. After a moment of uncertainty, he slowly lowered himself to his knees, suppressing noises of rage and anguish as he bent forward and put his forehead on the toe of the nobleman's boot. The shackles on his wrists meant he could do little with his hands besides tucking his arms underneath his body to demonstrate that he was at the noble's mercy.

"Learns quickly, doesn't he?" Grandmaster Norio's tone overflowed with disgusting smugness. If any of the gods were real, this would've already ended.

No. There couldn't be a single deity condoning this. Not Hikari or Kuro worshipped by Giahatians and Perenins, the fierce spirits of the Okami, and certainly not the Old Northern Gods the Nomads had once prayed to long before slavers invaded their isle's shore.

"I'm sorry." Daisuke's voice strained against the swelling wave of his emotions.

The collar squeezed at his windpipe. "Get up, boy."

Two
Shattering the Fractal

The auction carried on without Grandmaster Norio's presence. He dragged Daisuke toward the main house by the collar, ignoring his captive's attempts to squirm free, which further cemented the boy's resolve and added a stream of vehement protests to the physical struggle. Expectedly and infuriatingly, anything he said fell on deaf ears. Daisuke knew he could explain himself, apologize to him properly, and get out of trouble. He just needed the grandmaster to listen.

All the gods be damned, why didn't anyone ever listen?

Daisuke firmly planted his feet on the gleaming hardwood floor when they entered the building. Were he a little heavier, it might've made a difference instead of causing the master to falter slightly at the change in weight before continuing onward as if nothing had happened.

Norio set a relentless pace through the mansion's halls, keeping the collar's clasp clenched in his fist to prevent Daisuke from simply taking it off and running away—he knew his captive to be a clever one who frequently escaped trouble. He stopped long enough to roughly pull aside the sliding door to his meeting room. He hauled Daisuke forward after slamming it behind him until they approached his sturdy, cherry-wood desk near the far wall. Compared to the rest of the building, apart from the slave quarters, there was little here. The planks used for trims and flooring were Noshian pine, which meant they were durable with a price to match. Honda had volunteered to help stain the boards later this week to preserve their veneer.

Daisuke's eyes wandered to a potted bamboo plant near the open window as he tried to devise a way out; somewhere in the back of his mind, he simultaneously realized his deep denial and that he was refusing to come to terms with the gravity of the situation. He'd never caused this much of a mess before, despite a love for shenanigans and arguing with his parents. Grandmaster Norio had finally released him and was rummaging through a drawer for something on the other side of the desk. He eventually tapped the surface in front of Daisuke with a long, wrought-iron key to reclaim his attention.

"Show me your hands, boy."

This tiny opening could be his last chance to make an appeal. "Grandmaster Norio, I—"

"Your hands, Daisuke."

Grandmaster Norio didn't call many of his slaves by name unless they were particularly rebellious or had some form of favoritism, like pets. Daisuke didn't have to think hard to figure out which category he'd been placed in by now. Disgust pooled in his stomach, sloshing around with dread and fear as he raised his arms, shackle chains clattering from trembling he couldn't control. After the Grandmaster released the bindings and caught them in his hand, he placed them off to the side. Daisuke dared to examine the bright streaks of raw skin they'd left on his wrists. Although a touch of red poppy ointment would take care of them within a couple of treatments, the searing, burning pain they left behind steadily flared into an unbearable sensation, especially when exposure to the open air made them itch.

Daisuke's blood ran cold when he saw Grandmaster Norio take a long, polished bamboo cane from a vase in the nearby corner, examine it, and then put it away again before choosing a slightly shorter one. He paused again at the same drawer to retrieve a purple silk cloth. His bushy, graying eyebrows relaxed when he came to stand near Daisuke, which gave him a poorly constructed air of sternness mixed with regret.

As if you're actually sorry about this. Daisuke firmly reminded himself not to roll his eyes.

"You're Honda's oldest boy, no?"

"I am, sir."

"The stunt you pulled in the courtyard dishonors your father, Daisuke, a hardworking and dependable slave. But do you know what's worse than that? You've dishonored *me*—your *master*. You know this, don't you?"

"...Yes, sir." Daisuke's stomach flipped until he felt nauseous again. He hadn't had time to consider what his father would think or how he'd react to the situation. At least Akane's indifference was predictable.

"Bend," the Grandmaster icily commanded. "Elbows to the surface."

"...Yes...sir." The smooth wood gave off a threatening shine in the grey daylight to taunt Daisuke—this was a horrendously miscalculated loss, and his situation was worsening by the second. A tiny, helpless whimper accidentally escaped his throat as he complied. Grandmaster Norio either didn't hear or simply refused to acknowledge it. Whichever it was, it wouldn't have come as a surprise.

"You have committed a serious offense, which means I have no choice but to respond with an equally severe consequence. Since you are only a child, I will not give you as many lashes as I would for an adult, but all the same, I sincerely hope this will teach you to control your temper."

Daisuke glared at the far wall at the mere idea of such a suggestion. However, any cognitive awareness came to a grinding halt when the cane's first strike sent a cutting, throbbing pain resonating across his back. The Grandmaster ignored the involuntary yelp he choked out as a result.

"F-fuck you!" the words burst from Daisuke's mind to his tongue like a fiery eruption, burning through a disorienting haze of scattered thoughts. The tumultuous combination of sudden agony and his reemerging fury made involuntary tears well in his eyes once more. He covered his mouth with the limited range of motion he was allowed, determined not to cry out again—clinging to his last bit of defiance with a vengeance. *Fuck you all.*

The cane whistled in the air as Grandmaster Norio swung to deliver a second, more brutal blow.

THE CANING LEFT SIX long streaks of welted, broken skin across Daisuke's back—a light sentence, realistically—and the bruising results still hurt with every movement a few days after. He expected it'd take several more before they completely faded away. It didn't help that Honda's dreadfully familiar leather strap had left its own swollen, flaring red stripes alongside and over Grandmaster Norio's the same night.

In his body and spirit, everything ached.

Unable to watch him bear that pain, without prompting from his older sibling, Kulako summoned his courage and did his best to rub some of their grandmother's red poppy ointment onto any affected areas in the hopes of helping them heal faster. However good-natured, this endeavor didn't end well for the boy when Honda saw what he was doing. Understandably, Kulako was too afraid to try again after their father had stalked away, satisfied with the punishment he'd inflicted. Instead, he'd run off, and now Daisuke was stiffly ambling around, calling his name between interspersed attempts to listen for a response over the rain.

He'd lost him. He'd *never* lost track of his little brother before. Daisuke swallowed a lump at the back of his throat; nothing had been the same since auction day. Shun no longer seemed interested in speaking to him after finding the human scarecrow, as he actively avoided Daisuke whenever they saw one another. His mother must not have been alone in her longstanding opinion that their friendship wasn't for the best. In addition, arguments between his parents were becoming more frequent—as was Honda's aggression toward his sons—and now this. Although whatever small pockets of joy he had in life were rapidly disappearing, he forced his thoughts away from the temptation of abandoning the search and climbing over the wall in a haphazardly contrived effort to escape. He wandered further into the back section of the property, continually needing to divert his attention away from worst-case scenarios—still no sign of Kulako around the stables or empty horse carts.

Gods be damned, where was he?

Soaked to the bone, desperate, and exhausted, he gave it one last try as he stepped into the shelter of a storage shed. "Kulako, I'm not mad at you, and Dad isn't with me. Come see me...please?"

Movement in the back corner among a shelter of crates and canvas tarps jerked Daisuke's attention in that direction. Hair standing on end, he braced himself to jump with all his weight onto a rat, but thankfully, Kulako appeared instead, cautiously peeking at him from under the protection of his hiding place. Relieved, Daisuke sighed and wordlessly gestured for him to come to him, bending to embrace the little pest as soon as he was within reach.

"Don't you *ever* scare me like that again. Got it?"

Kulako shrank in his brother's arms. "I'm sorry, Daisuke."

There was a small, dried cut on Kulako's lower lip from where it and his tooth had met under Honda's wrath, along with a large mark on the right side of his face matching their father's hand. More of the same littered his arms, punctuated by a rapidly developing bruise on his wrist from when Honda had initially grabbed him to stop him from helping Daisuke.

"It's fine," he finally said once he felt he'd thoroughly taken in his brother's appearance and the fury that made him look that way. "Let's go inside."

Kulako sniffled and wiped his arm across his reddened eyes, then nodded pensively, but Daisuke didn't press him for details this time. Instead, he gently tugged his sibling toward the door, then poked his head out of the storage shed to check for wandering overseers who might have nothing better to do than harass them. He couldn't believe what he saw when he looked toward the wall again; empty crates sat around on a wooden slab tucked behind a pile of broken horse carts, which kept them elevated from mud and puddling water. A tree branch somberly waved in the wind above them, beckoning him closer. Most wouldn't be able to access the crates with all the bracken in the way, but with a squint of his eyes, Daisuke determined he might be thin enough to wriggle through.

Remembering his objective, he dismissed the idea beginning to take form and hurried back to the main house with Kulako. It was getting late; workers were starting to extinguish oil lamps illuminating the courtyard, which meant they should already be in their room. Unsupervised children weren't to be seen in the mansion's corridors after early evening hours.

Much to Daisuke's relief, the hallways were empty and quiet until they neared the kitchens, where he caught two voices he recognized distinctly; overseers wouldn't be happy to find them. He pressed himself and Kulako against the wall, grateful for Grandmaster Norio's fondness for decorating with potted bamboo plants. He wondered if this was a moment when people usually prayed for luck.

"—If it's what Emperor Akuwara wants, I suppose we can't say much, but damn," one said reluctantly.

Daisuke held his breath when they stopped on the other side of the bamboo, then took his brother by the hand and crept closer to the overseers, dipping low behind the plant. He motioned for Kulako to stay quiet, which he quickly remembered was an unnecessary effort since the younger more or less existed in silence as a default state. Daisuke shook his head and forced himself to focus—Kulako couldn't take much more today if somebody caught them, and neither could he. He leaned forward slightly, staying hidden while peeking through green stalks, and returned to the conversation.

"Sounds like their last campaign on Othakra severely impacted their numbers."

"It must've if they're holding recruitment near winter like this—if we're unlucky, it'll become a regular thing." A shuddering sigh. "Damned wolves ought to be thanking the Empire for bringing them civilization."

"Those savages slaughter Giahatian soldiers in cold blood. Hell, I say we do away with them all!"

The other snickered. "Go into town and register if you're so thirsty for Okami blood, then. Enlistment opens at dawn; by afternoon, you'll be on your way to Perena."

"Do I look like a moron?"

"Well, now that you've asked—"

"Fuck off. Besides, if I joined the military, I'd be more than just a grunt. I'd be a—" The men's voices slowly faded when they decided to move along again. Daisuke had finished listening by then, as his mind was already latching onto a dangerous tidbit of inspiration.

It won't take much to get me out of here. He shivered a little as excitement and terror crawled along his spine. While he had no interest in charging into battle with the Okami or leaving his brother behind, the recruitment event might be his one chance to go...*anywhere*. He *had* to take it. His mind cruelly reminded him of the risks by flashing to the human scarecrow, stripped of flesh by rabid dogs, and he glanced at his brother, who still acted out of sorts. *No, it's too insane. I can barely read or write, anyway, and I don't know if they'll let a slaveborn enlist—they'll just bring me back here. Then what?*

Daisuke subconsciously winced at the marks on his back, sighed in defeat, and gave Kulako a little nudge to urge them onward in the same heavy silence as before. Much to their surprise, Akane waited for them when they turned the first corner, not far from where they'd hidden. She tilted her head, deliberating as she pensively stared at Daisuke, then crouched in front of Kulako with a small, uncertain smile.

"About time for bed, isn't it?" she asked him, tucking a lock of her loose black hair behind her ear. After looking to his brother for reassurance, Kulako cautiously mouthed an affirmative answer, eyes wary, and let their mother lead from there.

Exhausted from how the day had unfolded and at last in dry clothing, it didn't take long for Kulako to drift off, especially with Daisuke sitting next to him on their cot, giving the smaller boy a safe place to rest his head in his lap. Akane watched them the entire time, as if she were trying to see...something. He couldn't identify whatever it might be, so he pretended he didn't sense her eyes on them.

"You heard what those men were saying, too, didn't you?" Akane quietly prodded when she noticed Kulako had fallen asleep. Once Daisuke hesitantly confirmed he had, she took a deep breath and added, "Then you should go to that recruitment event."

Daisuke forced out a short laugh, confident he shouldn't take her seriously; neither of his parents shared his love for humor, but it was an absurd statement. "What?"

The sorrowful look that never entirely left her violet eyes settled on him sympathetically, patiently—the most tenderness she'd shown in months. She knelt on the bed softly to avoid disturbing Kulako, sparing her younger son the same wistful smile she always did when in a clearer state of mind, as if her presence now filled the emptiness of thousands of other absences for either of her children. Daisuke could never properly word how it upset him; he only understood his nearly uncontrollable urge to scream at her for it. Tonight, as with any other time, he swallowed his feelings.

Akane ran her thin, delicate fingers through Kulako's hair without stirring him, then gently touched Daisuke's cheek, causing them to both instinctively retract. "The world is bigger than this plantation, and my dreams say there's more in this life for you."

He stared at his mother for a long moment, unsure how to interpret her statement. As a gift from the Old Northern Gods and one of the last secrets they kept from slavers, dreams held significant importance for Northern Nomads since they often showed glimpses of the future. Daisuke believed he had a healthy skepticism toward this claim, as he'd never experienced the phenomenon. He crossed his arms as if it helped deflect Akane's suggestion.

"Not to upset you, Mom, but how do you plan on taking care of Kulako without me? I mean, he makes it easy, but—" Daisuke stopped himself; his mother wouldn't hit him as Honda had for asking the same question, but he didn't know how to finish it without hurting her.

"You and that wicked tongue of yours, child," she chided breathlessly, eyes downcast, followed by a mirthless laugh.

While Akane wasn't wrong about his tendency to be blunt, everything about her expression and demeanor reminded him of how she frequently villainized him for it. Although the impulse to verbally lash out at her still thrashed around in his throat, he kept his composure; he knew he'd lost his turn to speak, even to apologize. Finally, she drew another breath that sounded more uneasy than her last, forced something into his hand, and stood before heading for the door.

She turned once more when she slid it open a little, her countenance emotionless again. "Give what I've said some thought, Daisuke. We both know you'll never be happy like this."

Akane didn't wait for her son's decision, nor did he expect her to—after all, she was right.

Moments after her departure, Daisuke began planning his, using the grim knowledge he'd gained through watching multiple failed attempts throughout the years. He knew going through the main gate was practically suicide, that he'd be less likely to run into trouble if he snuck out in the middle of the night, where to go to attract the least attention, and he was sure he could land the leap over the wall. He'd practiced from comparable heights with Shun. He debated if he should try sneaking his friend out, too, but the idea quickly vanished. All the same, that shiver of combined nerves raced through his body again.

Daisuke opened his clenched fingers to see what his mother had given him. A small, gold hoop with two dyed finch feathers—one green, the other pink—with tiny blue, green, and pink beads rested on his palm. In Northern Nomadic culture, this little helix earring symbolized one's rite of passage into adulthood at the age of sixteen. Infants received their two lobe piercings shortly before turning a year old—boys with studs, girls with hoops—and the choices in earring styles changed over their lifetimes, depending on the identity they grew into as time passed. Daisuke's grandmother had done his piercings and Kulako's. She was also part of a select few who knew how to make red poppy ointment used for numbing the skin during the procedure—she'd taught Daisuke, too, though the flowers were incredibly fickle and challenging for him to keep alive without an adult's help.

He tucked the earring into a self-made pocket in his shirt and decided to leave the medicine behind for Kulako. The Capital on Perena still received occasional imports of red poppy seeds from the Nomadic Isle, and he didn't have much else he'd need for supplies otherwise; rather, there was little else he *could* take with him. He stretched out on his back and crossed his arms behind his head before looking over at his brother, overcome with guilt. Kulako was too young for the infantry—he had to stay behind.

"Don't be mad," Daisuke whispered, rolling over to put an arm around his sibling. "I'm sure there's a way for you to get out, too."

Daisuke wasn't sure when he'd fallen asleep, but everything was dark and still when he became conscious of his surroundings again. Honda, Akane, and Kulako remained undisturbed as he quietly rose from the bedding, then groggily picked his way to the window. Nothing moved or made a sound outside, save for the delicate trickle of rainwater running down the grooved eaves to collection barrels waiting on the ground. No more precipitation fell, but no moon broke through the clouds to illuminate the Okaran sky, which meant his luck had halfway improved.

It was difficult to tell how long he had until daybreak. Daisuke firmly reminded himself of the unimaginable and numerous miseries he could suffer in this life, ones he'd witnessed far too many times, and picked up an old cloak of Akane's that he'd seen on the floor near the dresser earlier that day. There were frays along the hem, and a few holes had worn through the fabric, but it would keep him somewhat protected from the weather should it rain again.

Unable to bear looking at his family, Daisuke left without sparing any of them one last glance.

Guards, if one was bold enough to call them that, were placed at the house's main entrance, in Grandmaster Norio's meeting room, and outside his private quarters at night. A handful lightly patrolled the house during these hours, too. Thankfully, Daisuke knew of a neglected kitchen window he could easily fit through without drawing attention to himself—if the Grandmaster didn't kill him for trying to escape, Honda might. He had plenty of experience taking this route to sneak outside; the last time he did, about a fortnight ago, he'd met Shun by the koi pond, where the other boy surprised him with an awkward but no less sweet kiss on his cheek. He supposed it was at least *one* good memory he could take with him.

Gods, what in Kuro's Hells am I doing? He silently bemoaned his decisions once he'd wriggled through the kitchen window. *I can't see a fucking thing.*

Sporadically placed lanterns had cast dim lights in the mansion's corridors—he failed to consider what he'd do without their guidance before his feet touched the decorative courtyard stones. He gave himself a moment to adjust, then carefully approached the shed where he'd found Kulako. Using what little night vision he'd gained, he slipped around the carts and trudged through squishy muck until he reached the empty crates. Once properly stacked, he'd have to jump from the top to close the remaining gap to the branch.

The supports he'd crafted wobbled dangerously underneath him as he slowly made his ascent. Daisuke drew in a deep breath, then slowly released it as he carefully extended his legs to full height. He leapt for the barely visible tree limb, knocking over the mountain he'd climbed to get there. A deafening silence fell as he fixed his grip.

If one of the wretched dogs started barking, so did the rest. Daisuke swore as more joined in and swung himself from the branch to the wall, which was barely wide enough to find his balance. He stumbled a little, nearly slipping on the slick rock beneath his feet as he crouched down, then froze altogether when he looked up again and saw the threatening orange glow of lanterns trickling into view. Men were yelling at one another as their lights exposed the pile of fallen and smashed crates; snarling hounds already had their noses to the ground. Daisuke used the chaos to his advantage, as they hadn't yet figured out to point their lights upward and toward him. He steadied and lowered into a seated position, then, with all his strength, launched himself from the wall, letting the darkness below swallow him whole. He remembered to absorb the impact of the drop by bending his knees when he landed, and despite a misstep due to the muddy ground, he recovered quickly and kept running.

He could barely see anything. His eyes gradually adjusted to the nighttime, but he wasn't a Shifter like the Othakran wolf-people called the Okami, which meant he only had the pathway's vague outline against the grass to guide him. Just when he'd begun to shake the worry he wasn't moving fast enough, came the audible, distant screech of metal as the property's back gate opened; his heart leapt into his throat, then plunged back down to thunder in his chest. He tried to speed up his pace without getting lost, but abruptly stopped when a chilling, familiar sound broke through the still night air. He pivoted to search the surrounding blackness.

They'd let the hounds loose.

Panic surged through Daisuke's blood, binding his feet to the wet road as terror immobilized him on the spot—he loathed and feared those beasts worse than any monster his imagination could have conjured; they were already about to pounce on him. Grandmaster Norio had the mutts trained to bite or maul slaves on command. Daisuke held his breath, shaking, praying to deities he wasn't sure existed while the murderous animals drew closer.

The flap of wings and a raven's croaking caw from overhead startled him out of his shocked state, though he was soon equally taken aback when a pale mist formed in front of him and steadily converged into the form of a white wolf. She bared her gleaming, deadly fangs, then lunged forward with a menacing growl. Daisuke clenched his eyes shut and threw his arms in front of him to shield his face, but the frightened yelps of dogs forced him to look again. She'd leapt over him, and now gnashed and snarled at any of the mutts that drew near.

The wolf turned to him once more when the beasts had run off in the opposite direction, her deep yellow eyes lulling him into calmness until she noiselessly brushed past him like a silent rush of wind, turning his body in the same direction. By the time Daisuke blinked, the wolf had already disappeared, but left a trail of glowing paw prints on the muddy path in her wake. Unbelievable as the whole ordeal was, he didn't have time to question what he saw. Still stunned, he thanked her with an uncertain mutter, then followed the way she'd mapped at a full sprint, relieved when a glance over his shoulder revealed the prints rapidly fading behind him, helping him vanish without a trace.

Dawn's earliest hint of light touched the sky when Daisuke infiltrated Okara's singular town, lungs on fire, drenched in sweat, and ready to collapse from exhaustion. Feet numb from the cold and mud that caked them, he nearly praised Hikari when he finally found the port at the end of the white wolf's route; his legs were about to give out, and moving them felt like a chore. Fortunately, the military ship's folded black sails made it easy to locate—the seasonal emptiness of the place helped, too. Daisuke stopped to rest against a building while he watched from safe shadows created by the shop, trying to calculate how he should proceed.

Despite coolness in the morning air, a lone man dressed in what he vaguely recognized as a simple military uniform sat on a bench nearest to the pier, unfolding a cloth and revealing what must be his breakfast. A large wooden sign rested against the metal railing to the soldier's left, with several more to guide one's way toward the Imperial ship. Daisuke narrowed his eyes to decipher the words he could most easily see on the posting. He'd learned how to read what little he could from Akane, something the masters taught her so she could better entertain guests with poetry recitations, but improving the skill wasn't easy with the limited options he had.

What's the phrase again? In for a copper, in for a gold? Daisuke abandoned the idea of reading the signs, summoned all his courage, then cautiously stepped into the open, letting a foot scuffle against stones similar to those in Grandmaster Norio's courtyard.

The man paused instead of taking his first bite, his eyes tracking Daisuke as he slowly came forward, subconsciously hunched in fear as he drew Akane's cloak tighter. His counterpart already recognized him as a slaveborn; he could tell as much judging by the subtle, confused, yet suspicious expression the Perenin man had temporarily displayed. A heavy silence filled the air when Daisuke was mere feet away, but he couldn't speak or move.

The soldier cleared his throat, feigning disinterest when he asked, "Did your master send you for something?"

He wordlessly shook his head.

"I see." Dark eyebrows furrowed over pensive black eyes as the Perenin man scratched the stubble on his cheek. "A runaway from the plantations, then?"

Daisuke had no idea how to answer this time—if this man were cruel, he was in unfathomable trouble that would surely end in far worse than six strikes from the Grandmaster's cane. Thinking about it tied his stomach in knots. Eventually, too exhausted to drum up a clever lie, he nodded with a mumbled affirmative, surrendering to the fact that he couldn't predict or control what would happen next. Although his heart stopped when the soldier bid him closer, he listened to his intuition and obeyed. He wasn't sure what he thought would happen now, but unable to run any further, Daisuke begrudgingly accepted that his fate rested in this man's hands. They analyzed one another intently, weighing their few remaining choices.

"Quite the feat to get away from Grandmaster Norio's properties. It's about a two-hour walk to the plantations, isn't it? I'll bet it took longer with yesterday's rain. Roads must've been muddy—and I doubt that made it any easier."

Uncertain, Daisuke merely gave him another nonverbal confirmation.

"You must be hungry after all that. In my experience, a hungry soldier is hardly useful. Here." The man tossed Daisuke one of his three rice balls, his sternness softening unexpectedly, then gestured to the ship with a tilt of his head. "Eat that and get yourself settled belowdecks. If anyone has a problem with you, tell them they can come argue with General Aki."

THREE

ROUGH SILK

WARM CANDLELIGHT DANCED IN a flickering ring across the surface of an old oak desk, flagging the lone sign of life in the otherwise empty library. Fortified from the outside world by rows of shelves, stocked with tomes collected throughout centuries and wrapped in perfect silence, Obito breathed easily for the first time that day—no one would have a reason to come looking for him this late at night. He finally had a moment alone with a letter he'd received hours earlier. Although his hometown in the Wen Valley lay miles from Perena's Capital, seeing hints of his eldest brother's artistic flare in the envelope's wax seal brought everything he wanted to avoid uncomfortably close.

Obito's dark green eyes settled on the gleaming letters written in black ink without absorbing any meaning from the words they formed. It'd been six months since he'd last spoken to his mother, father, or siblings, and while it seemed his brothers and sisters were ready to make amends, he wasn't sure if he was—or if he *could*. In the half-year following his enlistment with Giahatian intelligence, he'd managed to emotionally distance himself from an unforgivable incident and find a small sliver of peace; he'd determined that also meant keeping out anyone else who knew about it, which eventually included *everyone*.

It was safer for his sanity this way.

Perhaps the reflex of shutting other people out had come too quickly, but Obito's natural preference for solitude drew him toward it, and he thought the daunting effect of a simple note from his family served as suitable evidence for why he'd done so in the first place. His heart couldn't take how any of this made him feel. Too many emotions that had taken him months to identify threatened to boil over all at once: guilt, anger, sadness, and distantly familiar senses of betrayal.

Obito purposefully folded the letter into a tiny square and placed it between the first two pages of a book he'd also brought along. Getting up to leave, however, was unexpectedly delayed as he sat with his head in his hands for a long moment, fingers gripping his dark hair out of frustration. Finally, he gathered the candle and walked toward the royal library's double doors. As this section of winding halls and corridors in the Palace had become familiar through several of these midnight excursions, he extinguished the flame he carried to let evenly spaced iron torches on the walls guide him back toward the onmitsu dormitories. He would've taken advantage of the many passages hidden within the Palace walls, but at this hour, he risked running into older, more experienced spies who didn't want their conversations interrupted—trying to save a few minutes of his time wasn't worth the potential hazard to his health that could follow.

Obito slowed to a stop when he came to a line of narrow slits carved into the Palace's outward-facing wall, an architectural relic from when Perenins controlled the Empire, made for archers to shoot at advancing enemy forces without exposing themselves. Once the Higia Dynasty became the established monarchy, Giahatian rule discontinued most Perenin military traditions, such as archery, from practice. These windows now merely looked upon an early season snow dusting the Palace grounds, the freshly fallen crystals shimmering beneath the moon's light. Obito's anxiety rose again.

About a year ago, during a cousin's wedding, a night like this had permanently reshaped his life. Although the mental images frequently haunted him, he'd spoken of the incident only once after spending the next few months processing it and then gathering the courage to tell his parents. Takato, however, soundly struck down all his amassed effort, unwilling to hold an audience for a terrible truth that now infected their lives and family. Shizune couldn't go against her husband, given that he'd already made the decision. Instead, they sent him to the Capital for voluntary military service earlier than planned, which meant he'd enlisted with intelligence by spring rather than autumn. Being the youngest of four boys, the middle of six children, and a nobleman's son, this was one of Obito's better paths. Still, he knew the immediacy with which his father acted had little to do with his son's safety—he hadn't shied away from stating the need to keep things quiet.

Upon arriving in the city, Obito stayed with an aunt who happily lived alone in the nobility quarter; though fiery in spirit, Aunt Kiko cultivated her home and presence to be quiet, safe spaces, and she was easy to speak to on nearly any level. She was also far more brilliant and analytical than she often let on, so she'd managed to piece things together quickly without ever blatantly saying so. Perhaps it was petulant to think in such terms, but acknowledging that didn't lessen his deep satisfaction at her declaration to send her younger brother a scathing letter for how he'd handled things. Being considered the family's matriarch gave her quite a bit of pull in that sense.

A frigid wind snaked through the archer slats to guide Obito back toward reality and ground him again. The note he'd stored in the book hadn't come from Takato, which meant he wasn't hurting his father by ignoring it, only his brothers and sisters. He'd address it after he and his assigned partner finished with training exercises the following day.

Even if things hadn't transpired the way they had, he'd likely still be standing in this corridor on this night, worrying about the things he couldn't control or upset over something else entirely. Despite the contrasts in his surroundings and the empty comfort of someone's absence, it didn't seem the beginning of his twelfth winter would yield much difference than that of his eleventh.

The hour was late. Obito turned away from the windows and returned to his room, unsure when sleep would come, but hoping it'd be soon.

MEMBERS OF IMPERIAL INTELLIGENCE didn't receive training in the same ways as footsoldiers or assassins; the onmitsu required their operatives to draw upon their ability to think critically and analyze information. They were taught hand-to-hand combat and mastered deadly accuracy with throwing knives and other weapons of individual choice, but those were treated as secondary priorities. Along with their wits, a spy mainly relied on stealth and poisons to fulfill their duties.

They came to the Palace as needed whenever the Intelligence Master asked noble families to send him their youngest sons, but this wasn't an act borne from the dedication of those houses like the Empire claimed. The boys who sought to carve their own paths in the Capital were generally around the age of eleven or twelve, which meant they already had a basic education in the various things they'd study and, therefore, didn't need to waste a trainer's time on reading or writing lessons. Perhaps most importantly, their families usually didn't miss them terribly if they went missing or died, a risk carried by anyone who became entangled in political affairs. If they didn't enlist, they were better as servants to their parents or siblings than they'd ever be as sons and brothers.

Although plenty of others were quick to dismiss or deny it, Obito thought acknowledging that last part as fact merely exposed one of many ugly truths in the Giahatian social structure. Most of his fellow students saw his observations as blunt, paranoid, or overly cynical, so it didn't take long for them to stop asking for his opinions, or at least learn to exercise more caution if they did. Not that he particularly minded; he'd never been above purposely saying something acerbic or biting enough to drive someone away, nor did he believe it was likely to change.

Unfortunately, this wasn't always easy to pull off; each onmitsu got paired with a partner with whom they carried out their various missions, which meant they spent most of their days together. These pairings commonly developed into close friendships or relationships rife with begrudging, mutual respect with little middle ground. His own partner, Itsuki, came from a lower-ranking noble family in Perena's western agricultural plains. He had a genuinely warm disposition toward others, which made him highly popular and well-liked among the onmitsu ranks, but he also had little grasp on the concept that some people preferred solitude.

A balled-up scrap of paper landed near his left hand. As this had become a familiar greeting—a joke to the effect of making sure it was "safe" to approach—he wasn't surprised when he looked up to find Itsuki's lanky form near the table. It was as if he'd accidentally summoned him by thinking about him. Obito had spent the last hour trying to focus on a destructive poison's delicate composition in the dormitory's empty communal area; he supposed if he'd wanted to prevent such annoying interruptions, he should've stayed in his room.

Plans foiled, he rolled his eyes, then scowled as he asked, "What do you want?"

"Good morning." Itsuki smiled pleasantly, ignoring the looming cloud of sleep-deprived irritability hanging over his partner.

"It's hardly morning anymore."

Somehow, this had also gained a sense of comfortable familiarity between them. Itsuki's smile didn't falter. "You'll be thrilled to know Master Yujin is the culprit this time—caught me on the way back from breakfast.

He wants us to go to the wharves today; he said he's expecting to receive a message from troops on Othakra."

It wasn't uncommon for the Intelligence Master to assign his first-years smaller fetch missions similar to this one. He saw it as an opportunity to encourage teams to collaborate and operate independently from his watchful eyes without giving them too much responsibility. If they earned Master Yujin's trust, they'd occasionally receive orders from further away to retrieve parcels or letters intended for their superior, which sometimes also added an element of secretive interception to their actions. Itsuki was certain they'd see changes in responsibility like those soon, but Obito didn't find much use in speculating. Master Yujin was one of the few military officials who could make his decisions independently, but Emperor Akuwara also kept his eyes on the hitokiri and onmitsu he favored, which meant Yujin didn't always get the final say in those moments.

"If I remember right, General Aki should also be returning around then." Obito paused to watch his partner process the information. The General himself wasn't much to be concerned with, nor was the troop of recruits he'd sought out, but the added chaos of two ships simultaneously unloading at the harbor would make their contact harder to locate.

"Has it been that long already? Well...the ship from Othakra should arrive first, so we'll find our contact fast and clear out as soon as possible." Relentlessly optimistic, but that was simply the Perenin boy's way of seeing life. "We're just getting a letter from General Xiang to Master Yujin, and I doubt we'll have much trouble figuring out which soldier is our messenger—rumor says the wolves got to him during a scrap and took off a good chunk of his ear."

Obito's eyes snapped to his again; it wasn't a malicious look, but the other boy still jumped a little at how suddenly it happened. Morbidly intrigued by this detail, he cautiously prodded for confirmation that he'd heard correctly. "An ear?"

"That's what Master Yujin said, and I don't see why either party would lie."

"You don't think anyone lies," Obito mumbled as he returned to his reading.

"And you think *everyone* does." Itsuki smiled and leaned over to obstruct his view once more. Sensing his growing agitation, he made his expression a little more sheepish, if not outright apologetic. "Those ships *are* coming in relatively soon, and as I said, it's coming from *Othakra,* which means it's a priority. We should get going within the hour."

Resigned, Obito rolled his eyes and closed the book.

WINTER WINDS CUT THROUGH the air and stung Obito's face as he and Itsuki approached the wharves; Itsuki was filling the silence with whatever went through his consciousness, as he usually did, though he knew Obito was only halfway listening. Most of the time, the other boy didn't need his participation, anyway, and he was perfectly content to let him talk at will. They had their differences, but he enjoyed his partner's rambles, although he'd often keep opposing opinions to himself. Assuming the matter was relatively harmless, he'd acted on his temptation to debate with Itsuki when they'd first met. However, after discovering how quickly it'd become an emotionally charged affair on his counterpart's behalf, he concluded that a new method was better for their team's overall well-being. He'd never been great with other people's emotions; his own could sometimes be enough of a foreign concept.

"—Shinta and Mika seem to think they're going to run a message to Genjing soon, but Master Yujin doesn't even trust them to run to Kurushima, and that's, what, five miles away?" Itsuki snickered. "They'll be pissed when it turns out to be any other team."

Obito considered adding a comment, but a salty, icy gust rolled up from the waters as they approached where the street opened into a large cobblestone square and the city met the sea, which decidedly ended his desire to talk. Like he expected they'd see, two ships were drawn to port on opposite sides of the pier, one with its black sails rolled tight and the other's crew still folding the ones billowing from its masts. As they drew closer, the roar of ocean waves, overlapping conversation, and moving rigging filled his ears as wood and steel hollowly echoed under his feet. Judging by neat three-man rows of soldiers filing down the loading ramp from the one on their left, it didn't take long to determine which one they needed; new enlistments wouldn't be so orderly. However, it also meant Obito's concern about General Aki's crew—an extra headache to work around—hadn't gone unwarranted. Fortunately, most of the general's prospective soldiers who had already found their way to the docks weren't moving far without further directions and waited in a cluster around that ship's ramp. Most of them likely hadn't been to the Capital before; it was wise to stick close.

"Let's stop here," Itsuki suggested when they came to a stack of crates slightly away from all the fuss, though still within sight of the ship carrying experienced military personnel. He followed Obito's eyes across the makeshift aisle that had formed between the two crews. "Good-sized bunch, isn't it?"

"Suppose it is," he replied. How should he know?

His eyes wandered, and became drawn to a boy wearing a tattered gray cloak. They were about ten feet apart, so it wasn't difficult to notice the violet of his irises when he looked in Obito's general direction. He quickly averted his gaze, though it wasn't fast enough to escape observation from Itsuki.

"A slaveborn?"

"—Northern Nomad—"

"Same difference, isn't it? Either way, I've never seen one enlist...then again, I doubt that's a useful metric." His partner shrugged, clearly not interested in furthering their discussion, as his black eyes were already lighting up as he spotted what must've been their contact. He waved to get the man's attention. "You there!"

The one-eared man stopped to search for who called out to him, head cocked and looking hopelessly confused when he settled on the two young onmitsu. He shifted the bag on his shoulder. "Y'mean me, boy?"

"Yes, sir! Would you happen to be carrying a message?"

"I am." He proudly puffed out his chest. "Los' an ear to those scruffy wolves, though, so ye might 'ave ta speak a bit louder."

Itsuki waved him a little closer, and they disappeared behind the crates. It might've been Obito's imagination, but he thought he saw the man swaying a little when he walked. Whether that was the alcohol he reeked of or a result of missing an ear, he couldn't say, nor did he know how badly he wanted an answer.

"So, youse two's Mas'er 'Ujin's hooligans, then?" the Giahatian soldier asked, then promptly belched and sent a nauseating, breathy cloud of stale and fresh ale into the air. Obito was positive he'd never been so offended by anything in his life as he watched the man wipe the corner of his mouth on his sleeve.

Itsuki didn't seem to mind. Instead, he beamed at the man and gave him a polite bow. "We are! My name is Itsuki, and this is my partner, Obito. Do you have the message from General Xiang?"

"Right 'ere." He wobbled slightly when he reached behind himself, pulled out a rolled scroll of parchment from his belt, and handed it to Obito.

He wrinkled his nose as he took the damp paper in hand. He forced a small smile through the urge to grimace and also bowed. "Thank you...sir. Do you need our help getting to a Healer?"

"Nonsense. A man oughta wear 'is battle scars. 'Ave a pleasant one, boys." With that, the soldier gave them a curt nod and strode toward the city.

Itsuki was silent for a moment while he looked off into the distance. "This may be a bit of a stretch, but do you mind if I leave that to you? I want to visit the baker's daughter today—we *were* meant to be off-duty, after all."

"Do her a favor and buy something this time; she should get *something* out of dealing with you for the last few weeks." Obito fought back a small smile when Itsuki rolled his eyes and shot him a playful scowl. He tucked the scroll into his cloak, and, preceded by the Perenin boy's friendly farewell, they parted ways for the afternoon.

THE INTELLIGENCE MASTER TRADITIONALLY lived in private quarters connected to his office, which also gave whoever occupied the position an access point to one of the major passages carved behind the Palace's walls. Some said there was a direct tunnel to the Emperor's study. Obito had no way of confirming or disproving these rumors, but it made logical sense to him, as did his decision to start his search for Master Yujin there. Luckily, his assumptions were correct, and his superior looked away from whatever work he'd spread across his desk when alerted to his presence with a gentle knock against the doorframe.

"Nakamura," the Intelligence Master acknowledged Obito by family name as he stood. "Stay there, please."

Master Yujin wasn't the strictest head spy to work for the Giahatio as the Emperor's right hand, nor was he the most adherent to certain customs, such as the overstuffed ones allegedly meant to convey respect, but the idea that no one should enter his office without his direct permission or supervision remained indisputable. Although this sometimes created inconveniences when he wasn't available, Obito saw it as relatively minor for a reasonable boundary.

"Where's Itsuki?" Master Yujin asked once he'd crossed the room and saw Obito was alone.

"Out pestering some poor girl, but we managed to get this first." Obito retrieved the scroll from its pocket and handed it to him, noting how his superior's brow furrowed as his eyes rapidly raked over the words mere seconds after taking it. The change in expression gave him an uncharacteristic shadow of worry. "Is something wrong, Master Yujin?"

"Not with anything you or Itsuki did," he reassured, no less distracted by the information as he stepped forward, wordlessly pushing Obito back from the threshold until he closed the door behind them. "I'm sorry, this seems to be a higher priority than I previously expected. If you'll excuse me."

"Of course, sir."

They exchanged bows; once the Intelligence Master disappeared down the corridor and his footsteps were no longer audible, Obito decided to retreat to his room for a bit. He also supposed it was time to sit with the letter from his siblings so he could adequately answer, though he didn't have much he wanted to say to any of them. In any case, he knew a simple greeting would keep them happy for now, and he didn't see much of a point in putting it off any longer.

FOUR
THE OPENED GATE

"CAN YOU SEE ANYTHING yet?"

Daisuke squinted hard into the foggy distance; the sun had barely risen yet, so he couldn't tell if he saw Perena's massive silhouette on the horizon or was imagining he did. He turned to Bunji, a comparatively giant young man originally from an island in the south called Itake, and mutely shook his head as his lips pressed together in a tight, worried line.

"Nervous, I take it?"

"Why wouldn't I be? It's not like I'm going somewhere I'm wanted."

"If you're aware of that, why'd you get on the boat in the first place?"

Wintry wind flapping through the sails behind them filled the silence while Daisuke considered an answer he'd already turned over several times during the voyage. Why *would* he think coming to Perena was a practical solution for escaping Okara? Was leaving his family and home ever going to be worth it? *Should* he have left? He'd acted entirely on impulse, after all...hadn't he?

All those concerns aside, if he shouldn't have gone, why was the sense that he'd abandoned his little brother the sole reason he felt even slightly guilty for his actions?

Memories of the pain caused by the caning flashed in and out as very real and visceral sensations on his skin; Honda's threats still boomed in his ears if he sat with his emotions for too long. Eventually, he quietly said, "Between my old man and the masters, staying home would've killed me."

"That's one hell of an answer." Bunji offered him a small, sympathetic smile, then wordlessly dipped his head to excuse himself from their conversation; he'd said the previous night that he had to ensure all his belongings were together before they landed.

Daisuke sighed and leaned over the railing, watching red and orange ribbons ripple across the water, the colorful streaks occasionally interrupted by a salty dark spray as the ship's bow broke through waves and brought them closer to shore, inch by crawling inch. The first few days of his trip hadn't gone over so well—he'd spent them curled into a pathetic, helpless ball belowdecks, horribly ill and endlessly terrified that General Aki had duped him into being returned to Grandmaster Norio. He'd prematurely cursed his stupidity for trusting the General's words during their first meeting. Once the period of misery passed, however, Daisuke forced himself toward the ship's upper deck and found himself surrounded by leagues of open ocean. Upon returning to the bunk area from this little venture, he was fortunate to meet Bunji, who'd been happily keeping to himself by reading as the sea swayed his hammock. He couldn't remember the exact questions he'd used to intrude on the peaceful scene, but doing so had benefited him well.

The friendship they'd struck bore no resemblance to the closeness he'd shared with Shun, but even so, they found common ground through storytelling. Sometimes, it was the ones Daisuke made up on the spot while they helped with tedious tasks around the ship; other times, it was Bunji reading to him in the evening hours while the other men aboard drank questionable ale and caused a mostly good-natured commotion. Somewhere along the way, Bunji announced that he wanted to work with Daisuke to improve his reading skills, and in turn, Daisuke taught him how to stitch repairs or improvements into his clothing. While the younger of the two felt it wasn't equal in value, the arrangement worked amazingly well for both.

As the sun rose to its midmorning position, sea fog steadily lifted away from the water. Daisuke could finally see the silhouette of Perena's Capital not far off from the ship's bow. Since his meager possessions consisted of the cloak around his shoulders and the helix earring in his pocket, he quickly found a spot in the formation when General Aki called his flustered recruits to assemble in neat rows a bit later. Daisuke saw glistening white snow blanketing the land as the ship prepared to dock. He looked at the flimsy sandals he'd fashioned during the voyage; he supposed that was why his feet couldn't stay warm.

"Experienced soldiers—your superiors—are returning home from a recent engagement on Othakra. You lot will do well to stay out of their way," General Aki had instructed in a tone that left no room for questions or additional commentary. He'd added more afterward, but decided to end his lecture when he made note of the glazed look on his recruits' faces from an overload of information.

Daisuke's eyes excitedly raked over the organized lines of soldiers filing down the other ship's boarding ramp once his feet finally touched the docks. It didn't take long for his eager gaze to wander, distracted as he noticed one of them break off to the side to greet a pair of younger, more formally dressed soldiers who likely weren't on the boat—one of them appeared to glance his way momentarily. Though he doubted the other boy saw him for what he was, it still sent a jolt of worry into his heart; he might've been safe at sea as an escapee, but dry land had separate rules. He went back to the first soldier. Dingy bandages with an odd splotch of red in the center were wound around his head several times. It took a moment, but Daisuke suddenly realized the crimson color was blood, and that the wrapping covered the area where his left ear ought to be. The three exchanged brief greetings he couldn't hear—it would've been impossible to try above all the noise—then went behind a stack of crates.

He quickly turned to Bunji, who must've followed his companion's eyes and also caught a glimpse of the man, judging by his mildly concerned expression. "What the hell happened to him?"

"How should I know? Do you want to follow him and ask?"

"Isn't that considered rude?"

"Yes." Bunji sighed, then laughed. "But do what you will."

Daisuke thought about it; in the end, he supposed it might be a little *too* impolite to ask the man directly. However, losing an appendage wasn't easy. Albeit extremely rare, sometimes Grandmaster Norio permitted the overseers to remove a slave's fingers or teeth as forms of punishment—gruesome, but it sent a message even Daisuke couldn't ignore. Gods knew it could've easily been him one day. A shiver ran through him at an unwelcome mental image of such incidents. Granted, he'd never *seen* it happen, but a few graphic stories and a wild imagination allowed him a vivid picture; unsettled by how easily those visuals had crept into his mind, he reckoned it was time to look at something else.

In any case, there was too much to glean from his surroundings to remain fixated on one small thing, and now was not the time to invite pain from a life that no longer belonged to him. In the distance, enormous black spires caught his attention, letting him move past his reflections. Since he'd seen plenty of depictions through ink paintings hanging on Grandmaster Norio's walls, he recognized the Palace easily; however, seeing the imposing structure from this proximity quickly made him realize how little those paintings managed to capture. He could've stared at the volcanic rock obelisks for much longer, but General Aki had come to address his men once more.

"We will stay together as we move through the city, and for today, I recommend that you hold off on any urges you may have to explore our beautiful Capital. When we get to our building, someone will show you to your assigned bunk and footlocker. Given our early arrival, you will be measured for uniforms today, and I expect you to bathe at some point—we'll go over expectations and more once we get to the barracks. For now, I believe this is a good place to start. Are there any questions?" A beat of silence passed, the few voices filling the space the General left open being those occasionally pushing forward from the background. "Good. Now, let's help the crew finish unloading and be on our way."

YUJIN'S SKIN CRAWLED AS he approached the door sealing the Emperor's private study, hand trembling ever so slightly before he touched the gold-plated handle; gods, his nerves made him ashamed of his title. The Master of Intelligence, head trainer and leader of all the Empire's spies, should expect to deliver unpleasant news to his monarch occasionally. However, anyone with the slightest sense knew to be as nervous as Yujin felt; Emperor Akuwara was a notoriously unforgiving man, cruel to the bone except with his son, Prince Akuko, though he was hardly an affectionate father.

Although the Prince was only nearing five years of age, he'd already been at the center of much controversy, particularly among elites who did not want bastard blood ascending the Giahatian throne one day. Yujin had heard rumors of noblemen refusing to send their sons for mandated military service if Akuko stood to inherit the Empire. He hadn't mentioned such reports to Akuwara yet, as they bore little threat for now, but he'd taken note of those who had spoken out; Imperial intelligence agents would eventually monitor them once he worked out who could handle the responsibility without bias. Should they unwisely choose to act upon their treasonous declarations, Yujin could just as easily make them reconsider.

For now, he had a separate matter to present to Akuwara. After spending his afternoon deep in discussion with the high-ranking generals who served as the military's primary tacticians—and bolstering his courage to speak with the Emperor—it was clear that the letter he received from Othakra couldn't be ignored or treated lightly. The wolf-shifters called the Okami, a race of warriors supposedly as savage as the predatory animal they emulated, were fiercely unyielding in their want to keep the isle free from Imperial advancement. While Yujin had never met any himself, he *had* seen the aftermath of battling them—the bloody, shredded remains of a Giahatian soldier were a familiar sight, yet highly contradictory to a carefully crafted, colorful beadwork pendant the wolves sent to Emperor Akuro in years past. He felt he didn't have a clear enough picture of who the Okami were. Unfortunately, one of their most recent engagements with the tribe over the summer turned out to be a significant misstep on the Giahatio's behalf, and resulted in many casualties on both sides. This follow-up report indicated things would escalate further if they continued provoking their opponents. Surprisingly, the tacticians had unanimously agreed with Yujin's assessment; the Giahatio couldn't afford more time or resources on Othakra.

Emperor Akuwara's study greeted him with low light and the scent of burning incense infused with lavender, one of His Highness's favorites and extremely difficult to find during winter months.

"Yujin? To what do I owe the honor?" Emperor Akuwara turned from where he stood by the window, watching snowflakes that had begun to fall from the evening sky. It wasn't nearly the pleasant greeting it sounded like—Akuwara's mahogany brown eyes already spoke of a great annoyance bubbling beneath the surface.

"My sincerest apologies for failing to notify you first, Your Highness—"

"I would think so. You must have something urgent to share."

"Yes, Your Highness," Yujin said tightly, trying to bury his own irritation. After a pause to collect himself, he continued, "A new intelligence report from our summer encounter with the Okami confirmed that one of our men slew Lady Okami. Lord Takeo is still furious and grieving—he announced that he'd give us one last chance to leave before they slaughter all Giahatians who set foot on their isle. He'll await our decision before he makes his—he says that since he has a young daughter to raise alone now, he does not want to choose war."

Thick black brows pulled together in a concentrated scowl, which Akuwara directed at the polished floor before his gaze shifted to the window again. The silver circlet adorning the Emperor's head gleamed in the warm light when he looked toward the heavens and placed his hands behind his back. "Have you spoken with the generals already?"

"I have, Sire."

"And what did they suggest?"

Yujin swallowed a dry patch in his throat. "We all agreed a temporary ceasefire—"

"No doubt bearing in mind that it is *my* word that is final."

"Of course, but if I may be blunt, Sire, our occupations in the North to quell the tax rebellions severely limit what we can do on Othakra. Under these circumstances, I believe it'd be madness to stay." Mentioning the minor uprisings wasn't the wisest route he could've taken, as tax increases on northern farmers to fund the war with the Okami were ideas of Akuwara's conception, but Yujin's sole concern was the strain placed on their forces.

A long pause steadily suffocated the life out of the room when the Emperor shifted to look at him again. The monarch studied his Master of Intelligence intently, weighing whether he should speak with the white-hot rage building on his tongue at the pathetic failure that had amounted to his Empire's predicament. At last, Akuwara relented. "Very well, then. You are dismissed, onmitsu."

His final words came out like acid. Yujin flinched before bowing deeply and wordlessly exiting the Emperor's study.

Isn't he done yet? Daisuke grumbled to himself as he stood with his arms stretched out to the sides, waiting with limited patience for the tailor to finish marking down the necessary measurements for his uniform. So far today, they'd toured the barracks and went through parts of the Palace they were allowed to enter—including the baths and the commissary he'd soon need to visit—and sat through a droning lecture about rules and expectations. The sooner he could get this fitting over with, the better. Occasional discerning noises from the tailor about Daisuke's small stature whittled away at his patience—as if it hadn't been humiliating enough to take in the baffled, questioning glance the man shot at General Aki when he'd stepped up for his turn. A steady, cold trickle of water from his wet hair dripped onto his back, brewing embarrassment into irritation with each droplet and stealing any delight he'd found in the warm bath he'd taken before this.

"You're a scrawny lad, aren't you?" the tailor remarked. To Daisuke or himself, no one else would ever know. "Then again, I'm not sure what else I expected; I've never met a slaveborn who *didn't* look a little underfed."

Daisuke scowled at the snowflakes piling up outside the window in front of him, sure his cheeks had turned as red as they felt. "Think there might be a reason?"

The older man peered at him from over the thin wire rims on his glasses as he returned his writing tools to a nearby table with the rest of his supplies. Daisuke tensed, fearful the tone he'd used would get him into trouble, and mentally prepared to talk his way out of it; the sole reason he didn't immediately run for it was the lack of animosity he saw in the man's eyes. Instead, he merely looked surprised, like he'd finally realized something.

"I'd better finish and let you get off to supper, then," he said as he passed Daisuke his original shirt, which he'd also washed during his bath. He'd hung it in front of the small mantle in the room so it would at least partially dry. "You need to build some strength if you want to be a decent soldier."

Daisuke hesitantly took his clothing back, watching the tailor in disbelief, especially when he smiled gently. He mirrored the expression half-heartedly, thanked him, and quietly slipped out while pulling his shirt over his head again. Now that he was free and the long day was ending, he wanted nothing more than to become one with the soft mattress on his bunk, but a persistent rumble in his stomach coaxed him into following a few faces he recognized toward the mess hall. The scents hanging in the air were somewhat familiar to him—*slaves* didn't eat well on Okara, but masters, overseers, and guests did—likely due to how often he and Kulako hid amongst Grandmaster Norio's kitchen staff when seeking refuge from their father. He hadn't been much of a student to those workers, as the temptation to cause mischief would eventually call his name and encourage him to run off elsewhere. However, he recognized the smoky smell of grilled tuna and simmering vegetables as the group he trailed drew nearer, which made him hungrier.

Fortunately, Bunji had the foresight and politeness to save him a seat, though Daisuke could barely find him among all the soldiers packed into the benches. He eyed a bright orange sauce covering the fish and vegetables he'd detected, all sitting in a bowl atop a mound of rice.

"What is this?" he asked as he picked it up, letting warm ceramic heat his hands as he breathed in spicy and tangy aromas from his dish.

"Donburi, I think they called it. I've never had it before, either," Bunji answered after swallowing a large bite, then gestured for him to do the same. "Did you sign the book yet?"

Daisuke's moment of bliss in tasting the delicious hints of sweetness and heat combined with the meal's other ingredients, easily the best thing he'd ever eaten, instantly became soured by this question. Without meaning to, he whined, "There's *more?*"

"Weren't you paying attention earlier?"

"If we're being honest, I missed at least half of that lecture."

Bunji sighed and pinched the bridge of his nose before letting a fondly exasperated smile touch his lips. "You need to sign the enlistment book for General Aki's records. Someone said they have one for Kurushima and intelligence, too, so it's standard procedure."

"Gods' sake. I just want to go to bed."

Complaints aside, once Daisuke decided he'd eaten enough—he hadn't realized his hunger, but the portion offered was more than he'd ever finish on his own—he let Bunji have the rest, then followed him to wash the used dishes. Afterward, he asked his friend for directions, and was soon on his way toward General Aki's quarters where he could find the book.

He hesitated when he finally found the general's half-ajar door. Unsure if he was meant to knock or let himself in, he hovered around the threshold, hoping to time his entrance with whoever came out next. Fortunately, luck was on his side for a moment. Two voices approached the other side of the door shortly after, and another young man pushed it open the rest of the way. Daisuke snuck in by ducking around the pair as they walked by, but when one of them purposely bumped into his shoulder, General Aki sternly cleared his throat at what he'd witnessed. They scurried away posthaste. The General gave him an apologetic smile, then gestured toward a small side table he'd left in the middle of the room.

Daisuke nervously looked at General Aki when he got to the table, then back at the open pages of yellowed and crinkly paper. An inkwell and pen sat beside them, but he'd never written anything with more than a stick in an available patch of dirt where the overseers wouldn't find him. This was more intimidating than Bunji originally made it sound.

"Do you know how to write your name, Daisuke?" General Aki sounded uncomfortable for asking, though he'd tried to make it a gentle inquiry. Daisuke merely nodded; his answer clearly piqued the General's curiosity. "What about reading? Can you read?"

"It's—well, I...I'm getting better at it."

"Then I'll have you sign under Chunta—right here, I mean." He pointed at a blank line beneath the ugly scrawling of a name Daisuke had only heard occasionally around the ship. He picked up the pen with his right hand, then, uncertain about how it felt in his palm, shifted it to his left, where it felt most natural. His focus broke when the General added, "I hope I didn't insult you by sounding surprised."

"*I'd* be surprised if you weren't...sir." Daisuke proudly beamed at his penmanship on the page as he put the writing utensil away once more—it wasn't the prettiest script, but it was a relief to see how well the skill he'd learned with sticks translated to using an actual pen.

General Aki scratched the stubble on his cheek. "Well, I'll do my best to ensure that part of your life is over, lad—no matter what anyone else tries to tell you, you are not expected to tolerate disrespect from your peers. Your superiors, either, but in that case, you will come to me first."

He turned to examine Aki's face more fully; he didn't sound insincere or appear to be hiding something malicious behind his words, but Daisuke didn't know what to do with what he'd been told. Instead, he uneasily thanked the General, checked his work in the book once more, and bowed before leaving. The hallways were much quieter now than they'd been all day, supplying a much-needed moment of peace.

"*Finally*," a voice came from behind him as he walked along. Daisuke turned to see an older soldier in a white nightshirt and matching trousers, though he didn't have time to register much else before the man thrust a lumpy burlap sack into his arms. "My bunk's in the east barracks when you're done washing those."

Daisuke gave him a bewildered look. "I'm sorry, I don't understand."

"General Aki picked you up from Okara, didn't he?"

Now I get it, Daisuke thought as he openly rolled his eyes. He shoved the laundry bag back into the soldier's hands. While he didn't enjoy feeling like he *needed* permission to defend himself, presumptuous people such as this man would always exist somewhere in his life. General Aki's reassurance had already done its part to encourage the bolder streaks of his personality.

"No, I don't think so, idiot."

His counterpart spluttered. "*Excuse* me?"

"I'm not your servant, and per General Aki, I will not be treated like one. If you have a problem with that, we can talk to him together." He grinned at the way he could see the other soldier trying to process what was said; somewhere in his mind, he wondered if he looked as wicked as his mother always told him he sounded when he spoke bluntly. "Or, we can go our separate ways and pretend this didn't happen. I'm sure that would be less embarrassing for you."

Heart racing with the instinctual fear that he'd be punished for his words, Daisuke didn't bother to wait for a response. He straightened to his fullest height and marched off as if he were expected elsewhere. Once he turned a corner, he paused and glanced over his shoulder, letting out a massive sigh of relief when no angered voices followed him through the passage. He scowled at the pools of orange intermittently illuminating the wooden floor despite this; silently, he cursed the man's audacity while lamenting the fact that he didn't get to enjoy how shocked the other soldier must've looked.

He deserved it. Daisuke readopted his confident posture and made his way back to the bunkroom. The warm, soft bed he'd set his stuff on earlier awaited him in the low-lit room, halfway filled with others who were already sleeping or had just turned in for the night. Bunji wasn't among them, likely off for a drink with the rest, which, by Daisuke's admission, was more than deserved after weeks of putting up with him while at sea. In any case, he assumed they would also be on their way soon.

He stretched out comfortably on his stomach and flexed his toes. They didn't go over the edge on this mattress; Northern Nomads weren't known for their towering height like Perenins or Giahatians, but he'd started to outgrow the cot he and Kulako shared, so this was a welcome change. Feeling pleasantly full and oddly safe despite being in an unfamiliar place, he readily sank into the softness beneath him, not waiting long for sleep to come.

DAISUKE FOUND HIMSELF STARING at the empty, gaping mouth of a cave, surrounded by swirling snowdrifts, but unable to feel the bite of frosty winds on his skin as he thought he should have. It was as if an invisible dome shielded him from the elements. A thick red rope hung across the cave's shrouded entrance, decorated with seven silver charms carefully crafted to look like spiraling dragons. Drawing on the sparse knowledge he had about religious symbols, he surmised they were for protection, intended to seal away whatever lay within the cavern.

Is this...a dream? He marveled as he glanced at a small, twisted tree to his left and squinted at the shredded black bark along its bare branches; he seemed to be on a mountain, which confirmed there couldn't be another explanation. He closed his eyes tightly and held utterly still, hoping he'd reawaken within seconds. When he sensed nothing change, he cautiously cracked his eyelids open again, alarmed when he caught sight of the large white wolf sitting before him.

Her golden eyes studied him as intently as they had when she guided him away from the plantations—penetrating and soul-deep. Then, tilting her ears forward, she asked in a warm, comforting voice, *"Is this your first time with the Raven God's gift, young one?"*

That's what grandma always called dreams, so I must've been right...but why *am I having one?*

Daisuke didn't harbor the same hate or fear toward the white wolf as he did for other canines, nor was he afraid of the fact that she'd spoken—*to* him, no less—in a perfectly articulate and human voice. Perhaps more inexplicably, he'd expected it. Even so, he barely managed to answer with a weak, uncertain nod. He watched in disbelief when he saw her tail thump against the ground, apparently amused by his response.

"There's no need for worry. Nothing can harm you in this realm."

The winds gusted again, sending the white wolf away in a burst of snowflakes that blew into Daisuke's face. He shivered and bundled against himself at the icy sensation rolling over him, though his eyes soon found the rope again. He swallowed, then stepped toward it. The charms delicately jingled when he took a section of the barrier in his hand to step underneath; he blinked when he appeared on the other side before he could complete the action. The soft music from the charms became a deep, resonant note until all sound faded once more. Ignoring his pounding heart, he kept one hand on a cold stone wall for guidance and forged ahead, increasingly aware of the ground's downward slope, which eventually became short steps carved into the mountain's insides. Finally, after ages of aimless walking, the cave floor abruptly plateaued, causing Daisuke to stumble and fall to his knees.

A pale green luminescence crawled across the antechamber's walls, soon bathing the room in the same light; it also revealed seven marble pedestals feet away from where he now stood. Each podium held an enormous statue of a jade dragon, with the one in the center being the most massive. Following a swirl of color in the floor, Daisuke inched closer until he could see their distinct features: scales on long bodies that looked tougher than iron despite several cracks running through their structures, dangerously vicious claws, fiery, angered eyes, and threateningly bared fangs.

Except for the one in the middle—its maw hung open, waiting for someone to place something there.

Daisuke eyed it warily; deciding he'd be better off not going near the ominous figure, he turned to the one flanking its left side. The surrounding soft glow of green revealed a carving on the pedestal beneath it, but it looked as though ages of sediment and other debris had caked over the original image. Hypnotized, he slowly stretched his hand toward it, though he stopped before he touched the sign to search the otherwise empty chamber once more, unable to shake the feeling that something wanted—or perhaps even dared—him to continue. He caught sight of his fingertips trembling from the corner of his eye, gaze then drawn back to the statue.

"What am I supposed to see?" Daisuke's words shook like his limbs. After another moment of watching the jade dragon, he swallowed his nerves and brushed the freshest layer of dust away from the plaque. In a flash, the green light became blinding as the ground went dark, broke apart, and swallowed him whole.

FIVE

HIVE-MINDED

EVERY MUSCLE IN DAISUKE'S arms shook or twitched as he adjusted the spear's shaft in his grip, hands aching from torn calluses on his palms and wrists equally sore after the last few hours of holding the weapon. His shoulders and forearms also hurt. He glared at the mannequin ahead of him, a vaguely human-shaped thing made of straw and bamboo; he'd heard a skilled assassin could cut one in half. He flexed his stiff fingers again.

It'd been at least two weeks since his arrival in the Capital, and while he'd expected training to be difficult, he never thought it'd be this outright impossible. The spear—a footsoldier's primary weapon in battle—was embarrassingly awkward in his grasp, too long for him to control, and not even the lifeless training dummies seemed threatened by his attacks. He'd made marginal improvements, as he supposed most people would after a fortnight of almost daily practice, though it never felt like he was doing enough to keep in stride with everyone else.

"Strike!" a man in his early twenties yelled from the other side of the indoor training hall.

Daisuke groaned and lamely poked the figure in front of him with the spear's tip before setting its opposite end on the wooden floor, leaning on it to catch his breath; he needed a break. Much to his dismay, the trainer leading spear drills for the day didn't show any signs of letting up yet. Daisuke's strength and health were also steadily improving, but it didn't take a highly observant person to notice that, although he was one of the youngest here, he was also behind his peers in this area. A glance to his right showed others in his row easily dislodging from their targets and positioning themselves in a ready stance again.

They've sold their souls to Kuro or something—we've been at this for hours. He heard a slight rattling noise behind him as he wiped the sweat from his brow with the back of his hand. Before he could fully register the sound, something hard whacked him on the left shoulder.

"Fuck!" he gasped, one hand immediately going to the swell of pain while the other struggled to maintain control of his weapon. Wincing, he turned to his assailant.

Junpei gave him a stupid, smug, ugly grin as he rested a shinai on his shoulder. The bamboo sword rattled as it moved. "Packing it in for the day already, silk-spinner?"

Daisuke glowered. There wasn't much he could say in return—Junpei and his four goons came from families with extensive military pedigrees. They were about to pass their second benchmark evaluation to become fully-fledged infantrymen, which meant they'd been training for at least a year. Although they were each around fourteen, Daisuke didn't doubt they'd earned their places as occasional junior instructors regarding raw martial skill. However, "silk-spinner" was a derogatory name thrown at Northern Nomads, whether or not they served a master, and hearing it instantly set his teeth on edge.

"What the fuck did you call me?" he demanded between heavy breaths as he tried to ignore the throbbing in his shoulder blade, though his bravery shrunk when he realized Junpei's gang of morons had come to investigate. Unfortunately, their positions as junior instructors allowed them some freedom, and no one in the group liked Daisuke—an entirely mutual feeling.

He was on his own until an adult took notice of the situation; none of the other nearby trainees would dare break formation to call for assistance. Junpei's strike with the shinai was well within the parameters of his job, as much as Daisuke wanted to accuse him of purely malicious intent. However, what he sensed was beginning to take place had nothing to do with those duties.

"There a problem here?" one of the minions asked threateningly, acting as if his voice hadn't cracked when he spoke.

Junpei smirked, now leaning against his shinai for support. "Don't worry, boys. This little *silk-spinner* doesn't like his name. Come to think of it, maybe we *should* call him something else."

"Why? Does the first slur have too many syllables for you?" Daisuke glanced at the door when he heard it slide open. General Aki's figure loomed at the threshold, which told him it was time to surrender. He rolled his eyes and pivoted to return to his mannequin, but one of the remaining idiots stopped him midway by gripping his upper arm so tightly he felt fingernails poke through his sleeve. "What do *you* want, stupid?"

"Take that back," the third underling ordered with a shove.

The fourth one chimed in, "You need to show us some respect."

Daisuke had planned to go about his day with good intentions, all of which he was more than happy to abandon now. He tossed his spear to the ground and used his free arm to push his captor in return, hard enough to make the unbalanced boy stumble as he seethed, "Fuck all of you, too."

The next few seconds were a bit blurry; before Daisuke knew it, he was curled into a ball on the ground under a pile of comparatively massive teenagers, right eye throbbing and arms shielding his face and head while they continued to swing or kick at him. Suddenly, the onslaught stopped, and soon after, someone dragged him to his feet by the shirt collar. Upon seeing Junpei's moronic face again, Daisuke's anger returned, and he swung his legs upward to kick him in the groin. A vicious, satisfied grin crossed his lips when the other boy collapsed to his knees, whimpering in pain and cursing through gritted teeth.

"All of you come with me. *Now.*" General Aki's forceful voice must've shaken the minions just as it had Daisuke, as they helped their ringleader to his feet without taking their wide, worried eyes off the man.

Aki didn't let go of Daisuke's shirt when he turned on his heel to exit, which was, admittedly, quite intelligent on his behalf; he also knew the scrawny boy didn't have any plans to do as instructed. None of the higher authority figures here had hit Daisuke *yet*, and he wasn't interested in that changing anytime soon. A caravan of excuses raced through Daisuke's mind as he and the other boys were marched straight to General Aki's private quarters. Once the General finished unceremoniously shoving the gang of morons through the door one by one, he finally released Daisuke and closed them inside.

"Attention!" he barked when he rounded on them, fury blazing in his dark eyes.

All six boys scrambled over one another to assemble in a neat row, standing stick-straight with their hands behind their backs. No one dared to try looking at whoever stood beside him, too terrified at the General's rare display of anger to move.

"I am absolutely appalled by what I saw back there. Fortunately for you lot, this is only your first offense. For showing such unacceptable and horrendous disrespect to your comrade, you five will report to the Palace groundskeepers after supper every night this week to help muck out the stables." It was a dark, cold, wet, and miserable job, to say the least—very few Palace staff members were interested in taking on a stableman's duties rather than their own. The mere suggestion had to border on insulting to someone from families like theirs.

"But, General Aki—"

"I expect far better of my soldiers, Junpei, and what you did in there was nothing short of disappointing and dishonorable. They'd have all six of you on the whipping posts for this at Kurushima."

"If anyone belongs on the whipping post, it's—" Junpei silenced himself this time, folding under Aki's intense warning glare within seconds of locking eyes with their superior.

"Unless you're interested in making it two weeks, do yourselves a favor and leave." The General's tone ensured the boys wouldn't take his statement as a suggestion.

Daisuke tried to join the ensuing scurry to obey the order—none of them were bold enough to test the man's temper beyond what they'd already invoked—but Aki gripped him by the back of his shirt again. Seeing his hope of escaping vanish, he sighed in defeat, then nervously turned toward his fate. After a moment, General Aki's eyes finally shifted toward Daisuke, who flinched under his gaze. Upon being released, he immediately took a few steps away and turned his back to the nearest wall, constantly scanning the other man for signs of movement. Gods, he felt like he was standing in front of Honda.

"Hikari's sake, lad, what's wrong?"

The question jarred Daisuke enough for him to realize his defensive posture and how utterly confused General Aki appeared. He glanced about the room as if frightened out of a dream—he hadn't noticed his current surroundings blending with haunting, familiar ones from home. For a moment, he *had* been looking at Honda, not the General. Self-loathing crawled into his chest.

The older man pressed a little further, "Daisuke, you aren't on the plantations anymore. Whatever the masters there did—"

"Fuck the masters. My old man was worse," he impulsively interrupted. Then, embarrassed by his words and unable to look General Aki in the eye, he turned his head slightly and crossed his arms over his chest.

"I see," General Aki's voice softened a little, though he looked uncomfortable with what their conversation had revealed. "I don't believe doing those things makes a man a better soldier. Like Junpei and his friends, however, you *are* expected to take responsibility for your actions and reactions."

Mistrust must've flashed in Daisuke's face as it traveled through his mind—Honda's interpretations of learning responsibility or showing respect sure as hell didn't agree with those sentiments, and he had no reason to expect anyone else believed otherwise—when Aki's expression grew sympathetic as he awaited the boy's response. It lodged in Daisuke's throat. He couldn't grasp what the General told him, nor could he stand the vulnerability he'd accidentally displayed to his superior in so few words. He didn't think it'd have the power to make him feel so disgustingly weak. Finally, he nodded as if he'd been considering General Aki's words all along.

"A few nights of scrubbing the training and dining hall floors should be enough to sort out your anger."

Being assigned a menial chore seemed like the least humiliating part of the afternoon. Daisuke's blackened right eye ached. "Understood, sir."

He didn't wait to be dismissed and turned to leave as soon as the words left his mouth, barely remembering a bow; he desperately needed to get away before he somehow made himself seem even more helpless. The grip of self-loathing and disgust tightened into a suffocating squeeze he wished he could release.

HARD-PACKED SNOW CRUNCHED SOFTLY under Obito's boots as he and Itsuki approached Zhao, a town about an hour or two down the Westbound Road from the Capital's sprawling edges. Both boys were sore from an exhausting day of weapons training, and small, circular bruises covered their arms where they'd practiced on one another's pressure points afterward.

Master Yujin must've been in a foul mood. He'd put those in Obito's age group through endless forms and drills all afternoon, and sentenced half of his older students to organize and clean the poisons room while the rest did the same in the library. Then, as if all that hadn't been enough for one day, just before Obito and Itsuki could head for a bath, Master

Yujin pulled them aside and told them it was their turn to deliver a letter to the magistrate in Zhao. Obito supposed things could've been worse—they could've been shoveling out the horse stalls or scrubbing floors as he'd heard General Aki had done the previous week to some of his soldiers still in basic training. Thinking about it added to his tiredness rather than mitigating it.

Unfortunately, Itsuki wasn't too exhausted to boast about some predictions he'd made not long ago. "Going to the next town over might not be a big deal to most people, but we're the first among our friends Master Yujin asked. So, I'd say we're doing pretty well for ourselves."

"This could've waited until tomorrow, which means he's still pissed about something—that's hardly good." Obito rolled his eyes as he ran a hand through his hair to shake out some of the snowflakes that had landed in it.

"You *assume* this could've waited," Itsuki corrected with a grin. Following a long, moody silence, he added, "Fine, you want to know what's *actually* bad about this? Mika knows, too; you probably didn't see him because you were too busy plotting a murder on the side, but he eavesdropped the whole time Master Yujin briefed us."

Obito scowled as Itsuki exchanged a greeting with the soldiers who stood under Zhao's entry arch. Although nearly every settlement on Perena had some form of military occupation, few had remnants of their original Perenin architecture, which included walls or gates surrounding them. Once the Giahatians invaded and sparked a civil war nearly two hundred years ago, most of the towns or villages affected also lost their defenses; even the Capital didn't have a wall anymore. In Zhao's case, the soldiers guarding the city—quite reasonably—liked having the option of getting out of the elements.

"Mika's jealousy is arguably less concerning than Master Yujin's temper," Obito said, continuing their conversation once they passed the guards.

"I don't get why you two hate each other so much. Maybe you need to talk it out or something. I mean, you're cousins, so—" Itsuki silenced himself when he glanced at his partner, meeting forest green eyes that dangerously dared him to finish his sentence.

He must've forgotten how much one bristled when someone mentioned the other, although neither would explain why. The closest he'd gotten was Mika telling him they were simply too different, and that Obito treated him as inferior since he wasn't from the main family; classic nobility issues or not, Itsuki didn't buy it. Mika acted like everything the other boy did was an ill-intended slight against him, while Obito did everything he could to avoid speaking with his cousin.

Realizing the unintended consequences of his expression, which he'd barely been aware of making in the first place, Obito sighed. "I'm sorry."

"Well, you wouldn't be you if you weren't cross about *something*." A wide grin brightened Itsuki's face when he saw Obito roll his eyes again, although it was softer this time than his usual, annoyed air. "Why don't I deliver the letter by myself? You look like you need some time to be alone, anyway."

Most people in the onmitsu ranks might've assumed Itsuki was trying to dismiss his partner from the mission. Although Obito wondered if he should've been one such person, he couldn't deny that giving himself space sounded better than arguing with the idea. They parted ways in a market area around the corner from the magistrate's mansion.

Obito found himself peering into the windows of nearby shops that were already closed for the night. He'd take his two younger sisters around during festival seasons to do the same thing when he still lived at home. The night would often start with them trying to trail their older brothers—Mika joined them, too, as his family always visited then—and wind up with them eyeing gleaming trinkets through the glass as he did now. A row of seven tiny, blown glass green dragons resting on a deep red cushion amid a nest of pearls caught his attention; Yumi and Hina would've loved them, though he'd ultimately have to neutralize their inevitable argument about what to name the things. He sighed, slowly and heavily. He missed his sisters and supposed the same went for his brothers, but physical distance aside, that part of his life never felt further away. Everything had changed so...violently and abruptly last year, he barely remembered what *he'd* been like beforehand. Obito doubted he'd ever know that version of himself again.

Suddenly, everything about the air around him became uneasy, like he could sense something horrendously negative stepping closer and closer. He drew back from the window and checked the street for logical signs of his otherwise unexplainable misgivings, though his mind kept turning to further irrationality. Snow drifted down from the rooftop above him, swirling before his eyes like a thick miasma before a breeze dispelled it. Snakes of fear coiled tighter around his insides with each fresh scan of his surroundings until he spotted a seemingly lost man, bobbing his head as if searching for something. By the time his mind caught up with his emotions, the mounting tension eased from his system at the sight of someone acting so ordinarily in a crowded market. Zhao's preparations for the Winter Festival were already in full swing, and its marketplace was sizeable compared to the rest of the city due to overall lower prices than most shops in the Capital, so the streets tended to stay consistently busy throughout the day.

Wait... Obito squinted at the man to get a clearer picture.

His blood went cold. Terror chained him to the spot where he stood when he realized he recognized the man as Mika's father—*his* uncle. The same person who was responsible for—

He shook himself, desperate to stay in the present, and forced himself into motion again. He sought the shelter of an alley and retreated into the alcove until shadows swallowed him. He wouldn't have enough time to get past Giichi undetected and knew he shouldn't stray too far from where he agreed to meet Itsuki; for now, stowing away in a cramped space would have to suffice.

His uncle paused when approached by someone heavily cloaked in all black; they'd also masked any discernable features on their hands with leather gloves. They exchanged a few indistinguishable words with Giichi before venturing closer to the alley's entrance, off the main street and presumably away from curious eyes and ears. Obito stiffened when they stopped in front of him, then carefully took another step back, pinning his shoulders to the brick wall behind him as he worked to slow his anxious breathing, softening it until he made no sound. One didn't need to be onmitsu to predict how this situation might end if they caught him.

"It took you long enough to find me," the cloaked figure's rasping voice criticized once the two were certain their conversation wouldn't be interrupted.

"Perhaps you're unfamiliar with the roads here, but traveling from the Wen Valley isn't easy during the winter." Hearing Giichi's voice for the first time in well over a year and tensely watching his every movement as he interacted with this stranger sent another icy wave through Obito's veins. Still, he stood his ground—not that he had many other choices. Panic couldn't win.

"Zandaka's Servant won't care for excuses, Giichi. Have you completed the task asked of you?"

There was a pause as Giichi's shoulders stiffened; he never liked being spoken to in that manner. Obito watched as he curled his fists, then slowly flexed his fingers to relax any reflexive anger. A twin set of ruby rings gleamed with restrained malice as they caught the light from the nearby shop's outdoor lamp.

"Yes, I have," Giichi answered, voice lacking an edge despite his previous reactions. "Hideo won't be able to leave his estates immediately as his in-laws are visiting for some time, but he'll bring the talisman to General Aki as soon as they return home."

"Good—I believe the Servant will find that satisfactory. In the meantime, you should return to *your* home in the Wen Valley; surely, your wife and son miss you by now. Never minding that, you'll have the Imperial army at the cult's heels in no time with how you like to bark."

"I am not the only one who believes Emperor Akuwara disgraces the Higia Dynasty and the Giahatian Empire by intending to leave us with an illegitimate heir."

"Enough. Zandaka's seal is far from broken, and we *must* maintain secrecy until then."

Tense silence ensued between them again. Then, without warning, the hooded person minutely tilted their head toward the shadows. They'd finally sensed someone was there, watching and listening. Their eyes settled on Obito, and he pressed against the wall in a futile effort to escape further detection should they come forward; just when he considered praying he could become one with it, Giichi distracted his counterpart.

"Where are you headed now, then?"

"I have also been away for too long, so I'll be heading further west to Zhu from here before returning to our base. The Servant needs me to gather some items from my contact there. Besides, the Winter Festival is next week—I need to be long gone by then."

"I see. Shall we part ways?"

"Preferably."

They gave each other a polite bow, then walked off in different directions—Giichi went left, while the stranger went right. Obito waited a moment to ensure they'd gone, then slowly dislodged himself from the alley. Looking in either direction, his uncle and the person he'd met had disappeared completely; it was as if they'd never been there in the first place. Tentative relief crept toward him, though an unexpected hand on his shoulder swiftly chased it away.

Itsuki snickered at the way Obito jumped. "*There* you are—I've been looking all over this stupid market for you."

"Sorry," Obito absentmindedly mumbled, eyes still anxiously searching the passing crowds.

"What were you doing, anyway? Hiding from someone?" Itsuki tried giving him a mischievous grin, which was an unnatural expression for him. Fortunately, since Obito looked as though he'd just seen a ghost, it quickly vanished. He snapped his fingers to focus his partner's attention. "What's wrong?"

Obito hesitated as he struggled with where to begin; explaining that he'd hid from his uncle and why the man had provoked such a reaction from him was out of the question, and he wasn't sure what to make of the conversation he'd overheard. He still needed to analyze it for himself before deciding what it meant. Moreover, he didn't think he could handle the emotional ramifications if no one believed him again; hell, he was barely functioning now. He straightened his shoulders.

"It's nothing. Can we leave now?"

"Sure." Itsuki's face fell a bit, hurt by yet another failed attempt to connect, no matter how small. They silently walked by several kiosks until he softly added, "You know, you're supposed to trust your partner...I mean, we *are* friends, aren't we?"

Obito turned his gaze toward the colorful stalls lining the noisy street as he stamped down the urge to say his thoughts aloud. Although he was hesitant to agree, that didn't mean Itsuki was wrong with either of the things he'd said, nor had he done anything to deserve a harsh reply. However, he was barely in the right mindset to acknowledge those things.

"Just...drop it, will you?"

"Fine." Itsuki rolled his eyes, then quickened his pace until he was well ahead of Obito, whose chest grew heavy with a familiar pang of guilt. Since he couldn't invoke the imagination required to amend the situation, he let their journey home continue in agitated silence.

Six
Solstice Night

THE WEEK LEADING UP to the Winter Festival was always a busy time on Perena, no matter where one went, so while Obito wasn't particularly thrilled about the increased activity around the Capital, he'd expected it, nonetheless. Aside from now, in the crisp, quiet early morning hours when soldiers cleared the streets from debris and snow, musicians played constantly in just about every sector of the city, replaced by the theatre guild's nightly productions at sundown. Acrobats who lived on the city's edge in a camp along the northern road to the Wen Valley were the final night's main attraction, along with other street performers who journeyed across the continent, and a blessing from the High Priestess to the Emperor and his subjects. The festival celebrated life's resilience through the darkest parts of winter, greeting the return of more daylight after the passing of the year's longest night—something along those lines, Obito thought, and it somehow tied into lore about the gods. He'd never paid much attention to why most traditions existed; they all seemed ridiculous if he analyzed them long enough.

Despite his skepticism, Obito didn't see a reason to ignore *all* festival traditions. It'd been a while since he'd seen Aunt Kiko, and bringing older relatives treats to enjoy on solstice night was generally considered polite. Since he'd be on patrol later that evening—mainly to help soldiers and guards with any disorderly citizens—he thought it'd be wise to drop off what he'd found for her at Itsuki's favorite bakery while he had time. The sweet smell from the sticky buns glazed with honey was plenty to make his teeth hurt, but his aunt would like them, and after their minor spat in Zhao, Obito knew he was lucky that Itsuki forgave him enough to suggest it. He didn't have the same benevolent streak.

Seeing his uncle had set off a row of miserable, anxious, irritable interactions with almost everyone he encountered. Unable and unwilling to explain his emotions, he settled for isolating himself more than usual when possible over the last few days. Now that his feelings of murderous rage and pathetic cowardice had subsided a little, the idea of socializing didn't sound so daunting.

Of course, the universe wasn't shy about reminding him of the many annoyances that went with it.

Two women—either still boisterously drunk from the night before or already drinking for the day—stopped him when he wasn't far from the nobility quarter, only to swear at him through slurred words and raucous laughter. Rolling his eyes, he wordlessly disengaged and carefully stepped over an ice patch in the road as he went around them, adjusting the cloth-covered basket in his hand; the scent of stale red wine that had wafted off them like perfume stuck to the air around him the rest of the way to Aunt Kiko's home.

Obito readily welcomed the warm sense of relief that flooded him when his aunt opened the door to greet him. Her long, dark hair fell freely over one shoulder, and it was early enough that she hadn't yet changed out of her night robes. Even on designated days off, he rarely had the same opportunity—Itsuki usually did what he could to get him out of bed not long after sunrise. The faint scent of cigarette smoke rolled off her, a habit she generally kept to herself—not unlike his mother—as it wasn't exactly acceptable behavior for a noblewoman. The slightly stronger, much more pleasant smell of slow-cooking miso came from the direction of the kitchen when he crossed the threshold. Aunt Kiko's dark eyes were the same shade of emerald green as his siblings' and father's, and they brightened whenever she saw her nieces or nephews. Today was no exception.

"Well, now, this is a lovely surprise." She waved to him to follow her into the kitchen. "Mika yesterday and you today—it *must* be a holiday. What brings you by this early?"

"Paying the elder tax," he replied, extending his arm to offer her the basket of sticky buns. She paused to playfully scowl at him before moving aside her ashtray, then took the gift from his hand.

"I'll let you get away with that this time, but only because these look even more delightful than they smell." She beamed at the fluffy, honey-drizzled pastries topped with chopped nuts as she carefully peeled away the cloth covering them. Obito typically would've disagreed, but they were better than the scent of old wine he'd been stuck with beforehand. "I can't wait to share these with Retsuko later. She likes a good sweet after a performance goes well. That reminds me, I haven't the faintest idea what to wear. Any suggestions?"

Obito wasn't sure why she believed *he'd* be a good source of advice, but he tried his best. "Are you allowed to wish acrobats good luck before a performance, or is the same rule as with the theatre?"

"Well, if you ask *her,* the rules are exactly the same and non-negotiable. I know from your mother that it's all superstition, anyway, but you *have* given me an idea—I'll wear her favorite color. I *should* have something in blue around here somewhere."

"Did you want to see her before they came into town for the day? I can walk you out there."

Aunt Kiko's smile softened as she leaned forward to ruffle his hair. Obito froze at the unexpected, fond gesture. "I appreciate the gesture, but I've lived alone in the Capital since Sojiro was born, and that was nineteen years ago. So, while your brothers and father might disagree, I don't need an escort. Besides, I'd be in the way while she and the acrobats are trying to get ready, and *you* need to get some rest before patrol tonight."

"How did you hear about that?" Obito's brows furrowed; Aunt Kiko didn't have some hidden agenda to worry about, but it was still information he hadn't given her—he wasn't sure if she was *allowed* to know.

"Mika told me. He was thrilled it wasn't him and his partner. It sounds like the pair plan to cause some trouble in the dormitories, though, so maybe this is secretly a blessing for you and Itsuki." She cut off his chance to criticize his cousin's choices by adding, "Speaking of, are you two still...well, avoiding one another?"

He uneasily shifted his weight and glanced at a faded watercolor painting of red poppies in a field that hung on the wall beside her little table. As far as he knew, it'd been in the family for at least three generations, and she'd taken it with her when she moved to the Capital.

"Perhaps it's for the best," Aunt Kiko sighed, not in a disappointed way, as Obito would've expected from the rest of his family, but one that sounded frustrated toward the situation in general. "Your Aunt Miwa wrote to me recently. She said everyone in Kinumura and Kyuumura has been acting so strange lately, like there's something in the water, and her husband's the worst of them. She thinks he's been poisoning Mika with some new beliefs he picked up a couple years ago—the poor thing must not remember he's always been that way. In any case, it doesn't bode well for their marriage, so she might end up coming to live with your father again."

Obito couldn't say he was surprised by his other aunt's concerns. At the very least, it matched the timeline of when his uncle no longer let Mika write directly to him, and behaving differently toward him, which came well before other things happened. He thought about asking Aunt Kiko why Giichi might've been in Zhao the previous week, or if she might know who he'd spoken with, but the likelihood that she'd have an answer was dismally low. The two, frankly, hated each other. Besides, it would've been unfair to ruin her mood any further on solstice night; watching as she happily took in the smell of the sticky buns again, though, he surmised that he might be projecting his own emotions.

"Is something on your mind, Obito?"

He wasn't aware of how long he'd been quiet. "No, I'm fine, just tired."

A hint of doubt flashed in Aunt Kiko's expression before she covered it with something softer and more amused. "Sounds like I was right about you needing rest, then."

"I guess so." Obito smiled at her half-heartedly. "I'll try to stop by again soon."

"Anytime you'd like, love."

FOR ONCE, DAISUKE WASN'T disappointed in being assigned to help clear snow from the Capital's streets that morning. They'd finished their work by noon, leaving him plenty of time to thaw in a warm bath and attend to some reading he'd neglected before the festival's evening activities began. He'd surprised himself with how much he enjoyed getting lost in the stories and scraps of poetry Bunji discreetly handed him when finished. He immensely appreciated that his quiet friend had such interests, especially since the same pair of Palace guards had chased him off both times he'd tried to make his way toward the Royal Library; infantry uniform or not, they refused to believe he was allowed in there.

The treatment he received within the Capital's various districts was so wildly inconsistent that he never knew what to expect when interacting with a new person; nobles either sneered at him or ignored him entirely, and the average citizen acted more ambivalent. Either way, it wasn't the constant barrage of outright vitriol his father and former masters told him he'd get if he dared to venture beyond the plantations. For the most part, it seemed like most of his fellow soldiers didn't care where he came from so long as he pulled his weight.

In the small space of a few weeks, an entirely different part of the world had opened for him, one he was endlessly curious about, that made him want to explore every inch of the known and unknown. His combat skills weren't improving rapidly, but he *had* discovered how light on his feet he could be and was developing a layer of lean muscle. As a result, Junpei and his grunts couldn't push him around as easily now. Not that they sought it out often anymore; they were nearly ready to transfer out of basic training and had forced themselves to mature a little—thank the gods. Daisuke had to have hope that he'd be preparing for a similar reassignment by spring. If not, he risked dishonorable discharge should he fail again in autumn, which led to several other disastrous possibilities, and he'd lose his chance to gain citizenship. Military service or special designation by a highly ranked socialite fuck were the two ways Northern Nomads within the Empire could claim that status.

He doubted he would've made it this far without the acceptance he'd found in people like Bunji and General Aki.

Since enslaved people weren't allowed to participate in the festivities on Okara, openly enjoying it in the Empire's Capital came with a delightful hint of vengeance, as if he'd shamelessly shoved both middle fingers in the face of every authority figure he'd known. However, acknowledging that also left his thoughts lingering on his family for longer than they had in a while. A short year ago, he'd welcomed solstice night huddled with his brother under a canvas tarp in a storage room, hiding from Honda's inevitable wrath to befall them after he and Akane had spent the previous two hours arguing.

He'd finally figured out how to admit—strictly to himself—that he missed his sibling, and while he wanted to hope Kulako was doing well, the likely reality heavily loomed over his heart. He often wondered if he should, or *could,* ask General Aki to find him, but it was a massive under-taking to place on a man who had already risked his career by taking in one of them, and far too unrealistic to expect he'd do it. Since guilt gnawed on Daisuke's nerves for hours on end if he assumed otherwise, he forced himself to remain optimistic that a similar path to escaping slavery would find Kulako. It was the only way he stayed sane about it.

Come on, there's no need to get like this. Daisuke internally berated himself with a sigh when he realized how his throat had tightened around his emotions. He went to where he'd hung his new cloak in front of the bunkroom's hearth after the morning's work and pulled it off the line; although it was already dry, he shook it with a sharp snap of his wrists, as if doing so would also dispel his feelings, then draped it around his shoulders.

"You're coming out tonight, too, right?" he asked Bunji, who lounged on his bed in the empty bunkroom.

Bunji stretched long, yawned, and pulled his quilt under his chin. "You're on your own this time. I got in all the festive drinking I could afford last night—I'll be broke if I'm not careful. You aren't old enough to drink, so you don't have to worry."

"I'm not so sure about that. This week's put a huge hole in my pocket, too."

"Street food's expensive during holidays on *Itake*—double that, and you get the prices here. I tried to warn you." Bunji rolled over, facing away from him.

Daisuke rolled his eyes, helpless to stop the crooked grin on his lips; it wasn't worth explaining where his money had actually gone. "Whatever. Mother."

Aside from trainees at Kurushima, military personnel received a stipend based on one's age and rank. Although he still owed the commissary for his boots and hadn't yet paid off the tailor and seamstresses for his uniforms, Daisuke determined those tabs could wait until he purchased a decent outer layer with his most recent earnings. The new cloak was made of thicker material than Akane's and lined with charcoal grey rabbit fur to keep him warm. Winter didn't bother him much so far—Northern Nomads, by claim of older generations, had a high tolerance to cold weather—but he knew the next couple of months would become bitterly frigid before the winds turned warm again. It didn't hurt to prepare.

I think this is the most I've ever planned for anything. Daisuke subconsciously took some of the cloak's soft fabric in hand to look at the material. He'd purchased it a few days ago; sometimes, he thought it was too well-made to believe it belonged to him now.

He hadn't chosen what he wanted to explore first tonight, but that didn't stop him from eagerly heading out the door for some sort of adventure; the options were overwhelming compared to what was available on Okara, and he wanted to take in as many of them as possible. He'd heard stories from soldiers who knew the festivals well. All the acrobats, silent theatre, dancing, music, and food and trinket vendors he'd seen this week were unlike anything he'd experienced. The Empire itself wasn't Daisuke's favorite thing in the world, but the festival—allegedly given its public vibrancy by Giahatians from the Perenin tradition of silent observation within families—seemed to be one of the few places where its existence intersected with humanity.

Light snowfall greeted him when he stepped into the courtyard outside the barracks. On his way through the training grounds leading to the Palace's main gate, he passed a group of advanced infantrymen using kusarigama to target solid oak posts dug into the ground; chained scythes were a weapon Daisuke doubted he'd ever master, as he could barely keep a spear in his hands. Never mind the onmitsu's honored and intricate kyoketsu-shoge. The mere sight of a weapon few could master made a disgusted pit form in his stomach. He subconsciously took his hands from the pockets he'd sewn into his trousers, turning them over to examine the rigid calluses on his palms—evidence of his efforts that still didn't wholly encapsulate everything he'd put into this so far. His fighting abilities sure as hell didn't, either.

Finally, Daisuke grumbled and shoved his hands back into his pockets. Nothing would change tonight, and he had to be fine with it; he supposed he could live with it for a little longer.

Celebrations happened in all corners of the city on solstice night, except for the small quarter where the hitokiri lived. However, the most popular attractions were on the white cobblestone street in front of the Palace he'd helped clear earlier that morning; as the afternoon drew closer, dark red tents were erected sporadically in the square. Now that evening had nearly fallen upon the Capital, smoldering red-orange coals in braziers provided a place for citizens to warm themselves as they enjoyed shopping for trinkets and food, milled about between musician performances, or placed offerings on the obsidian altar to Kuro and Hikari placed near the Palace's main gate. According to what he'd learned from his peers, people gave those gifts hoping the gods would keep one's health and fortune in good standing until spring. The High Priestess would appear there later in the evening to grant a special solstice blessing on Hikari's behalf and lead a prayer to the Mother Goddess, but Daisuke didn't care about the festival's religious aspects.

The tantalizing smell of fried pork dumplings wafted through the air while he listlessly browsed through some fabrics. Although he preferred the infantry's lighter diet of rice, fish, and vegetables, he couldn't pass up the opportunity to treat himself to something more indulgent than his usual fare. Besides, he hadn't eaten since that morning. Maybe he deserved it.

After a while of aimlessly wandering, Daisuke found himself on the ringside of an enchanting acrobatic performance. They flipped, stretched, and bent their bodies in seemingly impossible ways on the tatami mats they'd put down to prevent their performers from freezing. They wore all-black clothing with bone-white masks covering their faces, symbolizing the dance of balance between dark and light, the small space of existence in which Hikari could grant human life. Drums and flutes played, synchronizing everything to a beat, as their matron stood near the tent with a commanding presence, dressed in a kimono and mask to match her performers with another woman in a pale blue kimono at her side. He marveled at the challenging work one had to put themselves through to achieve such mastery of movement and balance. When the show finished, Daisuke instantly dug around in his cloak for whatever coins he had—primarily coppers, typical for someone still in basic training—and dropped a few of them into a large, glazed ceramic teal bowl on a small platform near their tent. Alerted by the clinking sound of coins in their collection pot, the matron winked at him from under her mask, followed by a giggle from her companion, before both women turned away again.

His vision went black when he stepped back to see if they'd planned an encore.

"There you are, little silk-spinner."

Junpei. What other fuck would bother? The woolen cloth itched at Daisuke's eyes and any skin it touched. He heard Junpei's lackeys snicker and jeer indistinguishably and could feel the rest of them closing in as the bulkier boy forced him to hold still.

"What the fuck do you want?" Daisuke grumbled, uselessly attempting to turn his head to glare.

"It's festival night—we're just looking to have some fun, aren't we?" Another round of obnoxious taunts agreed with Junpei's statement. Someone grabbed Daisuke by the arms; he felt their breath on his face.

Quite unfortunately, he could smell it, too. It was like having his head dunked into a tankard of ale.

Great. Fucking great. Who the hell was stupid enough to buy alcohol for these morons, anyway? Daisuke mentally whined as he simultaneously tried to decide which god he'd pissed off most recently. Junpei was the eldest of the bunch, but being his senior by two years meant he was still too young to drink. He wriggled in another bid to free himself, at the very least hoping to get away from the worst-smelling of the lot, but to no avail.

"What in Kuro's Hells do you think you're doing?" an unfamiliar boy's voice cut in; Daisuke's shoulders forcibly jerked back when Junpei startled at being reprimanded. "Basic infantry? Who's your commanding officer?"

Junpei tried stuttering out a response, but quickly abandoned the endeavor and shoved his blindfolded victim forward. Daisuke stumbled as he heard the idiots scrambling to get out of sight, which was probably the most brilliant thing they'd done all night. If someone reported them for misbehavior, General Aki would likely revoke his decision to promote any of them whether or not they passed their second evaluations. Just as he didn't tolerate Daisuke's smart mouth, he refused to put up with anything he viewed as disrespectful nonsense between his soldiers. He stuck his thumbs under the cloth to get it off his face.

"Did they hurt you?" the boy asked as he helped peel the makeshift blindfold away from covering his eyes, which he immediately scrubbed with his hands to relieve the irritation.

"No, I'm fine. I—" A strange, unexpected heat bloomed in Daisuke's cheeks when he could finally see who came to his rescue, immediately entranced by deep green eyes illuminated by the overhead light of dangling paper lanterns. He cleared his throat and awkwardly took back the scarf when offered. "I'm fine. Thank you for helping."

"That's...good." The other boy looked a little taken aback, too, though Daisuke couldn't imagine why. He, however, recovered more quickly and smoothly, aided by yet another soldier coming to *his* rescue; they must've been from a patrol unit in the regular infantry.

"The fireworks are about to go off," the newcomer said with a radiant, genuine smile. "Let's go find a good spot."

The first boy looked unimaginably unimpressed at the suggestion, but didn't have much time to protest before his companion grabbed him by the sleeve and dragged him away. Laughing, Daisuke waved at them as they disappeared into the crowds again.

He didn't fully realize the faint smile still tugging at his lips when a loud boom and crackle sounded from the skies, casting a pink light over the crowded streets as he nearly jumped out of his skin. He searched for the source as a high-pitched whistle filled his ears, which he traced to the sky as another burst of color exploded above him, the green peony glittering in midair for seconds before the sparkles faded into blackness again. However small, the act of kindness still warmed his heart, as did the bliss of an otherwise enjoyable day, so he decided to bask in it while it lasted as he watched the fireworks in peace.

SEVEN
PRIESTESS OF SHADOWS

NESTLED DEEP IN THE snow-covered mountaintops of Hikari's Range lay a cluster of hot springs, wedged between natural platforms left behind by glaciers that had melted from the primordial rockfaces long before humans set foot there. Many believed the first Perenins opened their eyes to the mother Goddess's gift of light here, and though pathways hidden from view of the well-traveled passes had become lost to the ages, the rough terrain was once home to holy lands. Early Perenins had built a temple into the mountainside around the springs, giving their people a place to heal as they bathed in the soothing, blessed waters.

Before disappearing into time's muddy memory, the temple had adopted several other faces to serve Hikari and her people. One of its final uses under such a designation was perhaps its most ironic—a health spa for the wealthy. However, because of its location, few outside those descended from the ancient bloodlines of its original caretakers knew where to go once they strayed off the main mountain roads—even fewer dared to make the perilous journey during the winter. Snowdrifts, whipping icy winds, and slippery trails threatened those seeking passage to the little haven. A thick wall of tall spruce and fir trees surrounding the grounds filled the air with a constant, earthy scent, and provided the hot springs with some shelter from the elements.

In recent years, the abandoned inn that now sat where ancestors built the original temple had steadily regained some semblance of life in its walls, and its new occupants had quietly reinstated its function as a bathhouse. Its doors weren't open to the public, but rather to a cluster of nobles who believed they'd found solace in their discontent with the Empire's state—citizens who quickly acquiesced to a new order would be the first among outsiders to visit. A sisterhood permanently occupied and ran the inn. They protected its age-old secret pools and concealed desires murmured by the noblemen who visited to air their grievances with a like-minded individual.

Lady Shadow stood on a veranda facing one of the larger pools, blankly watching her constituents while enjoying the rare warmth of winter's sun on her skin. The women and girls who lived here alongside her were also taking advantage of the daylight—it was uncommon to see so many of them in the courtyard all at once—but her thoughts were elsewhere, far away from her operations on the mountaintop. One of her most promising followers, a young lady named Misame, was due to at last return from a long and dangerous journey; she'd left for her crucial missions months ago, and Lady Shadow was awaiting her with bated breath. Unfortunately, getting back from Zhu in snowy conditions couldn't guarantee *experienced* mountain men their safety or success. Even trips to the nearest city, Baohu, for goods often proved too treacherous for casual travelers.

All thirty or so members of the sisterhood had prayed together early that morning for Misame's safe return. Lady Shadow anxiously turned to the towering red torii arch at the grounds' entrance. She'd sacrificed everything she once had to ensure her plan's success—she'd forsaken the name given to her by her mother, the one granted to her upon marrying her late husband, devoted countless hours to scouring the secrets of Perenin theology, and made contact with the disgruntled elite to help further her cause. If Misame didn't return, everything could be for naught while she ran from the Imperial army.

She glanced again at her sisters. They were other women who had also brutally lost their husbands and families or escaped terrible marriages with shitty men; other would-be victims of the Empire's making, and those who wished to break free of Giahatian tradition and control. When serving their occasional visitors as innkeepers, they dressed as any self-respecting woman on Perena should. If speaking with outsiders or acting in a more covert capacity for the sake of their goal, they shrouded themselves in dark cloaks with equally black veils stitched into the hoods; some wore masks to conceal their identities further, and a Healer changed their voices to a low, indistinguishable and guttural pitch. They met any demands to reveal their identities with cold, immediate dismissal. Lady Shadow did not compromise the safety of anyone who gave her their absolute faith.

Thankfully, after a few more moments passed, a silhouette manifested at the curved base of the path below. A cart pulled along by a strangely agreeable mule with Misame at the reins. Like always, Lady Shadow heaved a silent little sigh of relief, and others who heard the commotion along the trail became distracted from their activities one by one. Perena was dangerous for dissenters whether they lived in, over, or below the mountains that split the continent. Misame's homecoming was a massive weight off everyone's shoulders.

Lady Shadow smiled at Misame once a group of volunteers took her mule and the cart to the stable built with the inn. Despite how her youth should've made her socially timid and reticent, she was usually a maiden so fierce that Zandaka himself might become smitten. Her current, uncertain demeanor was odd, but the matron waved it off due to exhaustion. More than anything, she was grateful that the Demon King had guided Misame's way.

"Bathe and find some clean clothes," she gently told the young woman after they'd exchanged a quick embrace. "You've had a long journey."

Misame fretfully wrung her hands together as a hint of guilt played at her features. "Lady Shadow, I need to talk to you about the talisman."

Lady Shadow paused, a sinking feeling wriggling in her chest. "Which talisman? I sent you with two."

Misame looked afraid to provide an answer. She drew in the air as if she planned to respond, but her voice never came forward when her lips parted again. Instead, her gaze went to the springs, as if she hoped they could supplement her with an explanation. Lady Shadow's suspicion grew.

"Come, now. If we wish to purify the nation, we mustn't keep secrets from one another. What about Lord Saigai's talisman?"

"I...I lost it," Misame weakly confessed at last, although the way her statement caused everyone's interest to snap toward her made it feel much more like a shout. She winced under the unspoken, harsh criticism of twenty or more outraged stares, but Lady Shadow wrapped an arm around her shoulders, shielding her from the other women.

Lady Shadow lowered her voice to a soft, nearly whispered octave, though it now carried a sense of urgency. "That talisman could be anywhere between the Wen Valley and Zhu. Are you *sure* you lost it?"

Misame nodded meekly, now obviously terrified, and eyes unable to leave the large stone pendant at Lady Shadow's throat as the older woman twisted it between her fingers.

"Did you at least confirm with that pompous ass Giichi that Hideo received the talisman meant for him? Lord Hideo and General Aki served together in the military for a short time, but I've heard they're still close.

The general is our key to infiltrating army tactics and turning them against Akuwara."

"Y-yes, Lady. When we met in Zhao, Giichi said he'd already brought him the talisman, but Hideo couldn't leave with it immediately."

"I suppose that's a relief. I thought Giichi would make me regret letting you bring him a talisman." Lady Shadow straightened again, taking her arm away and folding her hands primly in front of her. "Bathe, change into fresh clothing, and beg the gods' forgiveness. I've much work to do."

"But, Lady Sha—"

"That is all," the dowager replied sternly, narrowing her eyes as she tried to gauge the reasoning behind such cowering reactions. This stunning display of incompetence wasn't what she'd expected of her protégé. Nevertheless, she needed to devise a plan quickly to convince the few nobles under her manipulation to seek the missing talisman for her. She knew one of Giichi's sons had enlisted with Imperial intelligence at the beginning of autumn, so perhaps she already had something to work with—the arrogant lord wasn't likely to tell her otherwise, and the boy would have invaluable access to a wide array of information. She'd also try to involve one of the Suzuki family's teenagers, as they knew the southern roads leaving the Wen Valley where Misame's route would've taken her. Lady Shadow glanced at Misame again, realizing she'd nearly forgotten about her, looking up just in time to catch her uncertain bow.

Perhaps she didn't need to outsource help after all.

Misame looked over her shoulder once after ensuring Lady Shadow had dismissed her from their conversation, heart pounding with every step she took toward the main building. She removed her soaked boots in a small mudroom at the inn's entrance, lifted the skirt of the simple white kimono all cult members wore, and ascended the half-step onto the main floor. The entryway was empty, and no sound came from anywhere within the sturdy old walls—everyone was still outside.

Misame heaved a sigh of relief, thankful for a moment alone with her inner world.

Her involvement in the cult was a decision made in a fit of passion that she profoundly regretted. She'd known for a while that getting close to Lady Shadow was vital for those who wanted permission to move about the world more freely, so she used that to her advantage and set to plotting her escape. After months of proving her devotion, Lady Shadow entrusted her with the mission to deliver one of the Six Talismans of Sin to the

Wen Valley while carrying another for protection. Upon parting ways with Giichi in Zhao, her next task was to collect information about where the other three talismans might be during her travels to Zhu, where her older sister lived with a kindhearted potter in married bliss.

Misame had lost her own lover to a military ambush on suspected traitors who supposedly followed a man known by his surname of Hinatako. Neither had known anything about him or his rebellion, but once the Giahatio caught and arrested him, his entire following fell apart, leaving their women—foolishly presumed ignorant and therefore innocent—behind. Marred by their affiliation with treasonous men, the desolated wives and children were left with no resources, money, or claims to lands or properties. Like Misame, they'd run to Lady Shadow's open arms when she promised them a chance at vengeance and safety.

No one knew with any certainty how old Lady Shadow was, only that she was the eldest among the ladies living at the abandoned spa, and that she'd immediately taken everyone under her wing. Determined that no sacrifice toward the downfall of the Giahatio would be in vain, she began building their lives anew. Like Misame, Lady Shadow was piloted by her despair, though sheer pride kept both women from admitting it was their driving force.

Misame supposed that pride was an utterly human trait. Almost inescapable, no matter how pious a person thought they might be. However, if Lady Shadow hadn't denounced the self-important attitudes of the nobles they dealt with, Misame might've forgiven her for also exuding one. Realizing their matron wasn't always a woman of her word, and often in the worst ways, had slowly plucked at the fulfillment of serving her in the cult.

Back to the present, Lady Shadow had insisted that meticulously crafted, sturdy vases would adequately store the remaining talismans as the cult collected them from across Perena. Misame had used the opportunity to reconnect with her sister and ask her for help. She'd left Lord Saigai's talisman with her, too. Misame knew that when her husband returned from selling wares at the Winter Festival in the Capital, Rin would surrender the artifact to him immediately, and had to believe the information would somehow reach the Intelligence Master.

This was the first time in years she'd earnestly prayed to Hikari and Kuro, but not for the forgiveness Lady Shadow said she needed—her entire spirit yearned for her plan to succeed, one way or another.

After a long, hot bath to soothe and warm her, Misame dressed in a freshly laundered, snow-white kimono. The inn was still hauntingly quiet when she returned to her room and knelt before the mirror to brush out her long black hair. Her door slid open, and she registered Lady Shadow's reflection behind her, eyeing her warily in the glass. The matron remained silent as she went to her, then got down behind her, holding her hand out to take the brush. Misame hesitantly surrendered it.

"We had three of the six talismans, and now we have one. Of course, scouts are constantly searching for where the remaining three are hiding, but you've managed to set us back by quite a bit upon...*misplacing* Lord Saigai. It could take several more years to recover the others," Lady Shadow spoke in a low murmur as if she were working these things out for herself. "Tell me, Misame, do you remember why they are so important?"

Misame swallowed, her eyes locking on Lady Shadow's expressionless gaze in the mirror. Her intuition screamed for her to run, but there was nowhere she could go, and with the grip on her hair, she couldn't try. "T-to revive Demon King Zandaka, my Lady."

"That is correct." A few more gentle brushstrokes untangled more small knots in the younger woman's hair, which Lady Shadow then gathered at the nape of Misame's neck like she would if preparing to style it. Instead, she clenched it hard in her fist, pulling Misame's head back and baring her throat. "And *why* do we need to revive Zandaka?"

"To eliminate the Empire. Lady, I—"

"Have you begged the gods for forgiveness yet?"

Fearful tears welled in Misame's eyes as she whimpered the affirmative; she'd never seen their matron so quietly furious, yet utterly cold and calculating. Her entire body quivered as her thoughts swarmed like locusts. If she pleaded with the Lady for her life, she'd admit guilt she did not wish to confess she carried, but she couldn't risk her sister's life, either. Lady Shadow knew *something* was off, though. She always did. A cool metal object touched her windpipe; she could barely see the glint of a blade against candlelight when she looked downward, but a strained glance at the mirror showed her the reflection of the knife Lady Shadow held.

Dear gods, Misame nearly screamed in panic, throat closing around her voice. *I'm going to die.*

"Whether or not you lied to me cannot be confirmed just yet, but you seem to have marked yourself as a liability. We *will* find that talisman.

Perhaps Mother Hikari and Father Kuro can forgive your failures, but I cannot, nor will Zandaka."

Lady Shadow did not compromise her cult's security, not even for a single member's slip-up; she responded swiftly to traitorous behavior and incompetence. The dagger's blade slit Misame's throat, her last, helpless gargles ignored as her blood spilled over Lady Shadow's hand, staining the silken kimono sleeve as it flowed down her wrist. Deep crimson flecks landed on the mirror.

"May the afterlife welcome you peacefully, Misame. Pity. I had such high hopes for you, too." Lady Shadow smirked mirthlessly, freeing the dead girl from her grasp and carelessly allowing her to slump forward, unflinching when Misame's head cracked the mirror. "If not, the demons can still feed off your soul."

Lady Shadow wiped the blade of her dagger on the inert body, placed it where she kept it stowed away in her obi, then removed a transparent glass vial she'd hidden alongside it. Throughout her scouring of religious texts, she'd encountered several summoning rituals to perform on the talismans. Although the books warned against summoning the creatures of the Between Realm—the consequences of manifesting a demon into the living world were unknown—she'd spotted at least one ritual she could feasibly perform. Confident that things had reached such a point, she uncorked the flask.

"Haruki," she called once she'd collected the dead girl's blood, face unchanging as she swirled the crimson liquid in its glass vial and blankly noted when tiny bubbles formed in the frothing meniscus.

As if summoned by magic, the door behind her immediately slid open, and a girl no older than fourteen stepped into the room with her. Lady Shadow turned slightly to observe her reactions at seeing her fallen sister. While Haruki was no stranger to death, her age sometimes reflected her naivety, and she'd retained enough of her sympathetic nature despite the harshness she'd experienced throughout her young life. Her light brown eyes widened, but she said nothing. Lady Shadow's eyes tensely yet imperceptibly shifted toward the sheathed katana always present at Haruki's hip, though she knew the sword's deadly blade would never turn against her.

Lady Shadow stoppered the vial and placed it in her obi, then rose from her knees and gracefully pivoted to face the girl. "We'll need to move her body."

"M-may I ask what happened, My Lady?" Haruki's soft-spoken question trembled as it left her lips. She and Misame hadn't been particularly close, but she tended to fawn over most people who treated her kindly. If nothing else, Lady Shadow supposed Misame had demonstrated plenty of that toward her sisters in the cult—kindness, however, wasn't the same as loyalty, though they often wore similar faces.

"Of course, my dear child. You see, Misame misplaced Lord Saigai's talisman somewhere between here and the Capital. To correct her mistake, she instead offered her blood to help us serve the Demon King."

Haruki looked between Misame and Lady Shadow for a long moment, clearly trying to process what had happened, then bowed to her matron as the older woman strode past her to leave. She paused to pat Haruki on the shoulder gently, but that was as far as her forced condolences went.

She retrieved a lantern and donned a cloak, as the receding evening sun had turned the air predictably bitter once more, then proceeded to a tiny shrine not far from the inn on an overgrown game trail. A couple of passages within the old texts led her to believe the shrine formerly belonged to the original temple, but she had no way of confirming her suspicions—it could've been from any era in this sacred place's history. She set the lantern on an altar made of rotting wood and brushed a layer of dust away from the surface.

Lady Shadow removed her necklace and shook it until the dark, flat stone pendant popped out of its bail; the necklace's chain was a lovely, helpful gift from their patrons as thanks for hosting them and originally home to a sizeable sapphire from Othakra, though she'd soon repurposed it. She adjusted the stone to sit neatly in the altar's center, then took the vial of blood out again and held it over the pendant, hesitant to go further. This ritual was the most basic of what she'd uncovered thus far, but awakening a slumbering spirit—if she was even successful in her attempt to do so—allegedly came with the risks of possession or death. She drew in a deep breath and finally uncorked the bottle, pouring a tiny drop on the stone's surface.

To her surprise, the blood rapidly disappeared as if absorbed by the talisman, and rays of bright green light burst from the stone. The light shrank into a single beam that carved the shape of a long, twisted red dragon into the talisman, along with the name Lady Shadow hoped to see.

"Kanashimi, Demon who wields the shadows of Hikari's grief," she said welcomingly, desperate to hold back a manic grin of delight. "I summon thee."

Wind from nowhere gusted in Lady Shadow's unflinching face, followed by an earth-shaking roar, and a black mist that rose from the talisman. Lady Shadow stepped back to make room for her visitor, whose enormous, clawed feet touched the shrine's floor seconds later. Excitement thrummed in her heart when the smoke steadily cleared away, revealing a massive dragon that nearly hit the shrine's ceiling with long, pointed horns on its head. A mane of flowing, pure white hair swirled around it, as did a shadow. When the shadow dissipated, the dragon wore a layer each of white, purple, and gold robes, along with an open black outer robe. A gold headpiece adorned its forehead, inlaid with six tiny rubies in the center. Two black streaks came down from the bottom of each eye like painted markings. A string of deep purple beads materialized at the demon's throat, with large pieces of rose quartz hanging in the center.

Lady Shadow couldn't help but stare in awe at the creature before her.

"Who dares awaken me?" the long, green dragon seethed, stretching sinewy arms and legs as a tail unfurled behind them. Pupilless, bright yellow eyes locked onto Lady Shadow. "You are not the Demon King."

"Master Kanashimi," Lady Shadow greeted as she sank to one knee with her head bowed. "My name is Lady Shadow, and I would devote myself to you if you allow it."

"I am not the Demon *King*, foolish human. My name is sufficient." The dragon demon narrowed their eyes and leaned forward as slits emerged in their irises, which shrank to a more humanlike size despite their reptilian appearance and sat against black sclera. Their snout nearly touched Lady Shadow's neck as they snorted a puff of hot breath and bared their fangs. "The blood you used to awaken me was not your own."

"It was not."

"That should be impossible...yet, here I am." Kanashimi straightened, head tilted as they continued examining Lady Shadow, expression—if dragons or demons made those—a mystery to the matron. "However, because you have found my talisman, you are more likely to try doing the same with my siblings, as well. I demand to know your purpose with us."

"I would act as the Demon King's servant and collect all your siblings' talismans scattered across Perena."

Kanashimi remained unreadable even when twin tendrils of smoke left their nostrils; their size slowly shrank so that they stood a foot over Lady Shadow's head. "A drop of your blood, and you may speak with me—it *must* be your blood. If you cannot provide that small sacrament, you are not worthy to act as Zandaka's servant in any capacity. I shall not permit further deception from the likes of *you*, human."

"You have my word."

Thicker puffs of smoke misted out of the dragon's snout, and their yellow eyes glowed a little brighter for the space of a single second. "You will do well to remember that I am a demon, a once-neutral spirit poisoned by the Goddess's sins, but powerful, nonetheless. As powerful as grief itself. You will command me as I allow."

"Will you stay confined to the talisman, then?"

"How well we bond will determine how close I stay." Kanashimi's flowing brows arched as they raised a long, curved claw and gently placed the pointed tip on Lady Shadow's forehead. "I sense you have great ambitions. If you wish to become the Servant of Zandaka, you must also become a Priestess of Shadows. What do you plan to do with such power at your disposal?"

"I will summon Zandaka and lay waste to the Empire," Lady Shadow replied confidently, with passion and anger she couldn't begin to describe burning in her chest. "It stole everything from me and *will* pay for the sins it has committed in the Gods' names."

Kanashimi became unreadable once more as they retracted their clawed finger, until a smirk curled their upper lip to show off their pointed white teeth again. "We've much work ahead of us, Priestess."

Daisuke's eyes flew open as he sat up in bed, barely awake as he clawed at the duvet and pulled it off. He stumbled when his feet touched the floor, but it didn't slow him as he rushed out of the bunkroom, dry-heaving and gagging as he clambered onto a stone bench in the hallway. He desperately pushed open the window above it. He could still see nauseating spatters of crimson on a shattered mirror, hear how it slowly dripped onto a wooden floor, and taste the stale iron scent heavily lingering in the air.

Gods, he couldn't stand the sight of blood. Thankfully, no one else knew—he could only imagine how someone like Junpei might exploit that fact.

He waited a moment to ensure he wouldn't be sick, then plopped down on the bench, resting his head against the cool stone wall behind him. His dream showed him something beyond the brutal slaying of a young woman; a vague symbol of sorts had crossed his vision, like faded lettering he couldn't read, along with the blurry figure of something long and winding floating through the skies. Daisuke paused his train of thought to ruminate over that image again. Though he'd only been able to focus on one, there were actually seven altogether, six of them much smaller than the first, and after he saw the bloody mirror, he stood in front of the jade dragons again. Cracks in the six flanking the one in the center had grown more profound, while the middle dragon seemed to have increased in size. One on the far left appeared brighter than the others, too. Blood poured from the statues' damaged surfaces when the dream abruptly ended.

There's no way anything about that was real, right? It didn't make any sense... Daisuke ran his hands through his hair with a watery sigh, then drew his knees to his chest and hugged himself, blankly studying the dark ceiling above him. *But, if it's never "just" a dream, then what the hell does this all mean?*

He stayed on the bench until he heard steady footsteps softly echoing in the hallway, alerting him to the unhurried pace of an overnight patroller. Daisuke supposed he'd better get back in bed if he didn't want to spend the following day running extra drills—his sore muscles complained at the very idea of it. His stomach and mind had finally settled enough for more sleep, anyway. He hoped there wouldn't be any more dreams; he didn't think he could handle another nightmare as wretchedly convoluted as this one.

SPRING AND EARLY SUMMER on Perena didn't act much differently than they did on Okara—nothing but fog and rainfall, often for days on end. This current bout had lasted nearly a week, with few breaks between trickles from the overcast skies constantly looming above. Emperor Akuwara's choice to reallocate resources usually devoted to upkeep caused the barracks to lose their former luster over the years, as experienced soldiers would loudly complain about, with plenty of evidence to support their statements. More crumbly places in the rough stone walls and foundation leaked in the thawing snowmelt and storms, and cool dampness from steady rain clung to the stiff air in stony hallways all day.

Daisuke's stomach had been in knots since the previous morning when General Aki announced the names of those about to participate in their first six-month evaluation the following afternoon. Overwhelmed by nerves, he hadn't absorbed much from conversations or his immediate surroundings once the general confirmed *his* name was on the list—he knew he wasn't ready. If he focused on the positives, the evaluation meant selected candidates got to skip the bloody, hellish sight of the Kurushima graduation that took place every spring. While it was true that he preferred this over the idea of watching new hitokiri slaughter one another, he couldn't find many other optimistic-leaning points; the weather hadn't cooperated at all over the week for the Spring Festival, and now he had to spend the last night of it humiliating himself in sparring.

He flexed his fingers to adjust his grip around the staff tucked behind his right shoulder, then forced himself to breathe normally rather than in the shallow manner he'd been using. As if he didn't have enough to worry about regarding the test, at General Aki's request, Junpei and a couple of his minions had returned from regular infantry for the evening to help. Daisuke thought the universe was having far too much fun at his expense.

"Daisuke," General Aki called, scaring him out of his skin. "You and Junpei."

Figures. He bit his cheek to hold back the nervous whine lodged in his throat as the young man who'd previously faced Junpei for his evaluation walked off, looking as glum as he felt. Bunji had already finished his match with a pass an hour ago and headed off for a bath and a celebratory meal; he doubted he'd be joining in similar antics tonight.

Despite his pounding heart, Daisuke met Junpei in the middle of the room. He spun the staff in front of himself once, held it slightly away from his body, parallel to the floor, and gave Junpei a proper bow while the other boy did the same. They both drew a foot back to slide into fighting stances, tilting their staffs from horizontal to vertical positions, which was when Daisuke noted the vicious smirk on Junpei's stupid face. At least that hadn't changed. The moron's last few months in the official infantry hadn't just matured his face and voice, however slightly, but also how he carried himself and behaved. He took himself seriously in a less insufferable way now. It was like he'd become an entirely new person.

"Come on; you can't be afraid," Junpei said.

Daisuke snorted. "Who said anything about me being afraid?"

"The fact that you didn't hear General Aki tell us to start."

A furious blush crossed Daisuke's cheeks, but he decided against digging himself in deeper. Instead, he tightened his grip on his staff again—while he expected this wouldn't last long, he still needed to put forth some effort and show he cared enough to try, because even the newest recruits knew he didn't stand a chance. He spun his weapon once more, and Junpei did the same before spreading his hands and thrusting forward. Daisuke swiped the attack away, feeling cautiously optimistic at how easy it'd been to block, though he immediately recognized how he'd failed himself by not planning a follow-through; Junpei had already turned himself around, stance low and knees locked for balance as he used the staff as an extension of his arm to strike.

Daisuke wasn't fast enough to pass the weapon into his right hand to defend that side. He stifled the noise he made when Junpei hit him in the ribs, then tried to chase him by retaliating with his own strike, but the other boy had already unwound himself and was launching another attack. Panic filled his chest to the brim like it always did in these situations. He realized with unmitigated dread that he'd put himself in a defensive position; now, he had no choice but to retreat from his opponent.

Junpei swung the staff low to sweep his feet, which fortunately missed, but Daisuke sensed how quickly he was losing ground as he stumbled backward again. No matter how badly he wanted to call him out for dirty fighting, Junpei's swift and sure strikes weren't overly aggressive, but the result of being a good student. Unlike Daisuke, who still couldn't grasp how to reconcile the ways his body naturally wanted to move with the training regimen, Junpei *was* a decent fighter.

Fuck—! was the first thing to run through his mind when the tip of Junpei's staff rammed into his solar plexus, stealing the air from his lungs as he lost balance and hit the ground. His weapon flew out of his grasp and spun across the floor; a brush of his fingertips knocked it further away when he twisted his body around to grab it. It revolved several more times—either for dramatic effect or to mock him, Daisuke felt he didn't need to guess—before a heavy silence filled the air.

"You lose, silk-spinner," Junpei sneered, dark eyes gleaming at his perceived cleverness. "I'd give you another chance, but why rub salt in the wound?"

Daisuke ran his fingers through loosened strands of hair that clung to a sheen of sweat on his face while he caught his breath.

"Gods be damned," he muttered through clenched teeth, unable to take his eyes off the floor until an outstretched hand entered his peripherals. To his surprise, it was Junpei. Daisuke cautiously accepted the gesture, expecting him to drop the act at any second and turn it into his usual maliciousness. However, his confusion grew when the other boy helped him to his feet without incident. He tensed, still expecting Junpei to lash out in some fashion.

"Overall, not the worst I've seen you fight, though," Junpei added, trying to be nonchalant over something he didn't want to admit. "Maybe you'll get it next time."

"Did you hit your head?" Daisuke asked incredulously. Moving beyond basic really had mellowed the older boy considerably.

"You fucking idiot," Junpei snapped, reminding everyone he hadn't changed *that* much. He looked ready to say something else, but whatever might've been on his mind never came out; instead, he simply told Daisuke to get out of the makeshift ring so the next candidate could step forward with a simple, "Get lost."

"Fine by me." Daisuke's attention had already gone elsewhere when he heard General Aki call someone else's name.

He had six more months until another chance to prove himself as a soldier came around; he didn't know what to do should he fail again. He didn't have the fallbacks or securities someone like Junpei did, such as a stable home—Kuro's Hells, he'd barely begun saving money from his stipend—which meant he had nowhere to go if served with a dishonorable discharge.

Since the end of his match meant automatic dismissal for the evening, Daisuke placed the staff he'd used on a rack on the wall and went in search of his cloak. The rain sounded like it'd stopped for now, and he thought walking some trails around the Palace might do him more good than moping around the barracks.

THE SCENT OF RAIN held onto the spring air, pleasantly stirring with that of blooming cherry blossoms whenever the breeze picked up a bit. Water ran along the Palace's outer wall on either side, flowing with a delicate trickling noise toward wherever it pooled downhill. The grounds would remain in their soggy state for several days even if it didn't rain more, but a distant chorus of singing frogs made the evening feel warmer than it was—the clearing purple clouds against the evening sun and pink sky added to that sense.

Itsuki had just finished regaling Obito with some roundabout yet utterly detailed story of what he'd occupied his time with during the hitokiri graduations earlier that day. Unlike his predecessors, Master Yujin didn't require every available onmitsu to attend the ceremony—his observations led him to believe it weakened morale instead of raising it as those before him claimed—so they'd enjoyed their extra free time separately. Although their current meeting had happened by pure chance, that hadn't stopped the Perenin boy from wanting to talk.

"What do you want from this year?" Itsuki abruptly asked after swallowing a mouthful of whatever tooth-rotting confection he'd been eating, then swatted away a swarm of spring insects in search of food.

Obito tilted his head, partly to think about his answer, but also to figure out how the hell they'd gotten to that question from where the other boy had last ended his fully narrated stream of consciousness. He'd barely kept up with everything his partner had said—not that Itsuki stopped long enough for questions. In spite of that, his natural energy and warmth made it feel as though Obito still had a place in their one-sided conversation; he'd grown fonder of these diatribes than he cared to admit, which would've been a much different case had someone asked him for his opinion when they first met this time last year.

In this instance, Obito couldn't answer the question, which he found bothersome. Finally, he admitted, "I'm not sure."

"You'll figure it out eventually," Itsuki said, beaming. He stretched his long arms over his head. "Anyways, I'm off for a bath. Are you coming, too, or are you heading somewhere?"

"You know I won't bathe when everyone else does."

"I'll never get why, but suit yourself. Later."

Once he was alone again, Obito decided he wasn't ready to head inside for the night, and ventured toward a path that wrapped around the Palace grounds and joined with a scenic route on the back end of the nobility quarter. From there, he followed a game trail down to a pond that was easily visible from the road, surrounded by constant streams of reverberating frog song. Regardless of its easy accessibility, Obito felt this was one of the few places he could be left alone in peace.

He skipped a stone over the pond's surface three times as he reflected on Itsuki's question again. Realizing that he still came up empty by the time he'd tossed four, he thought he should retire for the night and launched one more from the small collection in his left hand. This one sank as soon as it touched the water.

"What the hell did that poor pond ever do to you?" a voice asked from behind.

Obito turned to find a boy who appeared to be from the infantry. He'd stuffed his hands into his pockets, head tilted to one side, and a subtle, amused look danced across his face.

Isn't he the boy from the festival? Obito wondered as he searched through his memory. It'd been a few months since their encounter, which had lasted no more than a minute or two at best, but there was something about it he hadn't been able to shake from his mind. He watched the other boy's expression slip into one that mirrored his as recognition mutually dawned on them.

"It's you," the young soldier said; he sounded as surprised as Obito felt. After a moment, an uncertain yet slightly mischievous grin returned to the black-haired boy's distinct features. He glanced at his feet before he crossed his arms and leaned against a mossy tree trunk, then continued, "What are you doing, anyway?"

"I could ask you the same."

"At ease, soldier. I'm just out for a walk."

"'Soldier.'" Obito rolled his eyes, which made his counterpart's smirk temporarily widen. Military or not, that was hardly what he'd call any of the onmitsu—himself especially. "Is there a new ordinance against skipping rocks?"

"Didn't look like skipping to me."

"This is a lot of criticism from someone I don't know."

"Easy enough to change that, isn't it?" Before Obito had time to object or react, the boy had closed the gap between them and stood unnervingly close. "Name's Daisuke."

"Obito," he reluctantly introduced himself, though a half-grin tugged on the corner of his lips against his will. He handed one of his rocks to Daisuke. "Now that we know each other, please, enlighten me."

Daisuke looked at the flat, smooth stone resting on his palm, nervously chuckled as he bounced it in his hand, then turned toward the pond and tossed it in with a water-logged *plunk*.

"That was terrible," Obito commented.

"Leave me alone—I've never done this before."

"Never?"

Obito had learned by watching his three older brothers; it was how they'd spent calm evenings or blisteringly hot afternoons during the summer beside the creek running through the woods behind their home. While he supposed he shouldn't have assumed it was a given thing Daisuke would know, he didn't have much reason for otherwise—*most* people who'd grown up on Perena could point to a similar childhood experience. He was about to add another question, but a light shade of pink had softly colored Daisuke's cheeks, and he'd looked away, violet eyes now studying the rippling water to his left.

Even so, he quickly recovered by clearing his throat and straightening his shoulders. "Well, you know, not much time for it in basic...I guess patrol units aren't much different, are they?"

"No, it doesn't seem like it." Obito held out the remainder of his rock collection to keep himself from correcting the other boy's assumption—naturally, people were aware of the onmitsu's existence, but Master Yujin strongly advised against readily sharing such information. "Did you want to try again?"

Daisuke hesitated at first, then took another stone. "How did you do it last time?"

"Like this, watch."

Obito turned his wrist to give a rock a sideways pitch into the water, disturbing a frog that had dared to venture onto a lily pad as the stone skipped past. Daisuke's second attempt followed, this time bouncing on the surface once before plunging below, which was a resounding success according to him. After a while of them talking—perhaps more like griping—about their least favorite parts of military life while the sky gradually grew darker, it occurred to Obito that he wasn't normally this interactive, but spending the last year with Itsuki had helped him become a little bolder. Besides, he sensed something about Daisuke that was eerily similar to himself, though he couldn't point to whatever it was; for now, the ease between them felt sufficient.

"When did it get this dark?" Daisuke asked after they'd carried on for some time, pausing to look above them to where the first stars peeked through the deep blue expanse with a shy twinkle. "I guess that's curfew for me."

Obito also turned his gaze to the sky. "I should go, too."

Daisuke glanced at him, then threw the last stone into the pond, trying to sound casual when he suggested, "We could walk together, if you're going back to the Palace."

"Sure, why not?" Inexplicable panic surged through Obito's chest. He thought about rescinding his acceptance, but it was too late; he'd already agreed, and the pair set off together in tentatively comfortable silence.

GENERAL AKI'S FAVORITE METHOD of discipline became such a regular ordeal to Daisuke that he essentially expected it to be part of his nightly routine. He'd lost count of how many times he'd failed to keep his mouth shut throughout summer and early autumn—an unchanging trend in life he couldn't always control, not even when he wanted to—which never failed to land him in this predicament, sometimes with the addition of fifty or so push-ups if the General was in a particularly bad mood.

He hadn't been scrubbing floors in the vacant mess hall for long when he heard one of the heavy outer doors swing open with a maddening screech of its rusted hinges. Some believed the ghosts of deceased soldiers haunted the barracks, but if they'd had half a mind, they would've realized it was their superiors running errands or returning from less wholesome tasks at odd hours. Not that anyone paid that much attention. Besides, late evenings weren't a terribly strange time to hear these noises—the superstitious and paranoid lots would know that, too, if they weren't so busy smoking, drinking, or gambling in the communal areas.

Daisuke sighed heavily and straightened his back, looking around at the small corner of flooring he'd washed compared to what was left. He wished he wasn't missing all the fun he could hear from a few rooms over; he supposed that was the actual punishment. However, having an unfortunate number of rational adults in one place meant no one would let him join the games, so instead, he'd been relegated to watching his older counterparts play while Bunji explained the rules. As it turned out, his friend had plenty more interests than reading and boats, which surprised everyone else who had enlisted at the same time as him—perhaps there really was an advantage to being unassuming.

"Staying out of trouble, for instance," the boy grumbled, rolling his eyes. "I can't imagine what that's like."

Daisuke's nose wrinkled with disgust, though he knew he only had himself to blame. He probably shouldn't have openly—and loudly—criticized a trainer's decision to discipline a slightly unruly group with stupid drills rather than a verbal warning, but no one else would say it.

Footsteps echoing in the hallway brought him back to the present, and now aware they were coming closer, he pointlessly swept away the hair dangling in his face and returned to work. The unexpected arrival of a second set of clicking boots caused the first to halt, followed by a pitched noise of surprise, then low, indiscernible whispers. Things were finally getting interesting around here. Daisuke dipped his scrub brush into his bucket again as the men came closer, now able to hear their conversation better.

"A boy is cleaning in there, but we don't need to worry about him; he's deaf and won't be able to understand us unless we sign at him directly." General Aki—admittedly, not who he expected to see running around at this hour.

How fascinating. Daisuke thought with a subconscious, mischievous smirk as he continued washing the dark stones beneath him. *Better do as the man says.*

He circled the stiff bristles more quietly than before so he wouldn't need to strain to hear anything over the scratchy sound they made, firmly reminding himself not to acknowledge it when the general and his unseen companion entered the room. Then, sneaking a peek from under his hair, Daisuke saw a tall Giahatian man dressed in a layer of furs—more indicative of lengthy travel than the late autumn temperatures—which covered his pale yellow shirt. He wore his short dark hair slicked back, the shine of whatever oils he'd used catching in the lamplight. Shivering, the man removed his coat and gloves as he stood before the large fireplace across the room from where Daisuke worked. General Aki leaned against one of the tables Daisuke had pushed to the wall, dipping his fingers into a small canister he'd removed from his shirt, then tucking tobacco between his tongue and cheek.

"I apologize for my rude reception, Hideo, but one normally sends a messenger if they intend to visit the barracks." General Aki sounded entirely unimpressed, and Daisuke didn't need to look to know he wore a highly familiar expression to match—he'd seen it plenty of times. "I don't believe we make many exceptions to the rule."

Daisuke quickly glanced down when Hideo turned away from the warming fire with a grin, still hugging himself to fend off a chill. "Straight-laced as ever, I see, Aki. Don't worry about it. It was always more of an unspoken thing, anyway, wasn't it?"

"Actually—"

"Why dwell on it, old friend?"

"...I suppose. What brings you here? You didn't come this far for a social call."

"What makes you so sure?" Hideo paused, likely receiving Aki's familiar, scathingly impatient glower. Daisuke was beginning to like this side of the General...so long as he directed it at someone else. After a moment of nothing but the soft scrubbing of bristles rhythmically hitting the air, Hideo seemed to have bolstered the courage to ask for what he wanted. "You're sure the boy can't hear?"

"Am I sure? Of all the—" Aki sighed, clearly annoyed his friend didn't trust him, then called out, "Boy, are you listening?"

Daisuke didn't flinch, which was especially difficult when the general repeated his question more forcefully. He used both hands to wet the brush, this time to disguise the nervous clench of his fingers. *Whatever the idiot wants, it sounds illegal. Damn it. Why the hell did I get dragged into this?*

A drawn pause thick with tension settled between Hideo and Aki until the noble determined he could trust his friend's assessment. "Right, sorry."

"You're certainly nervous about this."

And the man has the nerve to call me blunt, Daisuke mentally commented, rolling his eyes. *Whatever.*

"Yes, well...I'm afraid I may be asking a rather large favor."

"Such as?"

"Here, take a look at th—*shit!*"

Daisuke's entire body twitched with the temptation to peek when the sound of a stone hitting the floor echoed across the room. After a moment of horrified quiet, Hideo fumbled out some pathetic attempt at excusing his clumsiness, and Daisuke finally dared to inspect the scene rapidly unfolding before him. He turned away slightly to pull his hair from its usual messy ponytail. When he bent over to pick up the brush again, the loosened strands gave him a discreet way to keep watch, helping him monitor the situation as he'd expected.

"By Hikari's Light, that's an awfully strange coin you have, Lord Hideo," General Aki murmured as he watched the nobleman stoop to retrieve the dropped object.

No one on Perena accepted Noshian coins or bills as legal tender, and money was an alien concept to the Okami and Oshoshans. Forging one's own was practically a declaration of war on the Empire—anyone with an ounce of wealth or power attached to their name would know that law; it was one of few things specifically designed to rein in the rich. Daisuke couldn't imagine any were so outright stupid to disobey it, no matter how arrogant a noble became. He took a chance by inching closer to the two men, dragging his bucket along, hoping to catch a glimpse.

Aki cleared his throat, "I take it you're here to report it."

Hideo must've gathered he wouldn't get what he originally wanted out of Aki, not with the other man's suspicions raised in this manner, so he began a miserable attempt to double back as he passed the mysterious object to the General. "Coin? No, this is a...it's a talisman—no! No, a token. A token of good luck. I wanted to give it to you for many years of friendship."

"That's exceedingly kind of you."

Why bother with a lie if you can't put in the effort to make it sound believable? Daisuke tilted his head as if concentrating on something stuck to the floor. General Aki clearly didn't intend to press the matter, which was probably for the best. *He knows Lord Horseshit is full of it, too.*

Now palpably anxious, Lord Hideo made his excuse to leave shortly afterward. "Do you mind if we take this conversation outside? I'd appreciate it if your infantrymen didn't hear me asking you for a small loan—gods help me if one of our former comrades did."

"You always did know how to make a fuss," Aki playfully criticized with a short chuckle, though he no longer appeared present in their discussion. "Why don't we talk more in my quarters instead? Think you can still outdrink me?"

Hideo smiled weakly, unalleviated, then nodded. General Aki imperceptibly tilted his head in Daisuke's direction, silently acknowledging him with a nod of approval, then quietly left the hall on Hideo's heels after discarding the "coin" on the ground again. Ruddy torchlight danced on its dark surface, antagonizing Daisuke's curiosity until he finally caved.

The coin weighed more than he guessed; it sat heavily on his fingers. It also seemed slightly too thick to be an actual form of money, though he wasn't sure what else it might be. Imperial coins had cherry blossoms engraved on their backs and the Emperor's profile on their faces. A coat of grime and general wear obscured the surface beyond Daisuke's ability to recognize any inscriptions, if they existed, which greatly strengthened the impression that whatever rested in his hand wasn't legal tender. Even on the off chance it *was,* it couldn't have come from Akuwara's reign. It didn't make sense to him why Lord Hideo felt compelled to show General Aki the odd thing in the first place; judging by his reactions, Daisuke wasn't alone in his confusion, which eased the sense that he was stealing it from the nobleman.

Daisuke waited for General Aki or Lord Hideo to return and snatch the coin away, expecting them at any second. When no one came, he tucked it into an unoccupied pocket, then looked around the room again.

"I'd better get out of here while I still can," Daisuke said to the empty hall, catching the abandoned bucket and brush from the corner of his eye. "Don't judge me. I've done *plenty* today."

OBITO SHIVERED WHEN AN icy wind blew through his hair and tried to burrow further into his cloak. Going to an unfamiliar part of the city close to sundown had *sounded* like a horrible idea when Itsuki brought it up after dinner; he still wasn't entirely sure how his partner had convinced him to tag along.

Well, I guess that isn't true. Obito wasn't exactly proud of the small pouches of white leaf they each carried in their pockets—he'd gone halfway out of curiosity for himself, with the other part stemming from an inexplicable sense that Itsuki would find trouble if he went alone. Hell, even with sticking together, they still risked the possibility of running into issues. Distribution of the recreational drug to anyone under the age of fifteen was technically illegal, though mostly just frowned upon in reality; how someone might react to a pair of thirteen-year-olds having it wasn't always predictable, and neither boy wanted to be reprimanded by Master Yujin for their choices. He glanced at the buildings around him, searching for a landmark to tell him how much further they had to walk. He didn't recognize anything.

"Itsuki, I think we're going the wrong way."

"You worry too much. I'm sure we'll find our way out of this area if we keep going." The other boy also looked at their surroundings, obviously not convinced by his own words. "Are we close to the assassin's quarter?"

"Hopefully not."

They paused at an intersection in the road. Obito squinted against the impending darkness and read the sign on an establishment not far from their right; another seedy-looking tavern, about the fourth they'd passed since leaving the white leaf seller's. Itsuki pointed to an alleyway on the other side of the street.

"Let's go that way. It looks like it could be a shortcut."

Obito's intuition instantly and viscerally resisted the idea, though he couldn't articulate why into words. He glanced over his shoulder at the street behind him, then shifted his attention to the one across the way. "I don't know...I think we should—"

"You're overthinking things again." Itsuki gave him an exasperated smile. "Come on."

There would've been more hesitation on Obito's part, but he didn't want Itsuki to get too far away from him. The feeling from earlier that had encouraged him to join his partner had festered all evening and became more insistent when Itsuki suggested their new path. As they drew further away from the tenuous comfort of the main road and wound their way through back alleys, Obito sensed exactly how far they'd isolated themselves from help.

Perhaps they weren't in the assassin's quarter, but the poor condition of some of the buildings they passed suggested they weren't any closer to a better part of the city, which meant they still had to confront the possibility of dealing with an opportunistic thief or a wandering assassin. A popular game with the hitokiri was to see how much they could obstruct the efforts of the onmitsu before incurring Master Yujin's wrath, as he had authority over both units. However, the assassins were often left to their own devices until a commanding officer distributed their assignments. Younger spies—or "little sneaks," as other military personnel liked calling them—were especially vulnerable to these antics, which often got far out of hand; some years ago, an incident had allegedly led to a few untimely deaths. None of the senior spies spoke of it now, but Obito wished they *would*; then maybe Itsuki would've exercised more caution when he turned the corner behind what must've been an inn and nearly stumbled into a meeting they shouldn't have witnessed.

Without warning, Itsuki swung out his hand and pushed Obito away when they reached a cross-section in the back streets. Obito's better senses made him bite back the urge to curse at his partner when he recovered his balance, as he saw Itsuki's shadowy form put a finger to his lips, along with a lantern's warm, reddish glow illuminating two sets of footprints in the snow from several feet away.

One set of impressions indicated an odd gait, but Obito didn't have much time to register the minute detail as his eyes followed the steps toward a pair of hitokiri conversing quietly—rarely a sign that something innocuous was underway. Obito knew they needed to make themselves scarce, so he grabbed the cuff of Itsuki's sleeve; instead, the other boy's head tilted toward the men in the narrow crossing, and his body shifted to get a better view.

Gods be damned. Obito barely kept his grip on Itsuki, who still wasn't willing to budge. His eyes anxiously went to the assassins again.

"You don't understand, Yin, I *need* that poison," the shorter of the two hissed.

The other assassin rubbed his scraggly beard in exasperation. "It doesn't matter how much you beg—I don't know how to make it, and I can't get my hands on any without causing trouble for myself. Quite frankly, I don't like you enough to risk getting caught by Master Yujin. Hell, I don't think anyone does."

"Does this mean you'll report me, then?"

"You can't be serious. This is one of those fantastic situations where keeping a secret helps the both of us; stealing from the onmitsu to assist you in someone's unauthorized murder won't end well for me, and *you* should pretend this conversation never happened."

"Fuck," Itsuki blurted, then gasped as he clapped his hands over his mouth.

The shorter assassin paused, body jerking slightly as he straightened, listening, and his counterpart swiftly dislodged a kunai from his belt, poised for an attack. Obito tugged on Itsuki's sleeve again and started running the second the first man's head turned toward them, flecks of red from the lantern he carried glinting menacingly in his black eyes.

"I fucking see you!"

"Quickly! Before Master Yujin hears of this!"

Obito ran faster through the alley and didn't stop until he felt there was enough distance between himself and the assassins. He looked around wildly to assess his surroundings; experienced, skilled hitokiri operated soundlessly within the shadows and were quicker than lightning when they struck. Nearly every angle in these back alleys favored the manslayers, so if he'd been followed by one, he had to prepare what few defenses he could find. His heart sank when he turned to where Itsuki should've been standing, only for his eyes to land on an empty spot.

"Itsuki?" he called out to locate his partner and to quell the panic in his chest. After what must've been an eternity passed without an answer, he tried again, this time with more intensity in his voice. "Itsuki!"

Obito took an uneasy step in the direction he'd come from; although he dreaded the sense that he already knew what retracing his footprints in the snow would reveal, he was sprinting as soon as he started to move again. He forced himself to take on a more rational line of thinking, despite the undeniable, terrible instinct that danger had befallen Itsuki upon their separation. When he returned to the intersection where they'd found the assassins plotting, a gleaming blotch on the corner of a building to his right caught his eye in the moonlight.

Obito's fears were confirmed before he faced forward again.

Shaking, he approached the boy lying on the ground and knelt beside him. Blood pooled beneath Itsuki's inert form. Obito stared in blank shock; the hitokiri had torn him open from shoulder to abdomen with a gruesome diagonal slash from their katana. Judging by the signs of a struggle in the snow behind him, the assassins hadn't allowed Itsuki to get far before they'd caught him. Dark shadows of indentations from chain links had deeply embedded in the other boy's skin at his jugular.

"You were right behind me," Obito whispered in disbelief. "How the fuck did they—?"

His throat closed around anything else he might've said as hot tears welled in his eyes.

"GENERAL AKI?" DAISUKE TIMIDLY poked his face through the slightly opened door. Aki's eyes shifted away from his book; his quick response made it clear he'd been expecting company, a sense that was compounded when he automatically waved Daisuke over the threshold. He stood a few feet away from the older man, squeezing the odd coin as he held it behind his back.

The General didn't bother moving from the comfort of where he sat beside his table, but he set aside his reading by placing the book in his lap, his thumb still marking his page. "Shouldn't you be in bed, Daisuke?"

"I'm sure I should," he admitted with a shrug, not fully meeting his superior's eyes. He uneasily bounced onto his toes, then padded closer to the General and held out his hand. "But didn't you want this from earlier?"

"That thing?" General Aki barely glanced at it and rolled his eyes before picking up his book again. If body language was a factor to consider, apparently the visit from his friend hadn't been a particularly happy reunion. "If it *is* a good luck charm, perhaps you ought to keep it—you may recall, evaluations are about two weeks away. It's not much time."

"Right. I'll keep that in mind."

"Dismissed, Daisuke. Go get some rest."

"Yes, sir."

Daisuke readily admitted that he found the General's reaction confusing, but also knew it meant he didn't want to discuss it further, so after another peek at the object resting in his palm, he carefully tucked it into a pocket. As he exited Aki's quarters, he became inexplicably drawn toward the nearest window at the opposite end of the hallway, and he couldn't force his body to change course; somewhere in the back of his mind, he realized he didn't want to, either. Upon looking through the glass, his eyes fell on the dark Palace grounds, lightly covered with fresh snowfall from earlier that day.

Still, he couldn't shake the unexpected, overpowering sense that something horrendous had happened.

TEN
THE INTERWOVEN THREADS

DEATH WAS AN INEVITABILITY—INDISCRIMINATE, uncaring, and unfeeling about whom it took and when. Pretty words, longing poetry, and love for the life lost gave a distinct beauty to the melancholy darkness death carried, though none of that splendor was present in the immediate wake of a tragedy.

Healers and medics from the infirmary worked for hours trying to resuscitate Itsuki, until they were forced to conclude there was no chance of saving him; he'd lost too much blood, and Healers couldn't revive a corpse. Master Yujin, naturally, questioned Obito at length during that time, but he couldn't have repeated any of the interrogation if he had tried. He didn't even remember how he'd gotten Itsuki's body back to the Palace in the first place, nor could he clearly recall anything after hearing the news that Itsuki had died from his injuries not long after receiving them. The heaviness of guilt gnarled and steeped into his consciousness for two sleepless nights before the day of the funeral, along with endless questions from his peers. So many fucking accusations framed as questions.

Obito moved through those two agonizingly long days as if there was an invisible wall between himself and the outside world, except, this time, he hadn't intentionally put it there. Everything felt colder and more distant than it had in almost two years; while Obito wouldn't speak of the last incident that put him in a similar state of shock, he remembered the feeling and its vice-like grip too well. He'd barely saved his sanity by finally learning to place it elsewhere in his mind, where he could pretend it didn't exist. Detachment from a situation often helped him accept the reality of it, but he knew he was far from fine—especially this time. Despite all his efforts to convince himself he was just that, and how he hadn't had a hand in Itsuki's death, all his emotions sat like a massive boulder on his chest that he didn't know how to move.

He still hadn't fully rejoined the present as he dressed for mourning on the day of the funeral, not until one of Master Yujin's advanced students passed him in a corridor, dutifully carrying a shiny memorial tablet carved from onyx, along with Itsuki's tanto. Grief swelled inside him. Knowing he couldn't bear to see his friend's pale, lifeless body burned on the pyre, he watched the procession of other onmitsu dressed in black formals for half a minute before deciding he wouldn't attend. Heartless as it probably seemed, the sight of Itsuki's blood on his hands flashed through his mind as it already had several hundred other times; he'd tried washing it off to the point of giving himself dried and cracked skin, but no amount of effort made the sensation or mental image go away.

Obito broke from formation and turned on his heel, going in the opposite direction of the empty hall where services would take place. He ignored the few quiet, mostly annoyed outbursts that his disruption caused and kept moving. He wandered the familiar back road toward the nobility quarter without stopping to look at the steel grey pond lying still in its ravine, although he was sure he'd originally meant to go there.

Soon enough, he knocked on Aunt Kiko's door. He didn't know what he'd do with her company now that he'd sought it, but intense relief flooded his chest when she answered. However unexpectedly the urge to wrap his arms around her rushed at him, he held back from acting upon it; he wasn't sure if he could handle that sort of contact. After absorbing his exhausted state, she ushered him inside with the same look of deep empathy she'd given him when he'd first arrived in the Capital, hurt and rejected by his family, along with a merciful lack of questions.

One of Aunt Kiko's favorite places in the apartment was the front tearoom, where she claimed the best sunlight came through in the afternoons; it was also her favorite place to play cards with a neighboring widow and where she liked to drink wine or smoke white leaf now and then when Retsuko came to visit her. Although the skies were overcast, and little of that light she loved came through the windowpane, she said they'd talk over tea in there.

"Your favorite is chai, right? Or was that your mother's?"

"Both, actually," Obito absentmindedly answered as he sat under the window at a small glass-top table. He shook his head, realizing why she'd asked, and started to stand again. "Let me help you."

Aunt Kiko firmly but gently pushed on his shoulder. "That won't be necessary. It won't take me but a moment, anyway, so you stay here and wait."

The minutes felt like hours, but Aunt Kiko eventually returned as promised.

"Mika stopped by to see me yesterday—poor dear was beside himself with grief," she said cautiously. Her eyes found his once she set the teapot down, aware she approached a sore subject whenever she brought the cousins up to one another. Her following statement also, inevitably, circled a sensitive topic. "He told me there's a funeral today for one of the onmitsu."

Obito's shoulders stiffened in the middle of him filling her cup. "He shouldn't have said anything. That goes against protocol."

"I'd better reconsider telling the neighborhood cats I feed, then." A gentle, teasing smile briefly warmed her features before they turned solemn again. She carefully touched his arm as he set the teapot down again. "Protocol or not, he also told me the boy who died was *your* teammate. Is that true?"

Obito helplessly averted his eyes from his aunt's, then leaned back in his seat with a slow, heavy sigh and nodded. He sensed her gaze stay on him for a long moment until suddenly, she stood and put her arms around him in an embrace. He froze, at first not grasping that she wasn't about to scold him for acting callously—as a rule, Giahatians didn't accept any reason for missing the funeral of a friend or relative. One's own death *might* be considered excusable. However, once he understood her intentions, he felt relieved that at least one person recognized his grief for what it was; losing Itsuki hurt like hell, but for whatever reason, Obito couldn't show it beyond what he was already doing.

ALTHOUGH AUNT KIKO DID her best to comfort him, it hadn't taken long for unease at displaying that amount of vulnerability to prickle under his skin. Obito didn't feel right with her trying to carry the weight of such an immense burden, nor did he want her to feel as though she had to hold it for his sake; he hadn't begun to untangle the emotions that had deepened from spending time with her. Of course, that wasn't her fault—he simply had no idea what to do with the anger, confusion, and sadness tumbling around inside him like a directionless swirl.

Despite any determination to keep himself together, Obito's eyes were raw from how often he had scrubbed annoyingly persistent tears out of them as soon as they brimmed at the rims. He'd all but raced back toward the dormitories to deal with this in the isolated safety of his room—while also hoping to avoid everyone else—but the heaviness of it all had slowed him near the old arrow slats. Obito's efforts to keep it to himself failed miserably, and he finally broke, a hand over his mouth to futilely repress his tears as they flowed down his face and over his fingers; their salt burned in the cracks of his broken skin. After spending a few minutes struggling to regain some semblance of control, he pretended he was ready to move again.

That was, until he heard solemn voices trickling into the corridor from the direction of the library. Struck with panic, he hoped they'd leave him alone if he stayed still and silent; his pessimistic half was also grimly aware he couldn't avoid them forever.

"Pretty bold of you to show your face around us after blowing off Itsuki's funeral," Mika's voice sneered from behind him, joined by a few differing expressions of agreement.

Obito rolled his eyes, but refused to give his cousin the satisfaction of acknowledgement by turning around to look at him. Instead, he forced himself to focus on the frost-tipped grass and hedges below; for the first time in a while, he didn't trust himself to stay calm.

Mika scoffed. "Nothing to say for yourself? Maybe that's better. *I'd* never get *my* partner killed just to get high off some white leaf."

"As if you don't steal some from Aunt Kiko every time you go over there," Obito impulsively muttered his retort, instantly regretting the slip in his restraint.

"Don't try to make this about something else. No one's died because of me."

Obito's anger rose like a tidal wave. He pivoted, pinning his cousin under his gaze. "My point is that you have no reason to act morally superior. You make so many mistakes that I'm surprised you *haven't* gotten Shinta killed yet. What happened wasn't my fault, and you fucking know it. Itsuki is dead. Now let him rest."

"Did he honestly mean that little to you?" Mika flushed as scorn filled his hazel eyes, a sign he was genuinely furious; unfortunately for him, so was Obito. "Where's your fucking heart?"

Obito glared. "You should know—you're the one who told me I don't have one, remember? Now fuck off and leave me alone."

At this point, the three behind Mika exchanged increasingly worried glances, the anxiety in their eyes a step higher than it'd already been when he first rounded on them. They'd noticed the second Mika struck at Obito's fragile defenses and appeared to understand how hard he'd hit, and were now equally as desperate for this exchange to end. Obito felt the same. He also saw no reason to waste more of his energy, and the ordeal had intruded enough on his emotions; he didn't fully believe himself when he told people Itsuki's death wasn't his fault. Before Mika had time to respond, he shoved his way past them and continued toward his room, accidentally slamming the door behind him when he reached the end of the hall.

Yujin sighed as he set his cup of tasteless wine on the table after placing a card in front of him; he should've known better than to buy a bottle from the city's cheaper markets. He threw a couple more coins on the table and waited for the general to draw, as well, unable to react when his friend beat him for the third round in a row. "I'm not sure what to do, Aki. The hitokiri murdered one of my boys a couple of weeks ago, so not only am I down an onmitsu, but I can't find a proper replacement."

Aki and Yujin had lost plenty of soldiers over the years, but neither found it ever became more manageable, especially when fate stole the younger lives in their ranks. The General's eyes lifted from his card to his friend, filled with genuine sympathy that Yujin solely trusted from him. "I'm deeply sorry to hear it. Do you know which assassin is responsible?"

"Not even close—I can't get anything out of his surviving teammate who was there."

"I see. You're down *two* onmitsu, then."

"That does seem to be the case, yes."

Aki didn't pull the two copper coins off to the side yet. He already had a small pile of the Intelligence Master's money—Yujin never was any good at these games, which was part of why he kept them low-stakes when they played—but there was little enjoyment in winning when their usual banter was missing. "None of the nobles have a son they can send?"

"So they said when I sent out a request at the end of summer." Yujin rolled his eyes and set another card down, along with a pair of copper pieces, when Aki finally took the others and put two of his own on the table. "Anything exciting on your end of things lately?"

"Not much to speak of. I wrapped six-month evaluations yesterday evening—nice move." Aki smirked as he acknowledged his friend's victory this time. They placed their bets once more.

"How did that go? Damn it, *again*?"

"Don't tell me you're surprised." Aki grinned at the liveliness finally infiltrating their conversation. "I'll admit, this wasn't the most impressive group I've ever passed, but they *did* fulfill requirements, so I can't do much else—His Highness and the main infantry generals care about quantity over everything else lately. I still had to fail one of the boys, though; the poor lad was on his last chance to show us what he could do, too."

Yujin knitted his brows, then took another drink to drown his humiliation at giving even more of his money to Aki. "Grounds for a dishonorable discharge, isn't it?"

"Yes, but...I'll be frank. I don't know what to do with him. He obviously won't be much of a soldier, but what he lacks in strength, he makes up for in smarts, so I think it'd be a shame to dismiss him entirely. Besides—another? Aren't you tired of losing yet? Besides, if I *do* discharge him, he'll either become a homeless drifter or some fuckwitted noble's unwilling servant. And he knows it. I'm almost positive those are the reasons he hasn't tried making a run for it yet."

Aki and Yujin momentarily stopped the game as their conversation also took on an uneasy pause, their silence creating a heavy bubble around them, though noise from the barracks continued outside the General's door.

The Intelligence Master regarded the General intently as he tried to parse through his companion's words. Finally, he opted to err on the side of caution and gently pressed the issue with, "No family, I take it? How old is he?"

"Twelve by now, I believe. He should be thirteen come spring."

"Aki, this boy...is he from Okara?"

Aki tapped the thin edge of the card in his hand. "Before you judge my decision, Yujin, remember that the Emperor permits generals to take on whatever men or resources are available to serve the Empire best. I picked this boy last year during the open recruiting campaign. I hope you'll understand—I couldn't send him back to the plantations or his slaveowners when he came to me."

"You *still* shouldn't." Yujin looked at his cup but didn't take it off the table. "What happens on Okara is a fucking shit-stain on our Empire."

"You know I don't disagree, but I don't have many other options with him now. I'm all ears if you have any suggestions."

Yujin lapsed into silence again, unable to decide if he should be looking at his friend, the table, or his sorry pile of coins near Aki's elbow, gleaming at him mockingly under the lamplight. He suddenly felt grateful that they bet with copper pieces or other silly things, such as extra buttons, when they played. The more serious part of his mind at work thought of the empty place on his roster, the absolute fit Emperor Akuwara would throw, and weighed if he'd regret the move he wanted to make.

"Perhaps it isn't *all* hopeless for the boy," he slowly ventured.

Aki raised his eyebrows, looking torn between amusement and disbelief that his attempt to goad him worked. "What, you want him?"

Master Yujin hesitated a little longer, then nodded, heart already in his throat at the verbal beating he'd be taking for this later. However, when he realized his next swig of wine tasted much better than any of what he'd previously drank, he felt he'd made the right call, even if it was a temporary solution.

"His Highness won't like it, but if I did everything he wanted, we'd still be losing soldiers on Othakra. Send the boy over tomorrow afternoon. That should give me time to prepare a few things."

MASTER YUJIN AND GENERAL Aki agreed they should frame the planned transfer in an official light, so bright and early the following morning, the Intelligence Master stood at the threshold of the Emperor's private study, frowning at the hastily written letter Aki had penned about an hour prior. On the one hand, he was thrilled that his friend had agreed to supplement his ranks, which meant somebody could avenge Itsuki's murder sooner. On the other hand, however, the boy Aki wanted to send over was guaranteed to needle the Emperor's temper. Gods, his knees felt weak.

"Care to share what's on your mind, Yujin? You've been glaring at that parchment for several minutes now," Akuwara invited with false warmth, immediately dashing Yujin's hopes.

The Intelligence Master swallowed and finally looked up; he hadn't realized how long he'd been standing there after announcing his presence. His eyes subconsciously drifted toward the young prince, seated on his father's lap while a nursemaid stood nearby. Prince Akuko had the late Empress's delicate features and fairer skin tone, but his true sire's deep black eyes, already unreadable and expressionless, looked back at Yujin. The prince seldom spoke, and this occasion was no different. An odd sense of relief washed over him. He carefully smoothed Aki's letter over the peace treaty draft he'd worked on over the last several months. Although it was nowhere near ready to present to His Highness, it'd soon be in good enough shape to show the tacticians, who could provide him with finer wording for details. Eventually, Akuwara would have no choice but to consider the words, his personal feelings about the Okami notwithstanding.

Yujin cleared his throat. "Of course, Your Highness. I spoke with General Aki several days ago regarding Intelligence's recent loss, and it seems he's willing to part with one of his younger trainees rather than sending him to regular infantry."

"Odd you found that news to be worthy of such a sour expression."

"Well, you see, the boy he's sending me will...likely seem less than desirable to you, Your Highness." Yujin hesitated, wincing when he added, "A Northern Nomad, to be exact."

Emperor Akuwara's eyes flashed with dangerous, silent fury, alarming Yujin with their sudden intensity. Then, without prompting, Prince Akuko slid away from his father and went to the nursemaid, who wordlessly left the room with him through a secret passage in the wall. Akuwara rose from his chair and prowled toward Yujin; infuriated puffs of air from his nose rattled the papers desperately clenched in the master spy's fingers. "A Northern Nomad, you said? Do you mean to tell me you've allowed a putrid *slaveborn* into *my* intelligence agency?"

"Your Highness, please, I—"

"This cannot stand—it *will* not. Contact as many noble or merchant families as you need, but I will *not* accept this...this...*insult* to the Empire."

"Neither General Aki nor I would ever intend to insult you *or* the Empire, Your Highness. I'd swear my life on it." All the gods help Yujin; it looked like he'd have a chance to explain, judging by the arch of the Emperor's brow. "I *have* contacted the nobles and merchants—only a few months ago, in fact. Of the few who responded, none could provide the help we needed. So, while I cannot vouch for the boy now, I must trust there's a reason General Aki does."

Emperor Akuwara drew back slightly, enough to give Yujin room to breathe, and folded his arms in front of him, the long sleeves of his pale blue and pearl-gray robes casually draping at his sides. Light from the crawling sunrise gave the Imperial circlet on his head a sinister gleam.

He waited until he'd collected his thoughts to say more, then narrowed his eyes and asked, "What do you expect to happen, Yujin? What do *you* want out of this?"

"An even number of trainees, Your Highness. No secret motives, no desire beyond wanting to ensure the best learning experience for *all* operatives—each one needs a partner, even if that teammate's purpose is to be completely disposable after all is said and done."

The corners of Akuwara's mouth twitched in a brief, smug smirk. "Why, Yujin, I had no idea you were so cold to your onmitsu; I'm amazed they show such loyalty to you."

"They are tools to the Empire's success, just as the hitokiri. We cannot mourn every life lost." It was a lie, but a fib Yujin was better off convincing Akuwara he believed. Since it was unlikely he'd ever father children of his own, the spies he trained held more value to him than any military member or any amount of gold. The impact of losing Itsuki and what his death had done to Obito wouldn't leave him for a long while.

The Emperor faced his desk, organizing his inner world once more. After a long, tense moment, he finally said, "If that disgrace's performance is anything less than perfect, feed him to the dogs. Alive. Should it come to that point, I hope you are also prepared for your dismissal."

EVERYTHING IN THE PALACE caught Daisuke's eye; from purple, jewel-encrusted tapestries lining the walls in one room to marble busts of previous Giahatian Emperors in another, his mind couldn't process everything he saw fast enough. The walls of lifelike nature oil paintings, verses calligraphed with careful brushstrokes, lush carpets running across stone floors, and gold and bronze artifacts all proudly on display vaguely reminded him of Grandmaster Norio's mansion. It was far more grandiose and elegant in design, no doubt, but somehow, the ideology behind the two felt the same. His skin crawled at the comparison. He rarely entered the Palace, and when he did, he made sure to avoid corridors with so many ornamentations.

He tensely watched the General, who escorted him through the long maze of halls to ensure he wouldn't get lost or encounter difficulties from guards. "General Aki, where are you taking me?"

"You're going to see an old friend of mine."

"...Why?"

"Because he's the head of Imperial Intelligence."

"Not to sound argumentative, sir—"

"—You'd never dream of it—"

"—But that doesn't feel like an answer."

"You'll see, Daisuke. Now, pick up the pace a little, would you?"

Now agitated and nervous, he stuffed a hand into his pocket to fiddle with the coin—it hadn't brought luck, but he hoped a distraction would soothe the sudden intrusion of self-doubt slithering into his chest. While he was grateful he hadn't been shipped off to Okara as his failure to advance should've promised, Daisuke couldn't help but guard himself more closely than he usually did. He didn't know what was underway, but he could tell no one thought he belonged inside the Palace—everyone he and General Aki passed said so by the contempt or confusion in their sideways glances.

Daisuke mentally shook himself and adjusted the leather sack hanging off his shoulder, which carried his clothes, a book about knots Bunji gave him as a parting gift before he'd gone to the main infantry, and the feathered hoop he'd pierce through his left ear in a few short years.

They took a sudden detour up a set of stairs, which set them on a path through another level of corridors, thankfully deserted this time, though the General's gait grew more relentless with each stride. They passed the library with barely a glance from the same guards who had chased Daisuke off a few times before, then turned around a corner to a narrower hall; eventually, this led them to strangely shaped, tall windows without any glass to protect this portion from the elements. However, despite the heavy, fluffy snowflakes dancing on an easy, wintry wind outside, none had accumulated indoors.

Daisuke couldn't stand his curiosity anymore. "Sir, please, this is killing me."

General Aki sighed in that frustrated, resigned way Daisuke heard from him all too often, specifically when they conversed. "I think it'd be better for the Intelligence Master to explain it to you. He knows the situation better, and since you're under his command now, he *should* be the one briefing you."

"I'm...what?"

"You are now a member of Imperial Intelligence. You might not be the best soldier I've ever trained, but that doesn't mean you don't have a place here. So, I spoke with my old friend, and we worked out a solution together."

Daisuke was stumped. Upon failing his second evaluation, he was certain he'd be returned to Okara on a dishonorable discharge, and had spent the last couple of days sincerely weighing if death would be better. When General Aki told him to pack his bags earlier that day, he wasn't sure what would befall him; his mind had raced even faster all morning, and he couldn't focus on much else. If the General hadn't assured him then that he wasn't going back to the slave plantations, he would've bolted hours ago. Being initiated into the elite ranks of the onmitsu was the last place he felt he deserved to go. A flash of panic made him question if spies used weaker members as bait for the stronger ones; rumors about Kurushima said the very same happened to hitokiri trainees who weren't meeting expectations. He didn't have the proper sources to say with any certainty if the onmitsu operated so brutally, but to believe anything else sounded naïve.

He knew the General didn't have much of a sense of humor; still, he had to ask, "You're joking, right?"

Aki groaned, and their journey continued in the same oppressive silence as before, though it wasn't nearly as long until they passed through what appeared to be a common area of sorts. A couple of desks, some old furniture, and worn cushions piled in a corner gave it a cozy enough feeling, as did a small fireplace on the far interior wall. As nice as it seemed, it was a direct contrast to the frenzied nerves still making Daisuke's hair stand on end.

They eventually stopped at a primarily empty room; its lone occupant was a man sitting on a stool with a small, wheeled cart at his side. He lounged against the trolley as he smoked from a long, curved tobacco pipe, utterly disinterested in the world, until the sight of General Aki and Daisuke standing in the doorway caught his attention. Startled, he scrambled to his feet and saluted the General.

"At ease, please," Aki said, holding up a hand. "This is Daisuke. Master Yujin told me he needed the initiation higanbana before proceeding with anything else."

"You've brought him to the right place, then." The young man smiled, relieved he wouldn't get reprimanded for how they'd caught him. Surprisingly, his grin didn't fade when he addressed Daisuke. "I'm Oko, a tattooist. Won't you come in?"

Daisuke went to step forward, but the General caught him by the arm. Aki pivoted to face him, and he copied the motion.

"Attention!" the older man barked after clearing his throat. He awkwardly straightened his posture, put his hands behind his back, his feet slightly less than shoulder-width apart, and nervously awaited the General's order. Aki's stern expression relaxed enough to give him a small smile. "Effective immediately, you are hereby dismissed from the infantry and formally reassigned to the onmitsu."

Daisuke blinked a few times before a slow, excited grin spread across his face. Though he knew this was how formalities wanted him to respond, he meant every word; he didn't know how the hell he could ever thank his former commanding officer, but the bare minimum seemed like a good place to start. "It's been an honor to serve under you, General Aki."

"There's a good lad. Off you go, then."

He bowed to General Aki, then entered the room without glancing over his shoulder. Although his heart sank a little when he heard the

General's footsteps grow quieter in the corridor, he couldn't repress a small smile that tugged on his lips. If it weren't for Aki, he didn't know where he'd be right now—certainly not preparing for a new and exciting phase in his military career. He planned to show everyone why General Aki thought a boy born as a slave was worthy of the onmitsu.

At first, he worried that Oko's pleasant demeanor might change now that they were alone, but he found a bit of encouragement when he noticed it hadn't; in the back of his mind, he wondered if that should've concerned him more. He knew what a tattoo was—the overseers he'd known and some of the other soldiers he'd met had them—but not how they got into one's skin.

Oko, however, gestured to a stool right behind the one he'd been using. "Set your bag wherever you like, but I'll need you to sit here. Please remove your shirt while I get my things ready."

"Why do you need me to take off my shirt?"

"A fair question. I'll need your upper right arm, so I suppose you don't need to take it completely off; do what makes you feel most comfortable, as long as I can get to it."

Daisuke hesitated, then did as instructed before carrying his bag and shirt over to the stool, setting them both in front of his feet. He rigidly lowered himself into the seat, tensely watching Oko the entire time as he rearranged the tools and some jars on his cart; he couldn't quite make out what he was doing, and a surge of fear returned when Oko turned around again. The tattooist pulled his cart over so that it was on his right side, nearer to where he'd be sitting beside the Giahatio's newest onmitsu—gods, that didn't sound right—wielding what looked like a stick attached to a metal point.

"S-so, why are you tattooing me?"

"Every onmitsu has a higanbana tattooed into his right arm upon initiation. It's an ancient tradition and a way for you to identify one another if need be—civilians don't know about this marking, nor do most other military personnel save for the higher ranks. I myself am sworn to secrecy in order to protect the identities of those I've worked on," Oko explained amicably, easing Daisuke's nerves when he set the needle aside again. He pulled a square silk cover off one of his jars and set up a miniature watercolor painting of the higanbana, likely to use as a guide.

Daisuke didn't have much experience with the flowers other than knowing they were toxic, but the depiction didn't look much like sketches he'd seen or the real ones used to keep deer out of gardens on the Palace grounds. "Is that what it'll look like on me?"

"Heavens, no. My master painted this one, so I put it out for his ego while I work in case he drops by. Believe me—mine are *far* prettier than his," Oko said the last part with a sly smirk and a wink.

He had a bucket of water stored on the bottom of his cart, and from it, he took a rag to wash the part of Daisuke's arm he intended to use before dabbing the moisture away with a dry one. He pulled two other cloths out and set one on his lap while slinging the other over the crook of his elbow, then measured a two-finger space below Daisuke's shoulder on his upper arm. He hummed as his other hand hovered over his set of slim tools made of metal and bamboo, fingers dancing in the air a bit as he selected which needle grouping to use. Daisuke cringed when he finally selected one.

"Will it hurt?" he asked.

"So many questions." Oko grinned, but didn't bother looking at him as he aligned the needles with Daisuke's skin, holding it barely an inch away from making contact. "Most people say it isn't bad. Now stop squirming, or it *will* hurt."

"W-what about bleeding? Will it bleed?"

"If I didn't know any better, I'd say you're stalling," Oko teased. "I'm going to begin now, so hold still."

Daisuke warily eyed the needlepoint, then Oko, and finally settled for looking at the furthest wall. He winced at the first jab into his skin and pulled away a bit out of instinct, but once he relaxed in his seat again, he found the process wasn't totally unbearable. He meticulously scanned each grey stone he could see, trying to count every speck and natural groove in the bricks as a distraction, when his eyes fell upon a black, silky banner draped across the wall.

Honor to the Empire; loyalty to the Giahatio; obedience to the Emperor; discipline to uphold them all.

Daisuke forced himself not to roll his eyes after mentally reading off the gold lettering embroidered into the banner. He settled for shaking his head at it instead and moved on to studying a map of Perena and the known world that were side-by-side on a different wall. At that point, Oko gently reminded him to keep his eyes off his shoulder area, which was greatly appreciated, though he was running out of patience to continue distracting himself. Fortunately, another diversion entered the room not five minutes later. Oko paused when he heard a rustle near the door, which made Daisuke's head turn toward two men standing near the entryway.

"No need for bowing, Oko. As you were," one of the men said.

"Thank you, Master Yujin," the tattooist answered. He sat on his stool again and resumed working as if nothing had happened.

Daisuke cautiously peered at Master Yujin, a tall Giahatian man wearing a black gi and shitagi; his undershirt was threaded delicately with golden patterns, and his presence rippled throughout the room. The boy swallowed as he stepped into full view, unable to look elsewhere. However, when Master Yujin opened his mouth to speak again, his companion cut off whatever either might've said.

"Are you sure you're tattooing the right boy, Oko?"

"This *is* the one General Aki brought to me, yes." Oko sounded nervous.

"It looks more like you're wasting *my* good ink on a slaveborn."

"Th-that isn't what I'm doing at all."

"Mind your tongue, Toshiro." Master Yujin's eyes flicked to the other man, then returned to Daisuke. "Oko is his apprentice; he wanted to observe his progress, which, as he may recall, was allowed on the condition that he'd mind his manners. As you may have heard, I am Master Yujin, your commanding officer and head of Imperial Intelligence. I'm afraid General Aki didn't give me your name, though."

"Daisuke," he introduced himself apprehensively, filled with anxiety again. Sensing it was warranted, he added, "...Akahana."

"I must thank you for agreeing to a transfer on such short notice," the Intelligence Master stated; either he hadn't been made aware of Daisuke's abysmal situation, or he was choosing to let him preserve a little dignity by not bringing it up in front of the other two in the room with them. "We've recently suffered an unexpected and excruciating loss in our ranks."

Daisuke froze at the news, which probably came as a relief to the man jabbing his arm. General Aki hadn't mentioned anything of the sort—was he in danger of suffering the same fate?

"You're here to take that boy's place," Master Yujin quickly continued, apparently noticing his fears. "You'll find your new teammate in the library once Oko's determined he's finished and says you're free to go."

Toshiro, who Daisuke still couldn't see, made a derisive noise. "Hikari help the poor boy you're forcing to endure with a slaveborn as his partner, Yujin."

Daisuke wondered if Master Yujin's neck might snap from how quickly he rounded on the other man.

The Intelligence Master straightened his spine to assert himself. "Toshiro, your lack of approval notwithstanding, this boy is now formally enlisted with intelligence, meaning he is under my direct supervision. You've stated several times—in my presence, no less—that you could never be close friends with a spy. If this is still your belief, we are not on terms for you to speak to me or one of my subordinates in such a manner."

Daisuke stared in wide-eyed shock between the two men—or, at least, he did his best to look at both. Oko kept working as if nothing had gone on right beside him. Toshiro's apprentice or not, it was clear whose authority mattered most to the tattooist; the gulf of difference between one who rabidly demanded respect and one who had earned it. Some shuffling about followed, and when Daisuke strained his neck to see, he observed Toshiro's form lumbering out of the room. Master Yujin sighed.

"My apologies, Daisuke," he said somberly. "It seems I've lost where we were. I'm afraid I must be going, but as I said, your partner will meet you in the library. He can help you get settled in for the night. I'll see you bright and early tomorrow for morning assembly."

"Yes, sir."

"Oko, if you're interested in a more permanent position here, I suggest you come to see me in my office once you've wrapped this up."

"Yes, sir." The cunning inflection in Oko's voice didn't go unnoticed by Daisuke, but Master Yujin ignored it entirely; after all, he'd just offered the apprentice a higher rank than his master's.

A little while later, long after the Intelligence Master left and that area of Daisuke's arm had gone numb, Oko happily chirped, "All done!"

Daisuke jerked his head sideways to look at the bright red flower now permanently inked into his skin. Long, crimson petals flowed and curved out from the center of his arm, as did three stamens, pronounced by yellow bulbs on the tips. As promised, Oko's work far exceeded the skill executed in the watercolor sketch he'd used as a guide. Daisuke wished he knew how to convey such opinions.

"Pretty," he whispered to himself as he kept rotating his shoulder to admire the artist's work further. Oko evidently overheard, as he chuckled while cleaning up his tools.

THE RUSTLE OF PAPER as Obito turned a book's pages to where he'd last left off the previous day provided a sense of comfort; he'd struggled to find enjoyment in...anything, it seemed, over the last couple of weeks, and finally experiencing it again was a welcomed relief from everything else that consumed him since Itsuki's funeral. Some of his peers had also come around since then, even offering condolences he wasn't sure he could accept, but Obito tried letting them know he appreciated their kindness. Although others still treated him harshly for their unit's loss, worrying about what they thought was pointless—they listened to whatever Mika said, anyway. He understood their opinions would never be worth his time.

He pulled out a folded sheet of notes he'd used to mark his place in the text and smoothed out the paper to examine what he'd recently written, only to be interrupted by a knock on his open door.

Hikari's sake. He suspected he'd regret not locking it.

Master Yujin cleared his throat. "It looks as though I'm intruding, so I'll make this brief."

Obito turned to face him, trying not to sound annoyed. "How can I help you, sir?"

"I've met with your new partner. Since I don't have time to give him all the proper introductions or tours, I'm leaving that to you. He's been instructed to meet with you in the library once he receives the initiation higanbana. Give him a few days to settle in, then brief him on the matter with the hitokiri." Master Yujin studied his student momentarily, then sighed before adding, "Try to get along with him, will you? No noble sons were of age to take Itsuki's place, so I had to transfer a soldier from the infantry—I'd like to show General Aki his generosity is appreciated."

"Yes, sir," Obito replied curtly. He had no interest in this newcomer, but that didn't mean he'd ignore the Intelligence Master's request. Whether he was emotionally ready for a different partner didn't matter; mourning Itsuki forever served little purpose.

Noticing the quiet that filled the room afterward, he finally looked away from pretending to concentrate on reading his notes and locked eyes with Master Yujin's tense gaze; perhaps he'd treaded a little too hard on his superior's patience, but it wasn't always easy to tell. However, as he prepared an apology for the way he'd spoken, the Intelligence Master squared his shoulders and quickly shed the expression. Obito also straightened his posture to give him his full attention.

Master Yujin crossed his arms, then glanced at the floor and shifted his weight between each foot. "What you've experienced would be a massive loss for any onmitsu at any age. I know Itsuki's death has been hard on you, but our organization cannot function without competent agents. Am I clear?"

"Explain Mika, then," Obito blurted with a roll of his eyes as he closed the book and left it resting near his right hand.

"That's twice, Nakamura. Do you really want to see what happens when you mouth off three times in a row?"

"...No, sir. My apologies."

"Thank you." The Intelligence Master tiredly rubbed his face. His irritation didn't lessen when he turned to go. "You *will* make sure you're in the library at the proper time. No excuses."

Obito wordlessly inclined his head as Master Yujin's echoing steps retreated down the passage again; nothing he'd said was up for debate, and they both knew the conversation was over, so he hadn't needed to wait for a response. He stared at the book and drummed his fingers on the front cover before finally surrendering to his sudden lack of interest in reading, then opened a drawer to pull out a small pouch of white leaf. Given everything else that transpired after its purchase, Master Yujin willfully ignored it—or had forgotten about it altogether—which meant he'd escaped having it confiscated. Once he finished greeting his new partner, he planned to slink off and finally enjoy it.

When he entered, Obito found an empty library, save for a few men milling about the shelves. Master Yujin hadn't given him so much as a vague description of who he was supposed to be looking for, which meant he had to pay more attention than usual to passersby. The Intelligence Master hadn't acted as if he were in the best mood, so perhaps neglecting to tell him anything about the boy had been a mere oversight; either way, he wasn't too interested in trying to ask.

At first, he tried waiting at a table close to the library's entrance, but impatience and anxiety soon had him standing again and browsing the nearby shelves. He couldn't concentrate on anything the spines of books or handwritten labels used to identify scrolls told him, nor could he figure out why he felt this way. In his opinion, he held a reasonable expectation that they wouldn't get along right away, if at all, so there was no explanation for his nerves. He hadn't even reacted like this when he and Itsuki first met.

He blinked when he heard how bitter those inner musings sounded. *Maybe I'm not doing as well as I thought.*

Obito jumped at a tap on his shoulder.

"...Daisuke?" He blinked. They hadn't seen each other over the summer except in passing, and there weren't many opportunities to interact other than shameless, enthusiastic waves from the other boy that seemed to serve no other purpose than drawing unwanted attention to both of them. This was the last place he expected to run into him.

"First time getting past those guards, too." Daisuke grinned. "So, you *do* remember me."

Obito rolled his eyes. "Obviously, but why are you here?"

"I'm looking for someone," Daisuke explained with a shrug, though he winced a little when the fabric of his shirt rustled against his right shoulder; he stopped mid-reach to keep himself from scratching that arm. "Maybe you can help me."

"I doubt it."

"I've been...reassigned, I guess, and need to find my partner."

Obito's eyes went to his, and a beat of silence followed before he said, "You're looking for me."

"You're serious?" Daisuke gawked at first, soon followed by a short burst of laughter. "You told me you were in a patrol unit, not intelligence."

"No, I just didn't correct you when you assumed it." Obito pinched the bridge of his nose and shook his head, as if he thought it'd help him absorb the information better. "*You're* my new partner?"

TWELVE
WHISPERS OF DECEIT

DAISUKE CROSSED HIS ARMS and glared, which, Obito could admit, was probably well-deserved.

"Is that so hard to believe? Coincidence or fate, take your pick, but Master Yujin said I was brought in to—" Realization dawned on Daisuke's features, and his posture slumped into a slightly less defensive stance as his expression softened. His eyes dropped to the floor. "I see. It was *your* partner who died, wasn't it?"

Obito also looked away without offering a response; internally accepting Itsuki's death still felt vastly different from saying it aloud, and while he didn't expect Master Yujin to keep it a secret, there was something surreal about having an outsider talk to him about it. Finally, he said, "It was."

Daisuke tilted his head to one side. "Were you there?"

Obito looked like he either wanted to throttle him for all the prying or walk away from him altogether. However, after a second pause, another slow nod followed. Daisuke tried not to seem too relieved; since it was undoubtedly—and understandably—a sore subject, he might not have blamed the other boy for lashing out at him this time.

"What happened?" he asked quietly. His insides wriggled with discomfort, but if what had killed his previous partner was still a threat, he felt he deserved to know.

Obito studied Daisuke's face—irritating as his prodding was, it didn't feel as if there was any malicious intent behind it. He forced himself to relax a bit; it wasn't like they *didn't* know each other. "Master Yujin said he wanted me to hold off on giving you exact details until you settled in more."

"That's stupid," Daisuke said before he could stop himself. However, something in the way Obito's lips ticked upward indicated he might feel the same, so he pressed forward. "I'll find out eventually, anyway, right? I'd rather hear it from you first."

"Why does it sound like you're trying to manipulate me into telling you?"

"'Manipulate' is a strong word to use." Daisuke grinned in spite of himself. "But, let's pretend I am...is it working?"

Obito hesitated again. If nothing else, it *was* vital information he'd need to share if he wanted help tracking the assassin who killed Itsuki, and after their tense meeting earlier, there was a certain satisfaction in ignoring Master Yujin's direct order. "We went to buy white leaf and ended up in a rougher part of the city. Itsuki thought he found our way back, but we ran into a couple of assassins instead...they didn't let him make it far after they saw him. I doubt they knew I was there. So now, Master Yujin wants us to find them and make sure they can't repeat what they did to Itsuki."

"Gods," Daisuke muttered at the ground, wishing he had a more intelligent or empathetic phrase to offer as condolences, though Obito didn't seem as if he planned to judge him for it. Rather than returning with either type of response when he looked at his partner again, he grimaced at a sudden, burning itch deep in his skin and went for his shoulder instead. "Fuck this stupid tattoo."

"Don't scratch it," Obito said, stretching a hand toward him to stop him, halting just short of grabbing him. He cleared his throat. "You'll hurt yourself if you do. There's medicine for it in the infirmary. I could bring you there—if you want, that is."

Daisuke's face turned warm. "If you're sure you don't mind. This thing's starting to hurt."

Grateful for the offer and a way to finally end the conversation about Itsuki's death, he happily kept his silence as he fell in line when Obito gestured for him to follow, then walked past him to lead the way out of the library.

A ROUGH PUB IN a poor part of the city was no place for a nobleman, which was why Hideo had sought its refuge. Pipes, cigarettes, opium, and white leaf all filled the room with a hazy screen of smoke as ruffians argued with the barkeep over the price of his piss-warm ale, thankfully far away from his booth on the far wall. If anyone recognized him for his status or as a retired military man, he might also end up with a fight on his hands—gods, the word "fight" implied he stood a chance in the first place.

While serving as a lowly infantryman, he'd made plenty of enemies on the Capital's streets. Before he'd met Aki, the group of soldiers he often accompanied tended to bully civilians for extra money or, more commonly, to see the fear and frustration in their eyes as they complied with blatant, petty attempts to grab a hint of power. He hadn't thought about it much then, nor did he consider potential consequences when he finished serving his required five-year term, but he had always acknowledged how Aki helped him become a better man and soldier for that short period. They'd maintained a casual correspondence over the years, and the General had attended Hideo's wedding. Even so, he hadn't tried contacting Aki again since their chat a fortnight ago. Hideo had to admit the cult was bold to assume *he* could talk Aki into abandoning his loyalties—the man, for better or worse, believed his duty was to serve the Empire as directed by Emperor Akuwara and his tacticians. He didn't seem to care whether that meant he'd eventually take orders from an illegitimate ruler.

With the loss of the talisman he'd taken on the responsibility for, Hideo feared the wrath he'd inevitably face when Zandaka's Servant found out about his failure. He shivered; their policies against killing the nobles working for them hadn't come to a solid conclusion, but he knew they slew any members who strayed—never mind Giichi, who would sell him out in an instant for his incompetence.

As she walked toward him, the barmaid's overpowering perfume and the rustle of her clothing drew his attention away from the questionable sake he'd been sipping. She slipped a folded square of paper onto his table without stopping, her tray of full glasses remaining perfectly balanced as she went by—women on this side of town were good messengers. They rarely asked questions and never repeated the answers unless one accomplished the impossible by earning their trust. Judging by the fat little pouch dangling from her obi, she'd been paid well enough not to give a damn about any of it. He figured it was for the best; he'd heard that the hitokiri had recently gotten hold of a young teenager and slaughtered him without mercy. Hideo knew he'd be little more than a corpse if one of those monsters found out his plans, and decided they wanted a swift way back into the Intelligence Master's good graces.

He tucked his hands under the table and opened the note, peering at it as inconspicuously as he could manage: a simple message stating to go outside and around the back of the building. He swallowed hard. His last moments may be nearing, but if he ignored the scrawled command, they'd be over sooner than he imagined.

Lady Shadow stood from her makeshift seat on a crate, Haruki flanking her as usual, along with the new addition of Kanashimi, though the demon attended as a vaguely human-shaped shadow while they watched from within the talisman; were it any lighter, a passerby would've easily noticed something odd about their form. The quick journey to the Capital had nearly exhausted their power as it was. Kanashimi had stated that it wouldn't fully recover for some time after years of slumber. Lady Shadow had to admit that she was pleasantly surprised by the aid she already procured from the demon, a perfectly sentient, humanlike spirit dedicated solely to her purpose, and all it cost was a drop of blood.

All three tensed as the bumbling nobleman rounded the pub's corner.

A single paper lantern hanging from a steel pole illuminated the alley, halfway filled with snow drifts. Lady Shadow wrinkled her nose as he approached her; he smelled of tobacco and cheap alcohol, and she sensed Kanashimi's amusement at her disgust as if she were laughing at herself. Hideo hesitated before getting closer, perhaps unsure of which cult member he faced. In this instance, her limited patience was a mercy from how she initially planned to let him squirm more. She reached under her cloak, pulled Kanashimi's pendant into the flickering light, and flashed its gleaming surface at the meek man. Only Lady Shadow had permission to always carry one of the demons' talismans on her, which made her presence in such moments undeniable.

"S-Servant of Zandaka, it's my pleasure to see—"

"Do you still have Demon Lord Tatakai's talisman?" To make up for the first summoning, Lady Shadow had given Kanashimi an extra offering once she'd summoned them to discuss this journey. As a result, the dragon now fed off her—specifically, her grief—as an energy source to regain control of their power faster. Her growing bond with the demon meant the trip had also taxed her; she was in no mood for blithering delays or unnecessary pleasantries, especially as she'd set out to ensure no one else would disappoint her as Misame had.

Hideo gawked at her, clearly surprised by the interruption—how typical for a nobleman. "N-no."

"Then it is with General Aki." Both a question and a statement, dripping with the threat of a venomous sting.

"In a manner of speaking."

Lady Shadow didn't like that answer, and neither did her guards. She had to catch Haruki by the wrist when she tried advancing on him, her dagger visible. The matron exchanged a long, silent look with each of her sentinels through the black veil sewn into her hood. Although Hideo had impressively managed not to cry out, he was frozen in place, staring at her with all the fear of a helpless rodent trapped by a starving, feral cat.

She slowly turned back to him. "Your answer makes me curious, my Lord. What could you possibly mean?"

"He...he said he needed some time to consider his options." Hideo wrung his hands together nervously. "I-I let him keep it in good faith. I know he wouldn't turn me in for suspicious activity, and I'm sure he'll come to his senses soon and find that he hates the government as much as we do."

Lady Shadow begrudgingly elected to grant the poor fool some grace. Although he'd sworn his allegiance, he likely hadn't expected direct responsibility for anything while cult members still worked to gather the remaining talismans. She couldn't imagine how it must've shocked him when Giichi arrived with the amulet of Tatakai and commanded him to go to the Capital. Realistically, he'd outperformed her low expectations. She twitched the first two fingers of her gloved left hand at her personnel, inviting them to ask any questions they may have.

Kanashimi watched for Lady Shadow's signal, then commanded the shadow figure to step forward slightly, calm and in control compared to Haruki, demanding in the same gravelly voice as the matron, "Did anyone else see you when you spoke with him?"

Hideo at last recognized that he wouldn't die tonight; his relief swelled into a sigh. "Yes, some help he had scrubbing the floors—hardly a threat, though. Poor boy didn't so much as twitch when I dropped it."

"He didn't hear you? You're sure?"

"He'd have to be as clever as one of the onmitsu to pull it off so naturally. Servant, I'd advise you not to place such hopes in slaveborns."

"That reminds me," Lady Shadow began. "Lord Giichi has a son enlisted with intelligence, does he not?"

"Yes," the nobleman hurriedly confirmed, anxious to escape trouble. "His youngest boy, Mika."

She smirked and let the inflection seep into her voice. "Mika? What a lovely name. Given his position, I think that boy could be useful to our cause—and being Giichi's son means recruiting him should be simple. I don't suppose you could travel to the Wen Valley to speak to his father about the matter?"

"While I doubt Giichi is opposed, I'd be careful adding another from Tanaka's family. He's related to the Nakamura clan through marriage, and their youngest boy also went into intelligence the same year as Mika—with good reason, too. Giichi's already managed to breed hate between the cousins, but all it'd take is for his boy to slip up a little, and our reliance on him is rendered useless. We'd have to wait for the right time to ask."

Lady Shadow paused to consider his words. Meek and foolish wasn't always the same as outright stupid, and though it'd be wise to skirt around the Nakamuras, she knew that boy would bring more value than his father or Hideo. "We only have my—*the* talisman of Kanashimi right now. If we ever hope to find those of Jihuang, Hinkon, Wenyi, and recover Saigai, we'd better move now."

"Something happened to Saigai's talisman?"

"According to one of my former followers, yes. It slipped through their fingers somewhere between Kyuumura and Zhu. We're scouting for it now while they repent for their sins in Kuro's Hells—I made sure of it. You know how I feel about failures and backstabbers."

Hideo hoped the surrounding darkness was enough to hide the disdain on his face. Zandaka's Servant didn't regret that they'd murdered in cold blood over a simple mistake; it prompted him to deliberate on the possibility of the same happening to the nobility who aligned themselves with this cause. After a moment, he finally found the courage to speak aloud, "I...I'll leave for the Wen Valley tomorrow morning, and I'll search for Lord Saigai's talisman while I'm traveling."

The cloaked figure merely dipped their head, satiated with his answer.

Daisuke stared at the dark ceiling, uncomfortably aware of how intense absolute silence felt against his ears. For the first twelve years of his life, he'd never slept alone, never mind having an entire room to himself. He couldn't imagine how anyone managed—it was so unnerving. The fresh higanbana tattoo on his right arm itched again, but it wasn't too much to ignore; the medicine Obito helped him procure from the infirmary was still working, for the most part, and it'd cooled the hot, prickling sensation under his skin. He thought that might be the one good thing about now, as lying like this while his mind raced through everything that happened that day was torture.

He tossed the covers off himself and sat up, feet dangling above the stone floor.

A small dresser sat at the end of the bed, shoved against the wall opposite from his desk where he'd stored the good luck charm, or whatever the hell it was. Cramming everything along with the bed into this one space gave the room a cozy feeling; the lantern he'd ignited before the "lights out" order from a senior onmitsu that night had illuminated it with a pleasant, relaxing warmth. Despite being told when to extinguish his lantern, Obito hadn't indicated any strict rules regarding wandering around after certain hours, prompting him to take advantage of what he assumed was intentional ambiguity. Besides, how *could* onmitsu be expected to adhere to a curfew?

In any case, some sneaking around to explore sounded better than lying awake and growing increasingly restless as his mind nagged about tomorrow's possibilities.

He pushed himself off the bed and found the familiar uniform he'd worn for the infantry where he'd left it strewn across the end. In addition to everything new he'd start learning the following day, he also needed a fitting for a different uniform. The onmitsu wore an outer gi ranging from black to light grey and a shitagi that matched their belt, though that color was their choice. Mainly. Obito indicated that wasn't exactly the case for the deep red one he wore—it'd simply been what the tailor had on hand and what fit.

He wasn't sure how they felt about each other. Although they had a casual acquaintance before, he recognized that was a wildly different relationship than being teammates, and that it might require extra patience from both of them. For now, he chose to take what small victories he could get, and be happy that the other boy still didn't act repulsed by the fact that he was a slaveborn, whether they were partners or friends.

No sound echoed through the hall when the door silently latched upon closing, which was a relief since he wasn't sure he had the mental stamina to explain himself or converse with anyone at this hour. Fortunately, most of his new classmates were already sleeping; Daisuke wished he was, too.

Burning candles with wax dripping into trays on wrought-iron wall mounts guided him toward the communal area, where he considered staying until he became tired. His plans abruptly changed when he became aware of a strange odor's faintest hints from the hall leading to the library.

What the hell? I'll probably find trouble either way. Daisuke shrugged and went toward it.

The smell grew stronger as he approached the long, evenly spaced slits lining the hallway's outer-facing wall. Upon seeing them yet another time, his curiosity finally won, and drove him to ask Obito about them as they walked toward the infirmary from the library earlier. He hadn't expected—but thoroughly enjoyed—an impromptu history lesson when his partner explained they'd been for archers to fire arrows from a safe vantage point. When they passed the first floor of the onmitsu dormitories not long after Obito's account finished, he figured out he now slept where those archers once had and commented as much. He couldn't identify the expression Obito wore when he heard Daisuke's conclusion, but he looked pleased that he'd made the deduction as quickly as he had.

Giving into a flutter of whimsy, Daisuke hopped over the pools of moonlight that peeked between the arrow slits, freezing out of fright when he caught sight of another silhouette; someone was watching him. Closer inspection showed him it was Mika, someone he'd met after dinner that evening. He heaved a silent sigh of relief at being confronted with a familiar face and, grinning, went to join him.

"What are you doing sulking around this late?" he teased as he plopped onto the floor beside Mika, which was when he realized his companion was the source of the unpleasant aroma.

The dark-haired boy blew a cloud of smoke near Daisuke's face, which was waved away, then mirrored his expression. "Shouldn't I be asking you the same thing?"

"Can't sleep."

"Me, either. Here, smoke some of this. You'll feel better."

Daisuke sniffed the burning dried substance rolled into the paper. "What is it?"

"White leaf. I stole—I mean, borrowed some from my aunt a couple of weeks ago." Mika arched an eyebrow when Daisuke copied how he'd taken a long puff off the paper, but came out gagging and coughing as a thick cloud of smoke erupted from his mouth. Once he'd regained control of his spasming lungs, he passed the cursed thing back. "So, I see you have the misfortune of being stuck with Obito. Try not to let him get you killed like he did with Itsuki."

Daisuke nearly choked again from the sudden change in Mika's speech. "Did *Obito* plan Itsuki's death or something? Because that sounds a little...harsh, I guess, if he didn't."

"Does the intent matter when that's the outcome?" Mika's hazel eyes became temporarily locked in some unspoken struggle. "Look, Daisuke, Itsuki was a core part of this class. We all loved him. Unlike my useless cousin, he was always out doing something for someone else. I'm telling you so you aren't surprised by it, but Obito never gave two fucks about Itsuki. Don't expect him to treat you any better."

Daisuke had a nagging feeling that the last part wasn't right—he and Obito might've enjoyed annoying each other earlier, but when it came to Itsuki and his death, it wasn't hard to see that he'd cared at least a little. He had a decent sense of when people weren't being honest, and there was something too raw in how his new teammate looked when speaking about his deceased friend. Maybe Mika needed to reevaluate his convictions.

"Are you sure? He doesn't exactly seem like the type—"

"You don't even know. We're two months apart, and since we're both the youngest sons in our families, we were close for a long time. He stopped hanging out with me right before my sister got married, though. My old man said it's some bull to do with him being from the family's main branch—I guess he confronted him at the wedding, but nothing else ever came of it, and now Obito won't talk to me at all. Just confirms things if you ask me."

Confirms what? That you're missing something? Daisuke took the roll once more when offered to him and said after a drag, "I mean, I obviously haven't known him as long as you have, but still, that's...strange. For any-one."

"You don't need to defend him." Mika looked as offended as he sound-ed when he took the white leaf back, smoked it, then handed it over again.

"I didn't mean anything by it," Daisuke said defensively, quickly in-haling another puff. Whether or not he knew Obito well was now entirely beside the point; the boy beside him obviously had an opposing picture painted in his mind and wouldn't be convinced to look at things differ-ently. How boring. He got to his feet again with a sigh and cursed under his breath as he handed Mika the roll. "Sorry, it's been a long day. I think I will go to bed after all."

"After a few hits of white leaf? I'm not surprised a little thing like you turned out to be a lightweight." Mika snickered.

He forced a laugh at Mika's comment. "I guess that's fair."

Daisuke was unfathomably relieved that his sudden exit hadn't sparked further conflict with Mika, but twice as happy to be away from the other boy and his unexpected anger. He paused as his hand touched his door's handle when he heard some shuffling from behind, then slowly turned. Obito was also sneaking back into his room.

He couldn't stop himself from shooting him a devilish grin and calling out, "You look like you're doing something you shouldn't."

Obito groaned and rested his forehead on the door he didn't have time to open; obviously, he wasn't expecting to get caught. He glanced over his shoulder, thoroughly annoyed, which incensed Daisuke's desire to stir some trouble. "What do you want?"

The scent of white leaf invaded Daisuke's sense of smell again. He snickered, this time genuinely, but decided to keep his brief conversation with Mika private—he doubted Obito was ignorant to the way his cousin felt, as it sounded like their issues were longstanding. Besides, if Obito's mood were similar to the light and slightly loopy feeling he had, it'd be rude to change it by mentioning anything Mika said.

"What were you doing?" Daisuke batted his eyelashes at the other boy, who rolled his bloodshot eyes and grumbled again.

"Smoking white leaf and enjoying a moment of silence. Is that al-lowed?"

"Not if you go without me next time."

"Then it won't be silent." Obito looked as if he hadn't meant for that sentence to live anywhere outside his mind, which made a flustered expression cross his features as he finally opened his door. He paused again when he heard Daisuke laugh a second time, but didn't add another comment before he quickly locked himself in his room for the night.

When Daisuke finally sprawled out on his bed again, a strange, irresistible force drew his tired eyes toward the desk drawer where he'd stored the stupid luck token until he could find a better place for it—like somewhere at the bottom of the ocean. Before he could decide if he wanted to act on the impulse to get up and dig it out, a heavy and thankfully dreamless sleep took him under its wing.

Fuck, fuck, fuck! Hurried footsteps loudly echoed throughout the corridors as Daisuke tore through them; he'd slept late for the fourth time this week and was frantically rushing to make it to morning assembly on time. It didn't help that last night's sleep had flooded with images of his childhood at the plantations—likely from some small part of him that was unable to let go of the notion that being placed with intelligence was a dirty trick of some kind. In any case, he'd awoken this morning upon being thrown into an abyss by his father. His mind hadn't settled since.

When he skidded to a halt at his destination, he found an open spot beside Obito at the back of the room, which was about the only thing to go right since he rolled out of bed.

"Can I sit here?" Daisuke breathlessly whispered as he knelt beside Obito, which forced away the tendrils of anger and bitter sadness lurking around him.

Obito looked at him as if the question was absurd, then rolled his eyes. "What if I told you no?"

"It wouldn't be very nice of you at all."

"I didn't think it'd take you this long to figure out I'm not nice."

"That so? Then how come you haven't already asked me to move?"

"You're so annoying," Obito mumbled before switching to a normal volume. "Keep it up. I won't be asking when I do."

"Would you two shut the fuck up?" Shinta rounded on them with an annoyed scowl. He faltered when he received the same expression from Obito in return, which made Daisuke's muffled snicker an outright cackle. Noting their reactions, Shinta determined further confrontation wasn't worth his energy, sheepishly adjusted his glasses, and left them alone again.

Obito cleared his throat once Shinta turned around, barely able to disguise his amusement as he went back to his partner. "Imagine how much easier this would be if you were on time."

"You're going to be so mad when you figure out that'll never happen," Daisuke muttered with another laugh, cut short when he caught Mika pointedly glaring at them. When Obito simply ignored his cousin and opened the journal he recorded anything he found useful in, Daisuke opted to do the same. He'd also received a black-bound book filled with blank pages during his first full day as onmitsu, but it barely had a few notes. He could never decide what to put in it—everything in lectures sounded important.

The door behind them opened again, and Master Yujin came through, boots clicking impatiently against the stone floor as he marched to the front of the room. He swiftly pivoted and rigidly stood at attention before his students, watching them intently until he finally opened his mouth to address them.

Once Daisuke realized they were listening to another update about a gang of bandits that had been terrorizing the mountain roads, he promptly lost interest in the discussion; the Intelligence Master's voice was low and calming as he read off status reports, and frankly, he didn't care to listen to the angsts of the nobility. His mind unintentionally wandered, eyes drifting toward the nearest page in Obito's journal without absorbing any of the words hastily but legibly scrawled on it; he doubted anyone had ever questioned *his* ability to read or write.

As Master Yujin's voice faded out, and with nothing to properly distract him, Daisuke felt his mind spiral toward the dark vortex awaiting him. Like in his dream, Honda's voice ruthlessly attacked him in a brutal assault. Fear and shame paralyzed him as echoes of his father's rabid rants speared through him—useless, hopeless, stupid, and a waste of skin. Air froze in his lungs when Honda screamed at him for dishonoring him.

Make it stop.

"Daisuke, move," Obito demanded out of nowhere, shattering his trance.

He stared at him blankly. "What?"

Despite looking unimaginably annoyed, Obito sighed to reel in his patience. "It's time to go downstairs."

"Where?" A steady trickle brought Daisuke's state of mind back to the present as they gathered their things and got to their feet, which soon became a rush that made the world clear again. He wished he could say he felt relieved, but that wrench of embarrassment returned when he noticed how perplexed, if not concerned, his partner looked.

"Were you with us at all during that lecture?"

"Lay off him, Obito," Mika jeered out of nowhere, arm hooking around Daisuke's neck and knocking him slightly off balance. Obito's shoulders tensed, but he said nothing as he stepped back from them. Mika tilted his head to display a chipped incisor in his victorious grin. "Come on, Daisuke. Master Yujin's teaching us how to make a poison today."

Daisuke nodded dumbly and followed Mika toward the back of the room, where one of the Palace's many secret passages awaited behind a half-wall that blended perfectly with the surrounding brick patterns from a distance. He didn't dare glance over his shoulder at Obito, who now walked beside an incredibly unimpressed Shinta; he'd lost the courage to look him in the eye, fearing the possibility of accidentally letting his vulnerabilities show. His companion was talking, but he didn't process any of it. Mika was enjoying his conversation with himself, anyway—who was Daisuke to interrupt?

They followed the passage downward to a dank room that faced the courtyard. Cross-hatched, deeply amber-stained windows let in little natural light, substituted by candles blazing from iron chandeliers above long, scarred wooden tables. Master Yujin waited until he was sure all his onmitsu were present, then went to a more cluttered table off to the side and returned with a tray, motioning for everyone to gather around as he set it down. He took several thin, metal tools from where they'd been hidden beside the flower. Curious and desperate for space, Daisuke took the opportunity to escape from under Mika's arm and push forward, though he hadn't expected to end up directly beside the Intelligence Master.

The tray held an odd, inky flower, prompting an inquisitive gaze at Master Yujin. Daisuke asked quietly, "What's wrong with it?"

"This is a black lotus flower," Master Yujin explained. "They grow along the eastern seaboard and create an incredibly toxic poison. No known antidote exists. Pink lotuses, on the other hand, have several health benefits—their roots and hearts are used in foods and medicines, and you can eat the seeds right from the pod. I don't recommend confusing the two."

Daisuke wrinkled his nose at the tiers of greasy-looking petals. "You mean this one's meant to look that way?"

The Intelligence Master chuckled, as did a few others. "I believe I once said the same thing. Appearances aside, before we get started, I'll remind you all that you're not to give poisons such as this one to outside entities like the hitokiri. They have their own list of rudimentary tinctures and *should* know to ask me directly if they need something like black lotus."

Daisuke unquestioningly took that as the warning intended. Despite the expectation to hear hushed, haughty comments from his classmates, Master Yujin held their attention with ease—he supposed it shouldn't come as a surprise; as the youngest sons of noble families, they probably felt they had something to prove, too. However, as their instructor diligently described how to use the scalpel, pliers, and tongs to milk the poison from the lotus's seed pod, those unwelcome voices encircled Daisuke again, bringing the lecture out of focus. Whispers told him he shouldn't be here. Gods, what he wouldn't give to make them shut the fuck up—unlike earlier, he *wanted* to hear this.

He barely registered a rustle of parchment at his fingertips. He blankly looked around and saw the others placing a sheet within the pages of their journals, a written form of what Master Yujin currently orated, likely penned by a set of his older students. Hands shaking, he also put his away before moving along with the group toward instruments set out on a different section of the long table.

He stood by a collection of translucent glass flasks and tubes on the outskirts of the small crowd. Master Yujin was still talking, but Daisuke was intensely, singularly aware of the cutting tools he now had easy access to—a clean scalpel in front of him grabbed every bit of his attention. The sharp edge beckoned. Impulse begged. Desperation to get this suffocating heaviness out of his heart lured him to the edge of sensibility. He glanced around to make sure everyone else, including Master Yujin, was still preoccupied, then slipped the scalpel under the soft blue cloth of his belt.

Although Daisuke was disappointed that they didn't get to try making their own vials of black lotus, he was also overwhelmingly relieved. He couldn't imagine trying to explain his distracted state when he fucked up, and it became obvious he wasn't paying attention, nor did he want anyone to know how much pain had swelled in his chest. As always, he intended to deal with it privately.

When Master Yujin dismissed them for the day, Daisuke wasted no time going back upstairs and headed directly for his room. Once inside, he bolted the door with the half-rusted chain to lock himself in, then sat on the edge of his bed, grateful for the same silence he disparaged at night. It soon dissolved into a different kind of quiet, where emptiness overflowed with the noisy chatter of a single, obsessive thought—anything to make it stop, something to escape the deep ache, rage, and self-hate seeping into his soul. His hands trembled again as he removed the scalpel from its hiding place. For a long while, he blankly stared at it.

The way Honda cursed and yelled at him while beating him after the caning flooded his vision without warning.

Stay the fuck away from me. Daisuke fought the memory, unconscious of when he brought the scalpel to the inside of his forearm as if possessed by another force.

He paused. What little remained of his rationality reminded him they'd be too visible there; he pulled off his shirts, then held the little blade over his right shoulder. Three cuts into his skin brimmed red with blood immediately as pain and shock at what he'd done shot a burst of head-clearing adrenaline through his veins.

Daisuke threw the scalpel across the floor in horror. The voices were gone now—he was alone, which meant he was safe. His whole body convulsed as he remembered the blood on his shoulder, driving him to his feet so he could dig around in his dresser for any suitable scraps of cloth. He stood in the middle of the room while he held a towel to his wounds, breathing hard and trying to resist the crying he couldn't stop. Cutting only broke the dam; the second wave was about to hit, bringing actual release. With the towel still on his shoulder, he slumped into bed, curled into a protective ball with tears still slipping down his cheeks.

"Daisuke, are you in there?"

He jolted upright at the call of his name, eyes stinging from crying and the rest his body desperately needed. Another set of three knocks from the other side of his door broke the daze Daisuke felt looking around the room—he didn't realize he'd fallen asleep—and he stumbled out of bed to answer it, barely remembering to discard the towel and throw on at least one of his shirts as he went. The fresh cuts on his shoulder stung, too, and he felt like he'd gotten his ass kicked by Junpei in a sparring match, but he forgot about their aching entirely when he opened the door for Obito.

"What are you doing here?" Daisuke asked him through a yawn as he threw his arms over his head for a long stretch, trying to convince himself that the friction between his cuts and the fabric of his clothing wasn't painful.

Obito remained silent at first as he examined his partner's frazzled form, then said, "Master Yujin cleared us to start tracking Itsuki's murderer...if you aren't up for it—"

"No, no, it's fine. *I'm* fine." Daisuke rubbed his face to dispel the fog in his head, which made him uncomfortably aware that he had no idea what Master Yujin expected or where they should start. Obito noticed his lack of conviction but chose to show that he had the restraint to let it go unmentioned.

"Good, because I think I already have some information that can help us." Obito forced himself to sound optimistic; something like gut instinct told him Daisuke had potential, but he had to give him a chance to prove it. He looked over his disheveled state again, unable to stop himself from raising an eyebrow at his appearance. "Why don't you meet me in the library when you're ready?"

"Sure. I'll be there soon."

Once Obito left, Daisuke hurriedly redressed for a more put-together look, gathered his untidy hair into a loose half-bun, and retrieved the scalpel from the corner it'd landed in, placing it in the same drawer where he stored his luck charm and helix ring. His hand hovered over the strange object, which he'd wrapped in a square of white fabric for safekeeping. Although it hadn't been in his possession for long, at times, he forgot it existed, while there were also moments when its presence was ominous and heavy, like the jade dragon statues he continued to see in his sporadic dreams throughout the last year. He tucked the "borrowed" instrument under the cloth and covered both with the bloodied towel from earlier, then went in search of his partner, not wanting to dwell on the dragons, his cuts, or why he'd inflicted them upon himself. He never wanted to do it again.

Daisuke caught up to Obito outside of the library, and from there, they agreed to find a section away from where scholars or some of the older onmitsu studied around solid oak tables in quiet clusters. When they reached the specific, secluded table Obito must've been looking for, he set out a piece of parchment, took an available inkwell and pen off a nearby shelf, then placed his journal in the center. He flipped open the book to a page he'd marked with a silk ribbon of braided red, black, and purple strips.

"This is really nice," Daisuke commented as he ran his fingers along the bookmark.

"My sisters sent it to me." Obito didn't know why he offered an explanation instead of thanking him and moving things along—he didn't exactly *need* the information. He pushed it out of his mind and scooted the journal toward Daisuke, who glanced at the few lines of neatly written script. "This is everything I know so far."

"It's not a lot." Daisuke flinched at his bluntness, but Obito seemed entirely unbothered by it. It hadn't taken long for each to realize they tended to speak the same way, although it sometimes came out hesitantly. Daisuke wondered if there wasn't something similar but different that they recognized in each other. Unfortunately for his curiosity, now wasn't the time to dissect it; he assumed his new teammate wouldn't be open to it yet, anyway. He reread his partner's notes, this time with more care. "There were two assassins. One was named Yin, and the other is unknown; the unknown assassin has a possible limp and wants black lotus. Maybe I was wrong. How do we look for this Yin idiot so we can talk to him?"

"You want to be that direct about it?"

"Why not?"

"Fair enough, but you need a better argument than that next time." Obito looked back at his notes while Daisuke chewed on that comment, unsure how he should take it. "As long as he isn't away on an assignment, it shouldn't take much. Raku should be able to help us there. We still need to figure out how to bait the other assassin out of hiding, though."

"It's about time for the Winter Festival, too, so we should keep that in mind. It could make things a bit messy if we're trying to corner this guy on the streets," Daisuke said. He paused when a new idea made his eyes narrow. "Wait, that's it. If we can talk to Yin and get him to work with us, he can make sure his friend meets with us somewhere quiet on solstice night."

Obito gave it a moment, then allowed the ghost of a smile to form as a hint of vicious delight flashed in his forest green eyes. "It should be easy enough to get him somewhere quiet, too."

"You like this idea, then?" Despite the teasing in his voice, excitement fluttered in Daisuke's chest as the other boy began jotting down ways to carry out their plan.

"Don't get used to it." That shadow of a smile didn't leave Obito's features, nor did he try to move away when Daisuke leaned over the table for a better view.

THE IVORY SNAKE WAS an inn on the north end of the nobility district. Raku, another of Master Yujin's onmitsu with about four years' seniority on Daisuke and Obito, told them to start their search there one evening. Since Yin couldn't out himself as hitokiri at an esteemed establishment he frequented—the inn's owners and the nobles alike would ban him for life—he wouldn't have his katana, only a hidden knife or two. It was about as much as they could control the situation, and with their combined levels of experience, Obito said they couldn't have asked for better.

Still, Daisuke's nerves were on edge. He couldn't believe they were about to go through with the plan, and Obito's air of calm disinterest didn't help much, nor did the obvious comfort and ease with which he moved through the streets in the nobility district, as if they were familiar.

Suppose he's been here a few times, though... Daisuke internally grumbled. It hadn't taken him long to determine the class preference emphasized when searching for new onmitsu recruits, although that also came with social intricacies he wasn't sure he understood yet. Not that Obito treated him as lesser for it, but there were a few who did. Mika, for instance, often had a condescending tone whenever he explained anything, even if doing so wasn't necessary in the first place. Agitated, he fiddled with the lower set of studs in his earlobes and forced himself to breathe deeply.

"Are you nervous?" Obito asked in a tone difficult to interpret.

"Uneasy," Daisuke slowly admitted. "But not about Yin."

In his partner's defense, he'd advocated for taking the back way from the Palace to avoid discomfort, but Daisuke had insisted they were fine to leave from the tea house where they'd shared an early dinner of onigiri and green tea. Since the route was more direct and made logical sense, and they were on a slight time limit before Yin drank himself into a useless stupor—both of which they'd taken turns pointing out to each other—Obito hadn't argued much beyond his initial objections.

"Stop worrying."

"Easy for you to say—*you're* allowed to be here."

"You are, too." Obito sighed and ran a hand through his hair. "Those policies didn't apply once you signed the enlistment book in basic infantry.

They definitely don't work now that you're onmitsu. Besides, using a family name isn't the same as having access to its privileges. We *do* have to be careful about entering the Ivory Snake, though; the owners are...well, bastards."

Daisuke groaned, a sentiment Obito sympathized with greatly.

True to its name, the Ivory Snake's exterior was painted pure white, as was the high wall surrounding it. The trailhead of the path leading back to the Palace lay not far from the property, so an easy escape wouldn't be challenging, though Obito doubted it'd be necessary. They slipped unnoticed into the courtyard cleared from snow and, crouched low to the ground, snuck into overgrown shrubs, which provided him and Daisuke with a small patch of dirt to kneel on while they plotted a way inside. Obito studied the building momentarily, but soon became distracted by a movement from beside him.

"There," Daisuke said proudly, setting aside the twig he'd used to sketch in the soil.

Obito titled his head at the crookedly scrawled, mostly square shape now between them. "What the hell is it?"

As expected, he received a rather unimpressed glare in response, with Daisuke's eyes fixated on his as he grabbed the stick and stabbed it into the center of his drawing. "We need to get inside without being noticed, right? I thought a visual might help."

"Is that what you're calling this?" Obito teased as he took the twig into his hands. Daisuke glowered at him again, but leaned in close when he made a few new lines in the frozen earth, now too curious to care about the insult any longer. His additions marked the entrances he could see from their vantage point. "We should be able to get in through a window."

"Think you can get me up to one?"

"We'll find out."

Balancing on Obito's shoulders was trickier than Daisuke initially envisioned. It took a couple of attempts to get it right—he hadn't guessed Obito had such a colorful vocabulary until the second time he fell and took them both to the ground—but once they figured out how to stay steady, he yanked the window open, pulled himself up, and slipped through the open space feet-first. Sometimes, being small and thin worked to his advantage. He twisted around about halfway through his descent. Although the smooth wall on the other side didn't provide much grip, he planted his knees and the balls of his feet into it and helped Obito through, mainly rocking on his hips for leverage. It hurt, but once they were both inside, all discomfort subsided, immediately replaced by alertness. They'd landed in a storage room of sorts. The dwindling light outside revealed their only company was a spare mattress with cotton and straw stuffing spilling from a torn seam, damaged cookware, and battered, discarded leather trunks. Obito quietly made his way to the door and slid it open a crack, gesturing for Daisuke to come closer.

"All clear," he said quietly after a moment. "There shouldn't be much staff to worry about now, so as long as we lay low, we'll be fine from here."

"Got it," Daisuke confirmed, his heart in his throat. "Let's go."

Locating the lounge where they expected to find Yin was a longer process than either predicted, but he hadn't bothered to style his hair in anything other than the long, high ponytail hitokiri generally wore, which made him easier to spot when they finally got there. He recognized their uniforms straightaway when they pulled back their cloaks a little as they approached his table, judging by how he spluttered and almost had to spit out his drink. Although visibly dispirited, he poured another drink and acted as though he'd expected them—just as well, since running from onmitsu who came looking for him wouldn't end in his favor. At least he was smart enough to recognize that fact.

"Fancy that, a pair of little sneaks," Yin muttered into his sake before taking a drink. Once finished, he reclined in his seat and looked at them with undisguised impatience. "Good thing you caught me without my katana, boys. What can I do for you?"

Obito didn't want to stick around longer than necessary, so he wasn't about to waste anyone's time. "It came to Master Yujin's attention that another assassin contacted you for a vial of black lotus. Perhaps you can tell us more about it."

"How did you know about the black lotus?" Yin's brows furrowed, face pale as his dark eyes darted between them. He cleared his throat. "L-listen, I heavily rely on poisons for my work; the other hitokiri know this. They'll frequently pay me to make one for them, but black lotus is one I don't know, and I told Haruto as much."

"Why would he ask for that specific poison without clearance from intelligence to possess it?" Daisuke's heart pounded as he spoke, but he sensed Obito's approval in a way he couldn't explain. In any case, it helped him remain calm—everything was still going according to plan.

Yin glanced at Daisuke, then topped off the alcohol in his cup, addressing Obito when he spoke again. "If a hitokiri wants an increase in pay and better assignments, he usually has no choice but to take out the one ahead of him in rank. Haruto wants a promotion, so he needs to off the assassin who's preventing that from happening. He figured black lotus was a surefire way to do it without risking his own life."

"Interesting. Haruto killed one of the onmitsu instead."

The scraggly-looking man nearly dropped his drink at Daisuke's remark. His eyes widened, and he took another look at both boys. While the military branches rarely cooperated well—a tension sowed by Emperor Akuwara throughout his long reign—there *were* consequences if the hitokiri killed outside their official orders, ranging from branding to an untimely demise. Either way, a slow and agonizing punishment awaited the guilty party.

"Th-that boy was...?"

"I suppose if you truly had nothing to do with it, however, we might be able to convince Master Yujin to let you live." Obito's calmness no longer felt infuriating; to the contrary, Daisuke found the coldness with which he applied it here quite amusing. "We need you to do something for us first."

"Anything." Yin jumped in his seat, eager to save his skin.

Daisuke and Obito glanced at each other, barely able to conceal the wicked delight they'd found in triumph.

"THEY'VE WHAT?" MASTER YUJIN blinked at Raku in surprise, eyes shifting to the teenager's silent teammate, Jido, with the same amount of disbelief. Jido curtly inclined his head as a means of confirmation.

"Nakamura and Akahana tracked the hitokiri who killed Itsuki," Raku calmly reiterated as he adjusted the patch covering his right eye. "It sounds as if they've determined the other person present that night isn't culpable. They plan to eliminate Haruto, as you ordered, but want to appeal to you about Yin after the dust settles—provided he doesn't betray them first."

"Which isn't likely if he knows that's part of the deal, but...Hikari's Light. When will they move in on him?"

"Solstice night, from the sounds of it," Jido answered.

Raku nodded. "Plenty of distractions for the general public and an effective way to isolate Haruto from other hitokiri who might suddenly work up the urge to help, which is also unlikely, but it seems they've thought this through. Would you like us to take over for them, sir?"

Master Yujin weighed his options. "No, at least not right away. I'd like them to try handling this on their own first. However, since this *is* one of the hitokiri, I'd appreciate it if you and Jido stayed close. I can't afford to lose three young spies in such a short time."

"We'll make sure they don't fail, sir."

"Thank you for the update, Raku and Jido. Please, return to your posts."

"Yes, sir," Raku said with a brief incline of his head before turning on a heel to take his leave. Jido also gave a curt nod, then pivoted and fell into step with perfect timing when Raku passed, and soon, Yujin was alone again.

Men who formerly occupied his position and most of the military's higher ranks might've considered their casualness an insult, as it was proper to bow. However, Yujin never emphasized etiquette so long as his onmitsu finished their assigned tasks correctly. Worrying about something so small seemed like an utter waste of time; his position as the Master of Intelligence afforded him a fair amount of unquestionable authority, but he preferred not to run his agency with mindless brutality. His master had believed otherwise, and not a soul had mourned Master Yao's death when he passed away due to old age, Yujin included. Few also obeyed his commands for unwavering loyalty and total discrepancy; it'd made Emperor Akuwara look like an absolute buffoon until he continued the war his father, Emperor Akuro, had started with the Okami years beforehand.

Yujin sighed. Most of Master Yao's problems were contained within the military's ranks. There were plenty of times when Emperor Akuwara didn't give the impression he was much more competent than his father, but at least he had the manpower to convince the public to keep their opinion to themselves. In any case, he supposed the letter he'd received from a potter in Zhu could wait; given the news, he couldn't bring himself to pay it the attention it deserved at the moment. An assassin with far more ambition than he deserved was about to face retribution—in the Intelligence Master's mind, that was plenty worth celebrating.

FOURTEEN

JINCHU

A WEEK PASSED AFTER their encounter with Yin. When the penultimate day of the Winter Festival dawned, Obito received confirmation that the hitokiri had followed through with his end of the bargain. Haruto would come to them the following night during the High Priestess's prayer to the gods. Relieved there would finally be justice for Itsuki—and nervous for the same reasons—he'd decided to take some time to himself to mentally and emotionally prepare before events unfolded.

He still sought solace in the library when he could; it fulfilled a need he hadn't outgrown for space and soothing quiet, occasionally broken by tolerable interruptions of distant, whispered conversations or rustling paper. It also provided better lighting for reading than the lantern light in his room, and if he at least *looked* busy, no one bothered him.

That wasn't entirely accurate—*almost* no one interfered with his unspoken requests for breathing room. Daisuke was a completely different issue, as he made regular intrusions that Obito begrudgingly supposed weren't altogether unwelcome. When at their most comfortable, they mainly read in silence, dotted by intermittent pauses to ask one another questions regarding the materials Master Yujin wanted them to study. Although he didn't know what to make of him—wonderfully snarky and quick-witted, but on the edge of trustworthiness as Mika's friend—no amount of stubbornness held off how much he'd already come to enjoy the other boy's company. As if merely thinking about him was enough of a summons, a familiar question came from the front edge of the desk.

"Can I sit here?" Daisuke asked, oddly tentative.

It was better than having wads of paper thrown at him. "Do you think it'd make a difference this time if I said no?"

"Hasn't yet, has it?"

"What an understatement."

After an uncertain chuckle, the black-haired boy pulled out the chair beside Obito's and joined him. Obito glanced over at Daisuke as he tucked away the letter from his sisters he'd been reading, waiting for one of them to find something to say, though nothing came forward from either. Instead, they sat in a strangely unpleasant silence for a while as they blankly observed others moving through the library. Daisuke finally felt compelled to speak when they accidentally made eye contact, a half-hearted but devious little twitch at the corners of his mouth.

"Are you constantly annoyed, or is that just your face?"

"Both, if you must know," Obito answered. "Does being this annoying come naturally to you, or do you have to work at it?"

"Yes, to both." Daisuke grinned in his familiar, cheeky way. After another moment, he confessed, "I'm nervous about tomorrow night."

"We'll be fine."

"What makes you so sure?"

Obito considered the question for a moment. So far, he'd observed Daisuke as an intuitive and intelligent person, traits he appreciated in anyone, but he also had a mischievous streak and a penchant for causing disorder if he felt things were getting too stagnant. Perhaps worse, sometimes he did those things *just* to see what happened. For example, a few days ago, he planted a frog he'd allegedly found hibernating in the dungeons on the shoulder of a visiting magistrate and then quickly dashed away to witness the fallout from afar. The public official flailed in panic, slinging streaks of wine from his goblet into the air, and accidentally struck a guard who'd come to his assistance. Obito wouldn't have believed it'd happened if he hadn't watched the entire thing unfold. However, that begged another question, concerning why he hadn't said anything to stop the incident. He'd had ample time to scrape the amphibian from Magistrate Arai's shoulder before things went out of control. Yet, he watched in fascinated horror when Daisuke left the poor creature to fend for itself, and ensured they made a smooth escape afterward with the frog tucked away in his partner's shirt. Something similar happened only yesterday while everyone was studying poisons; the same morbid curiosity had taken over when he saw Daisuke pour salt into a tincture of randomly selected oils, and he'd instinctively begun filling a pot with water. Master Yujin dismissed the class after they'd snuffed out the resulting fire. Whether or not he'd intended to make their master release his students early was still unclear, but Daisuke seemed thoroughly satisfied with himself either way.

Obito smiled a bit; the common thread was that his partner hadn't been caught or blamed for either instance, which he thought boded well for their future endeavors. "Truthfully? I'm not *that* sure. But, I think we have a good balance and can make this work."

"That's hard to argue with." Daisuke snickered as he pushed himself upright again. That playful little smirk reappeared, giving Obito a slight sense of dread. "Listen, I bought some white leaf off Raku earlier—"

"What?"

"I told him I would if he fucked off and didn't tell Master Yujin about the frog thing. Do you want to smoke with me?"

"Did you say you bribed one of our seniors?"

"Does it bother you?"

Obito paused—it wasn't right, but it *was* just white leaf. "I honestly don't know."

"You can overthink it on the way if you want, but we deserve to have a little fun now that we've gotten to this point." Daisuke's grin widened as he got to his feet, violet eyes gleaming as if he'd won something. A partner in crime in this scenario, Obito internally bemoaned his choices; nevertheless, he also stood. "There's a balcony two floors up from the lower dormitories. No one's ever there."

FLUTES, DRUMS, AND GUQIN played loudly throughout the Capital on solstice night. Once again, that sense of vibrant life in the dead of winter had returned to Perena, and light from a bright full moon glittering against the snow guided their way across the Palace grounds toward the Temple of Hikari. It was a rare sight on Festival night, but for once, Obito chose to see it as a sign of the luck they needed to handle the assassin.

Like the year before, Obito had dropped off Aunt Kiko's holiday treat much earlier in the day to avoid a conflict in his time management. However, given his last visit a few weeks ago—he found it hard to believe such little time had passed since—he'd stayed a bit longer so they could talk more. It was the right thing to do. Unfortunately, now that she knew about Daisuke, she'd politely yet sternly demanded to meet him. Why, Obito had no idea, as she hadn't been that insistent about meeting Itsuki, but he'd vaguely promised to bring him by sometime all the same.

"Have you ever killed anyone before?" Daisuke abruptly ventured, breaking Obito's reverie as they trudged across the empty Palace grounds.

"Can't say I have," Obito answered, taking a vial of goat milk mixed with charcoal shavings from Daisuke when he handed it over—they'd both considered it wise to bring a decoy of the real poison they'd promised the hitokiri. After several tries, Daisuke determined this tincture looked close enough to the real thing. "I've thought about if I could, though; it *is* part of our job."

"Your conclusion?"

Obito shrugged. "I'm not sure that's something anyone knows ahead of time."

"Fuck." Daisuke sighed and subconsciously adjusted the tanto at the back of his belt. "So, what happens to us after this?"

"If this goes well, we'll go back to regular training and studies by to-morrow morning. If not, they'll burn our bodies and replace us by spring."

"Grim."

"It is."

"This is probably a bad time to mention I'm not the best with combat training, isn't it?" Daisuke glanced over as Obito's unimpressed gaze settled on him—as if he didn't already know. "Wouldn't it make more sense for Master Yujin to assign another assassin to this? Why did he want us to take care of Haruto instead?"

"Don't you remember? He said having two involved was plenty." Obito looked forward again. "Time to act like we know what we're doing."

Haruto awaited them at the base of the stairs leading to the temple's sanctuary. Hitokiri weren't permitted to set foot within holy places, nor were Northern Nomads, regardless of their status. For once, Daisuke was relieved at an otherwise ridiculous social boundary set for his people. He had no interest in the horseshit spewed from the pulpit where priests or the High Priestess stood; a goddess who supported acts like slavery or the persecution of the Okami was hardly one worth worshipping.

A blade flashed brightly in the moonlight, followed by a kunai sinking into the hardpacked snow at their feet and stopping them when they were still about a yard away from the assassin. They looked at each other wor-riedly, finally questioning the full scale of what they'd gotten themselves into when they'd convinced Haruto to meet with them. Obito observed the assassin's limp yet again as he took a lurching step toward them, calculating as fast as he could force it. Trying to fight off one of the hitokiri brought on several issues; they were fast, highly skilled fighters up close and from afar, who rarely thought twice about who they murdered—the years they spent training at Kurushima or Genjing ensured as much. For two young spies who had little combat training compared to a hitokiri, this was basically suicide. He tapped the back of Daisuke's hand to grab his attention, bringing his partner's gaze toward Haruto's weak leg.

"Which of you miserable dogs has the poison?" he demanded with a ragged breath, glancing around wildly and shrinking in on himself, though likely not from the cold; he pulled his cloak over the bothersome leg to hide it. "Yin said you'd have it."

Obito ignored his nerves and wordlessly raised his occupied hand to show Haruto the vial; the man's eyes widened when he saw it. He quickly took out another kunai, aiming the deadly tip at Daisuke's throat as he gimped forward again. However, Haruto must've decided that was far enough, as going any further held a definite promise that he'd give away his blight despite his attempts to conceal it. Any threat to an assassin's functionality made them weak or useless—something a hitokiri willing to kill one of his own for advancement couldn't afford. The others of that rank would eat him alive. Whether that was literally or figuratively was anyone's guess. If he so much as suspected either boy had caught on, he needed to make them believe the illusion that there was little they could do to save themselves.

With these things in mind, Obito knew they had to gain an advantage from which they could properly dispose of him. A frontal assault wouldn't work, as Haruto would be too quick to react even with his injured leg, and if he ran, he'd have no choice but to take the cleared paths through the Palace grounds. If he chose that route, he may still attack them to ensure his secret was safe, which was a possibility Obito couldn't disregard and why he'd warned Daisuke to be on high alert before they'd left the dormitories earlier.

Daisuke laughed nervously, forcing himself not to look when his partner's shoulders stiffened. "What's with the artillery? We said you could have it—Yin's already paid us for it, too. Said you owe him for it later."

"Habit, I guess," Haruto casually explained with a shrug. "You'll notice I don't have my katana, though. Now, if your partner could bring me the bottle, I'll be on my way, and you two can get some sleep."

"Then you'll put that knife down, too, won't you?"

Obito cringed when a beat of silence passed. Daisuke would either successfully knock down Haruto's mental walls or piss him off trying. Fortunately, this time, the assassin glanced at his second kunai as if he hadn't meant to draw it after all, then chuckled. He dropped it without incident, subconsciously adopting an exaggerated, sheepish grin. Obito knew he was hiding more weapons and had no doubt Daisuke had realized it, too, but they had to pretend they trusted him for now.

"My apologies. The poison?"

The young spies traded another glance that went unnoticed by the assassin, signaling the next phase of their plan, then Obito cleared his throat and approached the man. Haruto grinned in pure, unabashed delight when he received the vial, but his expression quickly changed to one of shock that crumpled into indescribable agony after Obito, without warning, elbowed his injured hip.

"You little shits!" Haruto howled, swiping Obito aside with a powerful arm before he turned to run away. His lousy leg slowed him considerably, but not enough to eliminate his chances of absconding.

Daisuke froze at first, hand hovering over his tanto as he tried to decide what he should do. He shook himself, then went after him, no longer entertaining fear or doubt. Obito recovered quickly from the daze of an unexpected blow to his temple, and sprinted alongside Daisuke, tanto already pulled from its scabbard. Losing track of Haruto among the maze of paths through the grounds was out of the question. They pushed themselves to go faster until, with Daisuke in the lead, the gap between them and the hitokiri shrank. As soon as his footing was right, he launched himself toward the assassin, tackling him at the knee. White light erupted in his eyes when they hit the cobblestone path, glazed with ice and snow, at full force.

Daisuke heard a distinct *crack* when Haruto's face smacked the pathway, but it didn't appear to faze him in the slightest. Haruto thrashed around to try pulling out another knife despite a broken nose and Daisuke's tight grasp on his legs, which fortunately didn't last long, as Obito's foot unexpectedly came down on his neck. Repositioning, he took advantage of Haruto's turned head and knelt directly on his cheek to keep him still and prevent him from making too much noise, then stabbed him between the shoulder blades with his dagger and dragged it along his spine. Muscle and tissue squelched as the blade tore through in a deep, unforgiving line. Blood brimmed from the wound, a blackish-red pool under the moonlight.

Obito hurriedly set aside his knife and put his first two fingers on Haruto's neck, feeling for a pulse. Daisuke only now realized their heavy breathing.

"Fucking hell," Obito mumbled in disbelief as a resentment he hadn't fully been aware of carrying rushed out of his system. "He's dead."

"Is he? I think I've had enough excitement for one day." Daisuke pushed himself up, transfixed by the gushing laceration, but forced his attention away in order to search his partner's face as they turned the man onto his back. When Obito nodded, he sighed in relief.

Inexplicably, they broke into uncertain, nearly hysterical laughter when their eyes met again. For some reason, it was what best covered the array of emotions they were experiencing on top of rushing adrenaline. However, a sudden twist in the pit of Daisuke's stomach interrupted the rushing sense of camaraderie and a moment of triumphant relief. He scrambled to get as far away from Obito as possible, then retched from the sight of the dead assassin's pooling blood. He tried to hold himself together, but bile burned in his throat seconds before he spat it onto the ground.

"What the hell is wrong with you?" If Obito looked as offended as he sounded, Daisuke thought the universe was atrociously cruel by forcing him to miss it.

"I-it's—it's the—" He gagged, then, gasping, finally managed, "It's the blood."

"We've *got* to get that under control," Obito commented; he chose maturity by flipping Daisuke off when the other boy did the same to him.

Daisuke wiped his mouth on his sleeve when he was sure he'd purged what little contents of his stomach remained from that afternoon, then drew in a gulp of air to steady his breathing before glowering at his team-mate. "You know, I've never met anyone as sensitive or caring as you."

"That's nice. If you're done, help me get rid of the body—I'd like to go to bed at *some* point tonight, and we still need to write our reports."

"Fine, whatever."

Obito rolled his eyes and bent to loop his arms under Haruto's stiff shoulders, preventing Daisuke from seeing or feeling the large, weeping gash in his back while they carried him away. He pretended not to notice, just as he ignored the heat in his face at the strange but kind gesture. He'd come to expect that sort of oddness from what he'd already learned about military life, and it also seemed to be something Obito understood.

Neither spoke again as they hauled Haruto's body back to the Palace's underbelly for cremation, and instead, they let crunching snow beneath their footsteps fill the silence. It wasn't likely they'd attract attention, but they wanted to avoid it when possible, and Obito needed the space to deal with the fact that his emotions and morals hadn't collided in the way he'd expected. On the contrary, he felt better than he had in weeks, though he wasn't sure the same could be said for Daisuke, who appeared slightly shaken. Since he didn't know which words he should use to reach out to him, the silence went uninterrupted until they were near a side entrance to the Palace, when they heard a sharp whistle rocketing into the sky. Seconds later, purple and green fireworks burst overhead, leaving wispy black silhouettes that brushed against the moon's face in their wake.

FIFTEEN
INTERLUDE

THE ONMITSU TRAINING REGIMEN was more demanding than Daisuke had expected, though he'd already set his standards high, and very different than what he'd faced with the infantry. Between learning the various side effects of multiple poisons and their antidotes, the hundreds of pressure points the human body had, histories, politics, a variety of weapons, and techniques for taking down opponents, he felt his mind had little space left to absorb anything else. It was quite a statement to make, as his curiosity piqued at nearly every new thing he came across. Although he often collapsed into his bed at the end of these long days, he'd never felt so fulfilled and greatly appreciated how difficult true boredom was to find; if he kept himself busy, he also kept any urges to take the scalpel to his skin at bay whenever secret anxieties or self-hatred crept up on him.

Navigating his emotions—rather, the stunning lack thereof—toward Haruto's death nearly two months later wasn't as straightforward. No matter how he tried analyzing it, he found that he genuinely felt no guilt or remorse; it'd been the right thing to do. Moreover, although he hadn't held the blade that killed the man, his involvement alone had satiated something dark inside of him, even without the personal investment of knowing Itsuki. He wasn't alone in that, though. He noticed Obito also acted as if he was in a better mood as of late, which he considered far more understandable; Master Yujin was impressed with them for a job well done, and he'd done what so few people could by avenging a close friend's murder.

Not everyone believed Obito had held Itsuki in high regard, nor that he'd given him such a soft place in his heart; if Daisuke hadn't been allowed a chance to see differently, he might've believed the same, though he still doubted it. He supposed it was something Obito didn't need to explain, and he respected his partner's ability to quietly go about things far more than he cared to admit.

Presently, he stood across from Obito in one of the Palace's training hall reserved for indoor instruction during the winter. He faced his friend with his right foot forward, knees slightly bent, as his partner waited for him to signal that he was ready while in a similar stance with his feet in the opposite order. Daisuke tentatively reached for Obito's nearest outstretched wrist, then retracted the motion with a wince and eyed the tanto in his further hand.

"I don't know about this."

"Daisuke, come on, this is a very basic technique. You'll be fine." Obito tried not to let his exasperation show. Itsuki hadn't needed this much encouragement when performing novice-level training drills—or doing anything, for that matter—and trying his hand at it didn't come naturally.

"What if I end up hurting you?"

"That's sort of the idea, but at this point, I think I'll be more impressed than offended if you've managed to stall this much and still not do it correctly." Obito groaned when Daisuke mutely but firmly shook his head, messy black bangs exaggerating the movement.

"I don't *want* to hurt you, though."

"I'll be fine. You came over from basic infantry, right? How is this any different than the drills they run there?"

"I *flunked* basic. Fuck's sake, I couldn't get the marching right." Daisuke made a small, frustrated noise in the back of his throat. "Besides, how is defending against a *knife* considered a 'basic' technique?"

"Because you're onmitsu now."

"That's barely an answer."

Obito sighed—he didn't have the patience to explain, yet again, the different types of enemies they might face compared to an infantryman. "Do you at least remember the steps?"

"You mean for marching? Well, sure. There's only two."

Obito rolled his eyes at Daisuke, who was busily snickering at his terrible, stupid joke. Encouragement alone evidently wouldn't be enough; he had to find something the other boy's brain *would* respond to, but he wasn't sure what. However, after blankly examining the empty training hall to turn over the situation in his mind, he understood how he could get through to the little pest by the time they looked at each other again. He mentally prepared himself—this was going to get loud.

"You know, maybe you have a point."

"Explain." Daisuke's irises flashed with intrigue, challenging Obito to finish his thought, but he pretended he didn't see it.

"Well, if you flunked basic, you're obviously not smart enough to get something as easy as this. It's clearly too advanced for you—granted, the rest of us learned it in our first week, but you know yourself best."

"You're fucking with me, right?"

Obito shrugged, quietly daring Daisuke to prove him wrong. "It's a shame, too. I was starting to think you *weren't* incompetent."

"'*Incompetent*?!'" Daisuke's jaw fell open seconds before rage flooded his features. Gods be damned, Obito was sure he'd accomplished the impossible by managing to silence him for half a minute. "Shut your fucking mouth."

He shamelessly prodded further, "Then show me I'm wrong."

"Fuck you! I will!" Daisuke adjusted his stance again, eyes now blazing with fierce defiance. He motioned to the dagger. "Come on, let's do this."

"Finally." Obito fought the satisfied grin threatening to work its way onto his lips as he fixed his grip on the tanto and drew his arm back to prepare his strike. If he gave himself away now instead of saving it for afterward, Daisuke would figure out his plan, dig his heels in, and not perform the technique out of sheer stubbornness. While it wasn't the *worst* thing he could've done for a positive outcome, he had to admit that manipulating results out of his partner didn't feel great.

Obito stepped forward, and the dagger surged toward Daisuke, who pivoted to the left to avoid the stab aimed at his abdomen. Excitement thrummed in his heart as he realized his body remembered what to do from here. As if his feet and arms were pulled on the same strings, his right hand crossed over when he moved and hit a pressure point on the side of Obito's forearm, making his partner drop his weapon, but he didn't slow. Instead, he immediately turned to throw a left-handed punch at Obito, who caught his fist before a direct hit to his face, which Daisuke took as a signal to end the round.

"There," he proudly declared with a confident smirk. "How's that?"

"Not bad," Obito conceded. Just when Daisuke thought he'd won, he felt Obito's hands on his wrists, pulling him downward. Soon, his body jerked forward against his will. "But you forgot to finish."

"Fuck!" Daisuke yelped as the world spun around before he landed flat on his back. Once he regained his bearings enough to shoot a dizzy glare in

Obito's direction, his partner already had a hand outstretched to help him to his feet again.

TAKATO CHECKED OVER THE documents in his hands one last time, then placed them back in the small wrought-iron chest, content with the adjustments he'd made. He hadn't planned to sign things over to his eldest son this early, but the decision was more of a contingency, and highly practical. Dark things brewed behind the scenes for the Nakamura family, a sense he couldn't explain to anyone, but erratic behavior that emboldened his brother-in-law's cruel side as of late seemed to confirm it. Having Sojiro preemptively named the new family head would ease many worries for the townspeople in Kinumura should things turn sour, and he knew his eldest wouldn't allow the things Takato feared to come to fruition.

Unfortunately, it was one of many concerns. Divorce was a tricky subject to navigate in Perenin and Giahatian societies, especially within the nobility, but due to apprehension toward her husband's behavior, Miwa had asked to move back into the family home during her visit for the Winter Festival. Since everyone knew Takato couldn't deny either of his sisters anything, she'd been there ever since, and spring was now blooming everywhere in the Wen Valley. Takato's middle sons had already brought some of her things from Tanaka Estates in Kyuumura, which lay not far from their home in Kinumura. His wife, Shizune, and his daughters were thrilled to have her around the house, as was he; part of him wished Kiko would also move home.

His eldest nephew still vacillated between whether he wanted to follow his mother or continue occupying his father's home, which mostly lay empty these days, as Giichi had fired most of his staff and was rarely there. Takato couldn't fault the boy for it; at this point, he was biding his time until he received the same rights that had just been signed over to Sojiro. Besides, he couldn't imagine how unfair it'd be to ask the boy to choose between his parents, so instead, he assured Miwa and Ichiro that his doors would always remain open for them.

Takato sighed. Giichi hadn't always been the hateful and jealous man his wife and children knew—he would've fought tooth and nail to prevent Miwa from marrying him if he were. Somewhere along the way, Giichi's thoughts became poisoned by ideas of supremacy, and a twisted belief that anyone besides Prince Akuko should inherit the Giahatian throne. He'd been especially volatile toward Obito in the past, though the truth of that still made Lord Nakamura's stomach knot when he ruminated on it.

Everyone associated with his brother-in-law paid for the man's idiocy—the Nakamura name was still recovering from a tenuous history with the Empire despite being a driving economic force in the Wen Valley. The slightest misstep from the main branch or anyone associated with it could easily deepen tensions with the Emperor. However, Takato worried that Giichi was growing more unpredictable by the day; he acted restlessly, had angry outbursts, and was constantly on edge, as if waiting for something. He'd spent endless hours steeped in speculation, yet they hadn't guided Takato any closer to answers.

"Father?" Sojiro prodded softly from across the desk, peering over thin rims on his glasses, one eyebrow quirking with concern.

Gods' sake. Takato blinked. He didn't realize how long it'd been since he'd spoken. He shut the chest and secured the brass ward lock with a plain-looking key, which he slid over to his eldest son. "Put that somewhere only you can find. Your Aunt Kiko has its twin, so the contents should be safe until it gets to her."

"I'm sure she'll be happy to have the apartment in the Capital officially signed to her name, though I'm not sure how she'll take everything else." Sojiro smiled slightly, but the warmth didn't touch his eyes; his unease deepened. "Speaking of siblings...has Obito written lately?"

"Yumi said she sent him a letter a while ago, but I'm unsure if he answered her."

Sojiro's face fell a little more. "I see."

"Try not to dwell on it." Takato stood, shoulders straight with a practiced, dignified air, but heart heavy in his chest—it'd been two years since his youngest boy had departed Kinumura in the Wen Valley, yet none of the letters Obito sent home were explicitly addressed to him or Shizune; his own idiocy over time and when his son needed him most had landed him in such a spot. "According to your Aunt Kiko, I've done a fantastic job keeping him at arm's length from us. I suppose I deserve as much. As for you five, do your best to understand he can't reply to every letter you three or the girls send him."

"Right." His eldest son sighed, and Takato flinched—his relationship with the rest of his children remained rocky at best since he'd sent Obito away. "But I'm afraid I have one more question before you go, Father."

"As thorough as always, I see. What is it?"

"Why are we doing this now? You could've left the estate and business in your name for much longer if you wanted."

"Things are afoot that are not within my control, so your mother and I agreed it was best to organize some of our affairs. We can discuss this in detail at another time—I need to find a messenger soon, or this may not leave the Wen Valley for another week, perhaps longer. You may be my successor, but these burdens aren't yours to carry yet."

Takato patted him on the shoulder as he walked by, his eyes subconsciously falling on a red poppy mural painted on the wall when he came to the threshold. He sighed and continued on his way after a moment, realizing how much he needed to hurry to get to the town bordering his silk farm. The sooner the little chest was out of his hands, the better off they'd all be. A tearoom—more for Shizune's many sleepless nights than ceremony these days—sat adjacent to a large painting near the room he shared with his wife, ordinarily empty unless the lady of the house entertained visitors. That had become increasingly rare as former friends and allies got their hands politically dirty.

It's hard to believe this all came about because of the crown prince. Takato wrinkled his nose at the thought. Granted, the Empire hadn't been remarkably stable *before* Prince Akuko's birth, but his arrival managed to spark further controversy; he still wasn't entirely sure how Emperor Akuwara had avoided an outright war when he refused to remarry after the Empress's death and named an illegitimate son as heir to the throne. The Emperor was aging, but not particularly old, nor was he ill, so there weren't many logical reasons for his scandalous decisions aside from pigheaded pride.

Takato couldn't say his family had done much better in the past, although he believed their reasons were far more altruistic. For as long as the slave trade had existed on Perena, the Nakamuras had assisted in helping those enslaved escape to the far northern regions or to Noshe, where the practice was outlawed altogether. Now that the industry had mainly migrated to Perena's east and south as more northern settlements—especially those in the Wen Valley—decided against allowing it, that part of their history didn't come up nearly as often as it once did. Kiko now had the commemorative red poppy painting that had once belonged to their parents, given as thanks from one of the last groups of Northern Nomads their family had helped. While Takato believed it was his duty to continue this tradition, most days, he felt his hands were tied. Emperor Akuwara held a fleeting interest in indicting those caught abetting a slave escaping their master, though it'd been during the early years of his reign. The Imperial court rarely involved itself these days, but there was still an unspoken threat of it; Takato didn't know if it was worth risking everything his family had.

A smug voice broke into his inner realm from the tearoom, "You're telling me they need me in the Capital? Interesting. I suppose I'll be able to make other arrangements while I'm there."

"The leader is pissed. How can you sound so casual?" another man urgently hissed, drawing Takato's curiosity to peer around the corner.

"Lords Hideo...and Giichi." He shook his head in disbelief—what an unlikely pair—then continued walking forward. "I don't recall inviting either of you into my home, though I suppose this explains why I haven't seen my wife or sister all day."

"I was in Kyuumura to sign over the estates to Ichiro—is it such a crime to try reconciling with my estranged wife since I've already come this far?" Giichi's attempt at contrition was useless against his brother-in-law.

"I find it hard to believe you're here to speak with Miwa; she never mentioned the possibility of you showing your face here. For whatever you two are scheming, my home is not your base or an inn." Takato rolled his shoulders and adjusted his grasp on the chest as he collected himself. "If I am wrongly interpreting what's going on here, I do apologize, but *only* for that—since you didn't send word that we should expect you, you still have no right to barge in here."

Giichi bristled, as did Takato. Hideo looked helplessly confused—he always was a spineless sot when confronted. Though the Nakamura name was traditionally associated with the arts, education, and silk, weaselly people like him easily sensed a certain ruthlessness most of the family possessed.

"Th-these matters don't concern you, L-Lord Nakamura," the witless bundle of nerves tried to state firmly.

"You are on my property. *Every* matter concerns me. If you're going to insist on mucking about, perhaps I should find something more useful to you to spend your time on; in fact, I was just wondering how I'd get this little chest to Kiko."

"What's inside?" Hideo inquired, pitifully silenced by the glares Giichi and Takato shot at him in return.

"Some old trinkets from our parents I'd like my elder sister to have," Takato shamelessly lied as he raised the chest slightly; whether Giichi would believe him was an entirely separate matter. The man had politically lost his wits over the years, but he wasn't stupid. "The last few years have made it difficult for me to leave the estates, and it simply isn't feasible to send any of my boys at the moment."

Giichi had dogged Takato about his "share" of Nakamura properties for years—that which became his through Miwa, but she never accessed. With his marriage failing and the mounting suspicion from nearly all family members that he'd fallen into a secret society of sorts, Takato supposed omitting information when possible was the wisest decision. Besides, he never planned to announce Sojiro's official takeover of business matters, nor the things he'd assigned to his other two sons eligible for successorship. Doing so simply lessened the confusion for when Takato died, which, with the tension stemming from his brother-in-law, could happen sooner than he expected. He wanted Kiko to know what was going on, too.

"W-well," Giichi started indignantly, straightening his spine and crossing his arms. "If I'm carrying *your* important family trinkets to the Capital, then I believe I shall require an escort—that road is overrun with bandits, you know."

"Since when?"

"It's...recent."

"I suppose you expect me to supply the funds for one." Takato sighed when Giichi continued to look at him pointedly, his patience thoroughly tried. "If Lord Hideo could be so kind as to escort you to Kai'yei, I will pay for someone to send an escort from there to the Capital."

The road going away from Kai'yei branched off from the southern tip of the Wen Valley toward Lord Hideo's tiny cluster of copper mines. From there, it was about an hour's walk—perhaps a little over; he couldn't remember—to the Capital, which saved Takato money and hopefully spared him further dramatics on his brother-in-law's end.

"Very well," Giichi finally agreed with a roll of his eyes. "Since I haven't anything better to do, I suppose I can run Lord Nakamura's errands for him."

Takato ignored him. "I'll send a messenger now so someone will be waiting for you by the time you reach Kai'yei. In the meantime, I encourage you and Lord Hideo to either seek an inn or return to Ichiro's estates in Kyuumura."

Giichi knew he wouldn't receive the box until the moment he left for the Capital. Still, Takato didn't like the slow, self-assured smirk slowly spreading across the other man's lips as he signaled to Lord Hideo that it was time to leave. "Of course, whatever Lord Nakamura wishes. Tell the messenger I'd like my escort to meet me at the bridge, then."

"There is one more thing," Takato hurriedly added before Giichi could leave, letting Hideo escape. He swallowed, as he'd just begun confronting this with himself. "What Obito told me about the night of Himari's wedding..."

Giichi looked over his shoulder, but didn't pause otherwise. "You don't believe a child over *me*, do you?"

Takato slowly set the chest on the ground, then interlocked his fingers in front of himself and raised his chin a little as the other two men disappeared. He swallowed when guilt and resentment twisted deep in his gut, along with unspeakable fury.

KANASHIMI'S FORM WAS UNLIKE anything Lady Shadow had ever seen. Ethereal, graceful, imposing, and deadly. Yet, in some ways, fewer things felt as natural as the ancient demon's company. Their reptilian face was a welcome sight whenever they decided to appear of their own volition, familiar and comforting as an old friend might be; Lady Shadow had gifted them a glass hair ornament that they'd since used to help pin back some of their flowing white locks. The cult's matron wasn't sure what had brought on these changes, as with the revival of Kanashimi's strength, they ought to have become more ferocious—they remained stern and scathing in looks, but their personality hadn't shifted in the slightest. If anything, they'd become calmer.

That said, she ensured the talisman containing Kanashimi's spirit always remained around her neck, close to her pulse, and easily accessible within seconds if needed. Perhaps the near-constant proximity to her blood had bonded them more positively than she expected.

The demon seemed to have developed further interest in Lady Shadow's plans, as they often floated nearby while she studied maps and cross-examined letters she received from their few loyalists hidden throughout the nobility. Although they remained distant in some ways, the pair grew closer with each passing week. Kanashimi never offered counsel, nor did they try to convince Lady Shadow her goals were misguided; they merely tilted their head now and then as they listened or read from over her shoulder. They did, however, comment once on their admiration for her unshakeable patience while waiting for her pawns and puppets to fulfill their purposes.

"If you continue staring at me, I can't concentrate," the demon chided gently, cracking open one golden eye a sliver. They held a black folding fan with iron sides in one clawed hand, while the other stayed steady in front of them, fingers occasionally curling or flexing as if making a hand seal as they hovered above the ground. They'd stayed in this pose for what must've been hours, secluded in the shrine where they'd awakened. Transfixed once she'd come to check on them yet again, Lady Shadow hadn't realized how long she'd kept them company.

A small, involuntary smile briefly tugged at the corner of her lips. "What is it you've been doing this whole time?"

"You said your traitor last went to Zhu. I can't help but believe my brother's talisman is still there. My powers have recovered enough that if I meditate and concentrate, I should be able to use my shadows to search a little."

"A scouting mission, then."

"In a manner of speaking, I suppose. Tatakai is the demon of war; he would know best what to call this."

Kanashimi lapsed into silence again, though it didn't take long before a frustrated plume of smoke erupted from their nostrils. They flicked the wrist of the hand holding the fan, fluttering it with delicate movements like a dancer or actress might do onstage, shaking out balls of darkness twinkling with deep purple hues. The spheres looked incredibly soft, but Lady Shadow didn't dare put out her hand to touch them. When Kanashimi caught one in their open hand, she stood utterly still, waiting with bated breath as the demon finally opened their eyes to examine it while the fan dissipated into thin air after being snapped shut.

A dissatisfied snarl curled the dragon's upper lip, and their claws curled around the orb until it burst; it disappeared into a cloud of blackness that vanished before Lady Shadow's eyes as the fan had.

"I sense Saigai, but I cannot place him, and this exercise is still exhausting. I'm afraid that's all I can do for today. This is normally a simple trick for me—though I must admit, reaching as far as Zhu would be easier with Saigai's flute for assistance no matter the circumstances."

Trying to contain her excitement and resist leaning in close to the demon, Lady Shadow straightened her shoulders and knelt before them. "Is it something *I* might be able to learn?"

"I *did* say you would need to call upon the Between Realm if you intended to summon Zandaka once you possess all six of our talismans. In order to do that, however, you will also need us to lend you our power and control a fraction of it yourself, won't you?" Kanashimi mused as if talking to themselves before bright yellow eyes went to Lady Shadow again. Their clawed feet unfurled as they lowered themselves to the floor, and they folded their arms in their sleeves. "From the grief you share with me, I can sense you possess immense amounts of it. How could I call myself the Demon of Grief without showing you the extent of its power?"

Lady Shadow had placed a wedge between herself and her followers over the last several months partially because of Kanashimi, but also because as more feckless nobles joined her cause, she'd become busier. She'd heard it all before from the women who flocked to her—the heartbreak of loss and betrayal, the same abusive husbands, the never-ending stream of despair. If she wanted to keep her constituents at her side, Lady Shadow needed something to prove her words weren't empty, their suffering and pain weren't for naught, and that the Empire *would* fall under her diligence.

"A drop of your blood is all I need, Priestess of Shadows," Kanashimi said invitingly.

Lady Shadow thought of the dagger hidden in her obi, not realizing at first that her hand was already moving and that she was determined to retrieve it. She unsheathed it as soon as it was firmly in her grasp and pointed the tip at the pad of her ring finger.

SIXTEEN
THE BRIDGE AT KAI'YEI

THE HIGH PRIESTESS'S BLACK eyes swept over a cluster of purple-tipped flower buds. Their stems looked withered, and their color a sickly greenish-brown; this kind was always so fickle during their first emergence in springtime, but their silky petals and blue centers attracted many admirers once in full bloom. After inspecting her surroundings, she knelt beside them with her fingers softly pressing the warm flowerbed soil, willing a tendril of her energy into the dirt. She smiled softly when weak chutes stood tall, now a proud and vibrant green.

She continued her afternoon stroll through the Palace Temple gardens as if nothing had happened. Priestess or not, she didn't want to imagine what might happen if someone saw her and reported their findings to Emperor Akuwara, who feared the few types of magic known to the world; he barely tolerated Healers. However, if he learned the High Priestess could save small plants from the brink of death, he would doubtlessly demand that she abuse her abilities for his own gains and make foolish demands. Raising an army of the undead and reviving his deceased wife being among them. He would sacrifice blood, prayers, incense, and countless other offerings, but they'd all amount to nothing. When he discovered she couldn't use her powers in the capacity he wanted, he would denounce her as a fraud.

Too many questions would arise on execution day once they accepted death wouldn't take her. A demon's curse had restricted the High Priestess's spiritual energy to nearly nothing, but the same seal ensured she couldn't escape the mortal realm; two hundred years of the Giahatio were among the most exhausting centuries she'd spent in it.

She touched a thick, diamond-shaped pendant, inlaid with six tiny rubies, dangling from her golden headpiece. It felt heavier against her forehead than it had in ages, but she couldn't remove it to ease her discomfort—yet another result of the demon's curse.

Zandaka, the Demon of Balance, was not mentioned in religious practices, and scrolls written about him were presumed lost to time—it was as he wanted. While Hikari and Kuro ruled over the heavens and the underworld, he presided in the Between Realm. In this realm of shadows, demon disciples cleansed souls for ascension before reincarnation, all under the Demon King's guidance. However, Zandaka's roles were not limited to humanity's side of the afterlife. He maintained the universe's balance between Hikari and Kuro—each a proud and temperamental god in their individual ways. Whenever they made decisions regarding life or death, the universe required the Demon King to select a soul for either rebirth or condemnation into one of their realms, and his minions reacted accordingly.

A chill slithered down the High Priestess's spine, and her chest heaved as an ominous feeling wrapped around her. She folded her arms into her sleeves, facing the sun as she braced against an uneasy prickle searing her skin. Although her hair stood on end, she closed her eyes to invite the vision into her consciousness, as if recalling a buried memory.

Her mind filled with the image of seven jade dragon statues, each battered and cracked as if time had been exceedingly unkind to them; one on the far left glowed brightly on its stone pedestal, while the one beside it carried a dim, barely noticeable light in its forehead. Her eyes slowly raked over the largest figure on the center pedestal, a massive, spiraling dragon with an open maw. A bright flash illuminated its eyes, and then out of its snout came a wispy black smoke. The High Priestess blinked, hoping to awaken herself from this vision, and instead discovered a massive stone talisman sitting in the dragon's jaws. The talisman bore six inscriptions, but before she could read them, a screeching roar sounded overhead, reverberating against her eardrums; pressure built in her temples as the screech rose into a crescendo, feeling as if her head might burst.

Silence.

The real world materialized in front of the High Priestess once more. Sounds of singing birds and distant voices from the groundskeepers returned to her, and she glanced over her shoulder at the Temple. Shaking, she breathed deeply, then smoothed the wrinkles in her long red and white robes. Her fingertips lingered on the golden threads of a lotus embroidered into her clothing; she had to calm herself before someone noticed, and decided to return indoors to meditate.

The six names on the talisman belonged to the smaller dragon statues flanking the one who held it. When Zandaka punished Hikari for obstinately creating a new form of life, his dragon-demon disciples had sealed her powers within themselves by absorbing her sins; seeing any sign of them meant one had been brought to the mortal realm from their slumber in the Between Realm. If the High Priestess had no limitations on her spiritual powers, she could estimate how long ago the creature was summoned. She worried it'd been active for at least a few months by now. To make matters worse, whoever found that talisman and successfully summoned the demon might try to find its siblings; should the six talisman demons reunite and breathe life into their king anew, the High Priestess didn't know how she'd force their return to the Between Realm. Whatever this person had planned, she suspected they didn't understand what they'd brought onto themselves.

The High Priestess looked to the clear blue skies above, then reminded herself to school her anxieties—"Hikari's messenger" always maintained a veneer of serene composure, and she decided she'd already leapt to far too many conclusions. Only one dragon statue had glowed brightly enough for concern, and Zandaka's seal wouldn't break unless someone performed his summoning ritual under the rare blood moon. She pressed her fingers against the diamond-shaped pendant again as another bittersweet thought occurred.

This form of Hikari might not survive the Demon King's revival, but neither would His Highness.

THE SWEET, DELICATE FLORAL scent of cherry blossoms once again filled the air around the Capital as spring descended upon the land, stretching warmly over every inch of flora and fauna. The springtime rains had given way to pleasantly sunny skies a few days ago, leaving the forested trails surrounding the city a vibrant green, punctuated by a colorful swathe of early wildflowers. Obito generally didn't enjoy being outdoors, but all the same, he found peace in listening to various birdsong as he sat under pleasantly warm sunlight beside the pond. He mindlessly rolled a rock between his fingers, unsure where his thoughts wandered, while also disinterested in finding out where they'd gone. It wasn't often that his mind went this quiet—nor were his surroundings these days.

He threw the rock into the pond and leaned back on a soft cushion of damp moss, barely able to hear its small splashes as it skipped across the water. As frustrated as he became with Daisuke's love of verbal sparring, it wasn't all bad; the last few months with him as a partner had far exceeded expectations, which were admittedly too low in the first place. Obito had approached his peers with the same mindset before meeting any of them; it made more sense than blind faith in those he'd never met or whose families he'd heard about through his brothers. Though that cynicism came naturally, it also stemmed from how badly he'd been hurt beforehand. At least now, he could say he'd been proven wrong about some of them. He hoped he wouldn't regret giving Daisuke the tiny sliver of trust he'd earned.

Obito righted himself once more and threw a second rock—Itsuki would've wanted at least that much.

"Beating up helpless bodies of water again, are we?" that familiar, obnoxious voice asked from his right; Obito could practically hear the sly grin Daisuke wore.

"Being annoying as usual, are we?"

"I'm bored out of my skull, so probably *more* annoying than usual," the talkative pest said as he sat beside him. He tilted his head wistfully at the pond. "Did you think that was possible?"

Obito knew his feigned irritation hadn't convinced Daisuke in the slightest, which made a small smile cross his face. "What do you want? Weren't you working on something when I left earlier?"

"Just some reading; like I said, I got bored. Besides, since we're supposed to meet with Master Yujin later, I thought I'd see what you were doing—looks riveting, for what it's worth."

"Do you ever stop talking?"

"Sometimes."

"Prove it, then." Obito rolled his eyes and laid back on the ground.

Seconds later, he heard Daisuke flop onto a mossy spot beside him. Obito's initial prickle of irritation quickly faded, and he breathed easily as a familiar, oddly comfortable silence settled between them as they listened to trilling birds and the low hum of honeybees visiting a nearby patch of violets. Despite his contentment, a part of him remained vigilant at first. Since Daisuke didn't show many people this side of his personality, it sometimes caught him off guard, especially when compared to how exhausting his more chaotic tendencies were.

I guess that isn't fair. I'm usually the one enabling him for some reason. Obito didn't understand why, but he couldn't help himself. He just *had* to see how Daisuke would talk his way out of the situations he often created—sometimes, he prodded until the other boy swore at him and gave up or won. Other times, he made quiet comments that spurned a fiery defiance. Thankfully, most of those scenarios resulted from fictional arguments in his partner's imagination, though he'd come under the impression that would change the longer they worked together. He'd already been pulled into a few fights because of Daisuke's quick tongue.

Although Daisuke had taken his challenge to stay quiet, he rarely managed it for long, and eventually pressed for further conversation. "Do you remember when we saw each other here last year? I'd just failed my first infantry evaluation. Why were you back here?"

Obito opened his eyes again; although he was initially tempted to give a smart answer, something more honest came out instead. "Trying to figure out what I wanted out of the year—Itsuki asked me. I didn't have an answer...at least, not one I wanted to tell him."

"Sounds like we both needed a friend."

"...I guess we did."

"Well, if we're going to be friends instead of keeping it to partners, I'll have you know there's an expensive membership fee for this organization." Daisuke smirked in that annoying, self-satisfied way he'd mastered; Obito rolled his eyes again.

"Some fee. I know your price, and ohagi isn't close to expensive."

When Daisuke turned to look at him again, laughing and slightly flushed at his own nonsense, Obito's heart skipped a beat.

Intermittent chatter filled the late morning, though it was spaced far apart by blissful quiet—Obito caught himself dozing off a few times, and peeked at his right side upon stirring to find Daisuke had done the same. Between studies and combat training, they were hard at work nearly every day, even when they'd been marked as off-duty by Master Yujin. He'd needed this moment to breathe, but didn't expect how comfortable he'd felt with the other boy, nor did he know what to make of it.

Maybe I should let it be for now.

They rested a while longer as Obito tried to follow his own advice. However, his sense of conscientiousness reared its annoying head when the sun climbed to noon. He rubbed the sleepiness from his eyes.

"Come on," he said to rally himself and his partner; he lightly tapped the sole of Daisuke's boot with his foot once he got to his feet. "Up you get. You said Master Yujin wants to see us."

Daisuke cracked open an eyelid. "Suppose I did. It sounds like such a chore, now. Do you think it's necessary?"

"We might be getting paid. But if we aren't, we shouldn't test his patience, anyway."

"...Fine, but I'm going to complain the whole way to his office."

Obito chuckled, surprised by how helplessly fond he sounded. "I'd expect nothing less."

Daisuke begrudgingly sat up, the back of his shirt now damp from the moss, and grumbled an incoherent complaint—already making good on his promise, apparently—then also got to his feet. Despite his threats, he didn't have much else to add as he stretched, and they started toward the Palace, though the look of distinct displeasure never left his eyes during their entire walk.

Master Yujin was acting beyond frazzled when they arrived at his office. He sifted through a stack of papers, anxiously mumbling as he tried to sort through a mountain of parchment. Obito knocked twice, but both went unheard by their muttering and grumbling superior; he looked at Daisuke for an answer. His partner grinned when he caught the inquisitive expression, perhaps a little too confidently for comfort.

Daisuke loudly and obnoxiously cleared his throat after knocking. "Bit ironic since you lecture us about neatness, isn't it, Master Yujin?"

The Master of Intelligence's head snapped up, eyes immediately landing on Daisuke with a dangerously annoyed glare that made the boy jump while stifling a cackle. Seeing how ineffective his attempt at sternness was, Master Yujin sighed and straightened from the way he'd hunched over his desk, smoothing back the few strands of dark hair that had come loose from his normally kempt style.

"Happy as I am to see that you remembered to meet me, I strongly suggest you mind yourself, Akahana. I'll make this quick so you two can prepare to leave; I need you to meet a nobleman this evening at the Kai'yei Bridge and escort him back to the Capital."

Kai'yei wasn't far from the city—about a two-hour walk at most—nevertheless, Obito had to hold his breath as a dreadfully familiar, affronted expression crept into the arch of Daisuke's eyebrows. Surely, he could resist mouthing off for a mere five minutes. Much to Obito's relief, he noticed the subtle change in Daisuke's features when his partner decided he should remain silent, though the subsequent roll of his eyes wasn't what he'd call a significant improvement.

Master Yujin also seemed thankful for the restraint shown, and wisely chose to forge ahead without commenting on it. "I recommend an early supper and leaving as soon as possible—the nobleman expecting you isn't known for his patience."

"Great," Daisuke finally piped up, the dryness in his voice making Obito wince. "Aren't these escorts generally considered favors from the Emperor to the nobles?"

"Yes." Master Yujin pinched the bridge of his nose.

"Then what kind of prick—"

"Giichi Tanaka. Whatever your opinions, you will address him as nothing other than 'Lord Giichi' or 'Lord Tanaka' while you are with him. Have I made myself clear?"

"He sounds like a horse's ass—"

"Daisuke!"

Obito's blood ran cold at the sound of his uncle's name, coupled with disgust that tasted like swallowed bile when his titles were listed. Whatever argument had ensued between Master Yujin and Daisuke, Obito couldn't say. Their voices grew distant as if someone had plunged his head underwater—it was probably something about etiquette and respect, though. The Intelligence Master was wasting his breath if that were the case. His partner didn't care for the definitions or implementations of either; Obito wasn't sure where his feelings resided on the matter, though he usually shared the same views as Daisuke. Not when it came to his uncle, whom he hoped he'd never see again upon enlistment. Now, duty interfered with that perfectly reasonable plan—resentment bubbled in his chest because of it. Finally, with a resigned sigh, he reached around Daisuke to put his hand firmly over his mouth, drawing him close to keep him muzzled despite muffled protests and attempts to squirm away.

"We'll leave early, sir," Obito told Master Yujin flatly, hoping uncertainty didn't seep into his voice. He stiffly bowed to the Intelligence Master, then dragged his struggling partner from the room.

Summer's first half sometimes brought periods of drought on the heels of springtime's rain, which shrank rivers such as the one at Kai'yei into trickling creeks retreating low into their mucky beds. However, in spring, melting snowpack from the mountains nearly overflowed the river. Daisuke hadn't ventured far outside the Capital since he'd landed on its piers, so once the forest thinned out and opened to a stretch of road bordered by fields of tall, swaying grass, he was surprised at how much gentler the land looked compared to the flat, dusty turf of Okara's dry months. He glanced at Obito to say something, but the other boy didn't react nor notice; Daisuke struggled to match his long strides as a silent, moody cloud of gloom towered over him. It'd been present since they left the Intelligence Master's office.

As he'd done with Bunji and Kulako, Daisuke learned to parse through the differences in his companion's silences. Realistically, few were out of anger or annoyance as most others thought, and the real answer was much more straightforward; Obito preferred keeping to himself most of the time, which he understood. Sometimes, he had nothing he wanted to add to a conversation, such as when everyone else created a ruckus at the long table in a room off the Palace's kitchen where they shared meals, and the noise was more disturbing than entertaining. Daisuke sensed something peculiar in this one, though, like a pending volcanic eruption of emotion—he felt it like a weight in his own gut. Even *he'd* never managed to upset Obito to this point. Something was very wrong and had been since they'd received their orders.

When they arrived at the bridge, they wordlessly agreed to rest at the center as the sun steadily sank west of Kai'yei on the river's far bank. They rested by leaning over thick, carved wooden rails painted with a faded red hue. Cooled by the evening breeze, they shared water from a bamboo canteen while awaiting their charge, though it didn't go unnoticed that Obito still couldn't place where his mind and feelings wanted to settle.

Daisuke tried minding his own business, but couldn't take it anymore after several minutes of prolonged, tense quiet. He took another drink from the suitou to buy himself a moment as he bolstered up to confront his friend. He didn't think he'd be responsive if it were him on the other side of an unprompted interrogation, so he wasn't entirely sure what he wanted or expected from Obito.

Honesty, Daisuke decided. That was also how he needed to approach it. Not unlike him, sometimes Obito was blunt about things to a fault, especially when given free rein to do so. Finally, he looked over at his partner and tried a mischievous inflection as he said, "You're hiding something from me."

Obito rolled his eyes in response; not a bad sign, all things considered. He seemed like he *wanted* to say something. Perhaps he didn't know how.

"It's about this idiot noble, isn't it?"

"What if it is?"

Progress! Mean as hell, but still progress! Daisuke internally cheered. He decided to take what he could get and forge onward. "Well, *if* it is, then maybe you could explain why this meeting's making you so tense."

"Because he's an asshole," Obito returned, a snappy edge to his voice. When he heard his tone, he dropped his gaze and continued more evenly, "And my uncle."

"You know that adds more questions instead of answering the one I already asked, right?" Daisuke sighed as it became clear his partner still wasn't keen on communication. "I know this emotional shit isn't a strong point for either of us, but...maybe we should try sometimes."

Obito gripped his hair. He desperately wanted to drop the conversation and leave things as they were; it didn't matter if it meant enduring several days—or an entire career—of awkwardness from this single moment. However, when he cautiously raised his eyes to Daisuke's again, wide and innocently awaiting a response, something inside him broke, and his wall of defenses crumbled.

"I..." His voice died in his throat, and another heavy pause ensued. "I don't know how to talk about what happened—not anymore, at least. My father got so pissed off when he heard about it that I haven't bothered trying since, and I prefer it that way."

Daisuke's heart sank at the distress on his partner's face despite the ease he'd tried putting into his voice. "Your uncle did the really bad part, though, right?"

Obito turned away slightly.

"...Was it fucked up?" Daisuke shuffled closer, not letting him hide.

Obito hesitated before nodding slowly. Daisuke's question brought them dangerously close to the point where he didn't know how he'd react to further inquiries, which his partner evidently recognized. Although his heart jumped when he felt the first two fingers of Daisuke's left hand hook around the ones on his right, he didn't fight it as his first instinct wanted him to—the weight that had pounced on his chest upon realizing he'd have to face Giichi lessened with his partner's unspoken reassurance.

"You know, my family's also pretty fucked up, so whatever it is," Daisuke's voice was soft, but solemn. "I believe you, even if no one else does."

Stormy dark eyes settled on Daisuke for a moment, uncertain, but ultimately relieved. Their conversation ended right on time, as it wasn't much longer until they heard someone clear his throat from Kai'yei's end of the bridge. When they turned, a nobleman wearing fancy black and blue robes with a silvery belt at his waist impatiently awaited their response. Daisuke bit his tongue to keep himself from immediately charging at the man with his tanto. With how similar he and Mika were in appearance and how Obito's shoulders had instinctively tensed, he knew without introductions that this man was Giichi Tanaka.

Giichi pulled at his short, neatly-trimmed beard, his upper lip curled into a snarl, then adjusted the satchel hanging off his shoulder. "I see Master Yujin no longer takes me seriously—I politely request an escort, and he sends me the family disappointment and a slaveborn."

"What a horse's ass," Daisuke grumbled through his teeth; Obito stifled his laughter.

"Let's get this over with," he muttered to his companion before stepping forward to address the noble with a bravery he hadn't felt in a long time. "A pleasure to see you, too, uncle. Shall we?"

Giichi scoffed, but stepped onto the bridge without another word.

THEIR JOURNEY HOME WAS much more reasonable than the walk to Kai'yei, as the sun's disappearance below the horizon gave the cooling air a pleasant chill and dewy scent. Crickets chirped, and frogs warbled in the distance, but aside from listening to their chorus as a light breeze rustled rich green leaves on nearby trees, little else transpired among the three walking toward the Capital. A crescent moon provided scant lighting on the trail. However, they didn't need to rely on it for long, as flames from torches at the Capital's back entrance signaled them from only yards away, as did strings of lanterns from the acrobat camp in the field to their right.

"Where are we taking you, anyway?" Daisuke abrasively asked as he turned to Giichi, who skulked behind him and Obito. It was the first time any of them had spoken since their initial exchange on the bridge.

"It's awfully rude to address a man of stature so informally," Giichi replied indignantly, lifting his chin. "I would think *you*, of all, would know how to speak to someone who outranks you."

"What the fuck is that supposed to mean?"

"Boy, if you aren't smart enough to know, then you definitely aren't smart enough to be with intelligence."

"No, I get it. I just want to see if you have the balls to say it—plainly—to my face."

Obito wordlessly reached for Daisuke and gripped his upper arm to turn him back around in one furious motion. However, Giichi wasn't excluded from incurring his wrath, judging by how his partner's eyes darted between them. While Daisuke's first reaction was a returning glance loaded with resentment to mask a sudden surge of profound, ingrained fear, he understood after a second of critical thought kept him firmly planted in the present. At the end of everything, Obito was the one who would face any backlash for the way they acted, and most of it—if any at all—wouldn't come from Master Yujin.

"Fine," he quietly relented to his partner. However, he conveniently forgot to adjust his tone and ensured he sounded snarkier when he asked at a normal volume, "Where are we taking you, *Lord Tanaka*?"

Obito sighed, but didn't bother correcting his behavior.

"I need to visit with Lady Kiko Nakamura before going anywhere else. Get me to her apartments, and I won't need anything further from the likes of you two." He dipped into the bag he carried, eyeing Obito smugly. "Lord Takato Nakamura has a present for her—I imagine it has something to do with his will."

If Obito cared, he didn't show it; he turned, shrugged, then faced forward again in cold dismissal. "As far as I know, my father isn't ill, so I highly doubt it. You could only hope, though, couldn't you?"

The group lapsed into the familiarity of tense silence once more. It continued until they passed through the whitewashed wall guarding the nobility district and stepped onto streets illuminated by the occasional oil lamp blazing high above their heads. Daisuke felt just as uncomfortable around the sheer size of these single-family abodes as he had a few months ago when he and Obito went after Yin. "Thankful" wasn't a strong enough word to express how much he appreciated that Obito wasn't like other nobles he'd met—that included Mika. He'd met far too many like Giichi.

In fact, that difference between himself and most of the nobility seemed to be a point of pride for his partner.

Daisuke's mind wandered back to a week ago when Master Yujin caught him trying to purposely start a fire in the hopes of dismissing a poisons lesson early—the Intelligence Master saw him pouring off different, flammable compounds into a flask while Obito held it steady. Knowing they didn't stand a chance once apprehended, his partner admitted to their mischief straightaway; sure, it'd earned them a less severe punishment, but at the time, Daisuke was too pissed to care. Not an hour later, as they were elbow-deep in hot water and suds to clean every instrument in the room, he'd asked Obito why. Still fuming, when he received an answer based on principles, he'd immediately shot back that nobles couldn't possibly care about those. Maybe it'd been out of line, but Obito looked amused. Even so, he made sure to splash Daisuke with soapy water to make him pay for his comment and to shut him up for a bit.

After a few twists and turns through the streets, they arrived at what Daisuke assumed was the house in question. Like most of the nobility's housing, it was old in structure, but family wealth had allowed upkeep and repairs to come on schedule or as needed. Neatly maintained flowerbeds blooming with hyacinth and tulips lined the façade, punctuated by a short shrub on each end, and a twisted tangle of ivy arched over the doorway. Daisuke imagined a peaceful summer evening sitting on the steps while listening to far-off conversations and tending to a modest collection of plants. This brief, blissful escape from reality was boorishly interrupted by Giichi's loud knocking and calling out to Obito's aunt.

"Who is it?" a light, playful voice cooed from the other side moments later.

"Giichi," the nobleman stiffly replied, fists clenching with annoyance. Obito swallowed another snicker.

"Giichi? Dear me, this *is* a surprise. I'm afraid I need a moment, please. I'm not decent—Retsuko, stop giggling. You'll give away how much we've had to drink."

Another period of silence passed as they waited, clearly testing the nobleman's patience and temper, which Daisuke found wildly amusing. All the while, he and Obito didn't dare look at one another—they knew they'd burst out laughing if they did. He already liked this aunt a lot. Then, finally, just as Giichi prepared to knock on the door again, she appeared. Kiko was a lovely, dark-haired woman with wise, soft eyes, dressed in a simple, pale pink robe with a white jacket strewn across her shoulders. She held a half-empty glass of wine in her right hand that she quickly set aside on a surface that must've been hiding out of Daisuke's line of sight, meanwhile shushing the giggles of another woman who remained unseen.

"I hate to sound short with you, but did my brother forget to send word that I'd be expecting you?" Kiko frowned at Giichi once she'd sorted herself out, her gaze briefly darting around him toward Obito, asking for help or clarification. When their split-second, wordless exchange confirmed that he knew nothing, she added, "That's unlike him."

Giichi squared his shoulders. "Takato *is* rather busy these days, Kiko; you can't expect him to remember every petty little thing *you* want from him."

"Of course, I would never. Shall we attend to business, then?"

Obito didn't like the anxious look in his aunt's eyes, but when Giichi rounded on the pair of onmitsu behind him, he knew he had to act in a more professional capacity by at least pretending to leave. When Giichi faced Kiko again, Obito bumped Daisuke with his elbow and waved for him to follow along until they were around the corner of the house. Careful of the flowerbeds, he pinned his back to the wall, listening intently.

"You *are* tense tonight," Daisuke teased in a whisper from a few feet away. "Do you think he's going to kill her?"

"No, he's too much of a coward, and her partner's visiting. But I know Giichi. He probably wants whatever's in that chest; he just doesn't have a key."

"We should do this more often—your family is fun." The little pest snickered.

Exasperated, Obito pinched the bridge of his nose, then looked at him with a slight smirk. "It's fine, Daisuke. This is all too much for you. You should go home and turn in for the night—you must be exhausted, and this isn't part of our assignment, anyway."

Daisuke's jaw slacked, but that devilish twinkle didn't leave his eyes. "This is manipulation, and I won't stand for it."

Although he wanted to play at arguing more, curiosity won him over, and he quickly went to Obito's side, waiting for Giichi to bid Kiko farewell for the night. As soon as they heard him go, they rushed from the shadows keeping them out of sight, hurrying toward the door. Obito cautiously knocked, then heaved an undeniable sigh of relief when they heard two women briefly converse before locks rattled once more, and his aunt opened the door again seconds later.

She beamed when her eyes fell on the pair, as if they'd dropped by for a casual visit, but she gave the chest a slight nudge with her foot, showing them where she'd set it on the floor. "I was hoping you boys hadn't left—far better than trying to find a messenger at this hour. Obito, won't you introduce your friend? I don't believe we've had the opportunity."

"Now really isn't the time, is it?" He gave her a pained look, which gradually became an outright grimace when she gave him the same firm, expectant expression he sometimes wore while waiting for Daisuke to tell him something. Begrudgingly, he told her, "This is my partner, Daisuke."

Daisuke grinned and bowed at the waist—as if he'd ever acted so proper in his entire military career, or ever would again. He'd heard more about Kiko from Mika than his partner, which meant this opportunity was far more than he could've hoped for when they'd headed off for the Kai'yei bridge. "Pleased to meet your acquaintance, my Lady."

"The pleasure's all mine," she said delightedly before facing her nephew again, maintaining her sweet smile. "I've no idea what your father's sent me, but that can always be for another time. Right now, I need this out of Giichi's sight before he has a chance to tell anyone else about it. I want you to take it."

"*Me?*" Obito didn't want to be responsible for essential family documents—it was one of the few advantages he could claim over his brothers as the youngest son. Taking the chest was more than he'd bargained for when Master Yujin assigned them the escort mission. "I...I don't think that's—"

"Appropriate? Nonsense." Aunt Kiko waved her hand dismissively and grabbed the chest. Despite its small size, it felt cumbersome when she hoisted it into his arms. "I know you don't have enough interest in this to take a peek, and I trust Daisuke will keep his mouth shut should anyone ask of its whereabouts. Won't you, dear?"

Daisuke hadn't expected to get dragged into this—whatever it was—so directly. However, the pained, exasperated expression on his partner's face was worth its weight in gold. He knew Obito wasn't impressed with the situation, but as an audience member having plenty of fun with it, he *had* to see if he could get his partner's expression to turn into outright murderous intent.

"You have my word, ma'am," he promised with a wide grin, laughing when he heard Obito mutter something foul under his breath.

Despite the blazing summer heat outside, the Palace's inner stone walls stayed noticeably cooler most days. Daisuke learned to hide away inside rather than trying to find shade in the training yard as he'd done during his time with the infantry. He longed for when the hot breezes on his skin would turn cool again in a few more weeks, when thunderstorms at last sapped the heat and humidity from the air to make way for autumn and winter. He couldn't wait for the natural changes that took place during those seasons, either, especially in autumn. Because of the plantations and its native vegetation, Okara was depressingly barren in comparison, and without the bursts of color in the foliage. Until then, he had few options besides waiting patiently. The days were already growing shorter and the nights less suffocating; now that he'd watched nearly three of these cycles pass on Perena, he took comfort in knowing it wouldn't be much longer.

Three years, Daisuke mused. *Has it been that long already?*

He decided his eyes needed a rest from watching over a little metal pot in front of him, and turned his gaze toward the dim, soft orange light peeping through the tinted windows. The Giahatio may never see his worth, but he knew Master Yujin did; sheets of notes on parchment under his charcoal-smudged left hand confirmed as much. He was fourteen now, and although he was only in his second year as onmitsu, his confidence with poison-making had grown into a developing proficiency that edged out most of his peers. As such, the Intelligence Master had given him the task—or test, depending on how one looked at it—of putting together a complex elixir for some nameless noble who, inebriated and stupid, had called out Prince Akuko's bloodline in front of the Emperor at a party. Understandably, at least from specific perspectives, this could not stand.

Daisuke didn't care about the Prince or the nobleman either way. However, since he'd been made responsible for helping Master Yujin resolve the aftermath of that disaster at the previous night's party, he didn't plan on making himself look useless. Emperor Akuwara wouldn't know to credit him if this went well, but he didn't need—or *want*—the Emperor's attention if he could avoid attracting it.

Anxious chittering and clanging metal drew his attention to the massive black rat a chef had trapped earlier that day. Assuming he was also Palace staff—and hysterical about the creature's sheer size—he handed it off to Daisuke when he'd incidentally passed through the kitchens in search of something light to eat before getting to work on this assignment. Knowing the tenacity of rats and realizing he'd need a test subject once the mixture cooled off, Daisuke decided to make the poor thing comfortable before bringing it downstairs. Some might have seen the gesture as a gracious act toward his victim, but he couldn't deny a certain element of sadistic selfishness in his actions. In reality, doing so made *him* feel better, though he doubted the same could be said from the other side of the cage's door.

"What do you want?" He didn't sound as annoyed as he'd wanted.

Watery, beady black eyes looked back at him—he could've sworn he caught a hint of desperation in them. Daisuke huffed and sat back a little on the bench.

"Look, it's nothing personal. In fact, I like more animals than I do people—except dogs, I guess. I do hate those. But we aren't talking about them right now. Anyway, while I don't really think you deserve this...you *are* a rodent," he explained as he used a thin metal rod to stir his tincture, giving it a glance to check for leftover steam when he pulled it back out again. "Listen, if I did this right, you shouldn't feel anything—not even a little pain. You'll go into a deep sleep and eventually stop breathing instead. How does that sound?"

"Daisuke, are you talking to that mouse?" Obito's voice interrupted from the entrance, tearing his eyes away from his experiment.

He straightened his shoulders primly, gathering himself and hoping Obito hadn't noticed how he'd nearly jumped out of his seat at being startled. "First of all, this is a rat, not a mouse. Secondly, his name is Squeaks."

"...You named the rat you're about to kill?"

"Anyone can make it sound crazy when they use that tone."

Obito now looked worried about Daisuke's mental state, which he supposed was a fair concern, with or without Squeaks as a factor. Daisuke's eyes followed Obito as he crossed the room, then wordlessly sat beside him on the bench. The pair watched Squeaks rummage around in the soft bedding Daisuke had placed in his enclosure for a moment before Obito leafed through the notes his friend had quickly scrawled across several pieces of parchment in charcoal. After comparing the new annotations to Master Yujin's original instructions—haphazardly tossed aside, as things usually unfolded when Daisuke settled into an inventive mindset—he peered into the cooling pot in front of them, noticing a slight crimson tint under the candlelight.

"Is it meant to be red?"

"Not exactly." Daisuke leaned forward, resting his chin on his hand as a familiar look of vague annoyance worked its way into his features. "The steps to this one are stupidly complicated, and I can't tell you how many of the ingredients are rare—we didn't have half of them on hand, so I had to improvise...a lot."

"If my math is right, your adjustments made this poison better than its original." Obito organized the sheets into a neat stack, then set them off to the side again.

A half-hearted smirk twitched at the corners of Daisuke's mouth. "There's a reason I don't let anyone else see my notes."

Their attention subconsciously went back to Squeaks, still busily throwing around the bits of wood shavings and cotton lining his cage, and they both sighed. Daisuke's attempt to stall the proceedings hadn't taken him as far as he'd wanted. He took out a paintbrush and a small jar from a leather bag stored by his feet beneath the solid oak table, then asked Obito to pass him a bowl of scraps he'd saved from his meal earlier. After Obito helped him pour off the tincture into the container, Daisuke dipped the brush in, then slathered it over the remaining grains of rice and little pieces of fish.

"You know, I've killed rats before," he commented as he stripped off the leather gloves he'd been wearing, then picked up a pair of tiny silver prongs to pass the food into Squeaks's cage, letting it land in the bedding. The rat's beady eyes watched him warily, pink nose and whiskers twitching as he tried to determine what was happening. "But not like this. Those vermin were getting into the rice bins, so my dad made me help him get rid of them by breaking their necks—we were lucky none of them bit us. I mean, they were looking for something to eat and a warm place to sleep, like Squeaks here, but that wouldn't have mattered to Grandmaster Norio."

"There's a rumor that some of the higher ranks use humans as test subjects, like death row prisoners. I'm not sure if that's a better practice than using a rat, though."

"They do that?"

"I just said it's a rumor."

"But if I *had* to..." Daisuke's brows furrowed. "I don't see where I'd have an issue with testing poisons on *certain* people, but I honestly don't know how I feel about it. It's mostly...well, *wrong* to consider. Isn't it?"

Obito shrugged. "Probably, but necessary."

Their conversation dropped off when Squeaks finally smelled the food in his enclosure, and silence ensued as they tensely watched him twitch his nose at the offering before eating his fill. Daisuke's thin fingers tightly gripped Obito's sleeve when Squeaks finished his last meal, then lumbered to the other side of his cage and curled into a ball, long tail poking through the gap between the bars. Mere moments later, his sides stopped going up and down, and he remained perfectly still.

Daisuke sighed sadly and almost leaned into his friend, but pride forced him upright when he sank toward Obito's shoulder. Instead, he gently eased his vice-like grip from Obito's shirt and shifted his attention toward gathering the materials used to make the poison, unable to look at anything except what was directly in front of him.

"Do you need me to take care of Squeaks?" Obito asked, sounding oddly sympathetic about the whole ordeal.

Daisuke paused at the unexpected question, then slowly nodded, watching from his peripherals as Obito lifted the live trap from the table. As soon as the cage disappeared from view, he pushed out a heavy puff of air, then went to pump water into a metal dish for boiling and cleaning his tools. His hands shook when they gripped the lever, slipped, then hurriedly grasped it again.

Obito didn't think it was wise to bury Squeaks due to the poison in his body; plus, he couldn't see Daisuke taking it remarkably well if he somehow found out a scavenger dug up the deceased rodent. Burning was the easiest way to prevent either scenario, so he went to the woodstove in the back corner of the room and set the cage beside it while he messed with its finicky handle. Hinges on the stove's door screeched in protest as it opened and greeted him with a blast of heat from the fire, and he took another look at Squeaks.

"Emotional over a fucking rat," he heard Daisuke scoff at himself over the metallic clangor he created in the background. "Fucking hell."

Obito glanced over his shoulder in time to see Daisuke dumping a tray filled with used instruments into a pot of warming water, then turned back to discard Squeaks's inert form and the fillings inside his cage into the stove as gently as possible. The empty trap quietly rattled when he set it on the ground again and closed the door. He worried he'd make things worse by trying to comfort him, but still called out, "Daisuke, come here."

Despite his grumbling, the little nuisance was at his side within seconds, keeping a scowl trained on the floor.

"Do you know why Perenins and Giahatians cremate their dead?"

He sniffed and shook his head, messy hair carelessly exaggerating the movement, but finally looked up from his feet, cautiously showing Obito the slight redness around his eyes. "It's some spiritual thing, isn't it?"

"It is. Traditional beliefs say that the soul can ascend to the heavens when the physical body gets burned."

"I didn't take you for the religious type."

"Well, you weren't wrong—I'm far from it—but...this seemed like the right thing to do."

A faint smile pulled at the corners of Daisuke's mouth, and he finally gave himself over to the temptation of leaning a little on his friend; Obito's shoulder was a comfortable spot, and this was permission few others on the entire continent had. Unable to help the soft chuckle that escaped him at acknowledging this, his smile soon turned into an unusually half-hearted attempt at a more devious smirk. "Don't worry. I won't tell anyone about how much you loved Squeaks."

"You're an embodiment of the Mother Goddess's kindness." Obito rolled his eyes and nudged him off his shoulder. "Sitting in this room's fumes all day must've gone to your head."

"Rude, but fair." Daisuke snickered, secretly enjoying the warmth creeping into his face that he couldn't ignore.

Besides, he was confident the wall-mounted torches disguised any redness in his cheeks in the rapidly fading daylight. He hadn't known Obito for as long as he'd known Shun, whom he was close with for years before running away from home, but he liked this better. It'd seamlessly gone from a partnership to a much closer and raw human connection than anything he'd ever experienced before, apparently slipping past the defenses they'd both otherwise carefully crafted with barely a fight from either of them; their tendency to choose honesty first with each other lent itself to a unique brand of trust. Daisuke knew Obito's relationship with his emotionality was complex, and maybe even a little twisted, but that seemed to help draw them together. Hearts battered by past experiences so vastly different, yet similarly painful and life-altering, that something such as the untimely death of a rat solidified the safety they could seek in each other.

"By the way," Daisuke began as he shuffled away to check on his boiling instruments. "Where were you all day?"

"With Aunt Kiko," Obito answered; after a moment with the space to decide if he wanted to, he explained further, "I didn't like having the chest in my room. When I told her, she had me take it to Retsuko. We both think it'll be safer with her at the acrobat camp."

"You've had it for over a year," Daisuke commented, briefly looking away from his task. "Why now?"

"Remember Mika interrupting us when we were studying the other day? I'm pretty sure he saw it then. If nothing else, I'm sure Giichi's told him about it by now."

"Going to Retsuko if neither of you want to keep it around is smart—no one will think to ask her. Your aunt's basically married to her, anyway, isn't she? So she probably knows about all the fun stuff as is."

Obito chuckled. "We aren't supposed to talk about it."

"Right, the whole dysfunctional family thing." Daisuke shot him an impish grin as he swiped the stack of papers from the table, then tucked them between two pages in his weathered journal. His features slipped into a more serious expression when he glanced at the vial. "I *really* need to get this poison to Master Yujin before the Emperor holds court with the nobles tonight, and I still need to clean up here. Do you mind bringing my book back upstairs for me?"

"You're not asking me to go near your natural disaster of a desk, are you?" Obito dryly asked as he snagged the journal from Daisuke's outstretched hand, trying to ignore how much he enjoyed those brief looks of outrage and then confusion on the other boy's face. "Fine, but you'd better get moving if you still want to meet at Shiba's later."

"Please. I'll get there before you."

"What's next? You'll finally show up to morning assembly on time?" Obito grinned at the scowl Daisuke gave him. "I'll see you there."

The path to the onmitsu dormitories had ingrained itself into Obito's memory at this point, as was a secret passage that shortened the way there from the lecture hall; he frequently snuck into it to avoid other people. He wished he hadn't lost the map he'd so carefully sketched out of all the different backways he'd found—not only was it incredibly unlike him to misplace it, but not having it was a considerable disadvantage to their team, as any of the more experienced spies would tell them. While they weren't wrong, he and Daisuke would be going in circles if they tried exploring more than the few Obito had learned by heart.

Another time. Obito reminded himself as he let himself into his friend's room.

He paused when he opened the drawer where he knew Daisuke usually stored his poisons journal—where he stashed any additional ones was any-one's guess—as his eyes fell upon a white cloth with russet-colored blotches dotting nearly every inch of it. Soon after, he found the handle of a scalpel, evidently hastily tucked away beneath it, and at the back of the drawer was a second cloth that Daisuke appeared to have wrapped around something. The second one caught his attention for a moment, but couldn't hold it; his focus kept returning to the haunting implications of the dark red stains. Something in his mind wouldn't let him deny what he saw.

Obito usually didn't pry into other's lives—he liked too few people to bother. All the same, a magnetic force drew the tips of his fingers to the spotted cloth. He gently pulled down on it to avoid shifting it too much, and dread rapidly filled his stomach when this bit of closer inspection confirmed he was looking at patches of blood. His heart sank as he set the journal in its proper place without closing the drawer again right away. He wasn't sure how to—or if he *should*—address this with Daisuke. Did the same intense, dark grip of self-hate that held him after the incident at his cousin's wedding also torment his friend? Or was he simply missing context that would blow the whole thing out of proportion if he said something later?

The second option didn't sound realistic; optimistic, sure, but barely what he could call grounded.

Voices ricocheting in the corridor alerted him to the world outside his inner thoughts, and he abandoned them while hurriedly closing the drawer. The overlapping jokes and conversations sounded like they were growing closer, so Obito wanted to clear out of Daisuke's room as soon as he could manage. They'd likely come this way to search for him, anyway.

Of course, the universe never liked him *that* well.

"Daisuke, do you want to come to get some food with—" Mika stopped short at the doorway seconds before he and Obito collided; his eyes widened as he timidly finished his question, "...us?"

The usual group of idiots who had closely trailed Mika turned on their heels to ensure they'd quickly disappear from Obito's sight. His cousin's chipper demeanor fell away when he fully absorbed his friend's absence, and a short but heavy silence fell. He crossed his arms over his chest without stopping the unimpressed way his eyebrows arched.

"This is an interesting sight. What in the hell do you think you're doing here?"

"You don't need to know," Obito replied calmly, knowing a bland response always worked best. The flush and glower on Mika's face intensified when he added, "Besides, I was just leaving. You should, too."

"Not until you tell me what the fuck you're doing. As far as I'm concerned, you shouldn't be here, either."

"Good thing this isn't your concern, then."

"I fucking hate you."

"That's nice, but this is still none of your business." Obito examined Mika's face for a moment, then decided—mistakenly, he internally grumbled as he spoke again—to ease back a little. "Daisuke asked me to bring up his journal from the poisons room while he finished cleaning. Satisfied?"

Mika spat on Obito's boot, which was no surprise; he knew whatever he said wouldn't go over well without Daisuke nearby to corroborate his story.

"How dignified." He stared at the foamy spittle in undisguised disgust.

"Spouting off horseshit doesn't earn you dignity. You and I both know Daisuke doesn't let anyone in his room without permission. Are you trying to say you have it?"

Although Obito was beyond frustrated, Mika wasn't wrong. While the little pest enjoyed regaling—or annoying, depending on who one asked—his classmates with entertaining stories or outlandish ideas, he drew a firm boundary about not letting other people in his room. Obito could approach that line as his teammate and friend, but never crossed it without Daisuke's explicit permission. Obito also thought about the russet-stained cloth and stolen scalpel he'd inadvertently uncovered; even if those weren't stowed away in his desk, it wasn't unreasonable for Daisuke to expect others to respect his privacy. While he was here, it was his responsibility to enforce that rule.

"Leave it to you to make stupid assumptions." Obito sighed. "If you're so worried, go ask Daisuke for yourself."

"Fine, I will."

"Fi—never mind. I'm not doing this."

Mika backed off when he forced his way forward and firmly shut the door. Since he didn't know where to place this swell of baseless anger at his cousin, he let Obito by without further comment. However, realizing he was about to be alone with an odd surge of jealousy beginning to mingle with his anger, he pivoted and jogged to catch Obito.

"Why do you always leave in the middle of a fight?"

"Is there another way to get rid of you?" Obito rolled his eyes and looked over his shoulder. "Mika, if you're so desperate for company, why don't you see what your father's doing?"

"*Because*, stupid, my father lives in the Wen Valley. Remember?"

Obito stopped short and turned around, evidently surprising Mika. He hesitantly asked, "Didn't he tell you he's in the city?"

"How would *you* know if he came to town?"

"You mean other than seeing him leave a silk merchant's store yesterday? Daisuke and I brought him down from Kai'yei at the beginning of summer. Last year. I assumed he'd left by now."

Mika's assertive stance retracted as disbelief rushed into his face, followed closely by resentment. Although Obito wasn't terribly fond of the other boy, he deeply understood the heaviness in his expression; a nobleman like Giichi would've had plenty of reasons to stay in the Capital for a while, from business to personal, especially given the distance between Kyuumura and the city. If Mika truly was his favorite child, as Obito had heard him profess, visiting him should've been one of those reasons.

For a moment, Obito returned to the wintry night he unexpectedly saw his uncle in Zhao, the cloaked figure he'd spoken to, and wondered if there were other, perhaps sinister reasons underlying his actions.

No. Without further proof, that was paranoia and suspicion, not a logical conclusion. Besides, an annoying bout of sympathy compelled Obito to follow up with, "When *did* you last speak to your father, anyway?"

"Fuck off; you know he's busy. When was the last time *yours* bothered speaking to you?"

"I guess that's fair—it's probably been about three years by now."

Truthfully, Obito was certain he hadn't held a proper conversation with his father in the fourteen years he'd been alive, which added to the validity of his cousin's point. Takato and Giichi shared the same range of emotional articulation at times. Mika desperately needed Giichi's attention and approval—although Obito could never fathom why, he also knew his cousin pursued them with total tenacity. He'd learned how pointless it was to wring them from his own father, so he'd eventually stopped trying, which might've been one of the most freeing things he'd done despite causing an even greater distance in their relationship. That had been present before what happened at the wedding ultimately split them apart.

Cutting off anything else they might say, Daisuke miraculously saved him by calling their names.

"Well, this *is* odd," the little pest commented with a half-hearted chuckle as he looked between Obito and Mika. He scratched the back of his head. "Are...are you coming to Shiba's with us or something?"

Mika wrinkled his nose and glared, his gaze not settling anywhere in particular. "I don't need a fucking pity invite."

With that, he stormed off, likely headed toward his room or to find the friends he'd initially brought along with him. Obito sighed heavily as he watched his cousin go, then turned to Daisuke, words lost on his tongue when he tried to speak.

"Fucking hell, he'll start a fight over anything," Daisuke mumbled as he awkwardly shuffled his feet, then slipped past Obito, his steps missing their usual bounce. He cleared his throat and switched to a more audible pitch. "Don't laugh at me, but...it turns out I forgot my money in my room."

Obito snapped back a bit from the looming cloud of guilt threatening to overtake him, only for one glance at his friend to remind him again of the bloodied cloth. He opened his mouth to say something about it while they had the space, but what came out instead was, "Good. That means *you* can deal with your desk this time."

Daisuke rolled his eyes at him.

"Stay on your feet, Daisuke. Don't look down. Eyes on your opponent—*always*." Obito swung the staff hard at Daisuke's midsection for emphasis, which he barely blocked. He feared the reverberation sent through the stick in his own hands might make it crack. The fact that he'd managed to stop the strike caught him so off guard that he didn't have time to react when Obito swept his feet. The other boy grinned and bent down, extending his hand. "And don't get distracted."

Daisuke scowled and huffed, but still accepted his friend's wordless offer to help. He groaned and dragged his palms along his face to wipe away the sweat running into his eyes once he was upright again. "We've been at this for hours. Can't we stop?"

"Hard to believe you were in the infantry."

"Fuck off—you know I'm not a fighter."

"Obviously. It doesn't make sense *why*, though. You know how to move when it comes to defense, and it *is* possible to fight from a defensive position."

Daisuke glared in earnest this time, but Obito didn't seem to notice...or care. Instead, he leaned against his staff, appearing deep in thought over something. Daisuke nearly jumped when those dark green eyes flicked toward him again. Intriguing; his partner might not say anything now, but he clearly had an idea.

"One more time, then we'll call it for the day." Obito spun his staff around once, as did Daisuke, both holding their weapons slightly away from their bodies, parallel to the ground at chest height. "Ready?"

"Fine, I guess," Daisuke complained, rolling his eyes as he slid his left foot back into the appropriate stance while Obito did the same with his right. He'd step forward again when he made the first move.

They spread their hands on the wood to prevent accidentally breaking one another's knuckles with a wayward hit. Something clicked in

Daisuke's mind—he only had to react rather than fight back. Obito was leading, sort of like in a dance, so it made sense to block with the upper end of the staff when his partner's weapon came between them for a strike, immediately followed by a second one with the lower half. A downward strike from the top, then another follow-up from the bottom, deflected by a simple turn of the weapon to a horizontal position; this had never come so easily. Daisuke's eyes locked on Obito as the following exchange began, exhilarated. Every spin and twist of the body came much more naturally with this new focus as they moved through the form, as did the way he needed to maneuver the staff.

They wrapped the day's session no more than twenty minutes later; a bath and a few hours of sleep would be necessary before their mandated overnight patrol. Obito also apparently had some other unspoken business he wanted to attend to, as he quickly placed his weapon back on the wall rack once they agreed upon where they'd meet at sunset and took off without many words exchanged. Were it anyone else, Daisuke might've felt suspicious, but he'd come to expect that, like him, Obito's mind sometimes worked faster than he could communicate.

THE TIME TO START a night patrol always came faster than Daisuke anticipated, and somehow dragged on slower than he could've imagined, no matter how much he mentally prepared himself for it. He *liked* being awake late into the night, but the preference was based on when something interesting occupied his busy mind, like an engaging text or developing theories on how certain poisons could be changed for different effects. Sometimes, those nights also involved conversations with Obito, though more often than not, he silently read while Daisuke played with his experiments. Either way, he was fond of the company.

He was exceptionally happy to have it now. For tonight's patrol, he and Obito were assigned to a section of the Capital near the wharves, where after several loops around a designated route, they settled at an old half-wall near a fabric store—from here, they could quickly provide reinforcements to the soldiers across the old square at the docks should they need it.

Unable to help himself, Daisuke scaled the wall that reached a little above Obito's head and found a decent spot to sit. The sea breeze gently rolled across his skin, and the steady crash of waves onshore lulled his mind. They stayed at their post for hours with nothing happening, aside from occasional conversation between the pair, but even those moments were unremarkable and passed all too quickly as they tried to keep themselves awake. Bored out of his mind as the uneventful night grew deeper, Daisuke finally stood and stretched his arms over his head before looking down at his feet; the wall was wide enough for him to balance easily and low enough that an accidental fall shouldn't break his neck or otherwise injure him too terribly.

"You know how I like to watch the acrobats whenever they perform, right?" he called to Obito, whose head tilted toward his voice as if he pulled the other boy's attention along on a string. "I've been practicing some things I've seen them do. Want to see?"

"If you fuck up and fall, I'm not catching you."

He snickered and chided sweetly, "Don't be like that. I thought we were friends."

Naturally, by now, Obito knew better than to trust his tone, though Daisuke didn't quite know how to handle the half-smirk his partner shot at him from over his shoulder before he pushed himself away from the wall and pivoted for a better view. He shook himself out of the odd, momentary stupor that washed over him and tried to regain his composure.

"Nothing better to do, right?"

"We *could* walk the route a few more times."

"After?"

"Fine."

Daisuke proudly grinned at how effortlessly he'd won this round. Normally, it wouldn't be *as* exciting if Obito didn't try to fight, but he learned to take his victories when and where they were given; for as much as he enjoyed arguing and banter, his partner was a well-matched opponent in that realm. He shifted his feet slightly to ensure he was well-balanced, then hoisted himself onto his hands and pointed his toes toward the sky. He walked a little in one direction, doubled back, then flipped into a bridge before standing upright again.

He spread his arms wide and bowed at his one-man audience. "Not bad, right?"

Obito smiled a bit. "Not at all."

"And now you catch me," Daisuke announced with another wicked grin as he spun around and let himself fall backward off the wall. In the back of his mind, he worried that Obito would stay true to his previous threat, though those words instantly became empty when he felt his descent stop. It jarred him a little at first, but soon, he registered one of his partner's arms under his legs while the other supported his back. He cautiously looked upward and met his forest-green eyes, thankful for moonlight to conceal the unbearable heat in his face as Obito righted him again.

"So much for letting me fall," Daisuke deflected, scrambling to find some semblance of his usual snark.

"You didn't fuck up," Obito answered with a shrug, though he also sounded distracted. He gestured toward the docks, the closest part of the loop they'd already walked so many other times tonight. "Let's get going."

Once again, Daisuke thought that Obito might be running through a calculation of sorts, though no words left his partner's mouth. He couldn't focus on it much, anyway, not with his mind feeling so erratic. There had been something so natural about the way Obito held him that, even though he tried his hardest to think about something else, he simply couldn't; he still sensed how it felt to have his friend's arms around him.

"Don't get me wrong, walks are nice, but where did you say we were going?" Daisuke asked Obito as they moved through the city three days later. As they drew nearer to the outskirts, the trust he'd learned to have in his friend became riddled with the doubt he'd placed in so many others no matter how he tried to control his anxiety.

"We're going to visit Retsuko," Obito calmly explained. At least he wasn't committed to being tight-lipped about the situation.

"Why?"

"Because I think she can give us some ideas on improving our combat skills." Obito paused. "I guess I should've asked if you were open to it first."

Daisuke glanced at the sky while he recalled their sparring match from the previous day; he'd done better than usual, but not until after he remembered what Obito had said about fighting from a defensive position. Something had clicked in his partner's mind that wasn't obvious to him yet, and he'd followed whatever inspiration he'd found to an interesting conclusion. Frankly, Daisuke was too curious about Obito's plan to play at being upset.

"I guess I don't mind this time," he answered in his best attempt to sound casual about it as he shoved his hands into his pockets. "Besides, who wouldn't want the acrobat matron to give them free lessons?"

"Well, they might not be entirely free," Obito said uneasily. "If Retsuko believes you're wasting her time, she wants something more...monetary than the work I volunteered to do."

"Which entails...?"

He winced. "One hundred silvers for her time."

Daisuke swallowed—it'd take *ages* to pay off that amount. He couldn't deny his admiration for the matron's ability to drive a hard bargain, though. He was impressed with his partner for arranging this meeting in the first place. She wasn't exactly known for holding an audience with outsiders. According to Obito, Aunt Kiko never got involved with Retsuko's professional matters, so it wasn't as if she'd had a hand in any of this.

Daisuke forced a teasing inflection into his voice as he said, "Look at you—I didn't know you gambled."

"I don't. I just know when I'm right. I wish I'd thought of this sooner."

Somehow, hearing that made Daisuke feel better and worse all at once. While he appreciated Obito's confidence in the situation, he instantly felt the immense pressure of being able to live up to those expectations. He enjoyed watching the acrobats perform whenever they graced the city's streets for festivals or funding. He could even mimic some of their basic tricks—as he'd demonstrated during their last overnight patrol—but he still didn't understand how Obito presumed they could help. However, he was willing to try anything that elevated him from feeling like dead weight.

Daisuke cleared his throat. "Retsuko knows we're coming, then?"

"Not exactly. She invited us to stop by whenever we had the time before summer ended, though. We have time today."

"That's incredibly vague. What's the reason?"

"She said her guild was invited to perform somewhere out west, so they'll be traveling soon and won't be back until sometime around the Winter Festival."

"How does she have time for this, then?"

Obito finally spared him a glance. "Aunt Kiko told me that teaching is one of her favorite things about what she does—she'll always make time for it."

Once they were on the road heading toward Kai'yei, it didn't take long to find the familiar circle of red tents where the acrobats lived and rehearsed; the Emperor wouldn't allow them to settle anywhere inside the city, but that didn't bother Retsuko if Aunt Kiko's interpretations were accurate. They had more room to practice in the fields, and Imperial guards wouldn't harass them for simply existing as they did with most buskers who performed in the streets. On top of those things, it meant that the acrobats showing was a rarer sight to the people, which created a larger draw to their routines.

Upon arrival, several people looked at or turned toward them, and Daisuke tried not to stare back. Some must've recognized Obito, as they paused mid-rehearsal long enough to at least wave at him, then tentatively do the same to Daisuke, curious about a newcomer. Although Retsuko wasn't expecting them, she was clearly on the lookout, as they didn't wait long for the matron to appear from one of the tents and greet them. It wasn't common for Giahatian men to bow to a woman of any rank aside from more than a polite incline of the head; most couldn't imagine bowing to a street performer. However, Obito's grasp on when to use the propriety he so hated never failed him when needed.

"This is your friend, Obito?" Retsuko asked in a rich voice as her light brown eyes examined Daisuke from head to toe. "Daisuke, right?"

"Y-yes, ma'am." Daisuke's heart thudded as it filled with worry again. What if this really did turn out to be a waste of everyone's time? Never mind taking on the burden of a debt as massive as one hundred silvers. He wouldn't be able to show his face around Obito for at least a month if he fucked this up—maybe two to play it safe.

"Don't worry, it's not close enough to a performance date for me to bite." She winked at him. "Since we're preparing to head west soon, I would like to get right to business, though. What would you say your skill level is?"

He helplessly shook his head, unsure how to answer; he suddenly felt quite self-conscious and embarrassed over what he'd learned through observation.

Retsuko smiled patiently. It didn't alleviate the nerves twisting in his stomach, though, and he had to force himself to breathe when she turned to Obito. "I'll take things from here. Don't worry, I plan to give him back in one piece."

Daisuke also looked at him, inexplicably alarmed. "You're leaving me here?"

"They need help getting ready for travel," Obito said as if that explained everything. After a pause, he rolled his eyes and added, "I told you about this on the way here. Don't be annoying and listen."

Retsuko laughed when they scowled at one another, then sent Obito off to a group of adults milling about crates and passing ropes near a cart. She returned her focus to Daisuke. "I know you're both onmitsu, but we'll pretend I didn't say that. We've done mock combat plenty of times in performances, though the few kunai I've scraped together aren't props—the most important thing you can remember is to be light enough on your feet to get out of the way."

Daisuke's brows furrowed; the infantry had taught him to get directly in an opponent's path and stab them with the spear. The onmitsu operated under the assumption that most of their opponents would be better trained than a band of rebel soldiers—possibly defects from their own organization, hitokiri, or those who had otherwise built their marital skills to a higher level than the average citizen. Most of his time sparring with Obito focused on blocking strikes or trying to hit a pressure point to interrupt the flow, which often meant he was desperately trying to keep up with his partner in hand-to-hand exchanges.

Have I seriously never thought of...dodging? Of all the things? Why—and how—the fuck?! He mentally berated himself as a scorching hot blush colored his cheeks, wishing there was a way to pull his hair out of frustration without looking like he'd lost his mind. Lightness on his feet was something he'd discovered early on—he couldn't believe he'd never found ways to explore that idea further. Thankfully, Retsuko didn't seem to detect his internal dilemma or ignored it entirely, as she clapped a couple of times and called names he couldn't make out above the noise in his mind.

"Basics first. You'll duck or roll out of the way when one of my helpers moves to attack you." Retsuko smirked as a clever glint entered her eyes, and two other acrobats flanked her on each side. "It becomes a sort of dance once you get used to it. Shall we start?"

Daisuke uneasily looked between the helpers who had appeared, then nodded. *Might as well get this humiliation done and over with so I can hide from Obito before he catches up to me.*

Being light on his feet frequently saved Daisuke from getting caught causing trouble or being on the receiving end of it. However, he'd never given much thought to other ways it could help him. He spent part of the afternoon demonstrating what he'd learned from copying the acrobats over the last couple of years, mainly things like flexibility and balance, until Retsuko decided she wanted to see more. Daisuke grimaced when she said it was time for one of the no-contact sparring routines they used in performances. He'd memorized several, but he didn't believe he was ready to participate in one.

"Remember," she told him as her two helpers readied themselves. "As a dance."

Daisuke wasn't given time to object when Retsuko stepped away, as both helpers were already moving in on him. However, for once, he didn't bother to block or otherwise defend. Instead, he rolled out of the way. When he anchored himself to the ground again, he was already facing them; if he'd had a weapon, he could've thrown it from this distance while keeping himself safe.

This must've been what Obito meant a few days ago when he talked about fighting from the defensive. Daisuke could now see where it would've been possible to formulate and execute a few counterattacks, especially if he kept his momentum. It didn't ease his frustration at how miserably he'd failed in the past, but he didn't want to dwell on it for long; armed with a new perspective, he had to build confidence for the future.

It wasn't anything like combat training, but all the same, he couldn't deny how utterly exhausted he'd become by the time his feet touched the ground again after one last backward flip that Retsuko requested to see—apparently, there was something about his form that she found interesting. Around the same time, Obito returned from the group Retsuko sent him off with for help.

"It looks like we're starting to get the hang of things," Retsuko said to his partner as she signaled to her assistants, wordlessly telling them it was time to stop. She addressed Daisuke again when she added, "You won't have these two, of course, but you ought to train on what we covered. I'm sure Obito will be more than willing to help you with that."

Daisuke nodded firmly through a few last heavy breaths. After everything he'd done today, he felt oddly confident that she'd given him a plenty attainable goal. "Yes, ma'am."

"I could get used to this politeness." Retsuko crossed her arms and shot a nearby woman a satisfied look. "I think that's plenty for today, though—you'll be sore enough as it is tomorrow, and we have a long journey ahead of us going west."

"Thank you again, Retsuko," Obito told her with a bow, which Daisuke copied this time.

"Of course," she said with a smile. After a moment of pause, a light flush touched her cheeks, and she added, "Now that business is over, could you run a gift to Kiko for me? I do hate leaving her for long trips like this."

Due to soreness already settling into muscles he didn't know existed, Daisuke lagged considerably on their way back to the Palace. Despite how hard he tried to push himself to go faster and keep pace with his partner while they walked along the road, he consistently fell behind; he sheepishly avoided Obito's eyes every time he glanced over his shoulder to ensure he was still following. Once they re-entered the city, it seemed as though his friend finally had enough of his slowness, as he stopped long enough for Daisuke to catch him. Much to his relief and annoyance, Obito looked far too amused to give him the disinterested lecture he'd halfway expected.

"Are you going to make it?" he teased.

Well, hell, he started it this time, Daisuke decided with a grin. He sighed dramatically and leaned against an old, long-abandoned market stall with a tattered awning barely clinging onto its posts. "I'm dying, Obito. You'll have to carry me home."

"No."

"Please?"

"No."

"Is it because I'm too heavy?"

"You aren't serious, are you?"

"Maybe. It's been a long time since you lifted me—the Ivory Snake was forever ago, now." Daisuke grinned again when Obito rolled his eyes. "And we still have to stop by that bakery for your aunt like Retsuko wanted. It's going to take *ages* at this rate."

"It won't if you stop complaining and just walk."

"You're the one who dragged me into this without warning."

Now unable to place if he was amused or annoyed, Obito shook his head and turned on his heel, prepared to leave the snickering little pest behind; he felt anyone else he told would've understood. Much to his surprise, Daisuke unexpectedly launched himself onto his back, nearly sending them both to the ground. With Daisuke's arms now latched tightly around him, there was little way of getting him to let go unless he threw him, which he supposed might be an excessive amount of force. Plus, in this part of the city, stirring up a commotion in the middle of any street might attract a crowd neither of them wanted to see. With a heavy, irritated sigh, Obito resigned. He hooked his arms under his partner's knees to support him and kept walking.

Nineteen
Ominous

W OOD AND GLASS RATTLED slightly as Master Yujin removed a wedge from the windowsill in his private quarters; the setting sun had invited in the evening's chill, and though the day had been pleasantly warm, he couldn't say the same for the overnight hours this late in summer. The scent of fresh air lingered in the room and left behind crisp coolness that Yujin found highly enjoyable—not long after, a timid knock soured his mood.

Just one. One moment of peace. Is that too much to ask? he wondered while gazing at the ceiling, trying to collect himself before he answered. Scowling and grumbling, he made his way across the floor, unable to change the stern displeasure etched into his expression when he opened his door to greet his unexpected guest.

"Oko? What the hell are you doing here?" Yujin usually wouldn't have felt as bad about his cantankerous mood if the tattooist hadn't already looked so terrified. He anxiously stepped over the threshold, slouched and cradling himself as if he'd seen a ghost.

"H-His Highness would like a word with you. I-in the throne room," Oko replied while absentmindedly scanning his surroundings as if searching for danger; relief spread across his face when he encountered nothing but warm lamplight in return. "I was the unlucky soul he saw first to fetch you for him."

His Highness must *be anxious—usually, he's bedding his favorite courtesans by now, not yelling at innocent Palace staff.* Yujin winced as he watched Oko sink into a seat at his table. In direct contradiction with the Intelligence Master's current misgivings, relief washed over Oko's face as soon as he was off his feet. He tried prodding more information from him with a simple, "What did he say?"

"That he's summoned General Aki, too." The tattooist took a fan from his belt and unfolded it with a gentle flick of his wrist, covering his face while some color returned to his cheeks.

"Hikari's sake, did he happen to mention why? General Aki is a terribly busy man."

Still quivering, Oko swallowed and shook his head; a person of his social standing didn't receive direct attention from the Emperor often—it was rarely good if they did. "Your guess is as good as mine, but I'd advise haste, sir. It doesn't take an Imperial investigation to see that His Highness is pissed off about something—and that's putting it lightly."

Yujin hid a roll of his eyes from Oko before he pinched the bridge of his nose, accompanied by a deep, frustrated sigh. He couldn't imagine what the Emperor's temper tantrum possibly involved this time. He'd had a few exchanges with a potter in the eastern city of Zhu, who was anxious about an item his sister-in-law had left with his wife, but those became buried as more urgent matters came across his desk. He'd barely remembered the potter's letters until now, and wasn't sure what had dredged them up this time. Surely those couldn't be the source of His Highness's anger—Emperor Akuwara had more significant concerns on his mind, didn't he?

Moreover, if this *did* have anything to do with Zhu—gods knew His Highness's connection there could ensure it—Yujin had intended to find a team to investigate those reports for a while. He didn't want to waste the skills of his better spies. However, picking from his less experienced ranks was trickier than he'd initially expected, as young onmitsu didn't have much business traveling across the continent. Yujin prayed to Hikari and Kuro that His Highness wasn't planning to launch another campaign against the Okami. Propaganda against the Wolves of Othakra hadn't stopped because of the cease-fire called on the Empire's behalf. The temporary truce had, however, only positively impacted the Giahatian military's numbers and seemed to restore at least a little of the public's faith in the Emperor's regime; he wasn't about to waste those things on nonsense...*was* he?

Finally, the Intelligence Master gave up trying to analyze the situation and turned to Oko. "I'd better go, then—I still haven't heard the end of it from the last time I kept His Highness waiting."

"Good luck."

"You need to leave, too." Yujin arched an eyebrow at his companion, who had made himself comfortable in his seat and looked surprised at being told he couldn't stay.

"Right. I'll...I'll be on my way, then."

Yujin rolled his eyes again as Oko fumbled out a farewell and hurriedly left. Then, bracing himself for whatever might come his way, he exited his quarters and made his way toward the throne room.

He calmed his annoyance and collected his uncertainty as he walked; as always, a neutral appearance would serve him best, as would shedding his assumptions. When he arrived at the throne room, General Aki was already on one knee before the dais, his right arm crossed over his chest to show his respect for the Emperor. Akuwara's eyes darted to Yujin, watching him with a predatory intensity. The spymaster exchanged a glance with his counterpart, bowed, and took the same position in front of their monarch. Whispers of anxiety flooded Yujin's mind again when Emperor Akuwara decided to rise.

"Stand, for Hikari's sake, both of you," the Emperor harshly scoffed.

Upon their compliance, he lifted his chin, subconsciously asserting his authority over them—he was, after all, the shortest man in the room, which never sat well with him. Bidding them to their feet was a futile attempt to state the opposite, and his gesture gave some weight to the rumors about lifts built for his shoes that were covered by flowing crimson and gold robes. He folded his arms in front of his chest, looking quite unlike his usual dignified persona.

"I have recently received some interesting information from our informants, Yujin. I understand there are some locals drumming up trouble in Zhu."

"Do you mean the potter and his wife, Your Highness?" Yujin fought the urge to groan when the Emperor curtly inclined his head. "I'd hardly call it trouble, sire. They're simply nervous about an artifact they inherited from the wife's sister."

"Why?"

"Superstition, most likely, Your Highness," General Aki supplemented.

"Spare me." The Emperor mirthlessly chuckled. "Zhu is a rich and thriving trade port, not some village in the foothills where the people honestly believe ravens are Kuro's spying devils. Besides, that still does not solve the mystery of why our military continues to fail to investigate the matter when my good friend—a prominent senator, no less—has called for it."

General Aki swallowed, apologetically looking at Yujin for a moment until he finally managed to say, "I didn't receive notice to prepare the infantry, Your Highness."

Emperor Akuwara's brows relaxed slightly as an indication that he'd accepted the General's answer, and he turned to Yujin, now expecting his—more specifically, awaiting the Intelligence Master's best excuse. Painfully aware this wasn't likely to end well, Yujin steeled himself.

"I wasn't aware Senator Hajime had said anything, Your Highness. I haven't received anything from him, concerning this matter or any others."

"It went ignored for so long that he wrote to me directly. Now, what excuse are you offering me this time?"

"It's been difficult organizing a team to investigate, Your Highness. I didn't believe this was a high enough priority to send—"

"Are you the final authority on which of our priorities matter most?"

"N-no. Of course not, Your Highness, but—"

"Then I'm afraid I still fail to fathom why there's this much hesitation on your behalf." Emperor Akuwara's lips tightened into a thin white line; he would've typically dismissed or belittled Yujin had he taken things more seriously in the first place, which was infuriating to acknowledge. The Emperor chewed, then pursed his lips and breathed slowly, emphasizing his limited patience. "You should both know that Senator Hajime's information about the object is mostly through secondhand tales he's garnered from his own half-witted intelligence network. He believes the artifact in question is of Okami origins and likely cursed, given those stories. If this is true, I believe it goes without saying how weak we appear by allowing such an object on our shores—today, it rests in the hands of a simple potter. Tomorrow, who can say what carnage it will have caused? Carnage, I must emphasize, which could have been prevented."

Yujin knew this wasn't the time or place to explain how little sense it made to suspect the Okami. Nor was it appropriate to state how flabbergasted he was that Akuwara allowed Hajime to contact him directly, but also have any form of intelligence at his disposal. Granted, they were likely the underbelly type the Senator and the Emperor would never interact with outside of necessity and who would never have access to sensitive information. Nevertheless, the words threatened the stillness of his tongue, and he struggled to repress them. He was grateful when Aki intervened by supplying the lead for the next part of their discussion.

"What do you require of my infantrymen at the time, Your Highness?"

"As we are currently in peace treaty talks with the tacticians, nothing overt; if word traveled to those wolves, we could face a potential disaster on our front. However, I would like to see *some* preparation—organize with the other infantry generals to ready a small unit to...speak, as it were, with Lord Takeo. Yujin, which of your teams could leave for Zhu within the next few days?"

"Akahana and Nakamura. They can leave the day after tomorrow," Yujin said begrudgingly after pretending to wrack his brain for the answer. No matter what he tried or who he moved around, he knew they'd be his best option to send away for some time, if not one of his experienced teams, but they were also his worst.

"The slaveborn and Lord Nakamura's youngest son?" The Emperor let out a short, harsh laugh. "What a perfectly horrendous grouping of uselessness. Are you sure you have no one trustworthy or *competent* at your disposal?"

"I'm sure they're plenty capable, Your Highness," General Aki surprised them with his interruption, though perhaps most remarkable was the concern on his face that only the Intelligence Master understood. "They *are* Yujin's students, after all. However, if I may speak openly, sending them to Zhu could be highly dangerous beyond what most onmitsu would expect."

Akuwara's eyes narrowed. "Excellent points, General Aki. But since Yujin still, apparently, thinks this isn't worthy of better operatives' time, these runts ought to encounter few issues along the way. This mission should be easy if either boy is worth his salt as onmitsu—practically child's play, I daresay. Right, Yujin?"

Yujin exchanged one more uncertain glance with Aki, then sighed heavily, surrendering to the possibility that one of his agents might not return from this assignment. "Yes, Your Highness. They're currently on overnight patrol, so I'll discuss this with them tomorrow afternoon."

Obito blinked in surprise once Master Yujin finished briefing them the following afternoon, a slight hint of outrage uncontrollably slipping into his features, infiltrating his voice with every word he spoke afterward; thankfully, it was only three at first. "*Zhu*, Master Yujin?"

"You heard correctly, yes."

"With all due respect, are you *mad*?"

Yujin paused, frankly shocked at the young agent's reaction. This kind of animation and backtalk was—for better or worse—common from Daisuke, but to see it from Obito was something no senior military member would've expected, perhaps making it all the more compelling. Daisuke apparently hadn't worked out what the issue was yet, although his obliviousness wouldn't last much longer. Pity and guilt sloshed around together in the Intelligence Master's stomach. He cleared his throat to try pushing it away, then straightened his shoulders, staring at them from the protection of being behind his desk.

"Do you have a problem with this assignment, Nakamura?"

Obito anxiously glanced at a thoroughly confused Daisuke; his eyes had clouded with warring emotions Yujin couldn't recall ever seeing from him. Finally, the boy reined himself in and spoke in a more strained version of his usual calm, "Zhu is the *busiest* slave port on Perena. *Why*, in Hikari's name, *would* you make us go there?"

Daisuke's eyes widened as his head jerked in his partner's direction first, then their superior's. Kuro's Hells. In an often impossible feat, the boy had been rendered speechless. Yujin sighed. Unfortunately, Obito was right; it *was* sheer madness to send any team with a Northern Nomad in the configuration to a city such as Zhu. Senator Hajime wasn't known for his kindness.

"You're fucking joking." Daisuke's disbelief hadn't yet subsided, but an expression of utter betrayal had taken over his features.

"I wish I were, boys." Yujin leaned back in his seat, hoping a lack of sternness and will to correct the way they'd spoken to him conveyed some of his sympathies—revealing the level at which he didn't want them to go wouldn't be good form on his part. "But this is for an errand. Emperor Akuwara wants it done quickly, so focus on retrieving the item from the potter and his wife, avoiding Senator Hajime, and returning home. Sounds simple enough, doesn't it?"

"Nothing is ever that simple," Obito pointed out, unimpressed.

"Onmitsu must learn the art of blending in."

Daisuke cackled, though it had a slight, menacing undertone. "You're asking me to keep my mouth shut and play nice with people who hate me."

"Then try to think of it as biding your time before you're both seniors." Master Yujin flinched as soon as the words left his mouth, then cringed when they looked at each other like they usually did when conspiring. He saw they were fully intent on making this as difficult on him as they could reasonably get away with; if it weren't for the fact that Emperor Akuwara would order their immediate deaths with a snap of his fingers, he would've suggested they take their issues to him instead.

"I want double pay," Daisuke announced.

Yujin nearly choked on the tea he'd started drinking. "Excuse me?"

"Triple," he ruthlessly added. "Think of it as coverage for if something goes wrong."

"Absolutely not."

Master Yujin helplessly looked between them; it was clear that Obito had no interest in his usual, self-appointed duties of talking sense into his partner. While he thought he *should* reel the team in and calm them down, he knew he couldn't internally force the latter, even if he managed to stop them outwardly. He wished he'd had the opportunity to speak with Aki once His Highness dismissed them the other day; their discussion might've sounded the same.

"Fine, Akahana. You'll get your double pay, but you won't see a single copper piece until you come home *with* the artifact. Lose it, and you'll get your regular stipend pay only—if you're lucky. You'll also do well to remember *who* the Master of Intelligence is. Now, it's a long road to Zhu. I want you two out of here as soon as possible."

"We'll be on our way early in the morning, sir," Obito said, now more complacent with the situation.

"I'll have supplies for the trip sent to your rooms later this evening, along with more details of where you'll stay and the allowance you'll use along the way." Yujin rubbed his temples, grateful those two would be out of his hair for a while.

Three. If I'm lucky, I'll have peace for three whole months. The Intelligence Master sighed again as he watched them exit his office.

As promised, the supplies Master Yujin said he'd send arrived not long after dinner. Obito returned to discover the items on his bed: a map, a pouch of coins, and a detailed explanation of what they were to do. Along with some other particulars, he triple-checked to ensure his tanto would also make it in with his supplies. Without their daggers, he and Daisuke would be mostly defenseless on the road to Zhu, which could mean death if they happened upon any bandits who habitually stalked the path. They'd need to be on guard from the second they left until the moment they returned and handed over their reports, along with the artifact, to Master Yujin.

If he were honest, he was still pissed that their superior hadn't chosen a different team or assigned a substitute to take Daisuke's place, as much as he wouldn't want to spend so much uninterrupted time with anyone else. While he understood the final decision may not have been Master Yujin's to make, the ordeal was exceptionally unfair to his teammate—cruel to some degree, bordering on sadistic. They'd need to be on high alert the entire time they were in Zhu. It felt like a waste to expend so much extra energy on vigilance alone when he was sure it could be spent better in other areas. He didn't know precisely what those were, but the whole idea soured his mood. The situations his mind ran through to prepare defenses for were things none of the other operatives would have to consider. If the worst happened, protocols dictated Obito acted in a way he wouldn't be comfortable with—prioritizing the mission over Daisuke's life.

He was already prepared to deal with the consequences of ignoring that rule.

Senator Hajime's name was familiar to Obito, but only because of his notoriety regarding the enslavement of other human beings. At one point, his father had openly scorned the Senator's practices, but a cynical twinge in the back of his mind told him not to expect the same these days—Obito mentally shook himself to force his mind away from such thoughts. He couldn't let himself assume that his father had abandoned his morals.

As for the Senator himself, his reputation was widespread amongst the nobility, though likely because it directly impacted a specific sector of the gentry. He ruthlessly and indiscriminately captured Northern Nomads wandering through his streets, sometimes selling them back to their original owners—what a ridiculous word to use—at a ridiculous markup and calling it a fine for letting them out without proper supervision. The whole thing was beyond disgusting in Obito's eyes, but he was painfully aware that his opinions didn't change reality.

A knock came from the other side of the door. Obito wasn't quite startled, but after being deeply lost in thought for so long, he'd nearly forgotten about the outside world. There had always been a sort of unspoken agreement between the other onmitsu on this floor, and it was to leave him alone; as far as he knew, that hadn't changed. He rolled his eyes once his mind caught up—there was *one* exception. When he answered the door, it was hardly a surprise to find Daisuke on the other side, but the glint of mischief sparkling in his expressive violet eyes made Obito wary of engaging.

He decided not to give the little nuisance the satisfaction of noticing, and responded defensively. "Shouldn't you be packing? We should plan on leaving early—rather, we *are* leaving early."

"You worry too much. If my calculations are right—and I'm sure they are—walking to Zhu takes somewhere around forty days, and that's if we *don't* have any issues along the way. What's the rush?" His lips worked into a devious grin. "Come see what I've done to my desk drawer."

"Why? What the hell are you doing over there?" Obito stepped out of his room and closed the door behind himself. "Better yet, why does it sound like I should be afraid?"

"You have such little faith in me."

"It's quite the opposite, actually. I always have faith that you're up to something."

Daisuke snickered and waved him along, further proving the point in Obito's opinion.

There's a word for people like him. Obito grumbled internally as he followed his friend across the hall, likely against his better judgement, but he was morbidly curious about what he'd spent the last hour or so engineering. Curiosity was a hell of a drug, and he could barely contain his sense of it when it came to the odd things Daisuke did. *Is it "chaotic?" No, that can't be it. It's too simple. Is demonic better? Whatever. It's close enough.*

TWENTY
THE WESTBOUND ROAD

OBITO KNEW HE WAS a fool for expecting better of Daisuke's organization skills, as if the few times he'd seen his room in total disarray were isolated incidents or that he'd cleaned it in the limited space between now and the previous night. The familiar pile of laundry on the floor and studying materials scattered across the desk came as little surprise, simultaneously comforting and maddening in the oddest way imaginable; one last look at something he knew before they set out for less certain encounters. A deep sigh of annoyance pushed out of Obito's lungs when his lantern light revealed Daisuke huddled under the covers, still asleep in his bed. He knew he should've been ready; they'd discussed their journey's logistics before dinner yesterday. Obito closed the door behind him and set the lantern on a small bedside table after he crossed the room.

"Daisuke," he gruffly said as he shook him. "Daisuke, get up."

"No," a half-awake protest grumbled from under the blankets—Hikari's sake.

"Gods be damned," Obito swore under his breath. He looked around the room for options, then decided he'd yank the covers off Daisuke, who shivered and curled into a ball before he rolled to his other side, stubbornly refusing to open his eyes. With less patience and twice the force in his voice, Obito repeated, "Get up, Daisuke."

"Gods, you're so fucking mean—the *sun* isn't even out yet."

"I'm *never* mean to you." Obito took a deep breath to collect his scattering patience. "But, if you don't get out of bed right now, I *will* drag you."

Daisuke's sheets rustled as he looked at him from over his shoulder, a scowl visible on his face between the shadows of dim lantern light. "You wouldn't dare."

"Are you prepared to test that theory?"

Daisuke's eyes locked onto his, and their battle of wills was officially underway.

RESTLESSNESS RELENTLESSLY PRICKLED UNDER Giichi's skin. Despite being in the Capital for over a year with no clear plans of when he would return home, he hadn't accomplished anything to further the ambitions of the Servant's little cult or his own. He'd even tried to covertly gather information on Tatakai's talisman to gain favor with Zandaka's Servant. However, that quickly became a wash and a waste of his precious time. None of Master Yujin's spies were stupid enough to help him unquestioningly, that hag Kiko had outwitted him by concealing the chest she'd received from Takato, and in the face of his repeated requests for an audience with General Aki, he'd yet to see the man in person. In addition, a couple of highly ideal business ventures with merchants had fallen through because of a few abrasive words his fuck of a brother-in-law once gave them.

He supposed he should be leaving again soon to check on Hideo and his end of things, but he needed one more thing from the Capital. Despite his lack of information on Demon Lord Tatakai's talisman or the location of Lord Saigai's lost one, he was confident that receiving this item would still help him and the Servant's overall goals.

Giichi wasn't sure how much he believed in the deeply buried religious aspects of the cult's plan, especially since it came from such obscure passages in scripture he barely followed to begin with, but the Servant of Zandaka had agreed to return Giahatian purity to the sullied Imperial bloodline and ensure the bastard crown prince would never reign. The promise of eventually sacrificing undesirable noble houses along the way sweetened the deal.

In any case, he decided he should prepare a gift for the Servant before his next visit to the mountain retreat—with any luck, he'd be able to test it on his brother-in-law first. It also allowed him to visit Mika, who had come by his apartment several times over the last couple of weeks, asking for such an opportunity—he wasn't sure *how* the boy learned of him being in town, but had a feeling that mouthy slaveborn was involved.

Mika now sat across from him in the pleasant sunlight warming the Ivory Snake's dining hall, looking lean and muscular from his time with the onmitsu, yet incredibly childlike in his nervousness. He prompted the boy for an explanation.

"I'm surprised you finally wanted to see me, Father. I...I heard you've been here for a while," Mika hesitantly answered.

"Who told you that?"

"...Obito."

"Well, I hardly think I need to apologize for not having time to waste. Besides, I'm here now, and I was hoping you could do something for me." Giichi smiled, knowing it'd be all he needed to soothe him. "You've learned about all sorts of potions and the like, haven't you, son?"

Mika preened at the chance to impress his father. "Sure have."

"Then you could make just about anything if someone asked?"

"Me? Heavens, no. Most of them are more difficult than you'd think to get right," Mika said with a half-hearted laugh, which abruptly ended when he saw Giichi's lips tighten. "B-but I know someone who *can*. He's got an entire journal dedicated to our poisons and medicines—really detailed, too. I peeked at some a few days ago during lessons."

"I don't suppose you could ask him to make something *for* you, then, can you? Your poor mother wrote to me and told me she's been having a wretched time getting to sleep at night, but since work keeps me here in the Capital and your siblings can't help, I wanted to send something back to her."

"He just left for a mission; he'll be gone for a while." Mika paused to study the look on his father's face, then swallowed, recognizing the creep of his crushing fear of disappointing this man. "H-he trusts me, though, so I shouldn't have a problem finding his notes."

Giichi smiled again, satisfied. "Could you bring them to me? I'll give it back once I've picked one."

"I...I don't see why not. I'll bring them by later."

"That's my boy."

Mika's fingers trembled as he reached for the handle of Daisuke's door later that evening. Although he knew everyone else was out, immeasurable anxiety wracked his nerves at the idea of someone seeing him. As far as he could tell, his friend hadn't yet swayed toward Obito's perception of him. Still, if anyone caught him in this room uninvited, word would inevitably get back to Daisuke when he and Obito returned to the Capital. Undoubtedly, this would forever shatter their relationship if he got caught; he'd be proving his stupid cousin right by doing what his father wanted. He would become the untrustworthy liar his father had heard Obito call him many times when he thought he could safely express such an opinion.

Besides, how could he deny a simple request from his father, who had finally begun taking an interest in him and his life over the last couple of years?

Even those idiots would get why I don't want my mother to suffer, wouldn't they? Mika's hand clamped firmly on the handle as he let himself into the room. A strange sight greeted him—Daisuke's room hadn't looked this tidy since his first week or so of living in the dormitories. The bed was perfectly made, with the sheets and duvet pulled crisply across the mattress; the resident pile of laundry that usually lived on the floor was picked up and placed in a basket at the foot of the bed, and everything else was put away neatly—it was more suspicious than its typical, haphazardly organized state. Was someone trying to hide a murder?

Mika shook his head to regain control over his rational mind, though a half-grin teased his lips when he envisioned how outraged Daisuke would act if he'd mentioned it to him. He ignored the pang of guilt that followed as he proceeded toward the desk, which was also tidier than usual.

He tried to delay what he was about to do. However, flipping through the few weathered scrolls and old texts left lying about yielded nothing as valuable as Daisuke's notes on medicines, poisons, and other tinctures. Gods, what Mika wouldn't give to have half the talent as his friend when it came to those things. He looked at the drawers again, all on the right side of the desk, tauntingly easy to access, and crouched in front of them. He discovered the bottom two drawers were mostly empty, save for some spare parchment and calligraphy tools, along with a couple of empty bottles, likely for something Daisuke had planned on making soon. Finding nothing, he sighed and stood again.

The top drawer stuck a little the first time he wrenched on it, but it came free with a second try. To his surprise, a cloud of pink powder shot out at him as soon as the drawer loosened. He coughed and spat the particles that had flown into his mouth as he blinked and waved them away, rubbing his face exhaustedly once everything finally settled. When he could finally peer inside the drawer, he saw a rounded measuring spoon like the ones used in the poisons room tied to a coiled copper wire as a makeshift spring, both sitting atop the black leather-bound book, along with a hastily scrawled note that read,

Get lost, fucker.

It wasn't in Daisuke's handwriting; the penmanship resembled Obito's. Now driven by fury, jealousy, and betrayal, Mika uprooted the journal with vicious tenacity, uncaring that he'd sent the trap flying. Something else lay wrapped in a white cloth beneath the book, but with his heart hurting for reasons he couldn't explain, he couldn't muster the curiosity to investigate, and left it alone. Mika stormed out of the room and slammed the door behind him, no longer worried about what Daisuke would think when he inevitably noticed the tampering in his room.

Not like he'll ever guess it was me, anyway. Mika wiped his stinging eyes, cursing that stupid pink powder as he retreated from the dormitory hall.

"SET MY TALISMAN UPON that stone, Priestess—it's under the moonlight and flat enough to serve as an altar. When you're ready, offer your blood and keep your first two fingers on its surface." Kanashimi wrapped their long body around Lady Shadow, barely able to contain their visible excitement as they instructed her. It was the most animated she'd ever seen the dragon-demon behave. "This works better when all six of us are together, but as I'm the strongest of my siblings, I believe we should still see success."

Lady Shadow's brows furrowed as she looked at the demon under the pale lighting. "I suppose I've never thought about it—are there really differences in strength between you and the others?"

"Grief is a powerful and ever-present thing, Priestess, and the result of much of what my brothers and sisters symbolize...or what happens when they are awakened. Starving to death from pestilence or poverty—never mind living *through* those conditions—causes grief, as does losing a loved one in battle or everything you own in a disaster. Remember, we are neutral spirits poisoned by the Goddess's sins. We are so powerful *because* of Hikari and her flawed creations, and she is why we wreak so much havoc when our spirits are abused or broken."

Lady Shadow turned the explanation over in her mind, then nodded and placed Kanashimi's talisman on the stone altar—if she overthought, she'd doubt herself, and that hint of fear could be enough to disrupt the ritual. She drew in a deep breath, then used a drop of her blood from a vial also stored around her neck to smear on the talisman's surface. Kanashimi had warned her when they first taught her about this ceremony that things could go wrong at any second unless she maintained perfect control. However, once she could communicate with the dormant spirits, she could summon other talismans from faraway places and unseal them once they arrived. She'd been warned that it might not be possible without Saigai.

Since they'd already determined they'd go to Zhu with Haruki to search for the Demon of Disaster, being able to connect with the Between Realm would be enough for now.

The talisman sat in a waning moon's light. Stained with the offering of her blood, Kanashimi and Lady Shadow each placed a hand over it and began to chant in an ancient language the Shadow Priestess never knew existed before her studies with the demon. She stayed focused on her goal—call out to Zandaka.

After a minute or two of their chanting, the talisman glowed the same green as Kanashimi's scales, and a displeased voice rumbled like distant thunder, *"And what purpose do you have for calling upon me, Servant?"*

Lady Shadow didn't care that she was grinning like an absolute fool. The story of the demons, as told by Kanashimi, said that after Zandaka battled Hikari and sealed her, an enraged Kuro flew onto the scene and challenged the Demon King. In turn, one sealed away the other, as well as the six demons. Because of the bonds inflicted by the God of Death and Darkness, Lady Shadow wouldn't be able to maintain this contact for long, but she was thrilled to bring the Demon King pleasant news.

"My constituents—rather, *your* disciple, tells me they've located Saigai's missing talisman somewhere in Zhu, my Lord. We will be leaving shortly to retrieve the Demon of Disaster and unseal him from his talisman."

"Is it Kanashimi who speaks to me?"

"I am here, my Lord, but the one you speak to is the Priestess of Shadows—a Servant foretold by your lectures in the Between Realm, and therefore the one who will unseal you from Kuro's curse."

A faint glow brought life to the pendant's surface, like a flash of lightning in a distant storm cloud, and cast a warming light on her fingers. Lady Shadow decided that, without a doubt, the Demon King demonstrated his approval in that one tiny flicker.

DAISUKE HADN'T SPOKEN TO Obito much during the first leg of their journey, tired and openly sulking over the fact that his friend had grabbed him by the ankle and dragged him to the floor to get him out of bed. At least he'd gotten the final "word" in by throwing his pillow—the fact that he'd missed was entirely beside the point. After a while, his attitude toward the ordeal had gradually changed to amusement. He still couldn't believe that Obito took the challenge seriously.

"Dragging me out of bed and forcing me to clean my room," he groused, unable to help bringing it up again; annoying Obito was, after all, one of his favorite games. "And to think, you insisted right before that you're *never* mean to me."

"You'll get over it." Obito had given him the same answer the first two times.

"Don't try and act dignified now. *You're* the one who put that note in my drawer."

"True, but watching you struggle over such a simple message was painful. I had to intervene."

"How humane." Daisuke glared at him, though he couldn't keep his laughter back for long. From the corner of his eye, he swore he caught Obito smiling, too.

Around noon, they stopped to rest in the shade by a creek. While Daisuke didn't want to acknowledge the wisdom of leaving as early as they had, it was hard to ignore as he thought of how much ground they'd already covered. He wrestled briefly with whether he owed his friend an apology for being difficult that morning, but something different came out instead.

"So, who exactly is Senator Hajime, anyway?"

Obito's brows furrowed as he snapped a sizeable stick in two. He stuck both halves in the ground like poles, then rummaged through one of their packs while saying, "I don't have a nice way of describing him."

"Fair enough, but not exactly what I meant. Aren't magistrates the ones in charge of towns?" He'd conjured quite the mental image of this man, wearing a priest's robes and an evil spirit's mask; while he was sure it was an exaggeration, what he now knew about Zhu made the picture seem reasonably accurate.

"*Most* towns or villages have a magistrate. Senator Hajime is in charge of his city and the few small villages surrounding it, which is why his title is different. Because of their sizes, those villages don't have a direct authority figure—I think there's one in the southeast swamps like that, too."

Daisuke watched as he attached a hook and bit of twine to each pole before setting each out in the water, noting the immense tension burdening his friend's face and actions. "What's with you?"

Those forest green eyes snapped up from focusing on his task, revealing an unexpected amount of agitation. He took a minute to gather his reasoning, then carefully said, "I know Master Yujin doesn't always have the final say on things, and this clearly wasn't his idea, but sending us—*you*, specifically—to Zhu is nothing more than cruelty for the sake of it."

"You're still upset about that?"

"Are you trying to say you're not?"

Daisuke's gaze settled on him again, emotions mixing in a way that defied possibility by rendering him silent, no matter how much he struggled for a response, clever or otherwise. While he'd known Obito's stances on slavery for a bit, he felt they were odd, considering his family background—he wasn't sure how he'd come to maintain them.

"Be honest with me, Obito—I mean, you're from the nobility, too. Doesn't your family own slaves?" he ventured, nervous about how his friend would react to the question or how he'd feel about the answer.

"As far as I know, we never have." He looked at Daisuke for a long moment, then returned to the creek. "I guess that's hardly a claim to decency."

"I think you're the first person I've met who's as hard on the nobility as I am." Daisuke laughed, which made Obito glance at him again, this time with a small, self-conscious smile on his features. "I knew there was a reason we got along."

As sundown neared, they'd already covered a good amount of territory on the Westbound Road. Obito realized there might've been some wisdom in Daisuke not wanting to rush, though he'd hardly admit it aloud. They could only go so far on foot in a single day, and no matter what they did, it'd still be over a month before they reached Zhu. The scent of impending rain filled the air not long after they found a comfortable spot to sit on a fallen log, and through the leaves, they pointed out how heavy the gray clouds above appeared. Despite shared grumbles and complaints, it encouraged them to get back to their feet and make camp quickly. They found a nice little thicket several yards back from the main road, hopefully far from the view of bandits or other travelers.

Since they'd followed the creek as far as it would take them and already had a second meal of smoked fish, they concluded their supply of hard-tack would suffice if either one became hungry again. It also meant they wouldn't build a fire; they'd leave again in the early morning.

Rain pattered gently against the small tent. Despite their bickering to get it correctly set up and tied down, they were proud of their success, as neither would dare to call himself a survivalist. They dug a hole big enough to wedge their lantern in, perfect for keeping them warm, providing light, and hopefully minimizing the risk of everything catching fire. After a few bites of the terrible, crumbly hardtack, they decided it was time to settle in for the night, but hadn't moved much beyond sitting across from each other on dry bedrolls, idly chatting as Obito made notes in a blank journal he'd brought along. Master Yujin expected them to draft a report about the mission when they returned to the Capital, as he did with any onmitsu or hitokiri; Obito didn't want to wrack his memory for things later.

Daisuke bore no such concerns. The most eventful part of all this would be whatever happened when they got to Zhu, which he was sure would be as unremarkable as the walk there—rather, he *hoped* nothing noteworthy would arise while they were in the city. Very few things he might become entangled with had the possibility of ending particularly well, which, Daisuke guessed, wasn't entirely unexpected at this point in his life. Still, he had a *slight* sense of self-preservation that told him when to stay out of trouble.

Daisuke wrinkled his nose at the idea, mind buzzing through several things with no clear path and refusing to settle on one consistent thing. Instead of dwelling, he let his hair down from its messy ponytail and stripped off his shirt to prepare for sleep. He'd once spent the night hiding in a utility shed on the plantations to avoid his father; while that was hardly the same as camping in the woods overnight, Daisuke didn't have the apprehension toward it he was sure he should've felt. If anything, unbeknownst to his friend, he was looking forward to getting some decent rest from not sleeping alone.

"Can I ask you about something?" Obito cautiously ventured once he finished folding his shirt and placed it on the end of the bedroll, catching his attention again.

"Sure, shoot."

"The scars on your arms and shoulders."

Daisuke paused, knowing he shouldn't be surprised that Obito had observed the cuts in this small space. The collection of marks on his skin hadn't grown too much since the first time he'd hurt himself, but his feelings of anger toward the world had.

Still not looking at Obito, who usually wasn't one to prod about these things, Daisuke answered with his own question, "What of them?"

He sighed heavily as soon as the words left his mouth. If he'd remembered his scars in the first place, he wouldn't have removed his shirt, but seeing them daily gave them an odd permanence in his brain. He hadn't wanted to show proof of his self-inflicted outbursts to anyone—according to public opinion, those who harmed themselves were dangerous and deranged—but he supposed if anyone had to know, it should be Obito; he'd heard plenty about Daisuke's life before the military by now.

"I won't make you tell me," Obito said quietly.

"No, I want to. It's just...*hard*." Daisuke mulled over how he could best explain himself. "Do you ever feel just...pissed off at the world? Or like there's so much negativity inside you that you can't figure out how to make it go away without *something* to release it?"

"Those voices *telling* you that you're nothing?" Obito unexpectedly added as one who deeply understood might. Daisuke's breath hitched in his throat as he watched his friend's eyes settle on his shoulder again, and he slowly nodded. The scars didn't mar the exceptional work of the tattooist who had placed the higanbana on his arm—Daisuke admired it too much to allow it, no matter how out-of-body he otherwise felt during those incidents of cutting himself. Finally, Obito took a deep breath and looked away, continuing with, "They're wrong, Daisuke. I'm not sure how much that helps you, but I hope you know it's true."

Something strange happened when Obito's words fell on Daisuke's ears; while General Aki and Master Yujin had their own ways of showing they didn't believe he was worthless, he'd never known anyone to state those things so openly. Because of how often Obito was blunt, he had no reason to believe it was anything besides honesty, but hearing it directly made a hard lump form in his throat and swallowing difficult. He couldn't take his eyes off his partner's while simultaneously worrying that his emotions wouldn't stay under control if he looked for longer. Obeying impulse, he remained mindful of the lantern between them as he stretched across the tent and tightly hugged Obito.

"They're wrong about you, too," he said softly.

Obito froze at the unexpected touch—before he could decide whether he liked it, or what it might mean if he did, he half-heartedly scolded, "Let go of me."

"R-right, sorry." Daisuke retracted and settled on his bedroll while Obito moved to pack away the journal. When he rested his head on his arms, he stole another glance at his partner, and a small smile tugged on his lips.

After a moment, Obito added, "When we get back, you should go see the medics in the infirmary at the Palace. They'll have something to make the scarring lighter."

In his dreams that night, Daisuke stood on a never-ending slab of smooth obsidian in a dark cavern—only, the surface didn't appear as lifeless as one might expect. Subtle, sparkling swirls of deep purple and blue weaved in every direction from beneath his feet, giving the cave a dim glow of the same colors as they gracefully swam around him like koi. From the stone came a circle of green light to surround him until they split into six columns. His hand rose, but he didn't feel as though he'd entirely controlled the action. The jade beams grew brighter, and six objects floated toward him from them, as if riding on a breeze he couldn't feel against his skin. They spun around him once in a glowing halo before one came forward, timid in a way as it landed weightlessly in his outstretched palm. When Daisuke peered at it, he noticed it looked startlingly like the odd good luck charm he'd left hidden away in his desk drawer. Although there were differences among them he couldn't fully make out, so did the others. Before he could examine it further, he sensed something else in the cavern; Daisuke looked away from the stunning display in his hand to see the white wolf charging toward him, shifting into a raven that burst into light as it crashed into his chest.

A concert of songbirds awoke him the following morning. Despite the odd nature of his dream, he'd slept more soundly than he'd initially predicted he would. Propping himself up on his elbows to lift his chest off the mat beneath him and look around, he soon became conscious of the fact that he was alone in the tent; he deemed it wise to get out of bed before Obito could repeat the previous morning's *horribly* rude awakening. Beads of dew and leftover raindrops noisily dribbled down the canvas flap when he pushed it aside to poke his head out, searching for his friend, whom he found several feet away. Obito stood with his back to the tent, adjusting his lapels and ensuring the knot in his belt was tight. Not wanting to startle him, Daisuke waited until he was sure he'd finished before slinking outside to begin the day.

"About time you woke up," Obito dryly commented when he rounded on his approaching companion.

Daisuke grinned, which quickly overruled the scowl he'd first attempted as a response and only intensified when Obito's expression shifted into suspicion. "And here I thought you'd be enjoying the silence."

"Fair point—you *do* talk a lot."

"Sometimes you answer, and I think that might be worse, so maybe I should start questioning *your* sanity now and then."

"My sanity doesn't have anything to do with it." He smiled a bit, as if to himself. "There's another branch of the creek that way, so you can wash your face before we go."

"How convenient." Still grinning, Daisuke started for the creek. "I'll be back in a minute."

When Daisuke returned, they didn't waste much more time on a conversation before deciding to pack their campsite. Since he understood Obito wouldn't compromise on leaving early—and wanting to show a bit of gratitude for being allowed to sleep in—he didn't fight much when it came time to leave. However, the prospect of inching closer to Zhu tied a knot in his stomach. Even if it went unmentioned, he knew Obito sensed it, and likely had the same feelings; it wasn't as if the outrage he'd displayed to Master Yujin was for show. That, at least, Daisuke could trust wholeheartedly.

They followed the Westbound Road through farming fields, up steep paths through the forest and some of the lowermost rocky foothills of

Hikari's Range, trudging through the last few hot days and taking shelter from end-of-summer storms when they could in the towns or villages they encountered along the way. Between fresh stream fish, foraged mushrooms, and wild loquats they found growing on bushes, the land cared for them well during their journey—a luxury they wouldn't have on the return trip home when they'd be racing against the year's first frost and snowfall. All around them, vibrant green leaves gradually changed to their fiery autumn colors, which indicated they hadn't gone too far off schedule.

For the most part, Daisuke had managed to push aside his misgivings as they traveled along, but when they came to a village named Kagechi, every bit of fear and anxiety rushed at him once more. Several miles remained until they arrived at Zhu when expected—give or take a day or two, as one section of the road was nearly impassable due to heavy rainfall, and they'd had to make their own detour around it. Thankfully, this far end of Perena tended to be a little drier during the impending season, which meant the dirt beneath their feet kicked up dust as they went and in slightly stronger winds. Daisuke waited until they were outside Kagechi, then set his pack aside, rolled back his sleeves, and knelt on the ground. Despite the traffic going toward the city along with them, he knew the early afternoon light wouldn't provide much of a way to disguise himself from those they passed.

Obito stopped his task of hiding away their sidearms—which had thankfully remained unused thus far—to watch as Daisuke patted himself with dirt, rubbing it into his skin before shaking off the excess. "What are you doing?"

"Old trick my grandmother taught me," he explained without pause—even for Daisuke, this was highly unusual behavior.

"Daisuke, people are looking. I didn't think we *wanted* to attract attention."

"Point taken, but I'll be quick. Listen, Nomadic skin doesn't burn in the sun, but summers can get ridiculously hot on Okara. We weren't built for those temperatures, so field workers do this to keep cool. Plus, if you find the right shade...."

He raised his arm to show Obito; from this proximity, it was easy to tell his slightly deeper skin tone was nothing more than dust from the road, but if anyone noticed him from further away, they likely wouldn't think twice about it. A strange, unidentifiable emotion wriggled in his stomach—this was a precaution he'd never assume to take, no matter which city he approached. He knelt in front of Daisuke and coated his fingers with dirt. Those intensely expressive violet eyes settled on him, watching with curiosity and mistrust at first, which soon gave way to something else Obito didn't recognize. He cautiously brought his hand toward a bare patch on Daisuke's cheek, streaking a heavy line across his skin.

Ignoring the jump to his heart, Daisuke said, "Figures. I always miss a spot."

"You shouldn't have to go through all this."

Daisuke blinked to shake away the surprised look that involuntarily came onto his face, then quickly patted extra dirt off his cheek before shrugging casually. "True. The tattoo probably makes me worthless, anyway—you know, like branded cattle or whatever."

Obito rolled his eyes in an effort to ignore such a painfully awkward fact as they started on his left arm. "Well, you aren't wrong, but that isn't what I meant."

He had to look elsewhere, letting their conversation dissolve into nothing as Obito turned to clean his hands on the nearby grass, and neither spoke again until they were approaching a guarded archway carved into the stone wall surrounding Zhu. Daisuke bit his lip; he was about to willingly march into a busy slave port with his wits and partner to protect him, and he wasn't terribly confident that Obito's presence alone would be enough to keep shady slavers off his back.

"We'll make this as quick as possible," Obito told him quietly. "We only need to stay long enough to find the potter, collect the artifact, and then get the hell out of here. We should be fine if we stick together at all times."

"I'm impressed—you almost sounded convinced at that last part."

Obito gave him a sour look, but the men guarding the gate swiftly stole any rebuttal on his part.

"Halt right there, you two," one gruffly ordered, glaring down his nose at them. Obito swallowed nervously, nearly ready to pray that Daisuke wouldn't snark their way into trouble with the soldiers. "You little sneaks are a bit young to be traveling by yourselves, aren't you?"

"We're here on behalf of Master Yujin," Obito responded quickly, cutting off his partner's chance to speak. From the corner of his eye, he thought he saw half a smirk appear on Daisuke's lips before his expression faded into a mask of neutrality. *What an annoying little demon.*

"I'll assume you have some documentation, then," the second guard growled.

"Right here, yes." He handed the towering men a rolled parchment Master Yujin had signed and tucked into the supplies left on his bed before they'd left the Capital; once he'd read it to confirm what it said, he'd kept it as separate as possible from everything else in his pack.

"*I'll* assume that settles matters between us, then?" Daisuke asked with a shameless hint of sarcasm, avoiding direct eye contact with the guards. Obito flinched.

The first guard didn't take kindly to Daisuke's tone, but let out a frustrated sigh after rereading Master Yujin's undeniable signature. "Fine, but if there's a peep of trouble out of you, you're getting sent back to the Capital in a prisoner cart."

"Understood, sir." Daisuke smiled. The guard snorted but begrudgingly stood aside so they could proceed. Once they'd placed some distance between themselves and the gate, he sighed with minimal relief, grimly aware the hard part wasn't over yet. "Pleasant sots, weren't they?"

"Not unlike someone else I know." Obito also looked as if he'd had enough for one day. "We should find where we're staying soon—it feels like we're already pushing our luck."

"Couldn't agree more," Daisuke said, subconsciously moving closer to Obito's side.

Twenty-One
Kill the Messengers

Zhu didn't have the same sprawl over the land as the Capital, but being the most prominent slave port on Perena meant it was still a city of impressive size and held great economic importance to the Empire. Its narrow, crowded streets did little to lessen Daisuke's anxieties about entering the city. Though he stuck close to Obito, he felt like so much as blinking would separate them and place him in unspeakable danger. His heart pounded with each discerning glance he caught from others—rationally, he knew those people likely hadn't seen them, but were looking elsewhere in the same direction as where they walked.

Gods, what he wouldn't give to listen to *that* part of himself instead.

"Daisuke," Obito said in a quiet but firm tone, jolting him out of his head. "Breathe."

He swallowed, then inhaled slowly, centering himself in reality again. However, unable to thoroughly shake his fears, he rushed forward a few paces and cautiously hooked his arm around Obito's—the more he looked like he "belonged" somewhere, or *to* someone, the better off he'd be. Daisuke heard a faint grumble from his friend, but when he looked up, Obito was busily scanning their surroundings instead of paying attention to what he'd done.

"Are we at the inn yet?"

"Not quite, but," Obito finally wriggled his arm free when he noticed a group of women near a storefront who had stopped their conversation to stare at them pointedly; a faint hint of red colored his cheeks. "We should be getting close if Master Yujin's directions are worth anything."

"Gods willing." Daisuke sighed as he straightened his posture again, grateful when he noted the ladies minding their own business once more. He'd forgotten that it wouldn't be enough to think about how *he* presented himself to other people while in the public's eye, but also how he interacted with Obito, although that didn't appear to be what concerned his partner when he pulled away. To exercise further caution, he pulled up his hood to ensure his face wouldn't attract further attention; at least the early autumn weather helped the action look natural.

Even so, the scattered responses they'd already received spurned Obito into asserting, "We should move faster."

After a few more twists and turns, they found their destination as early evening encroached, and hurried toward the main door. Daisuke didn't bother reading the inn's name, which was elegantly painted on a sign staked into the ground near a stone pathway lined with barren rose bushes and pagoda statues crawling with green lichen patches. Instead, he kept right at Obito's heels, daring to take his companion's sleeve in hand again as they pushed through the inn's crowd. In these smaller, less opulent establishments, the main room commonly functioned as a tavern and was where guests requested their accommodations. Fortunately, it also meant that their payment would cover at least one meal per day. The room suffered from lazy upkeep, as determined by the number of loose or rotted floorboards, cobwebbed corners, and a broken oil lamp with a pile of shattered glass sitting near it on a table, but it seemed like a pleasant enough place, given their budget and need to lay low.

However, as for the other patrons...

Daisuke and Obito both subtly tilted their heads to take stock of their surroundings while the frazzled innkeeper had his back turned to search for his guestbook and a key to the room they'd paid for; neither wanted to witness the fallout of when he spilled a half-empty tankard of ale onto his own feet, anyway. While Daisuke was by now all too aware of Zhu's most prevalent industry, it didn't prevent the surge of heartbreak and anger he felt when he noticed a few Northern Nomads in heavy chains attached to boisterously drunken men, who occasionally paused to demand more food or drink from their captives by yanking on their bindings and all but spitting the commands at them. His fists clenched as his body subconsciously shifted; Grandmaster Norio might've had a conniption if he saw these "quality-bred" slaves in a dusty tavern like this, but Daisuke was fully prepared to bash in the heads of every man he saw pulling on those chains like leashes.

Obito nudged him, breaking his state of mind, then handed him the wrought-iron key to their room as they moved away from the counter, although it was apparent where his gaze had also fallen.

"Come on," he said quietly as he tore his eyes away from the scene and placed his hand on Daisuke's to keep him grounded. "Let's get settled."

"I doubt that'll be possible until I can hole up in *my* room at home for a week...or a month."

Obito cautiously patted his friend's shoulder. As much as he wished otherwise, there wasn't much more he could do to mollify the situation on Daisuke's end, a hard truth they'd both begrudgingly accepted somewhere along the Westbound Road. At least, in surprising contrast to what they'd seen so far, their room was decent in size and cleanliness. After swiping a hand over the mattress to check for mites, Daisuke determined the bed was safe enough for sleep, and they both heaved a sigh of tentative relief while setting their bags on the floor.

"I have an idea," Daisuke announced as his partner checked the number of coals in an unlit brazier sitting in the corner.

Obito turned to him and raised an eyebrow. "I'm sure I'll object, but I'm also intrigued. Go ahead."

"Rude, but fair." The little nuisance snickered. "What do you say to white leaf and something better than hardtack for dinner? We already have more than enough money since we're sharing the room."

"That *is* stealing, you know."

"From the budget Master Yujin gave us—"

"—With the idea that it'd be more expensive, and have two beds—"

"—So *you* know that isn't much of an objection." Daisuke grinned in earnest this time as he removed his cloak, eyes bright with mischief. "Is it really that bad? If we're careful, we'll still have plenty left to stock up on supplies before heading back to the Capital while being well within our means."

Obito thought for a moment. "I'll be really upset with you if I go along with this just to find out that your idea of something better than hardtack is plain soba—and if you so much as think of shaking off all that dirt in this room."

Daisuke touched his face, then brushed his fingers along his skin and wiped away some of the fake color coating it. Unable to stop himself, he smeared it on Obito's cheek, receiving perhaps the most intensely outraged expression he'd ever seen his friend make. It took every ounce of self-control he possessed to stifle his laughter.

"You're such a fucking menace," Obito complained when he touched the grainy splotch on his cheek, then shot him a withering glare before he opened their door again.

"That's bathtime, I take it."

Daisuke tossed his hairbrush on the bed and flopped down on it once they'd both returned from a much-needed soak in a pleasantly hot bath, sinking into the softness beneath him as he stretched his arms over his head.

"Now what?"

"We send a message to the potter and his wife—Gero and Rin—in the morning; the innkeeper says a courier comes by early." Obito hesitated, looking as if he wasn't sure where to go, then sat beside him. "When they decide they're ready to hand it over, we retrieve the artifact."

"Right. The Okami artifact that, by some means, found its way to Zhu."

"You don't believe it, either, do you?"

Daisuke shook his head, then changed the subject. "How long do you think we'll be in this shithole of a city?"

"That depends on them, but at least through the Harvest Moon Festival. Don't you remember what Master Yujin said during the briefing?"

"That happened a while ago, so not really, no."

Obito pinched the skin between his eyebrows and huffed. "He told us to give them at least two weeks to answer since the husband is likely preparing stock to sell at the Winter Festival. After that, if they take any longer, we can show up uninvited and take it."

Daisuke huffed, staring at the ceiling with an affronted expression at the information. Eventually, he grabbed his brush and sat upright again, flashing his demonic grin at Obito. "If that's the case, it's a good thing we're on our way out to get some white leaf—sounds like I'm going to need a mountain of it to get through this. What's this harvest moon festival you mentioned, anyway?"

"It isn't much different than the Spring and Winter Festival. No one really celebrates it around the Capital, but it's still popular in the Wen Valley and other farming communities around Perena. Zhu isn't involved in agriculture, but since its surrounding villages are, and plenty of people from those places *do* come here for...other things, they probably see that as reason enough to celebrate," Obito explained. He blankly watched Daisuke comb through his shoulder-length hair, then carefully asked, "How are you holding up?"

"Fine for now, I guess." He set the brush aside, timidly peeking at his friend. That flash of vulnerability was incredibly short-lived before he hauled himself onto his feet and switched subjects again. "Come on, let's find some food."

Most apothecaries and medics knew someone who carried dried white leaf or had some of their own on hand. However, being underage meant buying it came with a hefty tax as a bribe for keeping any authorities oblivious. Obito was more than willing to pay a premium if it meant going through reputable avenues, which Daisuke didn't initially understand; thankfully, he stopped trying to argue with him when he explained why going to a back-alley dealer made his palms itch with anxiety. Although Obito knew the white leaf itself wasn't why the assassins had killed Itsuki, he also knew they wouldn't have gone down those unfamiliar roads if they'd accepted their circumstances in the first place. Nearly two years later—which seemed impossible—and certain things about that night still hadn't left him.

Even so, Daisuke and Obito admitted to feeling slightly more content with their surroundings once they'd procured their supply and ate their fill of a deliciously spicy curry they'd shared from a neighboring food vendor.

After walking about for a bit under the protection of nighttime and lanternlight, they silently made their way to the rooftop of another inn on the city's wealthier end; the building right beside it was a fabric store, while on the other side, separated by an alley, was a jewelry shop. Much to Daisuke's devious delight, once they were settled on their new perch overlooking the cityscape, now little more than layers of shadow with occasional spots of light, Obito surprised him with a long, thin metal pipe designed explicitly for smoking white leaf, with no explanation of where he'd gotten it.

Once they'd passed the pipe back and forth a few times, Daisuke asked through a fit of coughing, "What would happen if someone *actually* moved a mountain?"

"An avalanche," Obito responded, to which they both laughed.

Inspired by their ease of conversation and the buzzed, blissful feeling in his mind, another question popped into the shorter boy's head, "What's the most disturbing dream you've ever had?"

"I wouldn't know. I never remember them."

"Shame—mine are always so...*vivid*. I once dreamt about a girl getting murdered. Her name was Misame." Daisuke didn't know how he had that information, nor why he was so sure it was correct, but it was as clear as any other fact he'd come across. Not wanting to dwell on it, he took back the pipe when Obito offered it to him. "The ones about the dragons are better, but also scarier. It's never *just* a dream with Northern Nomads, you know."

Obito looked at him before his eyes fell to the street below as he turned a question over, until he finally said, "Isn't that a myth?"

"Trust me, I wish it was. I never had any until I came to Perena."

Obito remained silent for a moment, then took the pipe back from Daisuke.

The effects created by the white leaf began to wear off somewhere about an hour or more later, so they agreed it was time to return to their room for sleep. They helped each other from their perch, and Daisuke could tell by music and loud, overlapping conversations that the neighboring street was still quite lively; although further exploration tempted him, he knew Obito wouldn't be up for it, as their travels had already exhausted them thoroughly, and the allure of sleeping in a real bed was tough to argue against. Curiosity could always wait, and he'd gathered early on that acting impulsively could result in one of those disgusting collars strapped around his throat. The way the white leaf had relaxed his nerves was a welcome relief, but only a temporary solution to his restlessness.

Several windows along the inn's bottom floor facing the alley were aglow with warm lamplight from behind thick paper screens, and though they tried being stealthy, stacked crates lined the other building's outer wall. Daisuke's body still buzzed from the white leaf; he trembled or jerked uncontrollably, which hindered the carefulness of his steps despite having the help of slight illumination. A glance at Obito said he wasn't doing much better; they were further under the influence than they'd assumed initially. Normally, Daisuke wouldn't consider this a problem, but when Obito unexpectedly looked back at him, he had to muffle a snicker with his hands. Soon, they were both snickering again, which evidently pissed off some ill-tempered god who hated humans—a second of Daisuke forgetting to watch his footing ended with him tripping into one of the wooden boxes, jutting out slightly from its stack. Panicked, he stretched his hand out for Obito, catching his lapels in a fist, which knocked him off balance as well, and brought them together in a clumsy tangle against the jewelry store's wall rather than stabilizing the pair.

Gods, what a racket. Of all the thoughts that should've raced through Daisuke's mind then, he hadn't expected to feel such utter disappointment in the one that stuck. Obito started pushing himself off, but Daisuke realized they wouldn't have time to get themselves out of there when concerned voices trickled toward them from behind the windows. Thinking on his feet, he grabbed Obito by the lapels and forced him to lean in close.

"You know," he muttered with a slight, devious grin as he lowered his lashes to avoid letting the lights shine in his eyes, "with our faces this close, someone might think we're kissing."

"Hikari's sake, Daisuke." Obito rolled his eyes. However, when a window behind him inevitably slid open less than a heartbeat later, he held in whatever he originally wanted to say. He couldn't meet Daisuke's eyes. *This is ridiculous. But better than letting them believe we're trying to steal something.*

"What in Hikari's name is going *on* out here?!" A woman demanded. She irritably snapped her fingers for their attention after a brief pause. "You two! Take it somewhere else!"

Adding to the illusion, Daisuke wiped his lips as Obito drew back. He had to stifle a mischievous cackle beneath his palm. They glanced at two highly unimpressed women standing at the window with falsely embarrassed expressions before hurrying from the alley, not wanting to press their luck with other antics. Merely getting scolded for slinking around at night in this area was beyond fortunate—why test the gods when they chose to be kind?

"Teenagers," Daisuke heard the older of the two mutter in disgust when she felt they were out of earshot. He looked at Obito, who hadn't heard her, and snickered.

LADY SHADOW PEERED INTO the alleyway again once she was sure the boys had gone, then closed her window. She frowned at her empty glass once she settled into her seat once more. "Noisy, obnoxious teenage boys. Quite the odd pair, though."

Haruki's brows knitted as she poured her lady more wine. "What do you mean, my Lady?"

"Not that I have anything personal against the Northern Nomads, but Zhu isn't exactly the city where one would want to get caught gallivanting with a slaveborn. I know what I saw, though. That other boy *was* Giahatian." Lady Shadow's brows furrowed as she lifted her wine glass to her red-painted lips, allowing the scents of blackberry and oak to fill her senses. The image of that boy's face burrowed into her mind, morphing with another's from her past, one she wasn't prepared to confront. "I don't suppose he might've been from an abolitionist bloodline—at least, that would make sense."

"I'm afraid I'm no help this time, my Lady." Haruki set down the decanter and gave her a nervous smile. "Misame knew which families we ought to avoid better than I could ever hope to remember."

"Unfortunately, I suppose you're right, though I suggest you not bring that traitor's name into future conversations. *She's* why we had to come to this wretched city in the first place."

"R-right. Of course, Lady Shadow. I'm sorry."

Lady Shadow merely sipped the deep red wine Haruki poured for her, signaling that, for now, her words would remain unpunished. The girl struggled to hold her tongue at times, but the matron tended to exercise more lenience with her than she did with the average person; she was a skilled fighter, but only because the poor girl had suffered through childhood at Genjing. If anything bled pure evil, it was Kurushima's more brutal counterpart in Perena's northwest; they raised Haruki until the age of twelve, when her blundering idiots called "masters" finally recognized their mistake—they should've executed her. Instead, the cruel slugs left her to freeze to death in drifting snow; somehow, she'd survived and found her way to the cult. Those fools also never figured out that Haruki had a slight touch of healing magic—there was no reliable means of predicting whom it would bless—which she used to restore and roughen the voices of cult members without irreparably harming their throats. She'd done it to Lady Shadow before they entered Zhu, and reversed the effect once they'd settled upon staying at this inn. Thanks to the patronage of the nobility who funded them, they were able to afford a rather luxurious stay; rooms were spacious, with a small dining and seating area, along with a screen to separate the beds.

Lady Shadow's gaze settled on Haruki's katana leaning against the far wall.

"Haruki," she said. She placed her wine glass on the small table in front of her, the soft velvet in her natural voice bringing the young woman's dark eyes to her once more as she stopped worrying about gathering her hair into a messy bun. "Even if my assumptions about them are wrong, those boys looked to be wearing suspiciously military clothing, don't you agree?"

"Yes, my Lady, but it didn't exactly match hitokiri or footsoldier uniforms."

Lady Shadow's eyes narrowed. "Then we could be dealing with the damned onmitsu, which poses a more significant threat. The Emperor may be an egotistical, bumbling fool, but I can promise the Intelligence Master is *not*."

"If I may, my Lady, my former masters *did* say that, to keep their operations discreet, the onmitsu rarely contact stationed soldiers unless they need assistance or otherwise instructed. So, even if they are here for the Talisman of Saigai, they likely haven't told the commanding officer at the barracks about their mission or alerted him to their presence in the city—*especially* if one is a slaveborn. Even when they voluntarily enlist, infantry captains treat them as second-class citizens at best. It's pure horror if they get conscripted to Kurushima."

"I see...then, perhaps, this isn't all bad. Haruki, you clever girl, I believe you've given me our answer. We should seek them out so we can follow them. With any luck, they'll take us directly to our traitor's sister."

"But...won't *we* be the suspicious ones at that point, my Lady?"

"My dear, haven't you realized our advantage?" Lady Shadow patted her cheek. "No one *ever* suspects a woman."

Daisuke's dreams were always unsettling, never made sense, and frequently woke him from sleep in the dead of night drenched in sweat or trembling in terror. His mother once said the Raven God gave Northern Nomads a gift in the form of these nocturnal visions, but as things stood, he was certain they were a curse.

The night after they arrived in Zhu, his dreams took him back to his room in the Capital, standing before his desk that had all three drawers opened; the bottom two were covered in marks and cracks, splintering from the force with which someone had ripped them open, while a more careful approach must've been taken with the top. There was no sign of the trap he'd set. In fact, the drawer's barren insides made it appear as though no one had ever placed a single thing inside it. He blinked, and suddenly, his scalpel was there, coated in fresh blood and surrounded by a spatter pattern that indicated heavy violence. He sharply sucked in a breath and stepped back at the sight, then yelped when he tripped over something he couldn't see on the floor.

He caught his fall on the corner of the bed, but was now face-to-face with a small wooden box. The stone walls encasing his room fell away one by one as if they were poorly stacked wooden planks, eventually leaving nothing but the wooden floor he stood upon in a void. The box rattled, and the odd charm General Aki gave him rolled out from behind it, standing on end as if it were sentient. It did another lap around the container, this time stopping at the front, now facing Daisuke. His breath hitched, and the object rose above the box.

Daisuke cried out when both went up in flames, but a loud, otherworldly roar stopped him in his tracks when he reached out to quell the fire. When he blinked again, his surroundings shifted once more. He was staring at a reflection of himself, covered in bright red blood spots. Panicked, he looked down at his arms, unable to tear his eyes away from the crimson oozing out of half a dozen distinct self-inflicted wounds on each forearm. The bellowing call sounded overhead again, and Daisuke's skin slowly crackled and shattered like fragile glass. Black smoke billowed out from the cracks.

Daisuke awoke shaking in terror, nearly hyperventilating as he stared into nothing but the darkness swallowing the ceiling. Silence surrounded him save for Obito's deep, steady breathing, which took several minutes to fully register in his mind. He sat up in bed to confirm he was still wedged between the wall and his friend, clutching his heart as it hammered against his chest, silently begging for calmness to return to his body.

"Fuck's sake," he sighed into the quiet room when his heart and breathing finally slowed to their normal rhythm.

He heard shuffling and voices in the hallway, but judging by the cadence and slurred speech, it was merely a group of drunks returning from the taverns. Obito didn't so much as stir at the noise they made as they went by their door. Once he was sure they were gone, Daisuke maneuvered himself from the bed without disturbing his friend, went to the washrooms to relieve himself, and splashed some chilly water on his face. By the time he returned, exhaustion stung at his eyes—he'd examined how bloodshot they were in the mirror above the basins by the baths—and the heaviness in his eyelids made him feel as though he needed to squint to keep them propped open enough to see. It was a good sign.

Daisuke crawled back onto the mattress, relieved he still had enough wherewithal to let Obito continue sleeping, and decided his friend had the right idea. A shiver from the cold autumn night went through his body, even once he burrowed under the warmth and comfort of the quilt he'd picked out, so he huddled closer to the other boy. Thankfully, he didn't have to wait long for sleep to reclaim him, this time a deep and dreamless rest.

TWENTY-TWO
HARVEST

MOONRISE ON THE FESTIVAL night had Obito's mind on high alert; it'd been a week since they first arrived in Zhu, and they hadn't heard anything from Gero or Rin since he'd sent out a correspondence. On top of it, Daisuke had expressed a desire to interact with the ongoing festivities, which meant they'd be out in the open. While that was hardly the worst scenario, they'd tried to limit their trips outside the inn over the last few days, and he felt they'd press their luck by going into any areas where people might not expect to see a pair like them. In a vain and rather clumsy attempt to protect his friend's sanity, Obito had neglected to say anything about the end-of-harvest slave auctions impending after the enormous orange moon sank below the horizon for another year, but all jokes aside, Daisuke wasn't stupid—he could tell his friend had picked up on the signs of the preparations that were already underway. Truthfully, he thought they'd be leaving Zhu long before that happened.

He entered the quiet courtyard, lit by strings of paper lanterns overhead, at the inn's back in time to see Daisuke's downward arc from a no-handed cartwheel, using the form and grace Retsuko had instructed him to practice while she and her troupe were away. It might still take him some time to figure out how to apply the movements in combat, but Obito could already see the confidence he'd started to gain from this new perspective on training. The innkeeper, looking relieved to have some personal time and free entertainment, clapped delightedly from the overturned bucket he'd sat upon when Daisuke landed softly on his feet without stumbling. Daisuke turned to him and gave his audience a cheeky bow, which was also when he saw Obito standing near the entryway.

His cocky grin turned into an embarrassed little smile. "Not bad, right?"

"Not at all." Obito returned the expression as he felt the better portion of his worries melt away for now; it felt as if his mind had temporarily gone blank for some reason. "Retsuko might even agree."

"You think so?" Daisuke blushed at his own enthusiasm, then shoved his hands in his pockets. "Come on, don't tease me like that."

"We both know I'd do much better than that if I wanted to tease you about it."

"You're always so mean to me."

"There you two go again with the bickering. Don't you ever give it a rest?" the innkeeper playfully scolded with a smirk as he rose from his perch. Upon noting their blank stares, he switched the subject. "Now listen. If I can help it, I don't want to see a single soul around this inn for the next few hours, including either of you. You can give me that much, right?"

"We should manage." Daisuke looked at Obito. "Shall we?"

Obito rolled his eyes. "Fine."

The square where the city held the main festivities was already buzzing with activity by the time they arrived. As Obito had indicated when they first spoke about the event, it wasn't much different than what anyone might find on display during the Spring and Winter Festivals, but those were some of Daisuke's favorite times of year. Although he thought he'd gotten more than his fill of it for the year on their journey across the Westbound Road, the deliciously smoky scent of freshly grilled shioyaki tempted Daisuke toward the vendor selling it; Obito didn't argue with the idea, either, likely because neither had eaten yet. Besides, his agreement had the black-haired boy acting as though he'd won something—he didn't see a reason to douse his spirits.

Lively music plucked from koto strings caught Daisuke's attention as they quietly ate in a comparatively rowdy, densely crowded seating area. Bright-eyed with curiosity, he peeked out at the player from under his cloak's hood when the man accompanying her lifted a flute to his lips to join the song. He noticed some nearby women excitedly grabbing their partners by the shirtsleeve to enter a slightly larger crowd on the square's edge.

"Dancing," he commented, halfway to himself. He looked at his friend with a teasing smirk once they'd finished their meals, and gestured toward the others participating. "What do you say, Obito?"

"You're going to annoy me until I say yes, aren't you?" He felt alarmed by the idea, though the subtle flash of panic in his eyes quickly faded. He hadn't done that since his cousin's wedding.

"Such mistrust," he gasped, then genuinely smiled as he got to his feet. "Besides, why not? Just one? I'll lead."

"You're too short to lead." Obito tried not to grin when Daisuke shot him a dirty look. "Good thing this isn't a formal dance."

THE FOLLOWING DAY, OBITO was forced from sleep by a painful nudge to his lower back; he was barely clinging to the edge of the bed. Although he'd slept on top of the main covers while Daisuke slept underneath, he'd still somehow ended up with his friend's feet on his spine. He regretted letting him have the half shoved against the wall—it gave him too much leverage. Now begrudgingly awake and upright, he wrapped the quilt around himself and shot Daisuke a glare from over his shoulder when he heard a sleepy mumble, followed by the other boy turning onto his stomach.

Something tells me you did that on purpose, and I will *get you back for it.* Obito rolled his eyes, agitated. From one fourteen-year-old to another, he didn't think he needed to explain to Daisuke that he wasn't alone in how much he enjoyed sleeping. However, since mornings had been his best way to find time to be alone lately, and he liked being the first one awake, he chose not to rouse Daisuke yet. When the annoyance he'd felt at his rude awakening subsided, he decided to go for a bath while the day was still quiet; he wouldn't have much longer to enjoy this peace.

Daisuke was still slumbering when he returned, blissfully unaware the day had already begun, and his unrestrained black tresses were messily fanned out in every direction as if someone had spilled ink on his pillow. Obito watched him for a moment, then looked at the spot beside him, now occupied by his folded quilt, and for once indulged in the temptation to crawl back into bed for more rest.

MISAME HADN'T MADE MANY mistakes while in the cult's service—no other follower could make up for her absence. However, a piece of information she thought would never betray her turned into something far more detrimental than she could've imagined. She frequently spoke to Lady Shadow about her family, namely her sister, whom she'd spent many years profoundly resenting. Their parents had sowed the seeds while the girls were growing up, constantly comparing one to the other at every possible instance. Misame sought her own path away from them as soon as possible, leading her to the man who ultimately brought her to Lady Shadow.

Although most of the information Misame had provided became largely disregarded, Lady Shadow *had* remembered the sister's name—she'd known a girl in her youth called by the same. She'd devoted a better part of her week to searching Zhu for a potter's wife named Rin without much luck; her patience was wearing thin. As she solitarily roamed the streets on the morning following the Harvest Moon festival, watching for any signs of other life through the frosty early autumn fog, she finally found an end to her search.

A gangly-looking courier who ambled about in a half-drunken state from the previous night swayed with each step he took on the quiet roads, clutching his parcel bag as if it'd help him keep his balance. The dowager smiled and drew a small dagger from her obi, which she concealed in her sleeve as she approached the messenger. Perhaps bringing Haruki along would've been the wiser choice, but armed with the spirit of a demon, letting the girl sleep sounded reasonable. Besides, if they were against onmitsu who were skilled in combat, she wanted her rested and ready to fight.

Of course, if appearances were anything to go by, the spies she suspected they'd encounter were still young—maybe too young for the steps she needed to take to retrieve Saigai's talisman from them. She didn't believe in hurting children. However, they *were* Imperial agents, and the team's ages revealed that the Capital didn't grasp the plot afoot despite all the noise Senator Hajime had made concerning the matter. There was no other choice than to keep it that way for now, and if those boys insisted on standing in her way, she'd be left with even fewer options.

Lady Shadow hesitated when it seemed the courier noticed her. She swallowed her doubt, then marched toward him with a charming smile. "Good morning, young man. May I ask where you're headed?"

"Fine mornin' indeed, my Lady." He took his time examining her, clearly enjoying the view. She resisted the urge to make her displeasure known. "I'm runnin' a message to th' inn over by th' gold shop on the east end. Can I help ya?"

"As it turns out, you're the sole person who can." Lady Shadow pulled out the dagger and put it to his throat. His dark eyes went wide with fear. "Now, then, tell me everything you know about this message you're delivering."

DURING THE LATE MORNING, amidst one of their typical nonsensical debates—inspired by an intense round of bartering for some cigarettes they'd overheard in the main room—Daisuke and Obito were interrupted by a sharp rapping on the door, followed by an envelope shooting out from underneath it not long after. Daisuke's gaze flitted toward it from his perch on the bed, then briefly returned to Obito, who got up from where he sat on the floor to retrieve it. He scanned it silently.

"This should cheer you up," Obito told him as he offered his partner the letter to review for himself. "We have an appointment this evening."

"Well, well, isn't this fantastic news? That means we can go home," Daisuke commented when Obito sat beside him. He failed miserably to repress an excited expression from overtaking his features as he smoothly folded his legs under him in a single, graceful motion—not that he saw any reason to pretend he *wasn't* in a rush to leave. "We can also avoid more than one trip out today by getting our supplies in Kagechi tomorrow."

"They'll be cheaper there, anyway," Obito agreed. He looked at Daisuke again, this time feeling an inexplicable warmth in his face when he caught sight of his friend's easygoing expression.

Under Master Yujin's suggestion for all his onmitsu when running retrieval operations, Daisuke and Obito dressed in all-black uniforms meant to act as formal apparel before heading out that evening. Although Daisuke held little patience for trivial things such as etiquette, he had to admit the senior spy likely had a point; they looked as if they possessed some official authority, the color allowed them a little more freedom to sneak through shadows, and adding a tanto on each of their belts enforced their presence. Before Obito might worry he was staring, he continued packing a couple glass tubes filled with tinctures he brought along into loops sewn into the uniform's inside. Since he'd used these same tubes to size the fabric strips, they fit perfectly, and he was confident they wouldn't go anywhere no matter how he moved. He knew it wasn't likely he'd need them, but he felt more at ease having *something* nearby for defense.

"Do you think it's always this busy here?" Daisuke asked as they pushed their way through cramped streets.

"Worse this time of year." Obito yanked him from the direct path of an oncoming mule-drawn cart, showing the driver his middle finger in return for the curses and slurs he'd shot at them. "This whole town should be set on fire."

They skirted around a small square where what appeared to be an auction was underway, unaware of the woman and her consort whose attention they'd attracted. Likewise, both failed to notice the conspiratorial smirks the ladies traded before shadowing the two young spies.

After what felt like ages of wandering through the maze that made Zhu's streets, they came upon the house described in the correspondence. Obito grumbled some derisive comment about how cities needed to create a more efficient system than this, which became lost on his companion as they approached the modest home.

Daisuke hesitated; he hadn't considered it until now, but he wasn't sure how these people might receive him and had already prepared for the worst. Sensing something was wrong with his friend, Obito turned toward him, then extended his hand after taking a moment to study his face. He'd only meant to wave him closer, but Daisuke had quickly latched onto his arm and let himself be pulled forward with the motion. At the sight of his soft smile, Obito suddenly didn't have the heart to mention his original intentions.

A large Giahatian man with a short, bushy beard answered their knock on the door—not exactly the stature Daisuke pictured when he thought of meeting a craftsperson such as a potter. Then again, he supposed his own slight stature didn't give off the impression that he had a military background, so he adjusted his opinions slightly; he probably wasn't in a place to judge. The man cocked a thick eyebrow at them discerningly before he looked both ways along the street.

"Can I help you, boys?" he gruffly asked.

"Master Yujin sent us," Obito explained; he and Daisuke recognized the exasperated sigh they received in response. He swallowed, then added, "You must be Gero."

"We wait two years for an answer, and His Highness sends *children* to help." Gero rubbed his face exhaustedly. "Sorry, that wasn't necessary. You're only doing your jobs. Please, do come in—Rin just finished making tea."

"How welcoming," Daisuke dryly stated under his breath when Gero turned around to bring them inside. Obito's elbow wedged into his upper arm.

"Be nice," he sternly whispered before they followed Gero into the house.

Daisuke rolled his eyes, but wisely decided to keep his comment to himself; after all, Obito likely had a point, as did the potter. The Empire had forced them to wait for a long time, and if the artifact had caused the couple so much stress, he couldn't help but agree that they deserved better than a last-minute decision to send a pair of inexperienced onmitsu.

The small house's interior was cozy, and far more welcoming than their initial greeting at the door. A patchy green curtain to their right divided the bedroom from the main room and kitchen. A small doorway on their left led out to Gero's workshop; Daisuke caught a glimpse of his muddy potter's wheel and a few unfinished pieces on the visible end of a workbench. Rin, a shorter-than-average Giahatian woman with deep brown eyes, beamed with delight when her husband explained who their visitors were.

"It's such a relief to see *someone* from the Capital took our letters seriously. Finally." She looked between Obito and Daisuke for at least the third time since their introduction, her lips forming a thin, severe line. "I know it isn't customary to attend to business first, but if you'd please follow me into Gero's workshop. You can bring your tea in there—he won't mind."

Gero grumbled to himself a bit, but didn't complain otherwise. He seemed to share his wife's anxiety about getting rid of the supposed Okami artifact. All four managed to cram into the workshop, standing elbow-to-elbow around the potter's wheel as Rin took a small wooden box from a shelf near the quiet kiln. Daisuke's heart plummeted into his stomach; it looked exactly like the one from his most recent dream.

"I'm not sure what fate my poor sister met after she left this with me, but strange things keep happening to us ever since," Rin said quietly, hands trembling slightly as she surrendered the box to Daisuke. "It started slowly at first...random, strange little happenings we tried putting in the backs of our minds. L-like how Gero's work would sometimes burst even when it'd completely cooled. It's escalated, though. I have these terrible, bloody nightmares, we've been sick more often than we can remember, and...well, our business hasn't been the best recently. No one wants to come here anymore, and that includes our friends and neighbors—they say it feels like a demon's curse lingers here."

"A demon's curse?" Daisuke's expression became skeptical as his fingers flipped the copper latch so he could peek inside; thankfully, Obito placed a hand over it to prevent his curiosity from getting the best of him. "No disrespect intended, miss, but your neighbors sound more superstitious than my grandmother was—and that lady nearly fainted once when she accidentally broke a mirror."

"Perhaps, but there's been too much to deny that *something* isn't right with whatever Misame brought me." Rin smiled tiredly, as if it took all the energy she could muster, then brought them back into the main room. Daisuke briefly caught Obito's eye at the hauntingly familiar name.

"Have you tried getting rid of it?" Obito asked.

"Who would want it?"

"Then, did Misame ever say how she found it?" Daisuke pressed as gently as he could manage, hoping to avoid sounding confrontational.

Rin's laden steps faltered, and Gero offered her his hand, shooting the inquisitive boy a dirty look. After a moment, she shook her head, then whispered, "I tried asking, but she acted like she was too afraid to say. Please, get it back to the Capital as soon as possible...and take care of yourselves around that thing."

No matter how many questions they still had, Daisuke and Obito knew better than to linger; Master Yujin sent them to retrieve the artifact inside the box, not interrogate the couple—further actions could only be determined by him once he read their reports. As they thanked Rin and Gero for their time and bowed, preparing to say their farewells, a palpable darkness crept into the air. They slowly looked at one another, then at the homeowners.

"Kill." That same foreboding feeling rippled throughout the room as the disembodied voice spoke.

"No," Rin whimpered, huddling into Gero's arms. "No, please, leave us alone."

A sudden hiss directed Obito's attention toward the kiln while Daisuke looked around for the voice before they searched one another's alarmed faces for any possible explanation. Thick smoke petered out from the clay oven's mouth, and then it erupted into wild black flames that rapidly crawled up the vent pipe and spilled forth onto the workshop's floor. Despite the heat prickling against Daisuke's skin, he became aware through his panic that the strange fire wasn't scorching anything in its path. The wooden box in his hands violently jerked in every direction, but he held on with more tenacity than he thought he possessed. Obito's hands also clamped around it to help him hold it steady.

"Get that thing out away from here!" the potter shouted. They looked at him helplessly as a collection of small, artfully arranged jars on a shelf exploded into tiny fragments one at a time.

Steady crackling noises snapped from the wall behind the husband and wife as fissures split the plaster. Rin's eyes darted around madly as she stood, frozen in terror, until they finally landed on her husband in a silent plea for him to do something—*anything*. A loud *pop* sounded from the roof overhead.

"Out, *out!*" Gero barked at them, going so far as to herd them toward the front door with his massive arms and then out onto the street. "I thank you both for your services to the Empire, but I cannot deal with that thing in my home for another second. Good day, boys."

Any signs of the impending destruction dissipated when the door slammed in their faces, and Daisuke and Obito slowly turned to one another again, for a moment unable to express their confusion in words as they began to walk back toward the inn in a daze. The box had settled for now, and Daisuke briefly had to question if he'd been dreaming.

"That was...odd," Obito finally said, unsure if he should trust the unease clawing at his chest or the impossibilities they'd witnessed. "We didn't imagine everything that just happened, did we?"

Daisuke swallowed and slowly shook his head. "What the hell is in this box?"

"We can find out later." He paused. "Maybe we *should* leave tonight."

"Good idea. We'll pack for home as soon as we get back."

They agreed to take a less populated return route to the inn. Once they were down the street a little way from the house, Daisuke glanced at the tiny wooden box in his hands again; a while back, he found a dusty old book in the library about sealing evil spirits. He'd disregarded the concept as nonsense then, and assumed he'd picked an intriguing fictional read. However, whatever lurked inside this box made him wish he hadn't been so quick to dismiss the idea. He looked at Obito, though whatever comment or inquiry he might've made instantly died on his tongue.

Obito abruptly tensed and put two fingers to his lips, a silent signal, universal to all onmitsu—someone was following them. His dark forest eyes caught the fading sunlight as they shifted to Daisuke, then the dreaded box.

A cloaked figure swooped down from the long shadows above, halting them in their tracks. Daisuke clutched the box tighter to his chest as Obito moved in front of him, tanto already drawn; the newcomer shifted into a deep stance and placed their gloved hand on a sheathed katana previously hidden under their robes. Obito nudged Daisuke in the opposite direction in a silent order to make a run for it, but another black silhouette material-ized before them the instant they turned. A plume of darkness peeled away from the mysterious form like a breeze clearing thick smoke, revealing a second cowled opponent.

Daisuke's heart leapt into his throat when a deep, resonating chuckle filled the empty alley. He backed into Obito, certain he felt the other boy's heartbeat pound against him as the second enemy circled them, preparing to stand beside the first. They both now had a clear view of the potter's residence, frozen while they watched in fascinated horror as a shadow descended upon it.

Within the blink of an eye, the house exploded into black and purple flames. There was no time to scream or react as a third cloaked figure stood before them. Obito glanced at the first two, one with their katana drawn while the other pulled out a thick chain from their sleeve. That bone-chilling laugh came from the third figure again, and he pulled on Daisuke's shirt as if hoping it'd either bring him closer or allow them to escape.

"Look at this," a ragged, rasping voice taunted them. "Two young onmitsu cutting their teeth on their first solo mission. How absolutely darling. Unfortunately for you boys, I need that box."

"J-just the box, right?" Daisuke fearfully squeaked; out of hope or stupidity, Obito didn't know, but he was ready to throttle him all the same. The little wooden crate rattled and twitched around in his hands of its own volition. He desperately clung to his charge and whimpered a tiny, "Fuck."

Obito's eyes darted back to the house ablaze in the distance, then to the hooded person directly in front of them; a black veil stitched into their cowls obscured any chance of discerning their facial features, and the constituents standing behind him and Daisuke didn't provide any other helpful information. His heart was beating so furiously that he worried it might jump right from his chest; they had to stand against anything threatening their ability to fulfill their duty to Master Yujin, but he couldn't force himself to take any degree of action.

Gods be damned, why couldn't he make a decision?

"Saigai, *awaken*," that rasping voice boldly declared with echoing timbre, seeming to shake the foundation on which they all stood. Daisuke had already turned as white as snow and nearly jumped into Obito's arms from fright. "Kanashimi and the Priestess of Shadow now summon thee to serve thy King."

A black, smoke-like substance puffed through thin cracks in the box's lid, rolled downward before it crept along the ground and encircled Daisuke, then wrapped around him like a constrictive shroud. The way his arms were powerfully pinned against his sides forced him to drop the box; his breath stopped, and ice ran through his veins when the little latch on it shattered. He struggled to free himself, but the otherworldly binding made his figure flash before Obito's eyes, then disappear altogether. Obito tried calling out to him, but a violent wind unexpectedly tore through the alley in a vicious, inescapable tunnel, sweeping Obito off his feet and sending him to the ground several yards past the other two cloaked figures. Another gale followed the first before he could try getting to his feet. The second time he landed, the force of the impact left him temporarily blinded by white light and skewed his other senses until he recovered. By the time he could see again, he felt heat against his skin before he consciously thought to uncover his face from the protection of his arms. When he dared to look up, he saw that he'd somehow landed not far from the charred and burning remains of the potter's house, now barely more than its frame.

Obito's eyes widened at the sight. The entire house lay in ruin, still engulfed in black flame; the fire gradually changed over to the typical hues one would expect to see, leaving him to momentarily wonder if he'd had a violent hallucination of some sort, though his self-doubt quickly dissipated. There was no immediate sign of Gero or Rin, though Obito suspected he needn't look further than the piled rubble left by collapsed support beams, where what looked like a charred hand limply stuck out from beneath it. He pushed himself to his feet and stepped further back from the scene, grateful when concerned bystanders rushed past him to see if they could help with the chaos before him.

"Daisuke?" he weakly called for his partner as shock slowly drained from his system, allowing him to control his body again. No answer followed. He cleared ash from his throat and tried again, this time in a much stronger voice, "Daisuke!"

Still, the little nuisance didn't reply, and despite the frustration it caused, there was no reason to suspect he was playing any games. Not right now—after all, he had *some* sense about when to refrain from his usual antics, and this wasn't a time he'd be in the mood, anyway.

Where the fuck are you? Limping a bit from a flaring pain due to a rough landing, Obito went around the forming crowd to the building's other demolished side, hoping beyond reason that would be where he found Daisuke. No trace of his friend. Not even an imprint in the grass or dirt where he might've settled. Panicked shouts for buckets of water and whatever else nearby citizens could spare to help extinguish the blaze overlapped, sounding distant as dread and trepidation grew in Obito's chest. Eyes now helplessly searching the rushing, steadily growing mob, the question became heavier as it lingered in the air and came to rest on his shoulders.

Where was Daisuke?

THIS STORY CONTINUES IN

ACT II: TALISMANS OF SIN

ACKNOWLEDGEMENTS

OH, WOW. I DID the thing—I published another book. If you've gotten this far, that means you've *read* this new book. It only fits that the first thank you goes out to you, lovely reader! Your support is the main reason I do this (sheer madness is one of the others, but we don't have to go into that). Not only do I have my wonderful readers to thank, but also my amazing beta readers and friends in the indie writing community, who kept me grounded when I doubted myself. Last but never least, a special thank you to my husband and my best friend, who hold my hands when I need it, are patient hostages as they listen to me yap my way out of plot holes, and who are genuinely the biggest supporters I have this side of the pages. I love and appreciate you both more than I know how to say at times.

About the Author

Alyssa Lauseng is a married mom of two warrior princesses who lives in Michigan's beautiful Upper Peninsula. So much inspiration is drawn from a life-long love of marital arts, the pointy objects she's obsessed with, and the U.P.'s abundant nature.

She can be found on Instagram and BlueSky at 5FeetofRedFury.